To Kathy S. and Sabrina C., for your wonderful enthusiasm and support. And always, to John.

FULL
CONTACT

SARAH CASTILLE

sourcebooks
casablanca

Copyright © 2015 by Sarah Castille
Cover and internal design © 2015 by Sourcebooks, Inc.
Cover design by Sourcebooks, Inc.
Cover art by Blake Morrow

Published by Sourcebooks Casablanca, an imprint of Sourcebooks, Inc.
P.O. Box 4410, Naperville, Illinois 60567-4410
(630) 961-3900
Fax: (630) 961-2168
www.sourcebooks.com

Library of Congress Cataloging-in-Publication Data

Castille, Sarah.
  Full contact / Sarah Castille. — First edition.
    pages ; cm. — (Redemption ; book 3)
  (softcover : acid-free paper) 1. Mixed martial arts—Fiction. I. Title.
PR9199.4.C38596F85 2015
813'.6--dc23
                            2014040700

      Printed and bound in the United States of America.
              VP 10 9 8 7 6 5 4 3 2 1

Chapter 1

UP CLOSE AND PERSONAL

Priority: Confidential
Bay Area Underground Fight Club (BUFC) Fight Night
Pier 70. Abandoned Boathouse. 8 p.m.
Headlining: The Predator vs. Tiny Tim
Code Word: Massacre

THERE HE IS.

Stalking across the ring after his prey. Slow. Sure. Effortlessly patient. No wonder the fighters at Redemption nicknamed him the Predator. I could get off just watching his muscles ripple. Come to think of it, I already have.

The crowd in the run-down boathouse in San Francisco's Marina District erupts into muted cheers when the Predator knocks down his opponent, the not so tiny Tiny Tim, with a swift double leg takedown. Underground fights are illegal in California, and no one wants to attract the attention of the police, or worse, the California State Athletic Commission (CSAC). Most of the fighters here tonight are licensed MMA amateurs or pros, and being caught at an underground fight is a serious offense.

And still they come.

As do I.

There is nothing like the ugly, gritty, absolutely electric atmosphere of an underground fight. No rules. No mercy. Pure testosterone. Man, stripped to his primitive essence. And the occasional woman.

How can I resist?

"Sia, I'm going for a drink with Blade Saw after the fight. Will you be okay going home on your own?" Jess's voice trembles with excitement. My best friend and co–underground fight enthusiast has been trying to get into Jimmy "Blade Saw" Sanchez's pants since the first night I dragged her to Redemption, one of the Bay Area's up-and-coming MMA gyms, to watch the Predator and my brother train. Unfortunately, for the longest time, Blade Saw was going out with Sandy, one of Redemption's few female fighters. Looks like Sandy's out and Jess is in on the rebound. Score!

"Um…no. I think I'll make you come home with me just to make you suffer for distracting me from the Predator's fight."

Jess gives a sarcastic snort and pulls out her ponytail holder, letting her mid-length dark hair fan over her shoulders. With her green eyes, curvy frame, and olive skin, Jess is exotic with a capital *E*. We met in the hospital when we were both eighteen, and by the end of the night, we knew we'd be besties forever. Shared trauma forms a bond like nothing else.

"The Predator's looking good tonight." She nudges me as we watch the fight unfold. "Why don't you make your move?"

"Because I didn't come here to pick up guys like some people I know. I came to get inspiration for my art."

Jess gives me a sidelong glance. "I believe the inspiration part, but I think your addiction to underground fights has less to do with art and more to do with the box of vibrators you have stashed under your bed." She adjusts the kind of cleavage I can only dream about and then tucks in her T-shirt as if baring it all isn't enough.

My voice drops to a low, irritated growl. "You're the one who told me about the online sale at the Pink Lady Emporium. And what am I supposed to do? I'm tired of missionary men who don't understand that women have more than one erogenous zone."

"Then don't go out with them anymore." She glances over at the ring where the Predator is pounding his fist into Tiny Tim's stomach. "Now, the Predator…he's in a different league. A man who can fight like that will not be boring in bed. He probably doesn't even know what a missionary is. You've come to every one of his fights for almost a year. Why don't you just admit you're crushing on him, grow a spine, and say hello?"

"Jess?"

She lifts an eyebrow.

"Isn't Blade Saw waiting?"

"No. He's watching the fight." She gestures toward the darkly handsome Blade Saw leaning against the wall beside a couple of his Redemption buddies: Doctor Death, Rampage, and Homicide Hank.

"How about you let *me* watch the fight?"

Jess gives my arm a sympathetic squeeze. "Sorry. It's just…one of these days you'll have to start trusting yourself. You're drawn to him for a reason. Just because he fights doesn't mean he's a bad person. Look at your brother. Tag is one of the hottest, sexiest, most protective, hottest, funniest, hottest guys I know. If he even noticed I existed, I wouldn't have to settle for Sandy's seconds. Not that Blade Saw isn't a nice guy, but he's not Tag."

"Looking at Tag is *your* job." Jess has been in love with my brother, a part-time trainer at Redemption and full-time pain in the ass, since the day we all met. Unfortunately, the feeling has never been mutual.

"Well…if you're too afraid to go after who you really want, what about Doctor Death?" She gestures toward Blade Saw's teammate, a blond Adonis with the chiseled face of a soap opera star. "He's always watching you at these events." She looks up and waves. "He's looking over here right now. Give him a smile."

"He's too pretty for me. And I've heard rumors about him and some of the women at Redemption." Doctor Death, a heart surgeon and sometime ring doctor who trains casually at Redemption, will hit on any woman with a working set of lungs. Still, Jess can't understand why I don't return his interest. But I like my men with a little edge, a bit of rough, and a lot of danger.

She sighs. "Fine. Lucky for you I've got something set up for you tomorrow night."

"No more blind dates."

"Yes. You'll love this guy. He's a fireman. Not Predator hot but still hot. Cute, funny, sensitive. Entirely nonthreatening. Beta male. Smiley. Four serious relationships. Doesn't play around. He's a little on the pudgy side, but I'll bet he knows more than one way to stoke your fire."

I groan. She laughs. The crowd cheers, but not for me.

After Jess leaves to flirt with Blade Saw, I lean against a pillar and focus again on the fight. The Predator is holding his opponent on the ground in a painful-looking submission, and by all appearances, he's just waiting the guy out. Disappointing. I like a bit of action, and usually the Predator gives a good show.

Although he does nothing to play to the crowd, his gruff recalcitrance and the speed and ferocity with which he defeats his opponents have won him legions of fans. No fighter has ever moved up through the underground league as quickly as the Predator. And I'm sure no fighter has ever had a more secret or dedicated fan than me.

Miraculously, Tiny Tim breaks the Predator's hold, rolls, and pushes himself to his feet. His freedom is short-lived. The Predator feints to the left and grabs Tiny Tim by the shoulders, using his momentum to carry him to the ground. Within seconds, he locks poor Tiny Tim in a quick triangle, his thigh against Tiny Tim's throat. He pulls Tiny Tim's arm across his body, tightening the hold, cutting off his air.

My breath leaves me in a rush and suddenly I'm Tiny Tim on the mat and the Predator has me in a different hold, his hand on my neck, his fingers splayed over my throat, forcing my head back. His grip is firm, but gentle, one finger resting in the hollow of my throat. My pulse kicks up a notch. Oh God. To be that vulnerable and not feel afraid. To trust. My ultimate fantasy.

Cheers echo through the boathouse, pulling me back to reality. From the camaraderie of the crowd to the glisten of bloodstained concrete, and from the sound of knees slamming into ribs to the crash of elbows against cheeks, nothing fires my blood or inspires my art as much as a good old down-and-dirty brawl. Nothing except the Predator himself.

Tiny Tim writhes and struggles, but in the end he succumbs, as all fighters do, to the power of the Predator.

The ref blows the whistle and raises the Predator's arm in a victory salute. Moments later the Predator disappears behind the screens set up as a makeshift changing room.

Show's over, folks. The Predator has left the building.

After saying good-bye to Jess, I leave through the side entrance and walk along the wharf toward my car. Water laps against the worn wooden pilings, and in the distance sea lions serenade the moon. Pausing for a moment to breathe in the salty scent of the ocean, I pull my leather jacket around me against the late-night autumn chill and tighten the red scarf around my neck.

And then he comes.

The *whoop whoop* of a police siren and the glare of headlights destroy my peaceful moment in the dark. With an irritated snort, I turn and continue my walk along the wharf. I always feel brave after watching the Predator.

The police car pulls up beside me, and the window slides down with a grating squeak. Eyes focused on my drab gray Volvo, only fifty feet away, I keep walking. Maybe I'll be able to make a clean getaway. He's not going to engage in a high-speed chase with so many people around.

"Sia. Stop." His voice hits me like one of the Predator's punches, stealing my breath away. I hate that tone of voice—bossy, commanding. The last thing it makes me want to do is obey.

So I don't.

When I hear the crunch of tires as the vehicle pulls over, I have to fight back the urge to run. It's not that I'm afraid of being taken down, but I hate confrontation, and I can smell it coming like my mother can smell a lie.

The car door slams. Police-issue shoes thud behind me, shaking the wharf. Although I know what's about to happen, I can't stop my heart from beating that little bit faster. When a meaty paw clamps down on my shoulder, my breath catches in my throat. Steeling myself, I turn around and glare at my brother, Tag.

"Seriously? Did you have to use the siren? Why all the drama? Everyone will think I'm a criminal."

My attempt to take control of the situation fails miserably in the face of Tag's anger.

"What the hell are you doing here? I told you I never wanted to see you at an underground fight again. It's after midnight, and you're walking alone in the dark."

Tag's glowering face ruins my evening, as it has ruined many evenings in my life, from my first kiss, to my first fumble in the dark, to my abruptly terminated first time in the basement of my parents' house when I was sixteen. Overprotective does not even begin to describe my older brother, and now that he's a cop, I can run, but I can never hide.

"Well?" His hands find his hips, drawing my attention to the weapon holstered on his belt, an unconscious gesture I'm sure, but effective just the same.

"Well…" I am very selective about the opportunities in which I defy Tag, but watching the Predator fight is always worth the drama. Not that I would ever tell Tag that I've been crushing on his Redemption teammate for over a year. I like my life. Sort of.

"I have a lot of fighter clients, and I needed inspiration. I've gone to sanctioned fights, but they just don't have the same ambience. My clients want gritty. They want real. They want something that reflects their primitive side. I can't find it in a sanitized ring with ads plastered on every surface and so many rules most of the fights turn into boring grapples on the mat."

Tag huffs and his cheeks redden, which means *I can see right through you* in Tag-speak. Jess, who practically lived at my house after we met, is intimately familiar with Tag-speak and thinks he's beyond cute when he's angry. If I weren't his sister, I'd probably say he is moderately handsome. Shorter and broader than the Predator, with a square jaw and warm brown eyes, he shaved his head when he joined the Oakland Police Department, and after six years, I've almost forgotten he used to have thick, dark hair like mine.

"Get in the vehicle." He raises his voice so loud, heads turn. My cheeks heat. But his anger isn't just coming from concern. Before he became a cop, he was a fighter and a damn good one. But he had to give it up because of me. And although it's hard for him to teach at Redemption, it is harder for him to be here because he loves the underground fights most of all.

"I brought my Volvo." I lean against the metal railing and sigh as the waves lap sympathetically against the wall below, sparkling under the light of the street lamp above me. Definitely not the car of my dreams, but safe, reliable, and acceptable to Tag, who helped me finance the deal.

His eyes narrow. "I don't like you driving alone at night. I'll take you home, and we'll come back tomorrow to pick it up."

"C'mon, Tag. I'm twenty-five years old, and you made me take every driving safety course in the known universe. I have no desire to ride home in the back of a police car like some vagrant you picked up off the street. I promise I'll drive carefully."

His jaw twitches and the pulse in his temple throbs as his foot taps an impatient beat on the cement. Uh-oh. Something else must have happened tonight because he's about to lose it, and in a big way. Tag has one hell of a temper, but it takes a lot to get him riled.

"You know where I was all night?" He thuds his hand on the metal railing and the clang of his watch rings down the dock. "I spent the night at the crime scene of an eighteen-year-old girl who was—"

Anticipating what he's about to say, I cut him off with a raised hand. "Stop. Please."

But he doesn't listen. He's ranting now, his face a mask of pain. The pain is why he's here. It's a pain he never should have been burdened with and one he should never have to experience again. Pain I gave him.

Turning away, I look out over the water, trying to tune him out, but I catch a few words I didn't want to hear: *sexual assault, knew her attacker.* He knows I don't want to hear this. He knows it brings back the nightmares. Whatever he saw tonight must have been bad, because Tag has never been anything but sympathetic and understanding about what happened to me.

I focus on my breathing, just like my therapist taught me to do in times of crisis. In and out. I hear nothing but the sound of my breath. I see nothing but inky black waves. I feel nothing but a gentle stroke on my cheek.

So gentle.

Looking up, I see the Predator with one hand on Tag's shoulder and the other drifting away from my cheek.

"You okay?"

My breath catches as I stare at my savior—strong jaw, dark with a five o'clock shadow; rough craggy face; and eyes as deep and blue as the twilight sky. Eyes that have haunted my dreams for almost a year. The face of my every fantasy.

The Predator. In. The. Flesh. Up close and personal.

"Hey," he says, meeting my gaze.

"Hey." I try not to melt into a puddle on the wharf.

His gaze flicks to Tag and he raises an inquisitive eyebrow. "You alright, Fuzz?"

Fuzz. Despite the tension thick around us, laughter bubbles in my chest. My poor brother has the worst ring name ever, given to him by his teammates to put him in his place because he is such a hard-ass when he teaches his classes. Soft and fuzzy Tag is not.

Tag's jaw tightens. "We're fine here."

The Predator doesn't move. "Man hears a woman yelling 'stop,' he's gotta investigate." His gaze drops to me. "You do something to get yourself arrested?"

I give an exaggerated sigh. "I didn't listen to my brother."

"You're Fuzz's sister?"

"Unfortunately."

The Predator studies me for so long I drop my gaze and twist my Claddagh ring around my finger, hoping he doesn't recognize me from the fights. Jess gave me the ring the first day we met as a sign of friendship, and I've never taken it off.

"You got a name?"

"Sia."

"I'm Ray."

Before I can stop myself, I blurt out in a soft voice, "I know."

Tag makes a choked sound, halfway between outrage and disbelief, and I cringe, knowing he has just figured out the real reason I've been coming to the fights. Sometimes having a close, overprotective sibling can really suck.

"Seen you before," Ray says.

My cheeks burn. How could he have noticed me in the crowd, especially when I made a point of keeping to the shadows at the very back? "Yeah. I…get inspiration for my art at the fights."

"Tattoos aren't real art." Tag recovers quickly so he can launch into one of his favorite speeches. "And the people who get tatted up are not the kind of people you should be hanging around."

Teeth gritted, I glare. We've had this argument a million times. Tattoo parlors rank on Tag's "Sia no-go" list, along with fight clubs, bars, parties, raves, racetracks, and restaurants where people have come down with food poisoning. And although I make an effort to play to his overprotective streak, I had to draw the line with my ink. Art has always been my outlet, and when my painting muse deserted me, I would have succumbed to the darkness if not for Jess's suggestion that I turn my talent to tattooing.

Ray gives me a measured look. "You got a shop? I've been looking for someone…"

My throat constricts. Ray has awesome tats; on the left, a half sleeve of a black, stylized, twisted lightning design that spreads over his shoulder, and an orange design on his right arm that I've never been close enough to see. Alone in my bed at night, I have imagined inking my own design into Ray's skin, marking him as mine.

"Maybe one day, when I have more experience. For now I work with Slim at Rabid Ink."

Ray nods. "I know Slim. He does good work."

Unable to help myself, I brush my finger over the lightning bolt wrapped around his left bicep. His skin is warm despite the cool breeze, and stretched tight over hard muscle. "Who did your ink?"

His jaw tightens. "Got it done overseas. Long time ago. Been thinking it's time for a cover. Get something new."

"What kind of cover?" My business brain kicks in. Despite the fact that I am having an almost uncontrollable physical reaction to Ray's presence—weak knees, racing pulse, damp panties, nipples so hard I'm amazed they don't pierce my jacket—he is a potential client and I'm desperate for cash. Mom lost her job at the florist a few weeks ago, and Tag and I are helping with the mortgage, so our parents don't lose their house.

A smile tugs at his lips. "Might need some professional advice on that."

"Oh." I am mesmerized by his smile. I don't think I've ever seen him smile before. Nor have I ever seen his eyes so warm. He looks beautiful to me—so beautiful I want to capture that expression in ink.

"You got a card?" His fingers brush my cheek as he reaches to tuck a wayward strand of hair behind my ear.

Oh God. He's touching me. Heat sizzles through my veins, numbing my brain and robbing me of the ability to move. Paralyzed with pleasure, all I can manage is, "Jacket."

With an affected sigh, Tag reaches into my jacket pocket and then hands Ray one of my cards. "You don't really need the card. She's inked half the guys at Redemption. If you want to see her work, just ask around."

Ray studies the card, then winks at me and places it carefully in his pocket.

"The things I do for you," Tag mutters under his breath.

"Ray!"

Ray turns at the sound of his name and waves to a woman in the distance. "Gotta go. Shayla's waitin' for a ride."

Ah yes. Ray and Shayla, a.k.a. Shilla the Killa. I've seen them together before. My heart sinks as he heads down the road. Well, of course he would be with someone like Shayla. She's one of the top-ranked female MMA fighters in the amateur league. Hard where I'm soft. Strong where I'm weak. She's smart, ambitious, successful, and has almost no body fat. If I didn't have a potato chip addiction, I could look like her. I'm sure of it.

Ray's gaze falls on me, focused, intent, as if no one exists in the world but us. "Later."

Later? Yes! My heart does a happy dance, but I play it cool. "Later."

Tag and I watch him go, and then I brace myself for the storm. But it doesn't come.

"Ray's not the right guy for you," he says as we watch Ray and Shayla walk away. "He works freelance as a private investigator, and you know what PIs are like: they've got an edge to them. Always walking the line, thinking they're above the law, and getting involved with the wrong people. He's a hard man, and he's got a lot of anger in him. He hides it well, but it comes out in the ring."

"He's thrilling to watch." What Tag sees as anger, I see as passion, fierce and barely controlled, an irresistible aura of danger. He fights as if he's trying to exorcise a demon, or maybe his past. And, *oh God*, those broad shoulders. Those narrow hips. That perfect, tight ass. And the lickable six-pack he's got going on…*yum*.

Tag ruffles my hair. "He's dangerous. Especially for you. I even heard a rumor he was with the CIA. Men like him easily lose control. I just want you to be safe, and that means staying away from guys like him."

"Sure." Yes, I want to be safe, but more than that, I want to be normal. I want to be able to look at a man like Ray and fantasize about taking him to bed with the hope that one day my fantasy could come true. Instead, I get panic attacks and flashbacks that reduce men to mush or scare them away.

"You can't protect me from everything." The unspoken words hang between us. A promise he made in a hospital waiting room seven years ago.

"I can try."

Chapter 2
IT'S ALL ABOUT PRESTIGE

"GOT SOME GOOD NEWS for you." Slim Jones, manager of Rabid Ink, perches on the reception desk while I hang up my coat. Our receptionist, Rose, a tall redhead with a diamanté nose ring and two full-color tat sleeves depicting birds of paradise, is already on the phone and gives me a wave.

"It's eight thirty on a Saturday morning. Unless you've got a triple shot latte and a chocolate croissant hidden behind your back, there is no good news."

He dismisses my grouchiness with an absent wave. A fedora-wearing hippie, tall and rangy, Slim took a chance on me years ago when I responded to his ad for a new tattoo artist. I had a portfolio full of drawings and watercolors from high school art class, and not one tattoo.

Although initially put off by his cavalier attitude, I soon discovered he was a very thorough and patient teacher. When I finally obtained my license, he gave me a full-time job, my own chair, and as many clients as I could handle. But only stencil work. The freehand jobs I dream of doing, he always keeps for himself.

"You're getting a promotion. Jay got himself in trouble with some street gang and had to go into hiding, so his chair is free. You're moving up to middle chair."

I glance over at Jay's untidy workstation, and his worn, red leather client chair, a cross between a lounger and a massage table. A giant print of a blue skull wearing a turban hangs on the exposed brick wall behind his scratched work cart, and his childhood collection of Hot Wheels lines the ledge beneath. His cart is a mess of cartridges, Kleenex, and assorted odds and ends—a huge contrast to my impeccably neat and tidy station.

"We'll clean it up," Slim says, following my gaze. "I doubt he'll be coming back."

Still on the phone, Rose draws a line across her throat mafia-style and then mouths the word *dead*, as if I might not understand her throat-slitting gesture. Rose is all crass and no class. She calls things the way she sees them, and apparently she sees Jay as having already checked out of Hotel Life.

Goose bumps prickle on my skin, and I regret my decision to wear my usual low-cut tank top to show off my tats. Pebbled ink is not a good look. But Slim seems unaffected by the fact that his employee has been marked or possibly killed by a street gang. Maybe because Jay was only here for a few months and we never got a chance to get to know him that well. Or maybe because he genuinely doesn't care. With Slim, it's always hard to tell.

"You don't seem happy," he says.

"I'm still in shock and stuck on the part about the gang and Jay going into hiding or, as Rose suggested, possibly being dead. These things happen in movies and not real life. How do you know all this?"

Slim shrugs. "He left a message."

"A message?" My eyes widen in incredulity. 'Hello. This is Jay. I'm being chased by a street gang. If I'm killed, please give my chair to Sia.' That kind of message?"

"Actually, he asked if I'd hold his chair until it all blew over. As if."

"As if the street gang would be forgiving?" My voice rises in pitch at the thought of poor Jay being pursued by a vicious, cutthroat gang. Although I didn't know him well, he was always friendly, if a little distant.

Slim taps his fingers against his leg. "As if I'd hold the chair. I'm running a business here. He wants to get in bed with unsavory characters, he pays the price."

My eyes widen and I shoot an incredulous look at Rose. Sometimes I wonder how I wound up at Rabid Ink with people whose sense of ethics is so diametrically opposed to mine. She hangs up the phone and laughs.

"I think your callous disregard for Jay's life has shocked our innocent Sia." Rose peers around Slim from her seat at the reception desk.
"I, on the other hand, was expecting this from day one. He had trouble
written all over him. Not something you artist types would notice. But
I always pick up on things, like the scar across his throat that looked like
a knife slash, cut marks on his arms, or the fact that he only had gang
members as clients."

Rose wanted to be a tattoo artist, but after three months as Slim's
apprentice, she realized her strength lay in her people skills, and she
took on the reception job instead. Over beer one night after work, Slim
told me he'd been incredibly relieved. He liked Rose and didn't know
how to tell her that she couldn't draw for crap.

Slim scowls at Rose, and then turns to me. "You're not dealing
are you? Owe anyone money? Pissed off the wrong people? In a gang?
Hooked up with the wrong kind of guy? I didn't screen him well
enough, and it's made me rethink my hiring process."

"Uh…no."

Rose snorts a laugh. "Her brother wouldn't even let her walk in the
wrong end of town, much less associate with evildoers like litterbugs or
jaywalkers or street gangs. He's got her so wrapped up in cotton, I'm
still amazed he let her work here. He came in once when you were away
to check out the safety of the building. He didn't like all those exposed
beams and pipes in the ceiling. Thought they were dangerous. I told
him decorating with natural elements is the in thing, but he wasn't
buying the modern vibe."

So true. If only she knew what I had to go through after Tag found
out I'd taken a job at Rabid Ink in San Francisco's Lower Haight
district. At one point he threatened to lock me in my apartment. But
after I brought him to meet Rose and Slim and the crew, he mellowed.
Especially when Slim assured him I would never be alone in the studio.

A shiver runs down my spine when I glance over at Jay's workstation. He's been gone for what…two days? The memory of him inking
a drunken frat boy on Thursday night is still crystal clear in my head. I
give Slim a weak smile. "Maybe I'll just stick with my chair."

"You'll be fine." Slim pats my shoulder. "Nothing to worry

about. If he comes back, he can take your old chair. You're a better artist anyway."

"Sure." I shoot Rose a quizzical glance. She puts two hands to her throat and makes a choking gesture, then closes her eyes and drops her head to her shoulder, limp. I guess she doesn't think Jay is coming back.

I follow Slim past the small, carpeted lounge area with its two worn, brown suede couches, flash racks displaying our portfolios, and permanently unfilled watercooler, and drop my bag on Jay's chair.

"Moving up a chair is considered a promotion," Slim says as he clears away Jay's works, tossing the needles and equipment into a cardboard box. "But we still operate on an eat-what-you-kill basis. I still take twenty percent off the top to cover expenses, insurance, and maintaining the autoclave. You're responsible for your own equipment and medical supplies. New clients are still fair game. Freehand work is mine."

My brow wrinkles in a frown. "Did I miss the part where there's a financial benefit to being middle chair instead of back chair?"

Slim laughs. "There isn't any. It's all about prestige."

"Prestige. Right." Rabid Ink doesn't scream *prestige*. Cheap artwork and faded band posters line the crumbling, exposed-brick walls. The windows are cracked and the hardwood floor, grayed over time, is decidedly uneven. Although he keeps the studio impeccably clean and brightly lit, Slim hasn't been big on maintenance or upkeep, and everything is tired and worn, from the chipped counters to the scratched workstations and ancient chairs. When I daydream about running my own shop, I always imagine clean, bright, and modern, with the newest hi-tech equipment, polished hardwood floors, art on the walls, and spacious private rooms for intimate ink.

The door opens and Christos walks in, tossing his bag on the first chair from the door. Our half-Greek, half-Italian piercing expert has shaved his hair into a bright-green Mohawk, and matching green snake tattoos adorn his muscular arms. When he's not at the studio, he's kicking it up with his thrash band, Cerebral Slaughter. He nods to Slim and Rose and then gives me a warm smile that somehow accentuates the prominent piercings in his eyebrows and lower lip.

"Sia's taking Jay's chair," Slim calls out as Christos heads for the coffeepot.

Christos's smile fades. "So that's the end of Jay then?"

"Yup. D-E-D," Rose says.

"Street gang got him?"

Slim and I share a glance, and Slim shakes his head. "How about next time everyone knows something about one of my employees, like he's in bed with a gang, they mention it to me, so I can make sure I'm not putting everyone else at risk? What about Duncan? Anything I need to know about him? He'll be in for the evening shift later tonight."

Rose, Christos, and I share a glance and come up blank. Duncan is just about the nicest guy anyone could meet. Although he looks like he's in a street gang, with his bald, tatted head; short, stocky body; and full-on swagger, he's the kind of guy who'll pick up a spider and carry it outside instead of stomping on it like everyone else. Although it is anathema to even think it, his art is wasted on skin. His designs should be hanging in museums or private collections, or traveling the world in exhibitions.

"Serial killer," Rose says finally. "It's always the quiet ones."

"Speaking of quiet"—Slim raises an eyebrow at Rose—"I noticed we had nothing in the book for this morning. How about Sia and I finish up with your boobs?"

My nose wrinkles. "Actually, I'm not really keen on inking Rose's boobs first thing Monday morning. I have a delicate stomach."

Rose laughs. "You're just jealous 'cause you got nothing worth inking up top."

"Sure, she—"

"Don't even go there." I fold my arms across my chest and glare at Christos, who is staring at my breasts in an entirely assessing, nonsexual way. So, I'm not well endowed like Rose. Not something I need to be reminded about before I've even had my morning coffee.

"If Rose isn't up for more work, I can finish up with you, Sia." Slim traces a line across my throat. "Didn't you want a collar connected to your sleeves?"

"I'm not ready for the collar yet." I rub my hands up and down my arms, exquisitely inked by Slim with an intricate rose and thorn design, so realistic the pink petals glisten. Although I had wanted a rose and thorn collar inked around my neck, when it came time to do it, I called a halt. For some reason, it felt too final, as if an ink collar would bind me to this world of needles, leather, ink, and skin. And I wasn't ready to be bound.

Christos agrees to work the reception desk while I assist Slim with Rose's ink and learn a new airbrush technique he picked up from a scratcher friend down in San Diego. Some tattoo artists excel at line work or calligraphy, others have a knack for the rhythms of tribals, and still others are better at peonies than pirates. Slim is master of them all, and yet he is always open to learning new techniques.

By the time we're done, Rose's left breast is red and swollen, but the feathers Slim has inked around it are so real, I can almost imagine they ruffle when I sigh. Not that I have any desire to breathe on Rose's breasts. She gets enough attention as it is.

Rose invites Christos to the back to admire her new piece and then hands him her phone to take a few pictures for her mom. I imagine getting my boobs inked and sending a picture to my mom, and almost collapse in hysterical laughter. The O'Donnells are *so* not a liberal family.

A steady stream of walk-in customers keeps us busy for the rest of the day. Rose maintains a good background music vibe with a mix of hip-hop, jazz, and house, and I relax into my work. Some clients bring their own music, but rarely does anyone complain about her choices. I ink a few college girls who have just finished exams, a Marine just about to ship out, and a bride and groom who want matching tats to mark their special day.

A few minutes before Duncan is due to arrive for the evening shift and relieve me for the day, I head to the back room to sterilize my equipment in the autoclave. Moments after I turn on the machine, Rose steps through the door.

"You've got a new client." She self-adjusts, plumping her breasts and tugging down her already-low neckline, which tells me the guy must be on the scorching end of hot. "He's drop-dead gorgeous, but in a rough, craggy kinda way."

Hand to my mouth, I groan. "I need the work, but I'm supposed to be off in five minutes. Blind date tonight. Do you think Duncan would do the consult, and I'll do the ink, and we can split the fee?" Not that I want to go on the date. They usually end with either an awkward peck on the cheek, if we make it through the evening, or an emergency text to Jess after five minutes begging her to come and save me. After a string of safe, vetted, but boring partners, I'm not looking for a relationship. Jess thinks I'm too picky, so every few weeks she fixes me up in the hopes I'll get, at the very least, some missionary action between the sheets. Two months without sex is a dry spell Jess can't handle. Twelve months, and she thinks I might as well just pack it in and give up on life.

Rose shakes her head. "He wants you and he's not the kind of guy who takes 'I'm off in five minutes' for an answer."

Shoulders slumping, I nod. "I'll do it, but Jess won't be pleased. She was pretty sure I'd like her blind date pick of the week. He's a fireman."

Rose perks up. "I'm free. I'll tell him I'm you, but with a boob job, an extra couple of inches in height, and about fifty extra pounds."

Laughing, she helps me collect my equipment, and we head back into the shop. But when I see who is in my chair, I freeze.

As all prey do when they catch sight of a predator.

Chapter 3

YOU LIKE THE FISH?

OH. MY. GOD. The Predator is sitting in my chair.

"What's the matter?" Rose grabs my elbow to steady me. "You know that guy?"

"He's my fantasy man," I whisper. "Except he stepped out of the fantasy on the weekend and it totally threw me off. He mentioned he needed a cover, but I didn't think he was serious."

Rose raises an eyebrow. "He looks serious to me. Maybe you're his fantasy woman."

"He has a girlfriend."

"The good ones always do." Rose gives my arm a sympathetic squeeze and then makes a show of placing my equipment on my workstation, which involves much bending over and a significant threat of chest overexposure.

"Hey, Ray. What's up?" I feign nonchalance, like men I have lusted over for the last year always show up at my studio at seven o'clock on a Saturday night wearing commando pants that are tight in all the right places and a kick-ass Affliction T-shirt stretched tight over rippling abs. Keeping my back to him, I manage to straighten my equipment without dropping anything and then stand awkwardly beside the chair, only inches away from his muscular forearm.

Ray's gaze travels over my body, from the pink streak in my hair I just added this morning, to my boobs, miraculously enlarged with a strategically padded bra and a two-sizes-too-small tank top, then down to my Jack Daniels belt buckle, over my leather-pant clad hips, and back up again. By the time he's done with his perusal, I'm sweating, horny, and ready to push him back in the chair and tear off his clothes.

"You done?" I lift an admonishing eyebrow, but Ray just smiles.

"Fucking awesome ink." He traces a finger up my arm, following the vines that extend from my wrist to my shoulder. His touch is electric. I bite back a whimper as every nerve ending in my body fires at once. His voice has a rasp that makes me think about sex. Rip-off-my-clothes, toss-me-on-the-bed, fuck-me-till-I-scream sex.

"Slim did it." I gesture toward Slim as he heads to the back of the shop. "He can do you. Tat-wise, I mean. Now. 'Cause he's free. He just went back to sterilize his equipment." I slam my lips shut. Could I possibly sound more like an idiot?

Ray frowns.

"Or not." Inwardly cringing at my lack of social skills, I cut myself off and vow never to speak again.

Ray picks up my portfolio from the cart on his other side and thumbs through it. "Saw your work when I asked around at Redemption. Decided you should be the one to cover me."

My heart hammers in my chest so hard I think I might break a rib. Ink Ray? Put my hands on that magnificent body? Although I have dreamed about it, even designed a tattoo for him in my head, seeing him in my chair now, I know I won't be able to do it. He unnerves me. Arouses me. My hands will shake too much to hold the tattoo machine. I'd probably ruin that beautiful skin for life.

"Actually, I…uh…was about to leave. But like I said, Slim's free. Or Duncan."

Ray tilts his head to the side and his eyes soften. "I want you."

Burn, cheeks, burn. "I'm sorry…I have…uh…plans." I should just tell him I'm going to a party, or that my bestie has set me up with her sister's best friend's cousin's wife's brother, and that I really shouldn't miss it because I only go out with people who can be vouched for by people I know and I'm running out of inventory. I could also easily tell him the date will go nowhere because they never do. But for some reason the words don't come out.

His eyes narrow. "Changeable plans?"

"Personal plans," I say, trying to hide my desperate need to get him out of my chair before I throw myself on him in a frenzy of lust or, worse, actually agree to do his ink. "And really, it would be better if you come back tomorrow, when I have time to discuss what you need and draw up a few designs. I don't want to do a half-assed job."

"Hot date?" Ray carefully places my portfolio back on the cart and folds his arms across his delectable chest.

I suck in a sharp breath. "I didn't say I had a date."

He gives me a smug look. "You didn't have to. You have a very expressive face and your body language says you're trying to hide something." He taps my folded arms. "The likely explanation is a date, and you don't want me to know about it." His lips curl into a sensual smile. "Why don't you want me to know about your date?"

Damn. Caught out. Me and my expressive face. This is exactly why I always got Tag to steal the cookies when we were growing up. I twist my ring around my finger and press my lips together as my temper starts to rise. "Maybe I'm planning to rob a bank or steal a car and go joyriding. Maybe I'm working a pole at a local strip joint. Or maybe I'm just meeting my bestie for a burger. There are hundreds of things I could be doing tonight."

"Definitely a date then. What's his name?"

"I don't think his name is any of your business."

Ray doesn't take the hint. "Ah. So it is a date." He winks and I am hard pressed not to smile. "First date? Second?"

My skin prickles with a flush of heat. What's with all the questions? He can't possibly be interested. He's the Predator. He has the body of a demigod. Beautiful women throw themselves at him after his fights. They are his for the taking. Which makes him perversely safe for an ordinary girl like me. Why order regular coffee when you can have a triple-shot espresso with cream?

"First date."

He gives a disapproving grunt. "You got a picture? Gimme a visual."

"I've never met him."

His face softens with a smile. "Good to know."

"I can't imagine why." But I can fantasize, and my imagination goes off the deep end. He wants me so bad, he came here tonight pretending he wanted a tattoo. He wants to fuck me, make me come in every dirty way I've read about and have been too afraid to try.

"Men like to know the lay of the land." He shifts in the chair, drawing my attention to the breadth of his shoulders, the thick biceps protruding from the tight sleeves of his T-shirt, his lightly tanned forearms covered in soft, downy hair. I have never been so sexually attracted to anyone in my entire life, and the feeling of not being in control of my responses is unsettling.

"I thought you came to get a tat, not to discuss my personal life, which I can guarantee will bore you in three seconds flat. You're almost as bad as Tag with all the questions. I already have a bossy, overprotective man in my life. I don't need another."

"Man's overprotective, he usually has a reason."

My blood runs cold. Would Tag have told him our secret? No. Never. We made a pact that night, and I trust him never to break it. "No particular reason. That's just who he is." Hopefully, my expressive face won't show Ray that I'm lying through my teeth.

A crease forms along Ray's brow. "He know you're going on this date?"

I heave a sigh and his gaze drops to my boobs. Christos was partially right. With the padded bra, I do have assets. "FYI, I don't report every detail of my life to Tag, but just in case you get any ideas"—I poke him gently in the chest, more to cop a feel than out of real annoyance—"it's none of your business, just like it's none of his." I emphasize each word and lean toward him in what I hope is a menacing way.

"Fuck, you're cute. Did you know your eyes go green when you're scared?"

Hmmm. Not really the look I was going for. I would have preferred sultry, sophisticated, or even badass. Who calls a woman pierced, dyed, leathered, and tatted *cute*? "First, my eyes are hazel, not green. And second, you won't think I'm cute if you say anything to Tag."

He stares, his gaze at once amused and intense. "Maybe not if you give me your ink."

"Seriously?" My voice rises in pitch. "You're blackmailing me?"

Ray slides back in my chair with the smug look of a man who knows he's about to get what he wants. "You want to ink me. You didn't, we wouldn't be having this conversation. You would already be out that door. Question is whether you want it more than what you got going on tonight."

The last of my inhibitions flutters away like a tattoo artist pursued by a street gang. "I don't."

"You do." His eyes glitter, and he licks his beautiful, sensual lips, as if daring me to make a move. And I almost do. I want him. I've wanted him for a year. And now he's here. In my chair. Making me think he wants me too. I could almost forgive his insufferable arrogance.

"Okay, I do. Covers are a specialty of mine. But are you sure you want to irritate a woman who'll be wielding a tattoo machine that could do some permanent damage to your skin, or worse, give you a tattoo that will embarrass you for life?"

He pushes up the left sleeve of his T-shirt and holds out his arm. "Sounds to me like you're saying yes. And it can't be worse than this."

My lips quiver with a repressed smile, and I trace my finger over the chubby orange smiley fish on his bicep. "I noticed it when you were fighting, but I was never close enough to see what it was."

"Otto the fish from a children's picture book. Got fucking drunk one night and must have mentioned it was my favorite book when I was a kid. A coupla my buddies dragged me to a tattoo studio, and I woke up the next day with Otto."

Laughter erupts from my throat and I pat tiny Otto's head. "I like Otto. And he was actually done by a master artist. Look how his scales glow and shimmer, and the way he ripples when you move your arm. It would be a shame to ink over him."

Ray slides a finger under my chin and tilts my head up, forcing me to meet his searing gaze. "You got a pretty smile. It lights up your face, chases away the shadows. And you got a lot of shadows."

My cheeks flame at his insight, and I look away. "Shadows" doesn't even begin to describe the baggage I've been carrying around—baggage that means I usually stay away from alpha males like Ray. "So how did you want to cover Otto?"

"You like the fish?" Ray says quietly.

"Yeah, I like the fish."

"I'll keep the fish."

My head jerks up, and I can't help but snort a laugh. "You can't keep a tat you hate just because I like it. You don't even know me. And it doesn't really go with your Predator image in the ring."

He captures me with his gaze, deep, dark, and delicious. "What would you cover it with?"

Without thinking, I stroke the tat on his bicep. I always get my best ideas through touch. So hard. So warm. So smooth. His muscle flexes under my fingers, rippling beneath the skin. But that is Ray. Hidden depths. Wild. Untamed.

"Sia?" His deep voice rumbles through me, and my hand vibrates against his arm. Instantly, I know how I would ink him. Grabbing my notebook and pencil, I sketch out a design, partially abstract, partially tribal, merging lines and patterns until they form the rough outline of a wolf.

"This." I hold up the notepad. "This is what I would do. This is what I see every time I watch you fight."

He takes the notebook and studies it for a moment longer than is comfortable. My pulse kicks up a notch and disappointment clenches my gut. He doesn't like it.

His gaze locks on mine, heated and heavy. "You *see* this?"

"It's the great wolf, Fenrir, from Norse legend." I shrug and grab the notepad from his hand. "Fenrir was a bit of a troublemaker so the gods decided to put him in shackles. However, Fenrir was so strong that there was no chain that could hold him. The gods asked the dwarves to create a magical ribbon that even Fenrir couldn't escape. But Fenrir said he would only allow himself to be tied if one of the gods was willing to make a sacrifice and stick a hand in Fenrir's mouth. And when one of them did, Fenrir bit it off."

Silence.

I cringe under his unwavering gaze and sit heavily on my artist's chair, which brings my eyes level with his strong chin. *Damn.* "I can come up with something else…"

"Did the ribbon have big hazel eyes and long, silky dark hair, awesome tats, and the sweetest fucking smile on the West Coast?"

An inferno rages in my cheeks. "Actually, it was a just an ordinary red ribbon."

"Like the scarf you wore the other night."

He remembers my scarf.

Ray pulls up his T-shirt to reveal his rippled six-pack and then points to a long, jagged scar running across his left pec. "Think you can do it here?"

My training kicks in at the sight of his scar. Taking a deep breath, I gently run a finger along the edges. Five years old, maybe six from the way it healed, and deep. His skin is smooth, warm over the hard ripple of muscle beneath.

"Yeah. I would have to modify it, make it bigger, but I could stretch it to cover the scar and then extend it and blend it in with the rest of your shoulder tat, but it would be quite painful. Scar tissue is more sensitive than skin, and you have a lot of it."

Ray draws in a ragged breath. "Not afraid of pain. Getting that scar was more pain than the needle would be."

My mouth waters at the thought of inking Ray's skin. "If you want to talk to Rose, she can set you up—"

"Now."

"Now?" My heart pounds in my chest. Now means freehand, which I'm not allowed to do. And I'm not ready for this. I'm not ready for my fantasies to become real. I don't want to find out Ray isn't all I imagined he would be.

Finding my tongue, I look up at Ray. "For a piece that size, you should really let me do a couple of designs and then a stencil, so you can be sure it's what you want. Everyone will see it when you're fighting. I want it to be perfect for you. Tattoos are forever."

A curious expression crosses his face, part longing, part disappointment, all sensual promise. "I've gotta go outta town for a coupla days, but I'll be training at Redemption tomorrow afternoon before I leave. You got time to bring me your designs?"

My throat tightens, burns. Tag forbade me from going to Redemption after Amanda, the club's attorney, was attacked in an alley a few blocks away from the gym. Even though I know most of the fighters, and would never walk around Ghost Town alone, Tag still added it to his "no-go" list. Of course, if I always listened to Tag, there would be few places in the Bay Area I would be able to go, and even fewer places I would get a chance to see Ray.

"Sure."

"Gimme your phone and we'll trade numbers. My line of work is not very predictable. Shit always comes up."

"What is your line of work?" I hand him my phone, and he does the number switch.

He hesitates for just a heartbeat and then shrugs. "Private investigator. But I got a bit on the side."

"A bit on the side?"

"A bit on the side."

"What does that mean? 'A bit on the side'?"

Ray chuckles. "Means I'll take on the odd job that might go outside the boundaries of professional ethics, so it doesn't count as official PI work. Mostly catching bad guys. Lookin' for one right now, but let it slide tonight so I could come here."

"I thought it meant you were having an affair. Not that you're the kind of person who would have an affair, or if you were, that you would tell me. I mean, it could be uncomfortable if you chose to share that information because I know Shayla, although—"

"Sia..."

Wound tight, I let my tension spill out in a nervous babble. "Not well enough that I would feel the need to call her up and tell her you've got a bit on the side, but you know, it could be awkward since I do go to all the Redemption parties—"

"Sia."

"And if I was talking to her and saw—"

He cups his hand around my neck, leans down, and kisses me. Soft and sweet, his lips press against mine, stealing my breath from my lungs.

"Oh," I whisper when he pulls away. "Is that how you shut babbling girls up?"

"Only the hot ones."

Stunned, I can only stare. I was kissed by the Predator. He thinks I'm hot. Fangirl swoon.

"I don't do that shit," Ray says, all cool and calm as if he hasn't just rocked my entire world. "Two women is two times the trouble. Got enough to do with work and training." He hands me my phone, and my stomach clenches when I see his name in my address book. *Ray.* No last name. But I'm not complaining. Until last week, I would never have imagined Ray's name would be associated with mine in any way. And cool. He's not into relationships. Neither am I.

"I don't know how you work your job, your bit on the side, *and train.*" I regain my equilibrium and pretend his kiss didn't just fry my brain. "Tag struggles with one, and he doesn't really train anymore. He just teaches."

"Passes the time." He slides out of my seat and tucks his phone in his pocket.

"'Passes the time'?" My voice rises in disbelief. "You're an amazing fighter. I'll bet you'd shoot right up through the amateurs if you got on the amateur circuit."

Ray's face tightens. "Underground fighting is more my style. A real test of skill and strength. Push yourself to the limit and let it go. Freedom. That's where it's at for me."

"That's how I feel about art," I say. "I see pictures in things, and I have to set them free."

Ray strokes a finger along my jaw, sending a delicious shiver down my spine. "What about Fenrir?"

"Like I said, he wants to be free."

Electric tension fills the space between us. Ray's corded throat tightens when he swallows, and he drops his hand. "He's not the only one."

He leans down and for a moment I think—no, hope—no, *pray* he's going to kiss me again. His breath is warm on my cheek. His lips brush over my ear. And then he whispers, "Tomorrow."

Chapter 4

YOU SCREAM SEXY

"Hey, Sia! Long time no see ya!" Rampage ruffles my hair when I walk in the front door to Redemption, a converted warehouse in Oakland's Foster-Hoover District—also known as Ghost Town—and one of the city's premier MMA training facilities.

I give Rampage a hug and wrap my arms around his belly, clad in a yellow happy face tank top. "Boy, I missed this place. Tag—"

Rampage cuts me off. "Ring names only in the gym."

"Sorry. I mean, Fuzzy banned me from coming here after what happened to Amanda. If it weren't for the parties and the guys who come into the studio, I would have totally lost touch with what's going on."

Rampage's face falls, bringing his scars into stark relief, and he leans his six-foot-two-inch super heavyweight frame against the wall. "Yeah. That was a rough time. Amanda hurt. Buncha idiots suing us for ten million dollars. But she sorted us all out, and sorted herself. You going to the wedding? Should be one hell of a party."

My stomach clenches. "Uh…I'm not sure." Amanda is marrying Jake a.k.a. Renegade, one of Redemption's top-ranked fighters and yet another of my fantasy men. Things got awkward when Tag tried to set us up by asking Renegade to look out for me at parties when he wasn't around. We definitely had chemistry, but after one kiss, I backed off. Not just because I thought I wouldn't be able to handle more than one kiss from such an über alpha male, but because it was so obvious he was still in love with Amanda and didn't know it.

Rampage gives me a sympathetic smile and walks over to the intercom. He knows everything about everyone at Redemption, and although he seems the most unlikely source of gossip, information always seems to find its way to him. "I'll let Fuzz know you're here."

My breath catches in my throat. "Actually, I think I'll try and fly under his radar. Ray…er…the Predator asked me to meet him here to show him some designs, and I'm pretty sure Fuzzy won't approve."

Rampage laughs. "He's not gonna say no to the Predator. First night the Predator took Fuzzy's Get Fit or Die class, he had Fuzz in a submission on the floor in the first five minutes. Didn't like being told what to do. Earned Fuzz's respect, which isn't an easy thing."

"Is the Predator here yet?" Butterflies flutter in my stomach. I still can't believe I had the nerve to come to Redemption. But how could I not after the verbal thrashing I got from my bestie?

Last night, after scaring away the ultra-conservative, dull-as-ditchwater fireman with my tats and piercings, I called Jess. After hearing about Ray showing up at Rabid Ink, she threatened to disown me as a friend if I didn't get my ass to Redemption. She also mentioned horrendous tortures she would inflict on me if I chickened out, most involving hiding my stash of potato chips or telling my mom about my secret piercings. In Jess's mind, any attention is good attention, even if he's got a girlfriend attached.

"Free weights. You can go find him if you like." Rampage raises a curious eyebrow, and I change my mind about looking for Ray right away. Maybe I should take a few minutes to chill and relax. Get my game on.

"I think I'll grab something to eat first. If you see him, let him know I'm in the café."

"Sure thing."

Taking a deep breath, I head down the main corridor toward the café, keeping a sharp lookout for Tag. The gym has undergone significant renovations over the last few years and now resembles a hi-tech military training facility. I pass the first aid room, equipment store, and a couple of workout studios before I spot Doctor Death heading my way. I contemplate pushing aside the plastic sheeting covering the entrance to what appears to be a new addition to Redemption's already vast space, but instead manage to duck into the little café unseen. A quick check of the menu yields disappointing results. Protein shakes of all varieties made-to-order and a cooler full of healthy treats.

After I buy a wrap and the least offensive-sounding protein shake, Choco Banana Whey Blast, I squeeze into the table at the back of the café beside a tall potted palm. Unless someone is looking for me, I should be well hidden.

"Sia. I almost missed you hiding behind that tree. Come out and say hello."

Or not.

Torment, the owner of Redemption, beckons to me from the counter. Without thinking, I leap to my feet. But then, Torment has that effect on people. He isn't just an alpha male. He's an über alpha. Crowds part when he walks down the street. Tables vacate when he enters a bar. He can make a man cower with the lift of his eyebrow. And in the ring…holy Hannah. It's no wonder he's being considered by the pros. The only person who has been able to tame him is his girlfriend, Makayla, the gym's first aid attendant. They went through hell for each other and now nothing could tear them apart.

"You here to see Fuzz?"

Holding up my travel portfolio, I give him a terrified smile. "Actually, I'm here to give the Predator a few designs. He wanted some fresh ink. But if that's a problem, I can meet him somewhere—"

"He's certainly impressed with your work." Torment snatches the portfolio from my hand and thumbs through the drawings. "All my boys are. The Predator dragged a few of them into my office this morning after I mentioned I was thinking of getting a new piece."

I can't imagine anyone daring to enter Torment's office without an invitation. "Is he still alive?"

"Barely."

"Thanks for not killing him."

"Pleasure." Torment drums his fingers on the counter, and sweat beads on the server's brow. He wipes his hands on his apron and doubles his speed as he prepares Torment's protein shake.

"Didn't want to deprive you of a potential client," Torment says.

"Thoughtful." The idea of Ray hauling fighters into Torment's office to show off their ink gives me a warm, melty feeling inside. Probably how Shayla feels when he kisses her softly, strokes her jaw with his finger, or brushes his lips over her cheek and says, "Tomorrow."

"I'm not sure why he would do that." I twist my ring around my finger and the little heart gleams under the light. "We've only met once…twice."

"The Predator is his own beast. He keeps to himself. I don't try to understand him. But I am impressed with your work. If you ever decide to leave Rabid Ink, come and talk to me. I have something in the works that might interest you."

The server rushes out from behind the counter and gives Torment an apologetic smile when he hands him his shake. Torment nods and stalks away. I collapse into my chair.

Ray hasn't shown up by the time I've finished my snack and I steel myself for a search of the main gym. But first, I check out the chalkboards outlining the weekly class schedule. Fuzzy is signed up to teach two classes this afternoon: Baby Boot Camp followed by Get Fit or Die. Sweet. He'll be tied up for at least another hour and a half, and by the time he's done, I'll be long gone.

Pausing in the doorway, I take in the twenty-five-thousand-square-foot gym, complete with fight cages, practice rings, and a full range of cardio, weight, strength, and endurance training equipment. Grapple dummies line one wall and punching bags another. In the training area at the back, exhausted fighter wannabes drag themselves around Tag's killer circuit while he scowls and peppers them with affectionate abuse. The air smells of stale sweat, lemon-scented disinfectant, and a hint of vinyl. Delightful.

Skirting around the equipment to keep out of Tag's line of vision, I head over to the free weights and catch sight of Ray drumrolling a speed bag in the corner. Sweat glistens on his body as he pounds the bag in a steady rhythm, his biceps flexed, the smooth skin on his lats rippling over the hard muscle underneath.

For a moment, I allow myself to imagine I'm a normal girl caught up in a normal fantasy where he dumps Shayla and takes me home, and we have wild, hot, animal sex until neither of us can move. I've never had wild, hot, animal sex, but I imagine any sex with Ray would be amazing.

Ray glances up and catches me watching. Without missing a beat, he gives me a wink that makes my cheeks flame and my toes curl. Instinctively, I do what all prey do when spotted by a predator. I run.

Safe in the shadow of the huge elevated cage dominating the center of the warehouse, I sit on a bench and watch from a safe distance where my drooling cannot be easily noticed.

Ray moves from the speed bag to the bench press and Homicide Hank offers to spot him. Wiry, tall, and lanky, Homicide seems ill suited to the job and is indeed rendered redundant when Ray lifts and lowers the massive weight bar without even a tremble of his arms. I try to keep my hormones in check at the incredible display of male strength, but Mother Nature has her own ideas, and within minutes my skin is hot and sweaty, my nipples are tight, and I'm wet down below. I am almost disappointed when Ray and Homicide Hank shake hands and Ray joins me on the bench.

"So how was the date?"

Momentarily befuddled, dragged out of a fantasy where Ray does push-ups over my naked body, I just stare. "What date?"

"The date you had last night."

My heart sinks. Ray is about the last person I want to talk dates with. "Well…it went as expected. One look at my ink, piercings, pink streak, and leather, and it was all over. It's like he was expecting Taylor Swift and got Lady Gaga instead."

His gaze travels over my Coldplay tank top and black leather pants. "A guy who can't appreciate a sexy woman isn't worth your time."

"C'mon." I give him a little nudge with my elbow. "This look doesn't scream sexy."

"You scream sexy." He strokes a finger along the strap of my tank top and my body stills, need gripping me so hard I can barely breathe.

"I'm not—"

"You got a gym full of men watching you walk across the floor," he says in a low growl. "Means you're sexy."

Oh God. Is he teasing me? Or worse, flirting? What about Shayla? Cheeks burning, I pull a folder from my portfolio. "Here are the designs I promised you."

But Ray doesn't take the folder. Instead, he gently strokes the little silver cross in my earlobe. "This what he didn't like? Your piercings?"

"Who?"

"The moron from last night."

Warm fuzzies spread through my body and I lower the folder. "Actually, I didn't tell him all the places I'm pierced."

Ray's hand stills, and his eyes darken almost to black. "Not letting that one go. Where else are you pierced?"

Delighted at finally gaining the upper hand, I lean in and whisper, "Secret."

His eyes bore into mine, drilling into my soul, as if he expects my secrets to reveal themselves if he digs far enough. But I'm an expert at keeping secrets. My fortress is impenetrable.

"Sia!" Tag's shout echoes through the gym and I groan. Although I knew getting in and out undetected was a long shot, I had still hoped.

"He doesn't like me coming here." I mumble under my breath. "He thinks it's too dangerous. I had hoped to avoid detection."

"Got it."

Pushing myself to my feet, I mentally prepare for the showdown. What I'm not prepared for is Ray, standing beside me, angling his body slightly to shield me from the oncoming Tag storm. Although calm and quiet on the outside, I can sense violence simmering beneath the surface. Is he protecting me? From Tag?

"What's going on? I told you not to come here." Tag's naturally loud voice attracts some unwanted attention and nausea roils my gut.

"Calm down." I hold up my art case, warding him away. "I don't want to cause a scene. I just came to bring Ray some designs."

He glares at Ray. "You couldn't have gone to her tattoo parlor? You had to make her come out to fucking Ghost Town?"

"Hey! You're outta line." I move forward, but Ray steps in front of me, blocking my way. The gesture is so subtle, I'm not sure if it was intentional. "I wanted to come out here," I say to Tag. "This is business. Plus, I miss hanging with the guys and watching you drill the new recruits and making them cry."

My joke falls flat and Tag scowls, but not at me. He huffs and puffs, and for a moment I wonder if he's going to blow Ray down.

"Not lookin' for a fight, Fuzz." Although his hands hang loosely by his sides, I've watched enough fights to know Ray is anything but relaxed. "I'll watch out for her," he continues, his voice low and even. "We got tats to talk about."

Before Tag can even splutter a word, Ray places his hand on my lower back and guides me toward the door. At least I think he's guiding me. My entire body is focused on his warm, firm hand pressed up against my back, sending waves of molten pleasure through my body.

"Sia."

Looking back over my shoulder, I give Tag a wink and a wave, profoundly grateful he is forced to exercise restraint in the gym. No shouting and hollering and storming about today. Just silent fury pulsing toward me in waves.

"Sorry about Tag," I say. "It was nice when I was younger to know he was watching out for me, but…"

"He's afraid to let you go."

Just like I'm afraid to let go of Tag. Emotion wells up in my chest and I stop in the hallway and hold out the folder. "You want to look at the designs?"

His fingers brush over mine as he takes the folder, electrifying my nerve endings. His hands are broad and strong, and for a moment I am captivated by his muscled forearms, the slight gleam of sweat on his tanned skin, the sprinkling of hair. How many nights have I watched him fight and wonder what it would be like to glide my finger along the ropes of those muscles, feel the hair tickle my palm?

He looks up and catches me staring, and although my heat rises, I can't look away. His eyes hide a darkness, a stain on his soul.

"These are good." He hands me the folder, breaking the spell. "But that first design you did? Fucking perfect."

"It was just off the top of my head." I take the folder from him and drop it in my case. "I didn't really give it much thought."

Ray cups my jaw with his hand and strokes his thumb over my cheek, sending a jolt of white lightning straight to my core. "Instinct. Trust it."

Not my instincts. And especially not now when my body is responding to his touch while my mind is screaming no.

"Ray, I was hoping I'd catch you before you left."

My eyes fly open as Shayla bounds over to us, all toned, sculpted muscles and not a jiggle in sight. Her gaze fixes on Ray's hand on my cheek, and she gives me a tight smile.

"Oh, hi, Sia. That was you at the fight the other night wasn't it?"

Oh God. How embarrassing is this. I give her an abrupt nod, then pull away. "I'd better get going. It's almost dark. Fuzzy will freak if I'm still here when the sun sets."

Shayla barks a laugh. "Why? You turn into a vampire or a werewolf or something?"

"No, but he does."

Her cheeks redden, and she licks her lips. "I'd like to see that. Fuzz as a werewolf. He'd be covered with fuzz for real. Fucking hot. What I wouldn't give for a bit of that."

I glance over at Ray, but he's watching me and doesn't seem to care that his girlfriend is lusting over another guy in front of him. Also, AWKWARD. Tag is my brother and he belongs to Jess, although he doesn't know it yet.

"I'll leave you two…together." I pick up my portfolio and head for the door.

"We're not together," Shayla calls out in an indiscreet, embarrass-the-hell-out-of-Sia tone of voice. "Me 'n' Ray are just friends. I'm him, but a girl. Not a good combo when you got two dominant personalities in the bedroom."

Stunned into inactivity, I stare at the front door. *He's not with her.* My brain gets stuck in an endless loop of wondering if he would ever want to be with me and knowing it could never happen.

"Uh…thanks for that." I turn and force a smile. "Actually, I was just here for business reasons."

Shayla gives me a sly grin. "Sorry. I got confused. I guess all Ray's petting was because you had something on your cheek, or maybe it's that perpetual lost-kitten look that has men falling at your feet."

What men? What the hell is she talking about?

"Shayla." Ray's warning growl does nothing more than egg her on.

Shayla grins. "And Sia was—"

"Leaving." No way am I sticking around to have my feelings brutally exposed, especially when I'm not used to having feelings at all. I'm used to bland firefighters and blander accountants. I'm used to cold sheets, hot fantasies, and a box of vibrators under the bed. I'm used to staying strong, staying safe, staying sane. And yet I'm inexorably drawn to Ray, body and soul, as if we somehow fit together.

"Sia." Ray's deep growl stops me in my tracks, and I look over my shoulder.

"Seven o'clock. Tuesday. We go late, I'll take you home. Keep Tag happy."

"Sure. I'll be there."

Ray gives a satisfied grunt and I turn and walk away. But I can feel his gaze on me, burning into my skin. A shiver ripples down my spine, but I don't know whether it's from anticipation or fear.

Or both.

Chapter 5

He didn't pee on my feet

"You're going to ink Ray tonight? Shut the front door!"

Jess shrieks after I tell her about my meeting with Ray at Redemption, the "sexy" comment, the cheek stroking, and my oh-so-exciting evening ahead. Of course, shrieks don't go down very well in tiny vegan cafés in the Haight District, and her outburst attracts a lot of attention. The unwanted kind.

"I kinda wish he was still a fantasy man." I stir my lentil chili and then take a little nibble. *Not bad.* Jess is always trying to convince me of the benefits of a vegan lifestyle, and although she's introduced me to some tasty dishes, I just can't give up my hamburgers. "He's a bit much to handle in real life. Very intense. Very dominant. And so damn hot I think I'll combust every time I'm near him."

"And taken."

"Well...no." I sigh and lower my spoon. "Which is a shame because I'm not looking for a relationship right now."

"You haven't been looking for a relationship for years." She gives a sarcastic snort. "Even when you were in a relationship, you said you weren't looking for a relationship."

"They weren't real relationships. What I had with Charlie and James was comfortable, and I was so grateful for everything they did for me, I felt I owed it to them to try to be in a relationship. And Peter was—"

"A pig." Jess curses as she has done every time I mention the name of the man who broke it off with me because I had too much "baggage."

"Seriously," I say. "I need to focus on my work so I can help out Mom and Dad, and save money so I can open up my own studio one day. And I've got to shake off the Tag shackles."

Longing flickers across her face. "Tag's overprotective because he cares."

But not about her. The unspoken words hang between us. Tag has always treated her like another little sister; never once did he give any sign he saw her as anything other than a friend.

She takes a bite of her tofu scramble. "If you really wanted to throw off the Tag shackles, you'd just tell him. You wouldn't call him up when you need help. You wouldn't ask his advice about everything. You wouldn't ride home with him after work. You wouldn't ride criminal-shotgun in the back of his police car. Of course, there are some of us who would die for a big brother like that, but if you want to throw it all away for a little independence, well, that's up to you."

"Sarcasm doesn't become you." I try for a withering stare and make her laugh instead.

"And anger doesn't become you. People with a smiley face generally look smiley even when they're annoyed, which I know you are because you've stirred that chili into mush."

"Okay then, man whispering genius." I dab my lips with my napkin and hold up my phone. "Ray offered to take me home if we go late tonight. How do I play it with Tag? He always picks me up when I work late."

Jess strokes an imaginary beard. "Tell him you have a date."

"I don't have a date. I have a client."

"Seriously?" Jess throws her napkin on the table. "He shows up at your studio demanding your ink, kisses you, then invites you to Redemption on the pretense of seeing your designs but in reality so he can show off his cut, half-naked, muscular fighter's body, then he says you're sexy, and you don't think you have a date?"

"Not really."

She shakes her head. "That's how the males of most species work. They show off the plumage in the hopes of attracting a mate. And as a vet's assistant, I would know."

Leaning back in my seat, I raise an eyebrow. "You know about dogs, cats, snakes, gerbils, fish, and other small city-type pets. You ever get a peacock or a baboon or even a lion in your clinic?"

Jess pouts. "Now you're just being mean. I took the job because I like animals. I read about them. I watch *Nature* and the Discovery Channel. I'm telling you, this is primal stuff. After the display, the winning alpha males make an assertion of dominance."

"He didn't pee on my feet, if that's where you're going with this." I bite my lip to keep from laughing because Jess is dead serious.

She frowns and takes another bite of her tofu. "Did he beat his chest?"

"No."

"Shout and wave his arms?"

"No."

"Drag you around by your hair?"

"No.

"Did he assume a physically superior position?"

"Ah…"

Jess's eyes widen. "Ah?"

"Well, when Tag came storming toward me, Ray kinda…stood between us. At first I thought I imagined it, but I wasn't too sure."

"Protective. Key alpha-male trait. He's marked you. It means he wants you on a primal level."

I give my lentil mush a vigorous stir. "How about if he just likes me on a normal level?"

Jess snorts a laugh. "I've seen him in the ring. That man is one hot, dominant alpha-male package all wrapped up with a fancy, badass bow. Men like that don't do normal. They live on the edge. Push it to the max. It's all or nothing. All out or all in. No mercy. No surrender."

"No control." I sigh and put down my fork. "Too dangerous for me. I need someone calm and predictable. Someone I can trust."

"You had that and you were bored out of your mind." Jess waves the waitress over. "And now the epitome of alpha male-dom is clearly interested, and you don't want that either. What do you want?"

Emotion wells up in my chest, and I drop my spoon on the table. "I want to let someone into my life without worrying that I've totally misjudged him or that I won't be safe. I want to be normal, Jess. I want to be able to trust someone, intimately."

"What's so great about normal?" She keeps her voice low. "Taking a bottle of sleeping pills and slitting your wrists at the age of seventeen isn't normal, but I do okay."

"Jess…" I've never been able to understand how she can be so candid about what happened to her the night we met, or about the abuse she suffered that led her down that path. But that's Jess. She puts it all out there, and if you can't deal, she walks away.

"He's perfect for you. Don't push him away like you have every-one else." She asks the waitress for dessert menus and another two cups of coffee. Jess and I share many things, a coffee addiction being one of them. "You need someone to shake you up, pull you out of your cocoon. He's the calculated risk your therapist told you to take. You need a little badass, but you know he's a safe badass. He's no stranger. Tag knows him. The guys at Redemption know him. And you like him. Who spends a year watching someone if they aren't drawn to them for some reason?" She leans over and grins. "A primal reason. Just like him."

I squirm in my seat and then take a menu from the waitress. "He just wants a tat, Jess, so let's talk about something else. What's good for dessert?"

"He wants you and you want him." She pulls out her purse and throws twenty dollars on the table. "Twenty says you make out by the end of the night despite all your hang-ups."

Hmmm. Can I afford to lose twenty dollars? Just the thought of making out with the Predator sends a delicious shiver down my spine.

"Okay." I throw a twenty on the table.

Jess grins. "And no turning him down just to win. If he makes the move, you play the game."

"No hardship there." So long as it's just a game.

The waitress arrives to take our orders and Jess points to my phone on the table. "Call Tag and tell him Ray's driving you home. I want to hear the explosion."

"Not this time. Tag's been acting kind of strange since last weekend. Almost punched Ray in the gym. And down on the wharf he was close to losing it. I don't know what would have happened if Ray hadn't shown up. I think it has to do with a new case he's on. He tried to tell me about it, but I just couldn't listen."

Her face creases with concern. "Poor Tag. He takes on too much. Sometimes you need a little help when you're trying to save the world."

"And sometimes you need a little help when you're trying to hide from it."

"Hi, Slim. Bye, Christos." I press myself back against the door as Christos sails past me and out onto the sidewalk.

"Got a gig at the Cage tonight. Have to run." He blows me a kiss and then races down the street.

Slim looks up from Rose's desk and shakes his head. "He's more about the music than the ink."

"That's not true. He's about both." I dump my stuff and perch on the edge of the desk beside him. "And if you think he's going to leave us, I can promise you he won't. He loves it here. He loves his work. And although I hate to say it, his band is never going to make it big. They're good but not that good. Plus, he's loyal. Like me and Duncan."

Slim sniffs and shoves his Fedora to the side. "You said you want to open up your own studio. Doesn't sound loyal to me."

"I'm talking years from now. Like so many years you'll probably be sick of me by then, and I'll have forgotten everything I learned in my business management course and come crawling back begging for a chair."

"That kinda attitude, you're right." Slim leans back in his chair and crosses his arms behind his head. "You gotta have confidence in yourself. Coupla times I left you running the shop, you did a bang-up job, but you were always second-guessing yourself. You got good instincts. Trust 'em."

Ha. If he knew about my lack of judgment, he would never say that. "You trying to make me leave? Bolster my confidence enough and I might just walk out of here."

"You're not there yet. If you were, I'd be hiding my client list."

We chat about some of the mind-blowing artists who have made names for themselves in the city with clever designs, crazy colors, and bold line work. I tell Slim they're killing at what they do while I'm stuck in the same place. Slim laughs and says they're all basically doing the same thing, scamming on the styles of the masters. True art is unique, pure creation. One day when I'm doing freehand, I'll understand.

I wish that day was now.

The little bell on the front door jangles and Slim gives my arm a warning squeeze. "Speaking of clients, here comes your man."

"He's not my man. He's a friend."

Slim laughs. "My friends don't look at me like they want to devour me. They also don't call up Rose, order her to clear your schedule for the evening, and offer to pay for the extra time. That kind of attention usually means something more than friendship." He winks and tips back his hat. "Just sayin'."

Pressing my lips together, I glare. "Don't you have an ass to ink out back? I thought Rose mentioned your favorite soldier got drunk again at a party and can't go home until you've covered 'Whore Lover' with his wife's name."

Slim scrubs his hands over his face. "Fifth time now. I'm running out of ideas for stylized versions of 'Ava' that are long enough to cover the tats he gets when he's on tour overseas."

He heads to the back and I spin around to find Ray in the doorway. He's wearing his usual delicious khaki commando pants, sitting low on his narrow hips, and a tight black Harley-Davidson T-shirt. His biceps bulge from beneath his short sleeves and my mouth waters.

"Ready for me?"

Oh boy. Am I ready.

When we reach my station, I pull out the stencil of the original design I finished up after Jess left for work. We discuss shading and the best way to make use of the design to cover his scar—a nice, professional conversation, although the thoughts going through my mind are anything but nice. Or professional.

Once we're done, I wash up and remove my sterilized equipment from the autoclave, then I pull on my gloves and bring the water, razor, and rubbing alcohol to prepare the skin I'm about to ink. By the time I return to my station, Ray has stripped off his shirt and is now lounging half-naked in my chair.

My breath catches in my throat. Dear God. His lightly tanned skin is stretched tight over rock-hard muscle and his tattoos shimmer under the overhead light. Seated, still, he is at the mercy of my slow, meticulous perusal. And boy, do I peruse.

After I've drunk my fill and calmed the raging desire in my blood, I adjust my artist's chair and pull it up so I am only inches away from his breathtaking body. "You can put your arm across my lap." My voice is remarkably calm. "It'll give me better access."

Better access? Cringe. I dip my head and swallow hard. How about I keep the mouth shut and just get busy?

He nods and places his forearm across my thighs, his clenched fist at my waist. Warm and heavy, his arm rests perilously close to the juncture of my thighs and I steel myself to keep my thoughts away from images of that hand between my legs, his fingers stroking my folds.

Taking a deep breath, I run a warm washcloth slowly over his skin. "Too hot?" I look up through my eyelashes and the intensity of his gaze as he shakes his head takes my breath away.

His muscles tighten when I dip the cloth again and gently wash his chest and shoulder. His skin is smooth and taut over rigid muscle. I silently curse the gloves that stop me from feeling his skin, and the soap that cannot mask the sinful, masculine scent that is driving me to distraction. When I pull out the rubbing alcohol, I curse that too because it means I have to stop touching him.

Except for the White Buffalo's cover of "House of the Rising Sun" playing in the background, there is no sound except the rasp of Ray's breath as his chest rises and falls under my hand. Although I've done shoulder and pec tats countless times, the intimacy of this position sends a shiver through my body. Longing grips me hard and fierce, and I scramble to regain some semblance of control. Maybe a little conversation.

"So, did you catch your bad guy?"

"No. Still after him."

When I look up, Ray is watching me. He is so close I can see the stubble of his five o'clock shadow, the thickness of his lashes, his eyes deepening to an azure blue. I force myself to look into them and swallow hard. "Everything okay?"

Apparently not. Jaw tight, muscles quivering, he captures me with his glance. "Your hair."

I give my head a slight shake and my ponytail swings back and forth. "What's wrong with my hair?"

"Take it down." He fingers a loose tendril beside my ear, his authoritative tone sending a wave of heat raging through me.

"I keep it up so it's out of the way."

"Down."

"I'll have to take off my gloves first, and then I'll have to…" My words die in my throat when he strokes his hand over my hair, front to back. With one sharp jerk, he tugs out my ponytail holder and my hair tumbles around my shoulders.

"Beautiful."

Trembling, painfully and desperately aroused, I pick up the razor and shaving gel from my tray. "I…have to shave you." My voice drops to a throaty whisper, and if that doesn't tell him what he does to me, nothing will.

Another curt nod. But then he's not a talkative type. I've never seen him hanging out with the other fighters after the gym closes for the night, and not once has he ever joined us for drinks after a fight.

Taking a deep breath, I still my hand, then smooth the gel over his skin. But when I dip the razor, Ray tenses, his fist clenching and unclenching beside my hip.

A smile tugs at the corner of my lips. "Don't worry. I've never cut anyone. I'll be gentle."

"Man lives the life I've lived, he's not used to gentle."

Tilting my head to the side, I meet his gaze. "You've never had anyone be gentle with you?"

"I usually scare the gentle ones away."

"I can't imagine why." My hand relaxes and I stroke the razor across his skin. Stroke and dip. Stroke and dip. The rhythmic movement calms my fraught nerves, but with every touch, tension builds between us until it is almost a living, palpable thing. "You're not so scary." I tease the blade around his nipple and Ray sucks in a sharp breath.

"Sia—" He chokes off his words so I continue talking, keeping my voice low and even, soothing the savage beast trapped in my chair.

"I have to admit, in the ring, you're pretty terrifying. You have so much power and yet you keep it so tightly leashed. But when you let it go"—I look up and my cheeks heat—"I think it's thrilling. But you keep it in control. You never go too far. That's where I see the beauty."

Ray stares at me as if entranced, heaving his breaths, his gaze focused, intent. Even when Slim walks past to grab some supplies and then heads back to the private rooms, Ray doesn't take his eyes off me.

"Slim ink the butterfly too?" He leans forward and lightly touches the butterfly on my shoulder. I yank the razor away in case he becomes my first ever casualty.

"Yeah, isn't it beautiful? I have one on the other shoulder too. Slim's a real master. When he was finished with the roses and thorns, I felt like something was missing. I wanted hope and freedom. And yellow, because it's my favorite color. He came up with the butterflies."

"Would have thought black was your favorite color." He gestures to my clothes. "You always wear black."

"Yellow is my secret favorite color." I give him a half smile. "Not many people know."

Ray gives a grunt of satisfaction, and I feel a little tingle at the thought that I've pleased him. He traces the outline of the little butterfly and pleasure ripples through my body.

"Looks just like a butterfly I caught when I was a kid. I watched it for hours. Learned a hard lesson that day. I wanted to touch it and I was too rough. Must've broken its wing. When I let it go, it couldn't fly."

"You can touch me. I won't break."

His jaw tightens, and I curse myself for being so flippant about what was probably an upsetting moment in his childhood. What the hell is wrong with me? He shares an actual piece of personal information and I show no sympathy at all. Not only that, but now I'm begging for his attention.

After a few more strokes with the blade, I wash him off, then spritz him with disinfectant. In my zeal, I spray not only the area to be inked, but the rest of his torso as well. Damn klutz side strikes again. "Sorry. Forgot to reduce the nozzle." Grabbing a sterile cloth, I dry his chest then work my way over his rippled abdomen. His muscles quiver beneath my touch as I pat along the soft, dusky trail of hair, following it down to his belt. Imagining where it might go.

He tenses when I near his buckle and gives a strangled grunt. "S'good."

My gaze drifts below his belt, to the bulge in his jeans. He is fully erect, his shaft straining against his fly. A naughty thrill of excitement shoots through my veins. He's aroused because of me.

"Um…do you want to take a break before I apply the stencil?"

He shakes his head, then leans forward and sweeps his hand through my hair, letting the strands slide through his fingers. A sigh escapes my lips as delicious sensations sweep through my body. I am on fire. And although I've been with men before, I've never been immobilized by a single touch.

"So soft." He runs his hand over my hair again, this time trailing his fingers along my shoulder. His thumb glides over my throat and he curls his hand around my neck. "So fucking delicate."

I am burning. Consumed by fire. A burst of need drives a whimper up my throat, and I choke it back as his thumb circles the sensitive hollow at the base of my neck. Firm. Unyielding. Dominant. With one squeeze, he could break me. The way I was broken before. The way he broke the butterfly. And yet nothing could tear me away from this moment.

"Sia." He says my name softly, drawing out the last syllable in a gravelly murmur, almost like a prayer.

My brain fuzzes with lust, and I surrender to the thrill of his touch, the pounding of my pulse in my veins, the desire that has haunted me since I first saw him in the ring. My head falls back, my lips part, and I drown in the depths of an azure sea.

With a low groan, Ray turns sideways in the chair, dropping his legs to the floor. With his hand still cupped around my neck, he pulls me between his legs, the casters on my stool squeaking in gentle protest. I circle my arms around his neck and my breasts rub against his bare chest. The press of his erection against my stomach sends a rush of moisture to my sex.

"Jesus Christ." His voice drops husky and low. "You're killing me."

He leans down and sweeps my hair behind my shoulder, then nuzzles my neck. Sensation sears through my body and I tilt my head to the side to give him better access. So unprofessional. What if Slim comes out? Overcome with the fulfillment of a year's worth of longing, I can't bring myself to care.

He feathers kisses over my cheek and I lick my lips in anticipation. This is really happening. He's going to kiss me again. A real hands-on-the-body Predator kiss.

A bell tinkles behind me. Damn front door. Damn customers who come after hours. I'm not turning around. I want my kiss.

Ray glances up and stiffens. "Holy shit."

Chapter 6

I HAVE NEVER REALLY, TRULY BEEN KISSED

POISED, BREATHLESS, ON THE cusp of the fulfillment of a yearlong fantasy, I half turn to see who is behind us. But before I get a glimpse at the door, Ray launches himself forward, taking me to the ground with a painful crash.

"What the...?"

"Down." He presses me against the cold floor, covering me with his body. I strain my neck to see, but my vision is blocked by the couch on the other side of Duncan's chair, beside us.

A crack. And another. Mortar crumbles from the wall behind us. Gunshots? My heart goes into overdrive as Ray pulls a gun from a holster around his ankle.

Ray has a gun.

"Who are they?" My voice is barely a whisper. "What do they want?"

Ray puts his finger to his lips as shots ring out around us. A jar shatters. Foam explodes upward from a chair. I tremble so hard I am sure they can hear the chatter of my teeth.

"What's going on?" Slim appears in the doorway to the back room, and Ray motions him away. But he's too late. Two shots crack the stillness and Slim goes down.

"No." I try to push Ray away so I can get to Slim. But Ray drops his weight, holding me still.

"Stay down. Don't know who they are or what they want, but they don't seem to care who they kill. You're going out the rear exit. Crawl or slide on your belly. Stay under the chairs until you get to that couch at the back. When you need to cross the floor, I'll cover you. Once you're out, call for help."

"I'll call Tag."

Bullets ring out around us. A mirror shatters. "911," says Ray. "Then Tag."

"Tag. I need Tag."

His voice drops, calm and even. "911. Then Tag. If he can't get here in five minutes, that call will kill him, and Slim needs medical attention."

"What about you?"

"Gotta stay with Slim. I'll meet you out back. Go."

My mom didn't raise any fools. Heart pumping, I slither under the chairs, staying close to the wall and under the ledge. When I reach the couch, Ray gestures me forward, then jumps up and shoots over the couch. Gritting my teeth, I crawl toward the door leading to the private ink rooms, staff room, and supply room out back. Thankfully, Slim has fallen back into the hallway, out of the line of fire. The soldier is with him, holding a wadded cloth to his shoulder.

"Is he going to be okay?"

"If we can get an ambulance here right away. You got a phone? I left mine in the treatment room and he needs pressure on the wound."

"Yeah." My voice wavers. "In my pocket."

His face softens. "It's gonna be okay. Took a quick look when the shooting started and the guy out there knows what he's doing. He'll keep us covered until the police get here. You get out. Call 911. I'll stay with Slim."

After a moment of hesitation, I give Slim a kiss on the cheek, then race down the hallway and out the back door. Leaning against a Dumpster, I pull my phone from my pocket and call 911. Then I call Tag.

His anguished cry almost breaks my heart. He is at least half an hour away. But Ray was right. He maintains his sanity only because I've told him I've already called 911.

Too afraid to leave the alley in case the shooters are still out front, I curl up beside the Dumpster, my nose wrinkling at the pungent odor of stale piss and rotting garbage. My heart continues to pound and I take deep, calming breaths as the wail of sirens grows louder and louder. Tires screech. Doors slam. Voices. Shouting.

"Sia." Ray rounds the corner from the alley leading to the street and runs toward me. Relief crashes over me and I shoot up from my hiding spot. Before I can stop myself, I'm in his arms.

For a long moment, we hold each other. Alone and out of sight. His warmth soaks into me, his arms tighten around me, and I breathe in his scent of sweat and soap, and the essence of him as he engulfs me with his body. The world fades away and we are completely still, connected, breathing together, our hearts pounding together. Despite the shouts and sirens, the barking of what must be a police dog, I feel safe—completely and utterly safe, in a way I have not felt since that terrible night when I went to a party Tag had warned me not to attend.

Finally, I manage to tilt my head back. Ray is watching me, his gaze intense, his face tight with an emotion I can't identify.

"Sia." My name comes out with the breath that releases the tension in his body. "You're safe."

Whether his words are meant as an assurance to me or to him, I don't know, but his stillness moves me. Ray is a man always in motion, like the Predator for which he was named.

"Are you okay?"

He nods. "Hit one of them in the leg, but they got away. Medics are looking after Slim. He'll be fine. Bullet just grazed his shoulder, and he hit his head going down."

"Did you see who they were?"

"Street gang. Nasty one. I recognized the colors and tattoos. Don't think they were there to kill anyone, just give a warning by shooting up the shop. Slim got in the way." His jaw tightens. "Someone in the shop must have done something to piss them off pretty bad."

"Jay, one of our senior artists. He left Slim a message saying he had to lie low and couldn't come to work. I didn't really take it seriously, but Rose did. She said he'd even inked some of them."

Ray scowls. "Anything to do with the street gangs is serious. Bastard should have known better than to let them know where he worked. Put you in danger. Next time I see him, I'll give him an ass kicking he'll never forget."

His ferocity makes me smile. "Will he be able to work after you're done?"

"You want him to work?" His voice softens.

"Yeah. I'm not really into revenge."

"What are you into?" His gaze drops to my lips, and I am suddenly and painfully aware of his body pressed tightly against mine, his arms around me, and his heartbeat quickening, as if it's oblivious to the fact the danger has passed. I've never been this close to him, never seen his eyes so dark, never imagined I would feel the power thrumming through his body. Because aren't predators supposed to kill?

Unspent adrenaline screams through my veins, turning my legs liquid. I ache with a desire I shouldn't feel. A painful, desperate hunger for a man I should not want—a man whose violent nature both arouses and frightens me.

"Ray…" His name is a whispered plea on my lips.

He threads his hand through my hair, tugging my head back so hard my eyes tear, but I have never felt such pleasure in pain.

"Christ. I'm barely in control as it is."

A soft moan escapes my lips. I am hot—so hot, I might combust—and before I can stop myself, I rock up, thread my hands through his hair, and touch my lips to his in a gentle kiss.

Ray stiffens and growls, the sound vibrating through my chest. He deepens the kiss, his tongue sliding between my lips to explore every inch of my mouth. My heart speeds to double time, but it is the way he holds me still—one hand tangled in my hair, his other hand firm around my back—that sends a wave of liquid heat through my veins. His lips are firm and demanding, forcing my mouth open as his tongue plunges deeper, stroking me into oblivion. Possessive. Demanding. Unyielding. A Predator's kiss.

Sliding my hands over his magnificent chest, taut and hard, and then along his broad shoulders, I drink him in with a never-ending thirst. Hot and hungry, my tongue tangles with his, questing, seeking, wanting more as I grind my hips against his thigh in an entirely uncharacteristic display of need.

My actions inflame him. In one smooth movement, he spins us and backs me into the cold, brick wall. His arm tightens so hard I can barely breathe. And then he ravages my mouth, his tongue questing deep, as if he has lost control and the beast within will settle for nothing less than devouring me.

I have never really, truly been kissed.

Until now.

I feel him with every inch of my skin, every breath I take. My breasts ache for his touch, my clit throbs for his attention, and my heart pounds in warning.

But when I moan into his mouth, he tenses and pulls away. "Condition I'm in now…it's like after a fight…I got no gentleness in me."

Bloodlust. The aftereffect of a fight. The edge of control. Tag told me about it, warned me to stay away from fighters immediately after a fight. But I have watched Ray for so long, lusted after him for so many nights, imagined I was the one in the ring pinned to the mat, I do the unthinkable and lean up and nip his lip. Hard.

"I don't want gentle." I've had years of gentle. Years of being treated like a piece of glass. Years of men who held my hand and wept with me when I told them about my past because they couldn't believe anyone would be capable of inflicting such pain. Years of wondering if my heart never pounded when I was with them because I wasn't capable of being loved or giving love in return. Ray is the opposite of gentle. He is the opposite of all the men I have been with. Dominant. In control. He is everything I fear and everything I have secretly desired.

"Fuck." He yanks my head to the side, exposing my throat to the heated slide of his lips. My blood turns to molten lava, burning hot through my veins, but when he grasps my hands and pins them tight over my head, clasping my wrists easily in his broad palm, the lava erupts in a high-pitched shriek.

Startled, Ray drops my hands and takes a step back. "Did I hurt you?"

Damn. Damn. Damn post-traumatic stress disorder. Damn psychological triggers. Damn therapists who can't make them go way. Damn Luke for putting them there.

Stuttering and stammering, I manage to get out a few words. "I…no. Just…like my hands to be free."

He studies me for long time, as if he knows I'm not telling him everything and then he takes another step back. "This wasn't a good idea. Especially now. When I can't pull it back."

I draw in a ragged breath, my arousal a living beast inside me, desperate, hungry, and howling at the possibility of being denied. "But…you didn't hurt me."

"Don't know what I was thinking," he says, half to himself. "When I thought you were in danger, and then you were okay…" He scrapes his hand through his hair. "Fuck…just…lost it. You're a sweet girl. This was a mistake."

Sweet? With my tats and leather pants? Doc Martens and pink-streaked hair? Broken isn't sweet, but he must sense I'm not normal because he's walking away. Normal girls don't shriek when mouth-watering, hot, sexy fighters hold their hands above their heads the way they fantasize about almost every night.

Maybe I should tell him it's just a quirk and I'm not looking for a relationship or even a date. Just one time. Here. Now. Him. But clearly it isn't meant to be.

"Sia." Tag rounds the corner and jogs up the alley toward me, stopping when he meets up with Ray.

"Don't know how I can ever thank you for looking out for my sis. The guys outside told me what you did. If you hadn't been there…" Tag chokes up and gives Ray a manly thump on the shoulder. Ray nods.

"Gotta go give a statement." He turns the corner. And then he's gone.

An hour later, I am sitting in Tag's squad car with a blanket wrapped around me and a coffee in my hand. Ray is nowhere in sight. Tag hovers.

"You need anything?"

"I'm good."

"Water? More coffee? Another blanket? You want me to sit with you?"

"I'm fine."

"You sure? I want to go find out what's going on, but I don't want to leave you alone."

I wave my hand generally around the area. "There are about twenty cops here. Nothing is going to happen to me, and I'm not allowed to go until the officer in charge has gone through my statement. Go get the scoop. I'll be right here."

After Tag leaves, I try not to think about what possessed me to come on to Ray and how I so obviously misread the signs he was giving me. Sure, he kissed me, but maybe it was post-shooting bloodlust, or he was just riding the adrenaline high. Clearly I took advantage of Ray in his "weakened" state, and as he came around, he realized he didn't want me, and gentleman that he is, he backed off.

For the fourth time that evening, I call Jess. I tell her my new theory as I pace back and forth beside the police car. She tells me she's never heard a bigger load of BS in her life. Maybe he didn't want to fuck his teammate's sister in a dirty back alley with a load of cops out front after he almost just got killed saving her. Did I consider that?

I tell her no, I didn't consider that. But what man in the throes of bloodlust turns down a sure thing just because she shrieks in terror because he tried to pin her arms above her head?

Ray, she says. 'Cause he's a nice guy. But I don't believe her. I've seen him in the ring. Tag has warned me about him. He has a gun. Maybe the rumors are true and he's in the CIA. Although he doesn't dress like the feds dress on TV. And why would he be moonlighting as a PI and fighting on the underground circuit? Not that I know anything about the CIA, but I do know my crime TV. I also know "nice" is not a word that fits Ray. He's badass bad. And badasses fuck in a badass way. I know, because I've just had a little taste.

Tag returns about twenty minutes later. I lean against the vehicle and he gives me a lecture about the dangers of working in the Lower Haight and associating with people like Jay, whom he confirms is indeed marked by one of the more vicious local street gangs. On a roll, he lectures about the dangers of driving at night, going to underground fights, and taking too many risks.

While he rants, I am struck with the realization that I won't be going to any more underground fights. No more watching the Predator from the shadows. No more cheering crowds, fists slamming into flesh, power unleashed. My fantasy came true, and it was nothing like I had imagined. It was better. And then it was gone.

"You're not listening." Tag's irritated voice cuts through my reverie.

"I've heard it all before. I understand how you must feel. But it's not my fault that I happened to be at the shop when that gang came looking for Jay. And it was a good thing Ray was there. He had a gun."

He rakes his hand over his fuzzy head and his jaw tightens. "Yeah, he did."

"Why?"

Tag shrugs. "You'll have to ask him yourself."

"Is he still here?" Not that I want to see him, but I do.

"No, he took off. Asked me to say good-bye. I hope you're not seeing him. I told you before, he's not the right kind of guy for you."

I slump against the vehicle and sigh. "No, I won't be seeing him again. He came in for a tat, but I have a feeling he won't be back."

Tag's eyes widen. "I thought you'd start screaming at me about interfering in your life. I know you like him and—"

"He isn't my kind of guy, and I'm not his kind of girl."

"If you say so." He pulls open the passenger door. "You can ride up front today."

"Gee thanks. No treating me like a criminal today. I feel honored." I pull my door closed and fasten my seat belt while he climbs into the driver's seat beside me.

"Can I stay at your place tonight? I don't feel like being alone."

Tag grimaces. "Actually, my place is a mess. I'll come and sleep on your couch."

"But your place is always a mess. It's never bothered you before."

He stiffens and glares. "I said I'll come to your place. I've found someone to take my shift."

When I startle at his uncharacteristically sharp tone, his face softens. "After a traumatic event you should be somewhere comfortable and familiar."

Emotion wells up in my chest at his oblique reference to the night I made the worst decision of my life. The night I didn't listen to Tag and my whole world changed.

He turns on the radio and the sad notes of No Doubt's "Don't Speak" fill the vehicle. Just what I need. A tear, unwanted and unexpected, trickles down my cheek.

"You okay?" He looks over and I shrug. But no, I'm not okay. Memories assail me. I'm outside the Psi Beta Pi frat house, eighteen years old, heart pounding with excitement that socially connected college bad boy Luke Rotherberg, star quarterback on Tag's football team, has asked me to go to the post-game party with him. Me—newly minted high school grad, starving artist, plain, and shy; the girl who just had her first art exhibition in the school gym; the daughter of a cab driver and a florist with none of his high-society connections.

Overwhelmed by the attention, I didn't listen when Tag warned me that he'd heard rumors about Luke and that it wasn't safe to go to the frat party alone. And I didn't pay attention when my skin prickled as Luke took my hand and told me he was going to show me the time of my life, or when my blood chilled when he winked at his friend. Instead, I thought about all the girls who were desperate for his attention and how Luke had picked me. So I told Tag I wouldn't go and I went anyway.

And when he pinned me to the bed and tore off my clothes, I screamed for Tag. Because he had been right and I hadn't listened. Because he had always been there to save me when we were kids. Because in my heart I knew he would come.

And he did.

But too late.

"Tag…" My voice is nothing more than a whisper. Too much emotion. Too many bad memories. Too much pain resurfacing tonight.

"Oh God. I didn't think." Tag reaches over and squeezes my hand. "I didn't mean to bring it all back. I'm just messed up right now. Fucking messed up."

"Join the club." A wave of sadness sweeps over me, not just for the part of me I lost that night, but because for a moment Ray found her, and now she's lost again.

Chapter 7

AND WHOOSH, HE IS GONE

FOUR DAYS AFTER THE shooting, the feds finally remove the police tape from Rabid Ink and let us back into the studio. Everything has been destroyed—workstations, chairs, tables, equipment…even the paintings on the walls.

Christos, Rose, Duncan, and I visit Slim, who has been discharged from the hospital. The bullets didn't hit any major arteries, and he is already up and around, although he can't move his left arm very well. Unfortunately, the shop reopening might be delayed because of issues with his insurance company. Concerned about losing clients, he asks us to find temporary chairs in other shops until he can rebuild, and, if possible, to stay together. Easier said than done. Four tattoo artists, no equipment, and a receptionist with an attitude. Not a recipe for success.

And neither is trying to forget about Ray.

Two kisses and I can't get him out of my mind. Two kisses and he is burned into my skin. At night, I dream about him. During the day, I hear his voice in every café and on every street corner. Alone in my bed, I fantasize about his hands on my body, his deep voice rumbling against my chest. Then I pull out my vibrator and make the fantasy real. And when I climax, I moan his name.

Always practical, Jess asks for her twenty dollars because she won the bet, then tells me to get over him. She points out that I barely knew him; I don't know where he lives or what he drives or whether he shares my addiction to potato chips. She thinks my inability to move on is a result of crushing on Ray too long before we met. I tell her she would know since she's been crushing after Tag for longer than that. We have a fight.

Of course, our fights never last long. By way of making amends, she offers to set me up with her brother's best friend's cousin's sister's ex. I tell her there is something about Ray that makes my heart pound and my knees weak, and until I figure out what it is, her brother's best friend's cousin's sister's ex will have to wait. Then I invite her to my parents' house for Sunday dinner because I know Tag will be there. I can make amends too.

Mom and Dad are delighted to see Jess. Since she practically lived at our house after we met, they have adopted her as a surrogate daughter. After a warm greeting for Jess, Mom turns to me.

"Oh, Sia." Mom sighs and gives me a perfunctory hug as she switches to her admonishing tone. "Did you have to wear leather? And those piercings?"

"This is how I've dressed for years, Mom. I'm not going to change."

She fiddles with her pearls and gives me a resigned look. "You used to dress so pretty, all those floaty dresses and skirts." She runs her hand along the pink streak in my hair. "Why do you do this? You have such beautiful hair."

"Mom, please. Can we not talk about my appearance and just have a nice dinner?"

Mom and Dad don't know about what happened at the party. Tag and I kept it a secret from everyone except Jess, who was at the hospital that night with problems of her own. So they don't know why I stopped painting or why I threw away everything that reminded me of the girl I used to be. They don't know why I needed a fresh start, a new me, Sia the tat artist who has no past and has suffered no pain. All they know is one night after a football game, Tag went to a party, fell out a window and dislocated his shoulder, and after that he couldn't fight anymore at Redemption.

"Sorry, darling. Sometimes I just miss the way you used to be." Her brow wrinkles and I know she's trying to think of a way to make up for her outburst. "You've added butterflies." She gestures to my shoulder. "Well…they're nicer than the thorns." Then her gaze travels upward, and her mouth tightens when she looks at my ears. "You have some new…piercings too. I like the little cross."

My ears and other places too indelicate to mention.

I smile because I know she's trying, and except for the changes in my appearance and my new career, we usually get along fine.

"Mom, leave her alone." Tag joins us from the kitchen, a scowl on his face. "Doesn't matter what she wears or how she looks; she's still our Sia."

I shoot him a grateful look, and Jess sighs and stares longingly at Tag. She always envied me having an older brother, although I told her many times, it wasn't all it's cut out to be.

Dad and Tag discuss the mortgage situation; in other words, Tag tries to give Dad money and Dad refuses to take it, while Jess and I help Mom set the table. Mom is very particular about the dinner table—linen tablecloth, expensive silverware, china plates. Everything properly arranged and in its place. Although we never had a lot of money growing up, she always bought the best we could afford. The pearls were my parents' only extravagance, a gift for Mom the day I was born.

Mom relaxes over dinner and gets us up to speed on the neighborhood gossip. She doesn't talk about her search for a new job as a florist, and I don't ask. I've already put an envelope with as much cash as I can afford in her purse, knowing she'll call me at home later and refuse to take it. But in the end she'll have no choice because they don't want to lose their house.

Dad regales us with stories about the people he's driven around in his cab. Always, I am amazed at what people will do in the back of a cab, and despite Mom's protests, he provides graphic details, sending Jess and me into fits of hysteria. Jess shares stories from the vet clinic that turn my stomach. I don't tell them my tattoo parlor was shot up by a street gang or that I kissed a hard-bodied underground fighter in a dirty back alley and would have fucked him if my PTSD hadn't chased him away. Tag doesn't talk at all.

Jess shoots Tag surreptitious glances from beneath her lashes, but Tag seems at best indifferent to her presence. After our meal, Mom and I head to the kitchen to prepare dessert and Mom tries to smooth things over between us with a girly conversation, asking why Jess and Tag never got together.

"He doesn't like her." I dump a carton of whipping cream in a bowl and fish around in the drawer for the beaters. "She's done everything she can to let him know she's interested. I've asked him a gazillion times. I guess she's just not his type."

Mom raises an eyebrow. "He does like her. And they're perfect for each other. She needs him in a way he needs to be needed. And he can give her the security she never had at home. He just can't see it."

After dessert, Tag offers to help Mom clean up in the kitchen, and Jess and I kick back and relax on the worn, beige sofa that has sat in the same place for the last twenty years. Dad turns on the TV, and we watch a few minutes of a survival show before my phone buzzes.

Priority: Confidential
Bay Area Underground Fight Club (BUFC) Fight Night
Jack London Square. 8 p.m.
Headlining: Misery vs. The Predator
Code Phrase: "Soon you'll be wanting to leave."

Underground fight promoters go to great lengths to keep their fights off the CSAC radar. They screen and limit attendee lists, text event announcements only two hours before the fights start, and require everyone to say the code word or phrase to get in. With so many Redemption fighters as clients, it wasn't hard for me to get on the list of the top BUFC promoter. And after seeing Ray fight at that first event, I pulled in favors to get on the list of every underground fight promoter in the Bay Area.

Jess takes one look at my face and then leans over to check the message. "Are you going?"

"No."

She glances over at Dad and then lowers her voice. "You've never missed one of his fights."

"I've never felt so embarrassed." I pick at a thread on the seat cushion. "I practically threw myself at him and he turned me down. I've never thrown myself at a man before. The whole panicking-because-he-pinned-my-arms thing was humiliating beyond belief, and just underscored the fact that I am not normal and never will be. My biggest fantasy is a damn trigger, and as expected, he went running in the opposite direction. Plus there's a boxing match on TV after this. Good wholesome entertainment."

The survival show finishes and the boxing match starts. Tag joins us in the living room, his phone in his hand. "You going out tonight?"

Jess and I share a glance. He must be on the promoter's list as well, although I've never seen him at a fight except to drive me home, and he would never step into the ring. Still…

"Uh…no. We're watching boxing with Dad."

Tag shakes his head. "Torment wants to see us at Redemption."

"Now?"

"You know Torment. He has a proposition for you, and he's not a man you keep waiting."

———

An hour later, Tag, Jess, and I are having a drink in Torment's office at Redemption. Despite the hour, the gym is still busy and the steady whir of cardio machines is interrupted by the occasional clang of weights and the thud of flesh hitting flesh. Of course, Jess insisted on coming with us. Although she claimed it was to give me moral support, I know she just wanted to spend more time with Tag.

Torment leans back in his chair and strokes his chin. Even such an innocuous gesture is threatening when Torment does it, and I shiver and dig my nails into my palm.

"I heard about your studio."

Is this Torment making small talk? I glance over at Tag, but he is lost in thought.

"Uh…yeah. It needs to be totally renovated. Slim's fighting with his insurance company, but he figures we'll be back in operation soon."

Tapping his fingers on the desk, he says, "What are you doing for work in the meantime?"

"We've been looking for somewhere temporary to set up shop so we don't lose our clients. Hasn't been going so good. Rent is expensive and no one wants to give us a short-term lease given the kind of work we do. We're thinking of splitting up and taking chairs with other shops until Slim has things sorted out."

Torment sniffs. "No one will find you if you split up. You're a team. Teams stick together. Isn't that right, Fuzz?"

Tag's head jerks up, and from his vacant expression, I can tell he didn't hear what Torment said. "Yeah…sure."

Torment scowls and Jess sucks in a sharp breath. What does Makayla do when Torment is angry with her? I'd probably run screaming in the other direction.

"Come." Torment stands so quickly, I almost fall out of my chair in my haste to join him. He stalks out of the room, and Jess and I scurry after him, trying to keep up with his long strides.

"What's with Tag?" She keeps her voice low. "He's not himself."

"I told you. I think it's his new case. I told Mom and Dad, and they tried to get him to talk about it, but he clammed right up. I don't know what to do."

We pass Rampage outside the snack shop and he gives us a big wave. "Hey, girls. You didn't miss anything at the fight tonight. Headline match got canceled. The Predator didn't show."

Jess and I exchange a puzzled look and then I pull to a halt. "He didn't show? When has he ever not shown?"

Rampage shrugs. "Never happened before. Misery's saying he was too chicken to face him. Called for a rematch next week even though he could have just claimed the no-show as a win on the underground circuit and moved up the ranks. He's desperate to fight the Predator."

"Rampage." Torment's voice booms down the corridor as he closes in on us. "I hope you're not discussing any illegal, unsanctioned fights in our licensed facility. You should also hope that I never catch you at an unsanctioned fight."

Rampage pales. "I thought the threat was from the CSAC."

Torment stops in front of us and folds his arms across his massive chest. "If I ever catch you putting your license at risk, you'll be begging the CSAC to take you in by the time I'm finished with you."

"He's one damn scary dude," Jess whispers after Torment stalks away. "It's like they've taken all alpha male-dom, rolled it up in one mouthwatering package, and called it Torment."

We break into a light jog to catch up to Torment, now on the threshold of the new addition to the warehouse. The plastic is gone and the corridor is bright and newly finished. Walls gleam and a warm, hardwood floor has been installed over the concrete. The sharp scent of fresh paint lingers in the air, and bright track lighting gives the hall a soft glow.

"What are you adding in this wing?"

Torment stops in front of a double glass door and pulls out a set of keys. "Newest thing. All the major MMA gyms have one." He pushes open the door and gestures for us to follow him. "All my boys get tats. Why not offer them a safe, clean, convenient place to get them done?" He flicks on the lights, and I behold my dream studio.

Spacious, light, and sophisticated, it is the opposite of Slim's cozy, stereotypically cramped and slightly garish shop. From the exposed beams in the ceilings to the angled alcoves, and from the gleaming hardwood floor to the polished oak reception desk, Torment's tattoo studio leaves nothing to be desired.

"This is amazing." I walk past the black leather hydraulic client chairs, trailing my fingers over the gray granite counters, and heavy-duty workstations, the best money can buy. He has everything I could ever have imagined in a tattoo studio. Bright lights, high-quality furnishings, antique mirrors, and tons of space for all our equipment.

"It's not quite finished." Torment leans against the reception desk. "I've commissioned murals for the walls and I'm trying to decide whether to go bohemian or exotic with the decor. I'd like to offer it to you and your coworkers rent-free until your studio is operational. You can help with the decorating, iron out the kinks, and I'll be able to test out its viability as a business in the gym."

Stunned speechless for a moment, I can only stare. "But...you would have no problems filling those chairs. Any tattoo artist I know would die to work in a studio like this."

Torment gives an irritated grunt. "Not looking for dead tattoo artists. Looking for live ones. Especially one who I can trust and who does good work. You fit the bill and if your friends trained under the same master artist, then I have no problem offering them the other chairs. I'll buy the supplies, and I have a team to manage the business side of things. You want to advertise or market, you let them know what you need. You keep what you earn minus ten percent to cover expenses."

So tempting. But I can't. Not while Ray is here. I can't deal with seeing him every day, knowing I could have lived my fantasy, even just for a night, if not for what happened in my past. And what if we bump into each other? What would we say?

My gaze flicks to Tag. He doesn't like me coming to Redemption. He'll make a lot of noise, put his foot down, rant about how it isn't safe for me to come out here, and for once I'll be happy that he does. I wait, but he doesn't speak.

"Tag?"

"Up to you," he says with a shrug. "As long as you aren't here at night and you stay away from—"

"Won't work." Torment folds his arms, cutting Tag off. "I need the studio open when the gym is busy, and that is mostly at night. I can make sure there is always someone available to walk Sia to and from her car, or I can arrange for transportation. My limo is usually available."

Hmmm. I don't know many tattoo artists who travel to and from work in a chauffeured limo. Might ruin my hard-core reputation. "I can drive, but I don't know…"

Torment scowls. "What are you afraid of, Sia? I'm offering you a chair, a steady supply of clients, the best equipment money can buy, and chairs for any of the coworkers you want to bring on board."

My cheeks heat. "It's just…"

"Are you afraid of Redemption?"

"No, of course not." I look up and catch a glint in Torment's eye and the slightest quirk of his lips. I don't know how he knows, but he knows.

"Every fighter who steps into the cage feels fear," Torment says. "The good ones use that fear. They control it, channel it, master it. They are the fighters who rise to the top. The ones who let fear control them never succeed. You know them right away because they have their backs to the cage, so worried about protecting themselves, they aren't even trying to win. What kind of fighter are you?"

"I'm not a fighter."

"We are all fighters. But sometimes we have to look hard at ourselves to find where our fighter is hiding."

I know exactly where my fighter is hiding—in the past. And maybe it's time to find her. Yes, it will hurt when I see him. And I'll wish that night with Luke never happened or that it didn't affect me the way it did. But I'll have my Redemption and Rabid Ink friends around me, and an awesome studio to work in, and money to help out Mom and Dad.

"So it's settled then." Torment shakes my hand before I speak. "Good to have you on board. I'll expect you to start tomorrow." And whoosh, he is gone. Discussion over.

"Um…I didn't say yes." I glare at the closing door. "Jess, did you hear me say yes? Or did you hear Tag say yes? Did anyone say yes?"

Lips pressed together, I yank open the door and shout, "YES."

"That's Torment," Tag says, coming up behind me. "Looks like you got a new studio. To be honest, although I don't like you coming to Ghost Town, you'll be safer here than you were in the Lower Haight 'cause I'll make sure everyone knows to keep an eye out for you. Just make sure you stay away from Ray."

"No problem." And I mean it.

Chapter 8

It was what it was, and that's all that it was

"Ohmigod. Ohmigod. I think I'm in heaven." First thing Monday morning, Rose plasters herself against the glass door to our new studio and stares out at the man candy on display. Torment has gathered the key members of his team in the hallway for a pep talk, and Rose is now physically unable to peel herself off the door.

"It's Redemption, not heaven," I say.

"It's heaven with you wearing that little black skirt and those fuck-me boots." Christos gives me a wink as he takes in my attire. "We'll have fighters lined up into the parking lot once they get a look at you."

I heave a sigh, but secretly I'm pleased. I love these boots. Soft, supple black leather, all straps and laces, with a stiletto heel. They set me back a month in savings last year, but every time I wear them, I feel like nothing can hold me back. And I needed a little confidence boost today.

"I've spent my weekends trawling bars and clubs looking for a replacement for my ex," Rose says, still staring out the door. "And now I discover all the hot guys have been hiding out here."

"Your ex was scum." Christos unpacks the new supplies Torment miraculously procured overnight: tattoo kits, paint, ink, tattoo machines, sketch pads, even an autoclave for the staff room. "Shouldn't be hard to replace him."

An affronted Rose sniffs. "He was the love of my life."

"He was the love of your bed."

Duncan and I share a glance. Christos and Rose have been fighting their attraction for years. Although he's never said anything to her, Christos confided in me that he was relieved when Rose's ex broke it off. He'd seen the bruises on her face beneath the makeup and he was finding it hard not to get involved.

"Do we have a name?" Duncan eases himself into his high-end titanium hydraulic client chair, the likes of which I have never seen before. With two headrests and two armrests, it allows clients to sit, straddle, or lay in multiple positions in padded leather comfort.

"Torment's Tattoos," Rose says. "To honor our benefactor."

Christos sticks his finger down his throat and pretends to heave.

"How about we stick with our old name?" I hand Christos a knife to cut open the next box, then settle into my new, cushy artist's chair. "I mean, this is temporary digs until Slim gets back on his feet and gets the studio fixed up."

Rose sighs. "How will we go back after this? I'm already ruined for tat studios for life."

"Because we're a team and we're loyal." I spin around in my chair, marveling at the lumbar support and padding where padding is needed. Maybe we can convince Slim to upgrade the furniture when he's done the renos.

The door opens—no tinkly bells in Torment's studio—and we go into full client alert.

"Hey, Sia." Rampage waves as he walks in. "Hope you're prepared to be busy. Torment spread the word that you're here now, and everyone's planning to come by to check you guys out. You're part of Redemption, and we look after our own."

Rampage does not lie. We have the busiest day we've ever had in the history of Rabid Ink. Fighters line up outside to book appointments weeks in advance after Rose tells them we've already filled our walk-ins for the day. I ink the Redemption logo at least six times on various body parts, including one ass, and accept four commissions for custom designs.

At seven p.m., Christos finally calls it quits to head out to a gig. Rose leaves with him, and I go to the café to grab some snacks to keep Duncan and me going for the next few hours.

By the time I return, we have three fighters in the fancy glass-and-leather waiting area and Ray is standing beside my chair.

I scowl at Duncan, who is making an appointment for Homicide Hank, and he shrugs. "He said he had you booked for the rest of the evening."

"He doesn't," I murmur through gritted teeth. "And I don't want to see him."

He lifts an eyebrow. "Look at him. I wasn't about to tell a guy like that to get lost. I'm an artist. I need my fingers unbroken."

With a huff, I hand him his food, and brace myself for more humiliation. But as I near the chair, humiliation is not what I feel. Instead, my body heats, my knees tremble, and my mind flies back to the moment we kissed in the alley and the searing pleasure of his touch.

Hot and intense, his eyes bore into me as I make my way to my station. But this time, I know where he stands, and it isn't anywhere near me.

"Hi." I fold my arms and lean against the counter, feigning a nonchalance I don't feel in the least. "Long time no see."

He draws in a deep breath and stares at me, drinking me in as if I quenched a thirst in his soul. "Sia." My name is a soft whisper on his sensual lips. "Jesus. Those boots—"

"Are made for walking. Which is what I was about to do. I didn't think you'd be back."

"Neither did I."

After waiting a few fruitless moments for him to elaborate, I say, "I heard you missed your fight yesterday. Didn't think it would ever happen."

"Had to clean up a mess. Sort myself out."

Puzzled, I frown. "Cryptic. My favorite type of explanation."

"It was what it was."

A smile tugs at my lips. "Even more cryptic. But then, that's you."

Ray laughs, easing the tension between us, and then his smile fades. "You weren't at the fight." A statement, not a question.

I give a casual shrug although I am already falling under his spell. Arousal floods through my veins, and my voice drops to an unintentional breathy whisper. "I had stuff to do."

He tucks a wayward strand of hair behind my ear, his fingers leaving a delicious prickle behind, awakening the memory of his hand in my hair, the caress of his fingers, the pressure of his hand around my neck. Pleasure ripples down my spine. If this isn't sexual chemistry, I don't know what is. But how can I be so attracted to the kind of man I've been so careful to avoid? And why is he touching me after he walked away?

"You never missed a fight before." His voice, deep, dark, and smooth, rumbles over me even as nausea grips my stomach. He noticed me at the fights. Does he know I was there to see him?

My hands clench and unclench by my sides. We stare at each other for so long, tension crackles between us, and I fully expect my cheeks to burst into flame. Finally, coward that I am, I break.

"Duncan said you wanted your ink. I won't have time to do the whole piece, but I could do the outline."

He nods and drops his hand. "Unless you got any other artists here who've been targeted by a street gang. Not keen on being interrupted again."

Although he doesn't smile when he speaks, his dry humor makes me laugh. "You think a street gang would dare set foot in Redemption? You guys would tear them to shreds."

Ray grunts in assent and slides into the chair. "Damn right we would."

He grips the bottom of his shirt to tug it off, and I beat a hasty retreat to the staff room, decorated in warm beiges and browns, with the excuse of needing to collect my equipment from the autoclave, but more to calm my nerves. For the last week, I'd resigned myself to never seeing him again, decided it was for the best. But now he's back, and as hot as ever, and I'm just as ready to throw myself at him as I was before he left me in the alley. I have no shame. How can I still want him after he made it clear he's not interested? How do normal people handle this kind of rejection? But, of course, they don't have to handle it because slightly kinky sex doesn't make them scream in panic and chase men away.

Ray is stripped to the waist when I return. Ignoring Duncan's appreciative raised eyebrow at the hunk of manly perfection in my chair, I go through the process of washing and sterilizing his chest and shoulder, and applying the stencil. Then I prepare the tattoo machine, placing ink in the ink caps and removing the needles and tubes from the sterile pouches. This time, I manage to keep cool. He's just an ordinary client.

I'll do his ink, he'll pay his money, and then maybe I'll see him once or twice around the gym before we return to Slim's shop. There are no unintended squirts with the disinfectant, no imagined electricity between us. I am the epitome of a professional artist.

At least, on the outside.

Duncan plays an eclectic mix of indie pop and rock, and I manage to put aside all lustful thoughts of Ray and concentrate on the line work. My first day on the job, Slim told me art is sex. I wondered, if that were true, what it meant when I locked my real art away.

After Duncan finishes up with his last client and leaves for the night, I steel myself to look up, and almost burn under the heat of Ray's gaze. "You want me to change the music? Not everyone likes Duncan's indie pop mix."

"I'm good."

When I turn to switch cartridges, Ray shifts in the chair. "You don't talk while you work?"

"Clients talk. I listen. I'm not really one for spilling all the details of my life to strangers. Rose, on the other hand, usually has them in the back room in less than five minutes to show off her tit tats."

Ray snorts a laugh, and I wait until he's still again so I can continue my work. "Feel free to talk, though. It won't bother me. I'm used to it."

"Not a big talker. But you can ask me a question."

"You want me to ask you a question?"

Ray nods. "I got nothing to hide. Ask me anything."

I return to inking his outline. "Okay. What do you drive?"

"Harley-Davidson Softail."

"Biker." I shake my head. "I should have known. I wanted to get a bike, but Tag helped me finance my vehicle, and I wound up with a Volvo instead. Not quite the same."

His eyes sparkle, amused. "Wouldn't have pegged you as a Volvo girl."

I pause and check my cartridge. "True. I'm more of a Nissan 370Z girl, or maybe an Audi TT. A sports car, but not a screamer. I don't want an eat-my-dust kind of sports car, but something more refined. Not that I have the money to buy one, but a girl can always dream."

"Ask me another one."

"Where do you live?"

"Loft apartment in a converted warehouse off Temescal Alley."

"Wrong side of the bridge," I say, half joking. Wrong because he's so far away from me. "I'm in the Upper Haight. Coming out here is one hell of a commute, but since it's only for a short time, I can manage."

He licks his lips, as if my answers are a tasty treat. "More."

"Favorite band?"

"Forest Rangers."

My head falls back and I groan. "*Sons of Anarchy* wannabe. Was that before or after you got your motorcycle?"

A half smile tugs at his lips. "Always had a bike."

"Of course. I'm sure you were born on a bike, like all bikers." I turn off the machine for a moment to give my hand a break. "Where did you grow up?"

"Army brat." His jaw clenches, almost imperceptibly, but I'm watching him so closely I see his corded neck tighten when he swallows. "Both parents. We moved so many times, I can't remember every place we were stationed. Also can't remember how many times we were all together, because they took turns going on tour. Both very strict. Very disciplined. Very focused on duty."

"Sounds tough for a kid." I give his arm a sympathetic stroke.

"Kids adapt. And when I turned eighteen, I did what was expected. Followed the family tradition. Enlisted as soon as I could."

"But you're not in the service anymore?"

His muscles tighten under my palm. "What about your parents?"

Puzzled by his reluctance to answer but not willing to pry, I shrug. "Mom is a florist. Very uptight. She came from a wealthy family, but she fell in love with my dad and her parents weren't happy about it so we never see them. Dad's a cab driver. Pretty laid-back except when it comes to me. Then he's overprotective to a fault. Small house in the suburbs. Never moved. Pretty normal until a few weeks ago when Mom lost her job, and then Tag and I found out they'd been living from paycheck to paycheck. We're helping them out with the mortgage so they don't lose the house, which is why I work the long hours and take on any client I can get."

"Nothing normal about you, Sia." He rubs his knuckles over my cheek and I melt beneath his touch. "More questions," he says, his voice gruff.

"Biggest vice?"

"You."

A hot wave sweeps into my belly, but I can't believe he's being serious. Me? After he told me the other night was a mistake?

I turn on the tattoo machine to finish the line work, and the fresh scent of ink mixed with musky male makes me shiver. "I meant it as a serious question. My vice is potato chips. Put a bag in front of me, and it will be gone in five minutes. I can't keep them in my house. The minute I see a bag of chips within reach, I lose all control. That's what I mean by a vice."

"Definitely you then."

His words do strange melty things to my stomach, and my voice flattens as I roll my artist's chair closer to his soft, black leather seat. "I'm nobody's vice. Arm on my lap, please. I've finished the outline and I just need to sterilize and bandage."

Ray drops his arm to my lap, but this time his fist doesn't clench on my hip. Instead, his fingers stroke my thigh, sending zings of sensation straight to my clit. The temperature rises and the air between us sparks, like the calm before a storm. But I'm not letting it get to me. Maybe it's just a casual brush of his hand as he settles it in my lap. Or a nervous twitch.

The bandaging takes forever, especially since my concentration is focused on the soft stroke of his fingers on my thigh. Good thing women are good at multitasking. Finally, I'm done. I give the bandage a last check and force a smile. "Okay. All finished."

Ray doesn't move.

"Usually when I say 'all finished,' my clients leap up from the chair, determined to rush home and rip off the bandage to see what's underneath."

Ray raises his hand from my lap and cups my jaw, brushing his thumb over my cheek as he tilts my head up, forcing me to meet his gaze.

"What's wrong?"

My cheeks flame and I try to pull away. "Nothing. I'm done. That's all. You can go. I have to clean up and lock up the shop."

He tightens his grip. "Is this about what happened in the alley?"

"There's nothing to say about what happened in the alley. Adrenaline was running high. We had a moment. It was what it was, and that's all that it was."

"You don't believe that."

"Sure I do." My heart pounds as the lie slides off my tongue, and I pray he'll just go and leave me to wallow in my misery. He is everything I have been running from. The ultimate temptation. The ultimate danger.

His jaw tightens and his body stills, like a predator about to spring. Then he leans so close I can feel his breath on my cheek.

"Tell me again that's all that it was. Tell me I shoulda stayed away."

I open my mouth to say just that, but before I get the words out, he leans down and kisses me. Shock, then heat, run through me, straight to the juncture of my thighs. He tastes of whiskey and coffee, sex and sin. All the tension of the evening, my confusion and indecision, coalesce into a red-hot ball of need. I thread my fingers through his soft hair and pull him down hard, deepening the kiss.

"Jesus," Ray murmurs against my mouth. "Don't know what I was thinking." And then he breaks our kiss and slides his arms under my shoulders, tugging me out of my seat. "Up on my lap. I wanna have you up close and personal like."

"I'm wearing a skirt."

"Oh, I know." His voice drops to a husky growl. "Been thinking about that tiny skirt and those fuck-me boots since the second I walked in the door."

"I might lose my job or, at the very least, a whole lot of professional respect if someone walks in and sees me on your lap."

He pulls me closer. "I'll deal with them."

"What if it's Torment? Or Rampage?"

Ray frowns. "You doubting my fight skills?"

"I'm doubting your sanity."

He turns in the chair and pulls me between his legs, his hands tight on my hips. "Man like me meets a woman like you, throws him for a loop. He's gotta take a step back. Get things straight in his head."

"What kind of woman am I?"

His hooded gaze locks on me; then he stands and pulls me into his arms. "The kind that can bring a man to his knees."

Mindful of the bandage on his chest and with my usual reticence washed away in a tidal wave of desire, I lean up and nuzzle his neck. "I don't see you as an on-the-knees kinda guy."

"Neither did I." His hands sweep up my body, in and out my curves, and then down again, curling around my ass, his fingers digging into the tender flesh as he yanks my hips against his hardened length. "But then I never met a sexy artist before, watched her put beauty into the world where most of us destroy it. Never thought I'd cut corners to get my work done early so I could see her again. Spent a lot of time thinking about you, so soft and sweet, your heart-shaped face, the way your eyes turn green when you're scared, your lips—"

"I thought you weren't coming back."

"I was coming back as soon as I walked away." His gaze fixes on my mouth. "It was just a matter of time."

One hand still on my ass, holding me tight, he traces my lips with his thumb and then slides it into my mouth.

"Suck, beautiful girl. Show me what those lips can do."

Oh. My. God.

Although I know I shouldn't, that this is taking me one step too close to the danger zone, I tighten my lips and draw his thumb into my mouth. His skin is salty, tangy, sinfully delicious. I suck, stroking him with my tongue, imagining it isn't his thumb in my mouth but something else. Ray curls his fingers under my chin, locking my head in place as he pulls his thumb out and traces the bow of my lips.

"So fucking soft. Perfect."

My body tingles, heats, my clit throbs, and all I can think about is getting more. And yet, this isn't me. I go out with nice guys who invite me for dinner or a walk in the park, and if things go well, then they give me a peck on the cheek and promise to call. Not once has a guy slid his thumb in my mouth and held my head, watching, breathless, as I did to his thumb what I desperately wanted to do to his cock. But, oh God, was it good.

Ray glides his thumb down to rest in the hollow at the base of my throat. His hand curls around my neck, his fingers stroking my nape, sending a wave of sensation cascading down my spine. I am at once unnerved by my vulnerability and intensely aroused by his control. A soft moan escapes my lips and Ray stills.

"That makes you hot."

"Yes." Understatement of the year. I've never had such an incredible endorphin rush. The dip in my throat seems to be directly connected to my pussy, and I'm pretty sure I've never been this wet in my life.

His hand tightens around my throat, and my sex throbs in response. Never could I have imagined such a controlling gesture would turn me on. I should be afraid, screaming, running away, but he is watching me so intently, I know that the second arousal turns to anxiety, he'll let me go.

With a groan, I fist his shirt in my hands and pull him toward me. Ray's hand drops, his mouth finds mine, and then we're kissing with a fierce intensity that takes my breath away. Tongues tangle and clash, lips bruise, teeth nip. His hands glide over my body, but when he pushes up my T-shirt, I freeze. And in that moment, Ray's hands become Luke's hands, his fingers cold and brutal as he shoves up my shirt. A violent tremble shakes my body. There's a reason I've never let any of my boyfriends undress me, but it's been so long since I let someone else take control, I had forgotten why.

"Sia?"

"I…thought I heard someone outside." Cringing inwardly at the lie, I place my hands over his and tug up my shirt, hoping that if we do it together, the PTSD will go away. "As you were," I say, mocking a frown. But Ray has been watching me too intently to fall for that kind of trick.

"I hurt you."

"No." I almost shout the word, terrified he'll turn into another Charlie or James, so afraid of hurting me that they treated me like I was made of glass.

From the set of his mouth, I can tell he doesn't believe me, and when he takes a step back, a sob wells up in my throat. Why can't I be like everyone else? Why can't I have what I want without the past getting in the way?

Maybe he just needs some encouragement.

Closing the distance between us, I slide my hands over his chest, and around his neck pulling him down so I can run my tongue along the seam of his lips. He groans and slants his mouth over mine, his kiss warm and deep and filled with passion.

"You wanting something, beautiful girl?" Ray grinds the steel of his erection against my stomach as I nuzzle his neck, breathing in his scent, tasting sex on his skin.

"You. I want you."

Ray covers my hand with his and draws it down, over his chest, skimming the taut muscles of his stomach, past his belt, to the bulge in his jeans that has grown significantly since the last time I looked. He squeezes my hand around his shaft, so hard I can't imagine it doesn't hurt, and whispers, "Bite."

So I do. I sink my teeth into the tender flesh at the join of his neck and shoulder blade, just a little nip.

Ray groans. "Harder."

Swallowing hard, I bite harder. His cock stiffens beneath my palm, and his obvious arousal almost makes me come right then.

He pants his breaths, and I curl one arm around his neck, pressing my chest against him, and bite so hard my teeth pierce his skin.

"Jesus fucking Christ." Ray rips himself away with a shout that echoes through the studio, and I am at once shocked by his outburst and mortified by my behavior, and the tang of blood on my tongue.

"I'm sorry. I'm so sorry. I've never done that before. I didn't mean to hurt you." I babble my apology, stumbling back until I hit my chair, and then I freeze. Nowhere to run. Nowhere to hide.

A curious expression flickers across his face. Self-loathing? Disgust? But it disappears so fast, I wonder if I've imagined it. He scrubs a hand over his face as if to wash away the sight of me. "'S'okay. My fault. I shouldn't have…"

But, clearly, it's not okay. What the hell was I thinking? This is the side of me that got me into trouble in the first place. Sia the thrill seeker. Sia the danger queen. Sia who has always wanted it rough and dirty and didn't learn her lesson the first time. Tag is right. Ray isn't the right guy for me, although not for the reasons he said. He's the kind of guy who makes me lose control, and that's not something I can do. Control is how I survived after Luke. Control over my life. Control over my emotions. Control over the men I chose to be with. But with Ray, control is just so damn hard, because the more he takes, the more I want to give.

"Lights are going out in the gym." I gesture to the door. "They're closing up for the night. You should probably get going." I draw in a ragged breath and will him to leave before I break down. "Rampage will be waiting. He offered to take me home."

"Rampage. Okay." He nods, but he doesn't move.

"I just have to pack up my equipment and put it in the autoclave. You don't have to stick around."

I imagine he flinches the tiniest bit at my awkward dismissal, or maybe it's just wishful thinking.

"Going out of town again tomorrow." A pained expression crosses his face. "Might not make it back for the fight on Friday."

Pleaseleavepleaseleavepleaseleave. Can this get more awkward?

"I probably won't make it anyway." I straighten the ink caps on the tray, grateful for an excuse to keep my eyes averted. "We're booked solid for the next few weeks, and I'm doing overtime because I need the extra work."

When I look up into the silence, his face has smoothed to an expressionless mask.

"Got it."

My stomach churns as he grabs his shirt and tugs it over his head. The tat on his shoulder has got to hurt, but if it bothers him, he gives no sign.

Still, I can't leave him with just an outline. I am a professional, after all, and although it will be incredibly awkward to see him again, I want to finish his ink. "Whenever you want me to finish up your tat, just call Rose. I'll tell her to squeeze you in."

"Sure." He turns and walks toward the door, eating up the fancy marble tile with easy strides of his long legs.

"Bye, Ray."

The door opens and then closes with a bang. If he said good-bye, I missed it.

Chapter 9

DANGEROUS MAN.
DANGEROUS BIKE.

Priority: Confidential

Bay Area Underground Fight Club (BUFC) Fight Night

Ex-machine shop, Jack London Square. 8 p.m.

Headlining: Misery vs. The Predator

Code Phrase: "I am your number-one fan"

FRIDAY NIGHT, FOUR DAYS after Ray left me in a state of aroused confusion at the studio, Jess and I are drinking beer with Blade Saw, Doctor Death, and Rampage in a former machine shop just off Jack London Square. Blade Saw has an arm around Jess's shoulders, and she is no longer annoyed at being dragged away from watching Tag torture his recruits at Redemption. Although she's told Blade Saw she's not looking for a relationship—she's still not ready to give up on Tag—he's happy to take whatever she wants to give, which means I'll be going home alone. Again.

But it's the best choice, as I've said to Jess about a dozen times over the last few days. I need to be with men who are sensitive and easygoing. Men who don't call to the thrill-seeking side of me that got me in trouble in the first place. Men like Charlie, my first serious boyfriend after the attack, who put up with my panic attacks and flashbacks and stroked my back and made me tea and even came to see my therapist so he could learn how to help me. At the time, I told Jess that men didn't get better than Charlie and that I probably would never have been able to have sex again if I hadn't met him.

Ever the pragmatist, Jess said Charlie and I wouldn't last. Although we were comfortable together, there was no spark. And she was right.

Just as she was right about Jason, another caring, sensitive man who was so concerned about my issues and triggers that he often couldn't perform in bed.

Still, she calls me on my BS. How could I possibly think the Predator would be put off by a little pain? Look what he dishes out—and takes—in the ring. Maybe he has his own issues. And didn't I tell her he got harder when I bit him? This is what I always do, she says. When they get too close, I push them away. And if I didn't want him, why the hell did I call her up and drag her out of yoga class when I found out he was fighting tonight?

Good questions. Too bad I have no answers.

"Never took you for a beer drinker." Doctor Death taps my bottle and I shrug.

"I'll drink just about anything with alcohol in it when I'm stressed."

His brow creases. Unbelievably, the slight frown makes him even more handsome.

"Stress can have some profound physiological effects on the body. What are you stressed about? Often it helps to just talk these things through."

"Uh…well…" I can't tell him I'm worried about Ray fighting Misery. And there's no way I'm telling him I'm lusting after a mercurial fighter who I just pushed away.

"I thought Misery was in jail for kidnapping Makayla and Amanda," Jess says loudly, finally coming to my rescue.

Dragging my thoughts away from my disastrous night in the studio, I nudge Rampage, who is trying to stay hidden in the shadows—an impossible task given his size and his penchant for wearing yellow. Both licensed MMA amateurs, Rampage and Blade Saw are taking a risk by coming to an underground fight, but like me, they can't resist. Redemption was an underground club for many years, and this kind of fighting is what they know and love best.

"Do you know anything about Misery?"

Rampage looks over and scowls. "He did three years and then he found himself a good lawyer for the appeal and got out for good behavior. They couldn't link him to the drugs or he might have been there forever." Rampage is very protective of the women in the club and took it as a personal affront when Misery, once Torment's biggest competitor in the underground league, kidnapped and beat up Makayla and Amanda when they inadvertently stumbled on his drug smuggling operation in the Menlo District.

"He's wanted to fight the Predator ever since he got out of the joint." Blade Saw pulls another beer from his bag and offers it around. "The Predator always refused and last week he didn't show. But for some reason he agreed to tonight's fight."

A whistle blows and we turn our attention to the makeshift ring in the middle of the shop. The fights are rarely held at the same location and this venue is rougher than most. Four metal poles with a thick rope strung between them mark the ring. Sawdust has been scattered over the concrete floor. The air smells of wood chips and diesel with a hint of sweat, and the only light comes from the glare of spotlights set up around the perimeter of the ring.

The first few fights are as bloody and gory as an underground fight lover could want. The concrete floor is responsible for one knockout and two broken arms. A medic tends to the injured in a corner. My skin prickles as if someone is watching me. I scan the crowd, but I don't see anyone looking in my direction, and I don't see Ray.

Finally, the promoter announces the big event and Misery steps into the ring. He must be at least six feet two inches tall and weighs over two hundred and fifty pounds. Rampage tells us he was once one of California's top-ranked amateur heavyweight fighters, but he threw it all away for a fistful of blow and a cup of revenge.

Anticipation ratchets through me as the crowd parts and Ray ducks under the rope. Although Misery clearly outweighs him, Ray dominates the ring through the force of his presence alone.

"He just gets better looking every time I see him," Jess whispers.

She's right. His muscles seem bigger and more defined, pecs protruding above his washboard stomach, his jaw firm, blue eyes focused and intent. His fight shorts, blue with white wolves on the sides, cling to his narrow hips, and for a moment I wonder if he got them because of the tattoo I might never finish, now a dark outline across his pec.

Hidden as we are in the corner, I don't know if he'll be able to see me, but I can pretend, and so I send him a mental kiss for luck.

At the sound of the whistle, they touch bare knuckles—no gloves in underground fighting—and then circle each other in the center of the ring. Already my heart is in my throat, and I feel the familiar surge of adrenaline that keeps me coming back time and time again.

"This is going to be a great fight." Doctor Death throws a casual arm around my shoulder, and I stiffen and pull away with an apologetic smile.

"Sometimes I like to wave my hands and jump around. Wouldn't want to hit you by accident." I cringe inwardly at my feeble excuse, but what if Ray looks over and sees us together? Although I'm mentally prepared for it to be over, hope still flickers in my soul.

Misery cocks his left hand and then, without warning, the Predator attacks, unleashing his power with a left uppercut that sends Misery staggering back against the ropes.

Rampage draws in a sharp breath, and my pulse kicks up a notch.

"That's not his usual MO." I look back over my shoulder at a rapt Rampage. "He usually stalks them first, then toys with them, lets them get in a few punches before he moves in for the kill."

Misery shakes his head, trying to recover, but the Predator doesn't give him a chance, exploding on him with shot after shot. Misery goes down and grabs for the Predator's legs, but he has left himself vulnerable. The Predator takes full advantage, unloading a flurry of big shots to his head. As Misery pushes himself to his feet, the Predator unleashes a powerful kick, striking the side of Misery's head and sending him back to his knees. Another few punches and Misery is down for the count.

Violent. Powerful. Explosive. I've never seen the Predator blitz an opponent before. Nor have I ever been as aroused by a fight as I am now. All I can think about is having all that power…on me, around me, beneath me, and…oh God, inside me.

"Sia? You okay?" Rampage turns me to face him and peers into my eyes. "You look kinda dazed. Too much for you? Never seen the Predator let go like that."

"Yeah. I'm good."

"We should get outta here." Blade Saw tugs Jess's hand. "The crowd was pretty loud for that last fight. Might have attracted the wrong kind of attention."

"Sure." I look back at the now-empty ring. Already the ropes are coming down and someone is sweeping bloody sawdust into a bag. Ray is nowhere in sight.

Doctor Death is paged by the hospital and pulls me to the side before I can follow Jess out the door. "You always disappear from these events so quickly we never get a chance to talk." He trails his finger over my shoulder, and I grit my teeth to repress a shudder. Not that he is in any way unattractive, but there is only one man I want touching me right now.

"Tag worries about me coming out to secluded areas at night, so I try to leave before he discovers where I am and comes looking for me."

"I can understand that." His voice drops to a soft growl. "A woman like you brings out a man's protective side. So delicate... with those big, liquid eyes...you just ooze vulnerability. Are you seeing someone?"

My skin prickles, and I scramble to think of a way to shut this down before it gets too awkward. No, I'm not seeing someone but there is someone I want to see.

"Sort of...it's...uh...complicated."

Doctor Death smiles. "So that's a no. Excellent. I'll come by your studio this week when I'm not on call and we'll have dinner and talk about that complicated situation."

"Thanks, but I...don't think I'm free this week. I'm doing a lot of overtime." My stomach clenches and I will him to get the message I'm so politely trying to convey. But, of course, he doesn't understand.

"I'm at the gym most nights I'm not working anyway, so I'm sure we'll find a time that works." He brushes a kiss over my cheek. "So looking forward to it."

We follow the crowd out the front door. Doctor Death heads in one direction, and I find Jess waiting for me near the parking lot.

"I'm going home with Blade Saw," she says. "Are you okay catching a lift with Rampage?"

"Are you kidding? He just bought a Hummer. I've been dying to go for a ride."

Jess snorts. "A Hummer in San Francisco? You won't be going anywhere fast."

"Doctor Death just asked me out." I follow her into the parking lot where Blade Saw and Rampage are waiting.

"Finally." She gives me a wink. "I was getting tired of running interference. Now you have options. Or, at the very least, you'll be able to make Ray jealous."

"I don't want the Doctor Death option." I sigh. "I want the Ray option. And I don't think he's the kind of man who does jealousy. He would probably just kill anyone who touched what was his."

Jess licks her lips. "Sounds delicious."

We stop at the edge of the parking lot and Blade Saw slides his arm around Jess's waist as we chat about the fights. Rampage is desperate to get into the ring but afraid of getting caught and ruining his fledgling amateur career. One of the few super heavyweights in the league, Rampage has a good shot at the amateur title, and he doesn't want to mess it up.

"Hey, Tag. Didn't know you were here." Rampage steps to the side to let Tag join our group and peppers him with questions about what he thought of the fight. Jess and I share a puzzled glance. Tag never comes to the fights because they remind him of what he lost when his shoulder didn't heal properly, and he had to drop out of the amateur circuit.

When Rampage pauses to catch his breath, I pull Tag to the side. "What are you doing here?"

"Heard about the fight. Knew you'd be here. Mom told me she'd borrowed your car for the day, so I came to give you a lift home."

"And you watched the fights?"

"Yeah." He glances over at Jess with Blade Saw's arm around her waist and his jaw tightens.

"You okay?" My question is directed at him watching the fight, but as I catch him watching Jess, I wonder if he thinks I'm asking something else.

"Yeah." He takes a step away from me to rejoin the group. "Jess?

You with Blade Saw?" He interrupts Rampage midsentence and everyone startles.

Jess swallows and I feel her pain. Tag has barely spoken to her in years, much less noticed her, and now, when she's finally sort of hooked up with someone, he decides to pay attention. "Uh…yeah."

"I lucked out, man." Blade Saw pulls Jess into his side and presses a kiss to her temple. A pained expression crosses Tag's face.

"Well then," I say too loudly. "I was going to ride in Rampage's Hummer, but it looks like I get to be a criminal again today." Only then do I notice Tag is not in uniform. But then, he couldn't show up in uniform at an unsanctioned fight without scaring everyone away.

"Cuff me, Officer. Or am I just a regular citizen today?" I hold out my hands wrists together, but Tag doesn't laugh at my joke.

Instead he draws in a ragged breath and then turns away. "Let's get going."

We wave good-bye to Rampage, Jess, and Blade Saw, and I follow Tag across the street. "She wanted you for years, Tag. I told you. But you didn't pay any attention to her. You said you weren't interested. What was she supposed to do? Wait forever?"

Tag jerks to a stop but doesn't turn. "I'm happy for her. Really. I've got too much going on right now to be getting involved with anyone. This case I'm working on is taking all my time and it's really tearing me up. I can't even look after myself, much less someone else, and emotionally, I got nothing left at the end of the day."

"If you ever want to talk about it, you know I won't tell anyone."

He sucks in his lips and sighs. "You're the one person I can't talk to about it."

"Well, thanks for coming to get me." I put my arm around his waist and give him a squeeze. "You didn't have to do it, especially the way you feel about the fights. There's always someone around to take me home."

"Gotta look out for my sis." He squeezes me back and we let each other go. "Only one I got."

We walk in silence down the road, and I spot Tag's Pathfinder parked across the street under a street lamp, only seconds before I see Ray heading toward us along the sidewalk. He's wearing jeans, tight in all the right places, and a gray T-shirt with a UFC logo on the front. Even slightly disheveled, he takes my breath away, and my heart ties itself in a knot when he stops in front of us. Is this a chance encounter, or was he looking for me? What should I say? Thankfully, Tag steps into the awkward silence.

"Good fight. No. Great fight. If anyone deserved that pounding, it was Misery." He dissects the fight, asking Ray about particular moves and strategies. Ray just shrugs and says he knew what Misery did to Makayla and Amanda, and the minute he got in the ring, all he could think about was pounding on Misery until he was mush. No strategy involved.

Of course, this does not go down well with Tag, who teaches about control and strategy in all his classes. He gestures me to his vehicle. "We'd better get going."

"I thought it was a great fight," I say to Ray after my tongue untangles. "I watched every minute."

"I know."

"You saw me?"

"I always see you." His deep voice rumbles through me, warming me to my toes. "You want…I'll take you home. I've got my bike."

"No motorcycles." Tag glares, first at Ray and then at me. "First, you can't ride without a helmet. It's against the law in California. Second, motorcycles are dangerous. The coroner's office has shelves lining the walls filled with motorcycle helmets from accidents. Look what happened last time."

"Last time?" Ray frowns.

"She has a reckless side," Tag says. "When she was seventeen, she started seeing some biker wannabe. I told her not to go, but she didn't listen. He took her up to Napa Valley at eighty miles an hour and then crashed his bike on the way down. Only reason they weren't killed was 'cause they were wearing helmets. Sia was so badly bruised up, she couldn't go to school for a week."

Ray lifts an eyebrow and I shrug.

"It was a mechanical problem, not a driving error. Other than the accident, it was the biggest thrill of my life."

"I brought an extra helmet." He glances over at Tag, the faintest hint of a smile playing across his lips before he turns those beautiful blue eyes on me. "In case you were here."

My heart lifts, sings, dances. Not a chance encounter. He was looking for me. I have a second chance.

"Sia." I catch the warning in Tag's tone. Dangerous man. Dangerous bike. It's been a long time since I did dangerous.

For a moment, I'm torn. Do I stay safe with Tag, or do I go with the man who makes my heart pound and my knees weak? A man who can make me feel both ecstasy and despair in the span of a heartbeat? Even though I feel I can trust him, how can I trust myself when I misjudged Luke so badly? Not once since that night at the frat house have I even considered being with a man as dominant as Ray. I thought I could never allow myself to be that vulnerable again. Instead, I went for guys like Charlie and James: risk free and risk averse. Easygoing to the point of always letting me take the lead, they demanded nothing and never questioned why I was holding back. They treated me like porcelain and under their sympathy, I cracked.

But since then, I never once really felt alive—the way I did that day in Napa Valley. The way I feel when I'm with Ray. Free. Normal. What if I had just one more taste?

"I'll go with Ray."

Chapter 10
SURPRISE

"YOU'LL GO WITH RAY?"

Tag launches into a rant to end all rants. Motorcycles aren't safe. Ray has just come out of a fight. I don't know Ray. On and on it goes until I want to melt into a humiliated puddle. Ray listens, amused, until Tag pauses for a breath.

"She'll be safe with me, Fuzz. You have my word. I would never put her in danger."

Only slightly mollified, Tag glances from me to Ray and back to me. Then he presses his lips together, huffs a good-bye, and walks across the street to his Pathfinder. Moments later, he drives past, revving his motor in displeasure.

"You wanna take a walk?" Ray slips an arm around me, as if that awful moment between us never happened. "I need to cool down before I get on the bike."

"Sure." My stomach gets all fluttery, like we're on a date, as he leads me down to the waterfront. We're going for a walk. A real walk. Like I do with my normal dates, except the guy has usually come from work and not a bloody underground fight, and smells of starch and laundry detergent and not blood, sweat, and sawdust.

During the day, Jack London Square, an open-air plaza on the Oakland waterfront, buzzes with activity. Jess and I have spent many Sunday afternoons at the farmer's market, riding around on our rental bikes and eating ice cream as we watch the container ships load and unload. At night, we've watched movies under the stars, danced, and closed down restaurants with groups of friends. Tonight, however, it is unusually quiet. A soft breeze blows off the water, bringing with it the faint scent of diesel and crisp ocean air, the quiet disturbed only by the loud clatter of the occasional Amtrak train.

"Sorry," I say, as we skirt around a couple walking hand in hand heading toward the ferry. "Having a brother is sometimes a bit of a pain."

Ray shakes his head. "He loves you. Don't take that for granted."

"Do you have a brother?"

His arm tightens around me. "Long time ago. He died when I was eight."

My heart squeezes in my chest and I stop in my tracks, forcing Ray to stop too. "I'm so sorry. I wouldn't have brought it up if I'd known."

He tugs me along, heading along the waterfront toward the archway. "'S okay. We were close, like you and Tag."

"What happened to him?"

Ray draws in a deep breath and looks out over the water. "For part of my childhood, before he died, we lived in Indiana. We spent all our free time riding the trails in the forest behind our house on our dirt bikes. There was a hill in the middle. Damn steep. Always the best part of the ride."

I slip my arm around his waist, just to let him know I'm here. And although I've walked the waterfront hundreds of times, I let him take the lead.

"I was older by a year, so I always went first. Checked the trail to make sure it was safe. One afternoon, Scott raced out of the house before me. I chased after him, but he was damn fast that day and he got to the hill first. I told him to wait, let me check the trail, but he didn't. There was a rock halfway down. He hit the front brake by mistake and went right over the handlebars. I saw it like it was in slow motion, knew it was going to be bad and there was nothing I could do to stop it. He landed on his head. No helmet. Didn't make it…"

"Oh God, Ray. How awful." I turn and wrap my arms around him, holding him still.

He shrugs. "My parents said it wasn't my fault. But I didn't believe them. If I'd just been a little bit faster that day…" He exhales a long breath. "Kinda shut everyone out after that. Couldn't imagine going through the pain of losing someone ever again. But then I did."

I want to ask him who else he lost, but this isn't the time. "I can't even imagine how it would feel to lose Tag." I lean up and press a kiss to his cheek. "I'm so sorry you lost him, Ray. Thank you for sharing it with me."

He studies me for a long moment, then brushes a kiss over my forehead. "You got a way of unlocking a man's secrets. Bad and good."

Swallowing hard, I pull away. I hope he doesn't unlock any of mine. I don't want him to think I'm anything other than normal.

We walk for half an hour until the light has faded and only couples linger on the waterfront. Ray leads me to the front of the machine shop and pulls open the door.

"Gotta grab the helmets and my bag from inside and then lock up." With a hand on my lower back, he directs me inside, then turns on one of the spotlights that had previously illuminated the ring.

While he gathers his stuff, I wander through the shadows, trailing my fingers over the cold, dusty machinery. The air is thick with the smell of wood chips and blood and the fainter scent of oil. A soft breeze ruffles my hair. Above me, someone has opened a window. I reach up to close it, stretching on my tippy toes.

"Don't move."

My body freezes, one hand on the latch. "Did you want me to leave it open?"

A sound escapes his throat, a cross between a growl and a groan. I look back over my shoulder and Ray comes up behind me, covering me with his body. Without a word, he slides his hands around my waist, warm on the skin bared by the rise of my tank top.

"Like you like this." His voice rumbles through me, thick with desire, washing away the memory of the studio and replacing it with warmth and the heat of arousal.

"Liked watching you in the ring." I stretch a little farther, giving him more to touch. "There's something about all that power, unleashed, that makes me…"

"Makes you what?" His breath in my ear sends a delicious shiver down my spine.

Emboldened by his hands stroking their way up my shirt and his erection pressed firmly against my ass, I say, "Makes me think about what could have happened in the alley…or the studio if I hadn't…done what I did."

His hands glide over my skin, beneath my T-shirt, to cup my breasts. "You drove me out of my fucking mind is what you did. Almost lost control. Had to get outta there 'cause if I'd stayed, I didn't know what would happen."

My lust-sodden brain is slow to process his words, but when it does, I draw in a sharp breath. He left because of him? Not because of me? "I thought you didn't like it."

Ray shoves my bra up and cups my naked breasts in his warm palms as he nuzzles my neck. "My girl, wantin' me so bad…nothing hotter than that."

My girl. I like it. I want it. For real. But his explanation, flattering as it is, doesn't really explain his reaction or the curious expression I caught on his face before he smoothed it away. "She wants you now."

"Don't want to scare you like I did before."

"You didn't scare me. I just have…issues with…my hands and…my clothes." Understatement of the year. But I'm not about to spill the whole sorry story of my PTSD and my triggers to a hot guy who is very obviously aroused and has his hands on my breasts.

"You gonna tell me about it? Anything else you need to tell me?"

My stomach clenches. "No. Just…a quirk. I don't let it get in the way of what I want."

"What do you want?" One hand presses against my stomach, pulling me against him, while the other tangles in my hair, yanking my head back, exposing my throat to the burn of his lips. "Tell me and I'll give it to you."

"I want to feel." I clench my hands against the windowsill. "Really feel. I want your hands and your mouth on me. I want your cock and your fingers inside me. Even if it's just now, tonight, and we're done."

His body quivers, vibrates against me, as if he is exerting great effort to hold himself back.

"Fuck me," he groans.

"I'm trying."

Wrong thing to say. Or maybe, right thing to say. His hand glides up and he squeezes my left breast, his thumb brushing over my nipple, making me ache with longing. And then he freezes.

"You're pierced."

"Yeah. Like Tag said, I've got a bit of a reckless side." Not quite the whole truth. When my therapist suggested I try to find other ways to reclaim my sexuality after one-night stands and a relationship with Charlie didn't do it, I decided to get piercings in the areas I felt had been most violated. Jess thought I was crazy, but my therapist was very supportive, especially after I told her about the cute new tattoo artist and piercing specialist at work named Duncan.

He gently strokes his thumb over the little silver ring in my left nipple and my sex clenches in response.

"Fucking hot."

"Glad you approve. I have another surprise for you, but I'm saving it for later."

Ray growls and scores his teeth over my nape, sending zings of pleasure through me. I moan and arch my back, wanting more.

"You like that," he says.

"No one has ever bitten my neck before, so it just might be the whole new-experience thing."

He licks over the bite, and I rub my ass against the bulge in his jeans. "More."

"So responsive. You're gonna be dripping by the time I'm done with you if you react that way to a lick."

My hands slide down the wall, and I look back over my shoulder, my eyes watering as my hair pulls in his grip. "I hope that's a promise."

"Christ." His breath is hot against my neck. "I pegged you wrong. Thought you were more reserved. But you're a little minx, aren't you?" He gives my nipple ring a rough tweak and I gasp. "How rough can I be with this?" He tweaks again like a kid with a new toy, and I shudder as the pleasure pain shoots straight to my clit.

"I don't know. No one has ever played with it before."

Ray stills and releases my hair. "No one?"

"You're my first. I'm a nipple ring virgin.'"

For a long moment, he doesn't move. I can feel his chest heaving against my back, his cock pressing into the cleft of my ass, then his hand feathers over my breast and he gives the ring a tug, his voice laced with amusement. "So." *Tug.* "How." *Tug.* "Was." *Tug.* "Your." *Tug.* "First." *Tug.* "Time?"

By the time he's done, my nipple is tight and peaked, my breast swollen, and I am so wet, my panties are soaked.

"Good," I whisper. "You never forget the first. But maybe you should stop playing with your new toy and see what other present I have for you under my clothes."

He presses a soft kiss to my shoulder, then backs away. "Clothes off and prepare to be searched." His voice is warm, lush, and filled with sensual promise. But I am oh so aware that, dominant as he is, he's mindful of my issue with being undressed. A warm, fluttery feeling spreads from my belly, beating back the memories.

"Help me."

And he does. His hands over my hands, we slide my shirt and bra up and over my head, his fingers tangling with mine, caressing my body as I am bared for his pleasure. When we get to my shoulders, I raise my arms and Ray takes over. Slow and sensual, his fingers glide over my skin, filling me with the sensation of his touch. When he reaches my hands, he yanks the clothing over my head and tosses it to the floor with a victory growl.

"Back in position." He smooths his hands down my arms and places my palms against the cool metal surface of the shop wall. And then he is everywhere, his hands roaming over my body, setting fire to my skin. When he has thoroughly touched and kissed every inch of my exposed skin, he tugs out my ponytail holder. My hair fans out across my back in a silken wave.

"Fuck. I love your hair." He strokes his fingers through the strands. "Don't put it up when you're with me."

"Guess that means I won't be with you when I'm exercising or doing ink." With a grin, I look back over my shoulder, but my smile fades at the intensity of his stare.

"You know what I do to girls who give me attitude?" He kicks my legs apart, then smooths his hand over my ass.

Desire, dark and delicious, curls through my body. "What do you do?"

His hand tightens, fingers digging into my flesh. "I spank them."

I make a soft sound, deep in my throat. Morbid fascination, dangerous desire—everything I've imagined but never thought could be real, he offers with a brush of his fingertips. "I've never been spanked," I whisper. "But I think I might like it."

His deep, satisfied rumble pulses between my legs. "You're gonna kill me, sayin' things like that." He circles my waist with his hands, his fingers lingering on the waistband of my jeans, skimming along the inside, his touch an erotic tickle that makes me writhe against him.

"Don't move."

"Then don't do things that make me want to push you to the ground and tear off your clothes."

He chuckles, amused. "We'll get to that later. Right now, you're taking off your jeans and I'm gonna help you, like last time."

With a vicious tug, he reaches around and opens the zipper, then positions my hands on my hips and covers them with his palms, guiding me as I push down my jeans. Although he is working around my trigger, he is still totally in control, and I tremble, overwhelmed with the knowledge that for the first time, I can have what I want without the past getting in the way.

He crouches beside me, offering his shoulder as I toe off my shoes and kick my jeans away. Then he licks his lips and barks, "Back to the wall."

My mouth waters at his tone—low, commanding, authoritative. Intensely erotic. He is so unlike any man I have ever been with. I turn without thinking, curiosity overriding reticence and my fear of losing control.

Crouched in front of me, Ray glides his hands up my legs, his fingers drawing lazy circles over the sensitive skin of my inner thighs, turning my thoughts to the throbbing between my legs. Unable to resist, I run my hands through the soft fuzz on his head.

He looks up, his eyes hooded with desire, then stands, dwarfing me with his massive body. With one hand pressed against the wall beside me, he glides a finger along the edge of my silky red panties, his lips curling into a satisfied smile when I whimper.

"You like red panties?"

"I like what's hidden by red panties." His naughty finger glides over my mound, brushing over the thin slip of fabric covering my aching clit. My breath catches in my throat, and I arch my back and moan.

"You want more?" His voice rumbles in my ear as he slides his hand down to cup my sex.

"Yes."

He wraps one arm around my waist, pulling my body against him. Then he kicks my legs apart.

"Open for me."

My cheeks flame, but the rest of me is burning so hot even the wetness between my thighs won't be able to put out the fire. I part my legs, and he shoves my panties aside, stroking through my folds with a thick, firm finger. Then he rips my panties away.

My lungs seize. My heart skips a beat. Flashbacks slice through my arousal, and I gasp, my fingers digging into his arm, nails cutting his skin. "Oh God…I…"

He cuts me off with a kiss, this one hard and urgent, his hand cupping the back of my head, holding me still as he forces my lips apart. "That's it. Use me," he growls. "If something is scaring you, holding you back, give it to me. I want your pain, Sia."

He does not lie. His cock, thick and hard as steel, presses against my abdomen, rigid beneath his jeans.

I tighten my grip on his arm, clawing his skin, imagining the memories are flowing through my fingertips and into him, where they are beaten away by the sheer force of his presence, solid and unyielding beneath me. My tension eases. I release him and gasp when I see blood on his skin.

"Good girl," he whispers. "And you didn't hurt me. The harder you hold, the more I get off."

Ray glides his fingers through my folds and up to my throbbing nub. I know the exact moment he feels my piercing because he jerks his hand away.

"Surprise number two," I say.

His sharp intake of breath, followed by an appreciative growl is all the reassurance I need, and I smile.

"Christ." Crouching down, he stares at the little barbell piercing my clitoral hood. "You've pierced your clit too."

"Just the hood. It's a VGH piercing."

He gently touches the top and bottom of the little barbell. My clit throbs in response and I moan.

"Does that feel good?"

"Oh, yes."

He touches it again—strokes, wiggles, plays.

"Why did you do it?" He pushes himself to his feet, his brow creased.

"I…" How do I explain my rationale without explaining what happened to me? And after Peter's brutal reaction, I am not telling him that story. I don't want tears or sympathy. I don't want to be treated like glass. And I don't want my past to be baggage that will chase Ray away. I just want to be normal. "It makes me feel…sexy."

Ray's eyes blaze, his breathing raw and ragged. "You are sexy. Damn sexy. You don't need anything to make you that way." Bold now, he cups my sex, pressing his palm against my piercing. I suck in a sharp breath and rock my hips against him, need coiling tight in my core. "What's it like?"

"Again…you're the first, but don't let it go to your head."

"Too late." He spins me around, one hand spanning my stomach while he pulls me back against him. "Arms up and around my neck. That work for you?"

"Yes." I do as he asks, my body arching as I reach behind me, my breasts thrusting up and out for his tormenting pleasure.

"Very nice." He cups my left breast, gently tugging my nipple ring as his fingers trace soft circles over my skin. "I don't know what to play with first."

Looking back over my shoulder, I brush my lips over his cheek. "Play with all of me."

"Oh, I will."

While he torments my nipple with one hand, he glides the other down my body, resting his fingers on my mound, just above my piercing. When I jerk my hips, trying to let him know I want more, he toys with the little barbell, stroking, pressing, wiggling, testing, driving my arousal up so fast, I am whimpering and rocking against his hand in minutes.

"You're so fucking wet. Hot."

His words fuel my fire and I moan. "You going to talk about it? Or are you going to do something about it?"

Ray chuckles. "Don't worry. I'll take care of you." And then he thrusts one thick finger deep inside me.

"Oh God." I breathe out my pleasure at the exquisite intrusion.

"Fuck you're tight." He groans and presses his finger deeper. "Been a while?"

"Kind of a personal question, don't you think?"

He draws his finger out and then drives two fingers into my slit. "Ah, well then. Wouldn't want to get personal while my fingers are in your pussy. Maybe I'll take them out and we can talk."

My sex tightens around him, and I moan when he strokes his fingers against my sensitive inner walls.

"Don't want me to take them out? You want me to fuck you with these fingers? Make you scream?"

Fists clenched tight behind his neck, back arched, nipples rock hard, I grind against his thrusting fingers. "Yes. Please. Yes."

"How long? Answer the question."

Panting, my wetness dripping down my thighs, so aroused I can barely think, I moan my answer. "Over a year. Gave up because the guys I met didn't do it for me."

"Because you needed me," he rasps, his cock pressed tight against my ass. "You needed a real man. A man who can drive you up and take you down until you are begging him to let you come. A man who can make you come with a flick of his fingers."

"Like you." I groan and rock my hips toward him. I've never needed to come so badly in my life.

"Like me. Now, touch your breasts." His voice is a sensual, husky rumble in my ear and I lower my hands and cup by breasts, alternating between squeezing and flicking my nipples with my thumbs. My head falls back against Ray's shoulder and I draw in a ragged breath.

"That's right." He presses a third finger into my sex, stretching me, filling me as he glides slowly in and out, pressing the pads of his fingers along my sensitive spot, his palm resting on my piercing, rubbing the tiny barbell against my swollen nub. Frantic with need, I ride his fingers, driving my ass against the steel of his erection. Tension coils inside me, building so quickly that, for a moment, I forget to breathe.

Out of control. My skin prickles and my chest tightens in warning.

"Come for me, beautiful girl." His voice, deep and low, coils around me like a rope, binding me to his will. "Come all over my hand. Give it up to me."

His words, his voice, sizzle to the most primal part of my brain. Naughty words. Dirty words. Arousing words. I writhe against him as he draws me to my peak, alternating the pressure on my clit with the deep thrust of his fingers until I am wound so tight my body trembles and the part of me that screams for me to run is drowned by the betraying thunder of my desire as it pounds through my veins. But it takes his hand tangling in my hair, yanking my head back so hard my eyes water, his lips hard on mine, to release me.

And then I'm gone, lost in the firestorm of a climax that sweeps through my body, a blaze of incredible pleasure that rips a scream from my throat and takes me past the point of no return.

After a panting pause, Ray withdraws his fingers and spins me around to face him, pulling me against his body. His erection presses into my stomach and I reach between us to stroke along his length. But when I tug on his fly, he stays my hand.

"Not tonight."

"But...don't you want...need?" I give him a tentative smile. "I'm not selfish, you know. And I have a condom in my purse."

Ray stiffens then places a soft kiss on my forehead. "I want you so bad, I can barely keep it together. But knowing myself, the way I am right now, if I take it any further, I'll hurt you."

"I won't break. Hard. Rough. I don't care. I want you inside me." For a moment, I am back in the dark years, when I thought mindlessly fucking strangers would wipe Luke's touch away. But Ray isn't a stranger. And I have no point to prove, except that I want him. I have wanted him since the day I first saw him in the ring.

Gaze locked to his, I tug on his belt. When he doesn't move, I pull it open, then yank on his fly. The button pops, and I draw the zipper down, inch by slow inch, letting my fingers graze over his shaft, which is straining against his fly.

He stills when I drop to my knees and pull his clothing over his hips. His erection springs free, hard, heavy, and so big it takes my breath away. Body tense and quivering, jaw tight, he makes no move to help me save for stepping out of his clothing when I drop them to the floor.

I lick my lips, wondering how he might taste, but when I reach for his thick shaft, he fists my hair and pulls me up, leaving me under no illusions about who is in control.

"This is what you want?" His voice is hollow, his eyes so dark they are almost black, and for the first time, I wonder if I've made the right decision.

"Yes."

He guides me across the floor to what must have been the main work area. Scrapes and patches on the floor indicate where the heavy equipment must have been, pieces of cardboard and small, gray piles of metal dust cling to the side of the wall. Ray stops in front of a worn, wooden workbench pushed up against the wall, the grease stains barely visible in the semidarkness. Then he pushes me down on the cool, hard surface.

"Don't move."

His feet thud over the floor. I hear the rustle of clothing and the crinkle of a condom wrapper. Then he is back. One hand presses against my lower back, holding me firm against the table, and the other twists in my hair, making me arch, my ass rubbing against his hips.

"I can't be gentle." His voice is raw, husky with need, low with warning. "For a coupla hours after a fight, I got no gentleness in me."

"You've been pretty gentle so far."

"That was the getting to know you bit." With a low groan, he kicks my legs apart, his fingers diving into my swollen pussy. I moan and rock against his touch, need building afresh. My breaths turn to pants, and he draws his fingers out, slicking my wetness up and around my clit, bumping against the piercing until lust fuzzes my brain, my body heats, and a cold sweat prickles my skin.

Nononononono. Not now. This is what I wanted. Hot, wild, rough animal sex. No strings. No attachments. Just pure physical pleasure.

Before the panic takes hold, he thrusts inside me, pushing through my sensitive tissue. Hard, fast, and so deep my breath catches in my throat. Before I can get used to his thickness, the fullness, the delight of having him inside me, he withdraws and thrusts again, deeper this time, hitting my cervix and making me gasp.

"You okay?"

Am I okay? Trapped between panic and desire, my body thrumming with need, my mind screaming of danger, I force a word from my lips. A lie. A challenge. A deep, desperate desire to be normal. "Yes."

"Don't lie to me, Sia." He reaches around and rubs his thumb over my bottom lip, then pushes it inside my mouth. "Bite. Give it to me, beautiful girl."

I bite. As hard as I dare. Ray groans and grips my hip with his free hand, then hammers into me, his shaft sliding over my sensitive inner walls. My piercing vibrates against my clit with his every thrust, and my nipples rub against the gritty surface of the table. Too much. Too many sensations. My arousal builds fast and fierce, spiraling out of control, and when he reaches around to stroke my clit, I am gone, screaming at the shock of an orgasm so intense I feel like I am being ripped apart by pleasure. Ray slides his thumb from my mouth and his rhythm quickens. Fingers dig into my hips and his body tenses, straining as he comes, his shaft pulsing inside me.

He collapses over my back, feathering soft kisses against my neck, but as my pleasure fades, something dark takes its place—the PTSD that will not go away. My lungs seize and I stiffen, squeezing my eyes shut as I rasp in a breath.

Ray pulls me up and wraps his arms around me. "I hurt you."

"No." Alarmed he would blame himself, I wrap my arms over his. If he would just hold me, make me feel safe, I'll be okay. But he pulls away.

"You should have told me to stop." He scrapes his hand through his hair. "You should have told me it was too much. I've got no limits. When I lose it, I lose it, and you threaten my control like no one else."

Curiously, his distress eases my anxiety. "It wasn't too much," I say softly. "You need to stop worrying you're going to hurt me. And I didn't want you to stop. It was just...very intense. I'll be okay."

But I'm not okay. Gritting my teeth, I try to breathe through waves of panic as I search for my clothes, drawing slow, deep breaths, counting in my head, taking comfort in the familiarity of getting dressed. I did what I had promised myself I would never do. I gave up control, left myself open, vulnerable, and my subconscious couldn't deal. I played with fire and I got burned.

Silence weighs heavy in the air between us. We tidy the fight area and lock up the building. I follow Ray to his bike, wishing for the first time ever that Tag was here to take me home.

Ray's Harley Softail is huge, heavily chromed, and oozes sex. Ironic how only a few hours ago, I would have killed for a ride on his bike, and now it is the last place I want to be.

Ray hands me the second helmet, and I fasten it under my chin and slide onto the pillion seat behind him. He points out the passenger pegs, two silver bars with little skulls on the ends, and I position my feet, then wrap my hands around his waist. Moments later, the engine thrums between my legs and we shoot off into the night. My body molds into his. My breasts press tight against his broad back, my hips grind into his ass. This is going to be one hell of a ride.

Too bad it will be my last.

Chapter 11
HAND

"What am I going to do?" Jess sobs, and grabs another tissue from the box on my living room table, an upside-down polar bear holding the glass with his feet. "How many years did I wait and then, suddenly, out of the blue, Tag shows up and expects me to still be waiting for him? It's ruined my weekend. No. It's ruined my life."

"Well…you *were* still waiting for him last week," I say. "And Tag wasn't expecting you to be waiting for him. He says he's too busy for a relationship, but he's happy for you."

She blows her nose and tosses the tissue at the already overflowing trash can. My bright blue area rug is already dotted with tissues as is the huge, overstuffed white couch she's sitting on. Although I always wear black when I go out, my house is a riot of primary colors, a throwback to the old me.

"There's nothing to be happy about. It's just casual with Blade Saw. I mean, I like him. If it weren't for Tag, I'd think about something more serious with him. He's fun, he's got an amazing body, he's hot in bed, he's a wicked fighter, and he's…nice."

"Nice?"

Jess shrugs. "He does nice things. He shows up at my office with a packed lunch. He picks me up from parties if it's dark, no questions asked. He'll lie for hours with me in the park while I work on my tan, pick up my dry cleaning, make me dinner if I'm tired, and rub my feet. He'll even walk my dog if I have to work late."

"He sounds like someone's dad."

She gives me an affronted stare. "Well, he doesn't talk like some-one's dad. His language is a little crude. *Hooters* and *tits* aren't my favorite words to describe my breasts, and I prefer *big* to *humongous*." Her lips twist to the side. "I especially don't like *juicy* or *cu*—"

"I get it. I don't need to hear it."

With a dramatic sigh, she throws herself back on the cushions—blue to match the carpet and drapes, and yellow to match the dining table that I forced Tag to carry home from a nearby flea market.

"I can't get serious with Blade Saw if there is even the smallest chance Tag is interested. And I think there is. Don't you think so? Did you see his face last night when he saw Blade Saw's arm around me? And the way he interrupted Rampage to find out what was going on? If that wasn't interest, what was it?"

"Friendship." I stretch out on the couch, basking in the late-afternoon sun. This is the closest I've come to relaxing since Ray dropped me at home after our encounter in the machine shop last night.

"Either way, I'm screwed." With an exaggerated sigh, she flings herself back on a couch that's a twin to the one I'm on. "They train in the same gym. How awkward would that be if I dumped one for the other?"

I twist my ring around my finger. "About as awkward as me having to see Ray at the gym after what happened last night."

Jess, of course, knows everything. Five minutes after Ray dropped me at home, I was on the phone to her.

"I need the potato chips." She reaches out her hand, and I lean over and hand her the bag.

"Chips don't make for a healthy lunch."

She stuffs a chip in her mouth and glares. "Look who's talking. You had them for breakfast and lunch."

"I'm depressed."

Jess snorts. "I thought you said it was the best, most mind-blowing sex of your life."

Hugging a pillow, I frown. "It was also the most terrifying. I felt totally out of control. It was like my body was chugging full-steam ahead and my brain was trying to catch up. Everything he said and did, the way he talked and touched me…it turned me on so much, I couldn't think. I was like a puppet. He said turn, I turned. He said spread 'em, and I spread. And afterward, I felt so anxious and empty inside. With Charlie and James, I felt closer to them after we had sex, even though I never came. With Ray, I came so hard I screamed, but I felt something was missing…me."

Jess crunches a chip. "You probably needed to ease into it, since it had been so long…soft lights, warm bed, a little music, lots of cuddle time, but unfortunately, you decided to dive in the deep end, lose your piercing virginity, and have sex in a freezing cold ex–machine shop with a fighter after a fight who warned you he would be rough, without telling him about your past. Does that about sum it up?"

She grabs a Twizzler and sticks it into her cooler, using it as a straw. Curious, I do the same and my tongue burns at the burst of sugary sweetness.

"He doesn't need to know about my past. I'm over it. I'm ready to have a normal relationship, but not with him."

"Seriously," she continues as if I hadn't spoken, "the entire thing sounds so hot that I wanted to combust while you were telling me about it. He's not Charlie or James, falling over themselves to make sure they don't hurt you or flip your triggers. Guys like Ray only hold back so much. They named him the Predator for a reason. He's like a wild animal. You've seen him in the ring. You only think you've tamed him, but show him a piece of raw meat, and instinct will override rational thought. You want a foot rub and a bubble bath, find a man like Charlie. You want someone to spank your ass raw and make you come so hard you scream, Ray's your man."

The sugar burn fades and I take another sip. "Nice. I feel so much better thinking I'm like a piece of raw meat to him. And he didn't spank me."

"I meant it as a compliment. And the spanking will come. Guys like him love to spank. It's the ultimate dominant trait. Marks you in the most primal way." She shoves a handful of chips in her mouth, forcing me to wait through her crunches for her more experienced insight.

I roll my eyes and grab the chip bag. "I hardly think having sex with him once means I'm marked as his. It was just sex. Raw sex. No emotions involved. It's exactly what I need. I'm not capable of sustaining an intimate relationship. I have trust issues because of what happened. I learned that with Charlie and James."

"They weren't right for you," she says softly. "That's why you couldn't have an intimate relationship. It has nothing to do with Luke. And not only that, you weren't honest with them. You pretended to come. You pretended to love them. Then you pushed them away. You never even gave them a chance."

"Since when did you become an amateur psychologist?"

Her cheeks brighten. "Blade Saw is taking psych at night school. He tells me lots of stuff."

"And did he mark you in a primal way?" Sarcasm imbues my tone, but Jess doesn't seem to mind.

"Blade Saw isn't like that. He's not an alpha fighter. He's a beta. He enjoys fighting, but he likes the social aspect too. So yeah, we have sex, but he's not going to pound on anyone who looks at me the wrong way, or attack someone if he found out I was cheating on him. He would be more like, 'well if he's what you want. I'm just glad you're happy.'"

"I can't see Ray chilling over something like that."

"Definitely not." She lifts an eyebrow. "I'm surprised he hasn't called you already. Alpha males are very possessive once they've marked their territory. He'll want to know you're still his."

I groan and drop back on the couch. "He did call. I just didn't answer."

"You should call him back." She grabs a napkin from the table and dabs her lips. "Invite him over to see your vast collection of sex toys. That should smooth things over."

"I don't want to call him. What if I've made another mistake? What if that was my subconscious saying, 'You fucked up again and trusted the wrong guy'? That dark feeling was a warning. Some part of me is trying to save me from myself."

"Is that how you really feel?" She tilts her head to the side, her eyes questioning.

"No." I wrap my arms around myself and meet her gaze. "It was utterly the most exciting and thrilling experience I've ever had. It was like he plucked my fantasies out of my head. Not only that, but he said he had no limits. It almost sent me over the edge. Imagine. He would make my deepest, darkest fantasies come true. All I have to do is ask."

Jess swings her legs off the couch and checks her watch. "I think you're just scared. You went from having nice, gentle sex with guys who only knew one position and were too afraid to try anything else because of what happened to you, to going full throttle with a man who is clearly vastly more experienced, very dominant, and drips sex appeal. You should have brought him home, where you feel safe. Told him what happened to you. Given yourself enough time for a post-sex cuddle."

"I'm not going to tell him." My chest tightens and I crumple the empty chip bag in my fist. "I'm not telling anyone ever again. That's over. Done. I'm going to be normal if it kills me."

My phone buzzes, and I fumble around until I find it on the kitchen island, then check the text messages.

"Who is it?"

"Rampage." My lips quiver when I read the text. "He's at Redemption. He says the Predator's there. He's all chuffed that the Predator had him track me down because he feels like the go-to man at Redemption. He said the Predator threatened to bounce him around the ring if he didn't find me and make sure I was okay because I wasn't answering my phone."

Jess stretches out on the couch again and crosses her legs. "Isn't Rampage a super heavyweight? Why would he even be worried about the Predator's threats? He could probably just sit on him to quiet him down."

"He's *the Predator.* You've seen him fight. Rampage wouldn't stand a chance. He's big but he's slow."

My phone buzzes again. Rampage says now that he knows I'm okay, everyone is heading over to Renegade and Amanda's place for a party. Since I have the day off, I should come and bring Jess too.

Jess and I debate the merits of going to the party. She wants to see Tag. No, she doesn't want to see Tag. She wants to see Blade Saw. No, she doesn't want to see Blade Saw because now she's thinking of breaking up with him for Tag. But what if Tag doesn't really want her?

She'll have no one. Or worse, what if they both want her and get into a fight? She licks her lips. That would be pretty awesome to watch. Okay, she'll come.

But I'm not sure if I'm going. What if Doctor Death is there? What if Ray is there? How will I explain why I just left him with a quick "good night" out on the street after he dropped me off? And what will I say when he asks why I didn't answer his calls? And what if he wants to talk about last night? What will I say? Normal people don't have an emotional crisis after hot sex. Normal people don't suddenly worry they've misplaced their trust.

Jess drags me into my bedroom and paws through my neatly organized closet. What if, she says, he's not the kind of guy to push? What if he just smiles and says hi and offers me a cooler, and we chill at the party and have a good time?

Two hours later, Jess and I are drinking coolers in the backyard of Renegade and Amanda's house. Renegade is manning the barbecue. Makayla and Amanda are chatting with Hammer Fist, and Torment is glowering by the fence, no doubt keeping the nonexistent predators away from his woman. Rampage has gathered a group of newbie fighters around him to share stories about Redemption when it was a gritty, underground fight club, and deliciously dark and ripped Obsidian is trying to out arm lift Shayla on a tree branch.

"See? We had nothing to worry about." Jess clinks bottles with me. "No Tag. No Blade Saw. No Doctor Death. No Predator. Although it's kind of a waste that we're all dressed up and the men who would appreciate us aren't around to…well, appreciate us. Maybe we shouldn't have worn skirts and heels."

"Jinx."

Jess widens her eyes. "Who's here?"

"Blade Saw. He's spotted you and he's smiling a *humongous* smile."

Jess glares and turns away. "If you need me, I'll be hiding in the crowd with Rampage's minions."

"Hey, kitten." Obsidian gives me a warm smile when I join him by the oak tree. Shayla is in the middle of a set of pull-ups, her ripped body glistening with sweat, yet she still manages to nod a greeting.

"So who's winning?" I sip my cooler and Obsidian lifts an eyebrow. "Me."

"Not. For. Much. Fucking. Longer." Shayla grunts out each word as her body moves smoothly up and down, her elbows operating like well-oiled hinges.

"You want to go next?" Obsidian squeezes my bicep between his thumb and forefinger. "Looks like you've got a bit of strength and she's already slowing down."

Shayla spits out a curse and increases her pace.

"I don't think I could even do one. Plus I'm wearing a skirt and heels. Not optimal attire for pull-ups."

"Hand." The barked command from across the yard startles Obsidian. He jerks back, ripping his hand off my arm so quickly he loses his balance and steps back into Shayla, knocking her off the tree. Shayla is on her feet in two seconds and battering at Obsidian in three.

"You did that on purpose. I was almost at one hundred. You knew I would win."

Someone yells *fight*. Someone else cheers. I am almost crushed in the stampede of excited fighters, saved only by a firm arm around my waist and an even firmer body protecting me from the excited horde.

"That was you?" I look up as Ray leads me to the safety of the patio. "You yelled 'hand'?"

"He had his hand on you," Ray says, unsmiling.

"He was just joking around." I wave at the crowd, now three deep around the tree. "Look what you did."

Ray scowls in Obsidian's direction. "He knows better. Would have dealt with him, but Shayla beat me to it."

And she is doing a good job too. Obsidian is already on the grass and Shayla is trying to twist him into a painful submission while everyone shouts encouragement.

Wrapping my arms around myself, I lean against the low, stone retaining wall. "I think it was a little OTT. I mean, it's not like we're... you know...together." I suck in my lips and look away.

"We were together last night." Ray lifts me and settles me on top of the wall, then eases himself between my legs. "If that didn't work for you, let me know."

Didn't work for me? What the heck is he talking about? Does he think I faked those orgasms? Or that I wanted him to go farther? Does he want an assessment of his A+ performance?

"I don't understand."

He steps closer, easing my legs apart and my skirt rides up, almost indecently, baring my secret for him alone.

"Neither do I," he says. "I never lose control. Never come on that strong unless I know it's something that gets you off. But when I told you to do something, you did it. No games. No pretense. It was like you wanted to do it. And it turned you on. Sent me over the edge and I went too far."

His words do strange fluttery things to my stomach. But he must be wrong. Sure I was turned on, but it was because of him and not because he bossed me around. The guys I've been dating would never dream of telling me what to do in bed. I don't allow myself to be that vulnerable. No one tells me what to do. No one sees beneath the surface.

"Look at me."

My head jerks up at his sharp tone and his eyes smolder as he cups my jaw. "There it is. That's why I can't stay away."

"I'm sorry about last night." I trace along his corded forearm, his hair soft beneath my fingers. "It wasn't you. It's me. And for me…it was—"

"Too much," he interjects softly. "Like breaking a butterfly's wing."

"I didn't break. I just"—a smile teases the corner of my mouth—"flew away." I lean into the warmth of his palm and he strokes down my hair.

"Come back to me, butterfly." He loops his arm around me and kisses me. Soft and warm, his tongue slides between my lips to caress the inside of my mouth. My lower body turns liquid and I am grateful for the seat.

Ray pulls away and trails his fingers up my inner thigh. "So fucking sexy in this skirt. Those shoes. Man sees someone else touching his woman when she's dressed so fine and it's hard to stay in control."

Blood rushes through my ears, drowning out the faint warning in the back of my mind that I am not someone capable of the trust needed to sustain any but the most fleeting of relationships. This is supposed to be light. Fun. The fulfillment of a fantasy. Nothing more.

Giving in to the rush of desire, I glide my tongue over the seam of his lips. He tastes fresh and minty, and a little of me. Our kiss is sweet and gentle. A touching of tongues. A murmur of lips. I close my eyes and drown in the softness of his smile.

"Hell."

My eyes snap open at Tag's irritated bark. Moments later he appears in front of me, his face a remarkable shade of purple, muscles quivering like he wants to punch someone. Likely Ray, who has already turned around, angling his body to form a shield between me and Tag.

"Get your hands off my fucking sister."

Ray doesn't move. "Nothin' to do with you, Fuzz. Back off."

"Tag, please." I glance around the yard and catch sight of Jess pushing her way through the crowd toward us. Fight groupies can always sense a fight.

"He's not safe." Tag's voice rises and a few people look over from the fight. "Not good for you. Why the fuck won't you listen?"

"I want to be here. With him." I look up at Ray, his jaw taut, and then over at Tag. "And it's not like you don't know him, Tag. He's your teammate."

"Thought you'd learned your lesson that just because I'm on a team with someone doesn't mean you can trust them." The bitterness in his voice slices through my heart, but his words make me gasp. Tag has never once been anything but sensitive about what happened to me. He's never used it against me in any way. The fact that he would do so now, and in public, takes my breath away. My mouth opens and closes, but in my shock I have nothing to say.

Lucky for me, Jess does.

"Tag O'Donnell." She shoves him in the chest, pushing him off balance. "I cannot believe you just said that. What the hell is wrong with you? What were you thinking? How could you bring that up?" She looks over at me and the sympathy and concern on her face tip me from barely in control to undone. Emotion wells up in my throat, and I push Ray away and slide off the wall.

"It's okay." My voice wavers. "I'm good. It's fine."

But it's not fine. I can't breathe. Can't talk. Can't think. Just have to get out of here.

Brushing past Ray, I walk into the house. Behind me, I can hear Jess shriek. "Look what you did to her. What kind of brother are you? She's the strongest person I know. She worked so hard to get over it, and now you take it and use it against her?"

Her shoes tap on the stone tiles, and then clatter across the linoleum floor, the sound slowing only when she spots me in the kitchen.

"You didn't have to do that." Curiously numb, I lean against the counter, my arms wrapped around my body. "I'm fine, really. I was just shocked he would bring it up, so I overreacted."

"Like fuck I didn't." Jess glares at the door to the backyard. "Someone needed to give him a shake. Something is wrong with him. He's never been so callous and insensitive. If I'd seen that side of him before, I don't know if I would have stuck it out so long." She shudders and then tilts her head and looks at me, her voice softening. "Are you sure you're okay?"

"Yeah." I fill a glass with water and take a sip. "I thought it was all gone, locked away with my paintings, but ever since I met Ray, it keeps spilling out. How can I have a normal relationship if I can't keep the past in the past?"

Jess wraps her arms around me and gives me a hug. "Maybe hiding it away wasn't the best thing to do."

Footsteps thud across the floor. I look up just as Ray walks into the kitchen. His gaze takes in Jess's arms around me and his face softens. "You want to go home? I'll take you."

"Thanks, but I can go with Jess." I pull away from her embrace but not before she pinches my arm.

"She gonna stay with you tonight?"

Puzzled I shake my head. "She's working tomorrow. I don't need anyone to stay with me."

"Not leaving you alone." He folds his arms in a "don't mess with me" pose, and his voice drops husky and low. "You wanna talk about it, we'll talk. You don't, that's cool. We'll kick back, watch TV. But I'm staying with you."

Jess makes a noise in her throat, something akin to a choked sob, like people make in the movies when they don't want anyone to know they are crying at a happy moment. But the feeling I have is deeper, warm, steadying; it curls low in my belly and then it gives my heart a little lick.

Ray looks over at Jess. "You got a way to get home safe? If not, I can drop Sia off and come back for you."

Jess beams. "So chivalrous. You could teach these fighters a thing or two. But I'm okay, thanks. We came in my car."

With a smug smile, Jess heads back to the party. Ray disappears and returns with a track suit, running shoes, and a helmet.

"Shayla had these in her gym bag." He hands me the clothes and shoes. "She said you could return them next time you're at Redemption. Not safe for you to ride without something to cover you up."

"Resourceful." I kick off my shoes and pull the track pants over my legs.

"Gotta get my girl home safe."

His girl. We've only had sex once and suddenly I'm his girl. But how can I set him straight when he's being so nice?

Once I'm dressed, I grab the helmet and follow Ray out to his bike, my mouth watering at his ass-hugging jeans and the battered leather jacket that clings to him like a second skin. The air is cool, fresh with the hint of an ocean breeze, but when we reach the bike, I shudder. Am I ready to take him home? Am I ready to go home at all? My past is everywhere in my apartment, and right now all I want to do is forget.

"Ray?"

"Yeah."

"Could we just ride around?"

He holds out his hand and helps me onto the pillion seat. "As long as you need. Just let me know when you want to go home."

Moments later he slides on in front of me, then reaches back and wraps my arms around his waist. "Hold on."

And I do. I hold him until the memories are gone and I know nothing but the whisper of the wind, the rumble of the motorcycle between my thighs, and the warmth of Ray's body in my arms.

For a little while at least, I can put the past behind me and pretend Ray is mine.

Chapter 12

GET OUT OF MY CUPBOARDS

AFTER TWO HOURS DRIVING around the city, with my ass numb and my hands frozen, I finally ask Ray to take me home. He parks outside my building and then follows me up the front walk.

"I'm coming in," he says, and I am profoundly grateful to be spared the usual awkward good night at the front door, the back and forth in my mind about whether or not I should invite him in, and the perfunctory farewell kiss. Ray always seems to know when I need him to take the lead. How could he not when I wrapped myself around him the second we got on his bike and didn't let go? Warm. Safe. Solid. I've never been so attracted to a man I know so little about.

Or maybe I do. After watching him for a year, I've picked up a few things. He's not a talkative type, keeping to himself before and after a fight. And he's got a philosophical bent. His fight shorts often have sayings from Nietzsche or Kant, musings about life, or abstract, thought-provoking designs. He keeps himself in tip-top shape, eats healthy, and rarely goes out drinking with the guys. So, basically, the opposite of me with my weekend indulgences on girls' night out, my weakness for potato chips and hamburgers, and my tendency to exercise only when my jeans get too tight.

When Ray closes the door behind me, all my tension leaves in a sigh. Motionless, I stand in the hallway and try to process the events of the evening without collapsing in a heap on the floor.

"What do you do to relax?" Ray comes up behind me and wraps a strong arm around my waist, pulling me back against his warm body.

"Other than drink too much, indulge in family-size bags of potato chips, and take bubble baths, none of which interest me right now?" I wriggle away and pull off Shayla's clothes, then toss them in the laundry basket. Hopefully I'll have time to wash them before work tomorrow. "Usually I call Jess."

Silence.

I turn around and Ray is gone. "Ray?"

"Hmmm." Ray grunts as he wanders through my apartment. "Checking your place out."

"Usually people wait for an invitation." I lean against the wall and fold my arms. "They don't wander at will."

"They aren't me. Getting to know you. Will report back in a minute."

For the next five minutes, he inspects my tiny apartment. First the bedroom with its four-poster bed, bright green throw rug and matching bed spread, and the closet where my clothes are all neatly arranged by color. Then he wanders into the tiny bathroom, turns on the taps at the sink for no discernible reason, opens the hall closet, and stares at my coats.

"Is this a territory thing?" I follow him into my living room slash dining room slash kitchen. "Are you going to mark it to keep other males away?"

His face hardens. "You bring guys up here?"

Exasperated, I say, "Yeah. Tons. It's basically a revolving door of hot, fit guys who come to service my needs."

"Not funny. Don't even joke." He frowns and opens my kitchen cupboards one by one, then peers into the fridge containing a surprising array of healthy foods, all purchased by my mother the last time she came to visit.

He makes a final lap around the living room and then returns to the hallway and tugs open the door to my storage closet. Easels and paintbrushes spill onto the floor from the overstuffed space.

"Hey! Get out of my cupboards." I race toward him and gather up my art supplies. "Most people get to know each other through conversation. You know what that is?"

"Not really one for conversation." He tugs a paintbrush from my hand and inspects the bristles. "You paint?"

"Not anymore. That's why everything is in the cupboard." With a harrumph, I shove past him and dump the art supplies at the bottom of the closet. Then I slam the door and lean against it, arms folded. "No."

His lips quiver with a smile and he lifts an eyebrow.

"Don't play that eyebrow game with me." I waggle my finger at him. "You can't intimidate me like you do everyone else. You're not getting in."

Ray takes a step toward me and leans his forearm on the door beside my head. Then he brushes his lips over my cheek and whispers in my ear. "If I really wanted in, you wouldn't be able to stop me." He curves one hand around my rib cage, brushing the underside of my breast with his thumb. My body heats to what I'm sure must be a million degrees and sweat trickles down my neck.

"I thought we were going to watch TV."

"You want to watch TV?"

My chest heaves as I pant. He is close—so close I can feel the warmth of his body, breathe in his scent of leather and soap and fresh ocean air. My chest tightens and I curl my fingers into his sleeve. God, I want him. But after last time, I'm not sure I can handle him again.

"Yes. TV."

A few minutes later, we are seated in front of the television. Ray grabs the remote with one hand and me with the other, tucking me against his body as he flips through the channels at dizzying speed.

"How can you see what's on if you go that fast?" I shut my eyes against the blur that is one hundred channels viewed in one hundredth of a second, or so it seems.

"Know what I like."

I tilt my head back, resting it against his arm. "What about what I like?"

"We'll get there."

We finally settle on a Discovery Channel episode about lions. We learn that lions can have sex as many as one hundred times during a twenty-four-hour period. Ray says he likes learning new things from the Discovery Channel and he never misses a show about jungle cats. I ask if he can have sex one hundred times in a day. He tells me to get the condoms. Slightly concerned he may not be joking, I suggest we watch some more.

The lions segue into sharks. Ray doesn't like the sharks. He thinks they lack class. Also they can't have sex one hundred times a day so, clearly, they are lesser creatures. Amused by this new, chatty, Discovery Channel–loving side of Ray, I slide down the couch and lay my head in his lap. Ray absently strokes my hair while mocking the sharks as they tear apart their prey.

"Why don't you paint anymore?"

An abrupt interjection into his muttering about sharks, Ray's question startles me and I jerk my head up.

"I paint in ink now. Skin is my canvas."

He waves his hand vaguely around the room, encompassing the giant abstract, colorful murals decorating the walls: oils on canvas, framed and hung, all in orange and deep ocean blue, bright reds and greens. "Did you paint these?"

"A long time ago."

"Beautiful." His voice drops to a quiet murmur. "Why did you switch to ink?"

"That was me then," I say. "I'm different now."

Hmmm. Somehow his hand has found its naughty way under my shirt and his deft fingers are fiddling with my bra. "Are you trying to distract me so you can seduce me?"

Ray chuckles as he unhooks my bra, then slides his warm hand around to cup my breast. "If you've let me get this far without slapping me, then I've already seduced you. Now you're mine to do with as I please, unless you still want to chill, and I'm cool with that."

I flip to my back to give him easier access and look up into sky-blue eyes. "It's hard to feel anything except the need to get in your pants when you've got your hand under my shirt."

A smile tugs his lips. "Never met anyone who teased me before."

"That's because you don't scare me, Predator." I grab the edges of my shirt and tug it and my bra over my head. "I know you have a good heart."

His jaw tightens almost imperceptibly. "How?"

"Because I watched you fight for so long I could tell when you were holding back. And you always held back when you had an unequal opponent. I figured you didn't want him to lose face by knocking him out in the first ten seconds, so you'd let him get in a few shots and dance around the ring before you took him down. Same thing you did the other day in the gym with Hammer Fist. I've seen you bench more than you did that night. But you held back so you didn't leave him in your dust, isn't that right?"

He traces my lips with the pad of his thumb. "You see a lot. Know what I see? Another Sia, all soft and sweet in a world of color, hiding under all that black."

"That Sia's gone."

"No, she's not." Ray leans down and kisses me. "She's here." His lips slide across my cheek, and he kisses each of the piercings in my ear. "And here."

My eyes close and I tilt my head to the side as he feathers kisses down my neck, following the tats down my arm. "And here."

Warmth suffuses my body, liquid pleasure flowing through my veins. My back arches, and his lips close around my left nipple. "Here."

Breathless, I sigh. "Where else?"

"You sure you want to do this?" Ray toys with my nipple ring, flipping it back and forth, the little tugging gesture sending every bit of heat rushing to my center. "When I said I was happy to just chill with you, I meant it."

"Hmmm." I raise a sarcastic eyebrow. "Maybe I should put my shirt back on and think about it."

"I have a better idea." Ray tweaks the ring with his finger and thumb, and I gasp as pleasure sizzles through me. "Paint something. Naked."

"You want me to paint for you...naked?"

Ray runs his hand through my hair and tugs my head back. "I'll make sure you enjoy every minute of it."

How many years has it been since I locked everything away? With the past already spilling out around me, do I really want to open that door? "I kinda made a decision to give it up. Couldn't we just—"

Ray slants his mouth over mine. This time his kiss is rough, demanding, his firm lips forcing my mouth open, his tongue delving inside, marking every inch. With his free hand, he sweeps his fingers under my skirt, and then teases me through my panties, his thumb tracing lazy circles over my clit. "Paint for me."

"Ray…" I rock into his touch, my thighs trembling. "I'm… It's been so long… I've moved on."

He twirls my pink-streaked hair around his finger. "Your apartment says you didn't move on. This"—he tugs the color in my hair—"says you didn't move on. And what happened in the alley behind Rabid Ink, and the other day in the machine shop… The things you aren't telling me, they say you didn't move on from whatever it was you're trying to leave behind."

With a rough finger, he shoves my panties aside and strokes over my folds, fuzzing my brain with delicious pleasure. "Paint anything. It doesn't have to be a picture. I'll be right here. I'll probably get off just watching you hold the brush."

My mouth waters at the thought of opening that door, holding the brush in my hand, splashing color on the canvas, the bold, wild strokes that can't be made with a tattoo machine. He's offering me freedom in the safety of his arms.

What are you afraid of? Torment asked me not so long ago. *What kind of fighter are you?*

"I won't let anything happen to you," Ray says. "Trust me."

I hesitate for only a moment longer, and then I give in to longing and step into the ring. "Okay."

Twenty minutes later, I have set up my easel on the dining table. Ray has thrown a drop cloth on the floor to protect the carpet. I've added a few oils to my palate—the only ones that haven't dried out—softened my brushes, and arranged my canvas. For a long moment, I just stare at the whiteness in front of me. A lump forms in my throat when no pictures come to mind. Maybe I won't be able to paint again. Maybe skin will always be my canvas and the tattoo machine my brush.

Ray jolts me out of my confusion with a soft caress. Warm hands on my breasts, his breath a whisper on my nape. "I'm going to undress you. Don't think about me. Don't think about what scares you. Think about that canvas and what you're going to paint. Think about the brush in your hand. The colors on your palate. Think about what inspires you. Think of something you can't do in ink. Then do it for me."

As he talks, his hands glide over my rib cage, his calluses sending sensual shivers across my skin. He presses his thumbs along either side of my spine, rubbing deep concentric circles, easing my tension as his fingers stroke the sides of my breasts. Such a feeling of warmth and contentment suffuses me that I lean back against him, only to have him growl a warning in my ear.

"Paint."

"Bossy."

"I haven't even started."

My body tingles. "Is that a promise?"

"You play nice, it could be a reward." His subtle assurance warms me to my toes. He may be a predator, but he has soft fur.

With slow, gentle movements, he unzips my skirt and eases it down over my hips. Cool air brushes over my heated skin, like the wind on my face when I'm on his motorcycle. But even with that happy image in my head, a familiar tension rolls through my body. My breaths come out in pants, and I tremble.

"Use it," Ray whispers. "Let it out. I've got you."

Heart pounding, muscles coiled tight, I grab my brush, dip into the oil, and streak black across the middle of the canvas. The first stroke is always almost orgasmic, the realization of a vision, desire exposed. But this time it is my fear splashed across the canvas, a black streak marring the pristine white surface, the memory of a night I have wished a thousand times had never been. A sob rips from my throat and I drop my brush.

"Shhhh." With a low growl, Ray runs his hands along my curves, and my breathing hitches.

Damn Luke. Damn that night. I'm going to turn my fear into something beautiful. Gritting my teeth, I lift my brush and the black streak becomes a wheel, two, and then I join them with a band of red.

"Fuck." Ray pinches my nipples between his thumbs and forefingers, his chest warm, hard against my back, his belt buckle a deliciously pleasant pain on my skin.

"Watching you paint is fucking hot."

PTSD crisis averted, I manage a smile. "Might be your hands on my breasts is what's making you hot."

He grinds his hips into my ass, his erection stiff between us. "Touching you makes me hard. Watching you makes me hot."

Gray for the chrome, more red for the fairing, abstract strokes but my brain can't fill in the detail with Ray's fingers grazing the bare skin of my abdomen.

"I can't paint anymore."

"You can." He cups my sex from behind, spreading his fingers, easing my legs apart. "You will."

I hiss in a breath when his fingers slide into my panties, grazing over my mound. My arm drops and I rock into his touch, willing his fingers to delve deeper.

"Steady," he says. "Don't want to ruin my bike."

I glance over my shoulder. "How do you know it's your bike? It's just a collection of brush strokes on canvas."

He buries his face in my neck, his five o'clock shadow scraping over my sensitive skin. "It's my bike."

And then he rips my panties away.

Shock steals my breath, but before the fear can take hold, Ray is on his knees in front of me, backing me away from the easel and filling the space with the breadth of his body.

"I got you," he murmurs as he presses my thighs apart.

"Ray?"

He doesn't answer. Instead he glides his thumbs over my folds, parting them, exposing me to the heat of his breath.

"No." I gasp and my hands tremble. "You can't. I won't be able to stand—much less paint."

"You stop. I stop." He presses his thumbs upward, exposing my clit from its pierced hood, and then he gives it a lick.

Warm and wet, his tongue rasps over my throbbing nub. A low, guttural groan rips from my throat. Wetness trickles down my inner thighs, and I steady myself on the table and moan.

Ray pulls away, looks up at me, his eyes hooded. "You got it together?"

Drawing in a deep breath, I nod.

"I'll ease up on you. Let you paint."

I shudder and nod. Then I grab another brush and pretend a hot, sexy fighter isn't kneeling in front of me, licking my pussy.

Red. Orange. Some yellow. My painting fills with heat as Ray slicks his tongue through my wetness, teasing and torturing me with the hint of how it would feel to have him inside me.

"Brace yourself," he whispers. And then he thrusts two thick fingers deep inside me.

I can't breathe. Can't move. I certainly can't paint. There is something sinfully erotic about standing naked in front of a half-painted canvas. Wanton. But this time my sexual curiosity is bringing me pleasure, not pain. "I can't...need to sit."

"Not yet." He withdraws and thrusts again, curling his fingers against my sensitive tissue as he flicks his tongue over my piercing, sending a wave of pulsing heat to my clit.

"Oh God." Panting, I paint quickly, fiercely, blending shape and form, drowning the black in a sea of color. So much color. Swirling through the canvas in an effort to be free.

My brush clatters to the floor and Ray eases me back onto the chair behind me, lifting my thigh over his shoulder, opening me for him, while he moves his hand faster, plunging in and out with hard, firm strokes. Braced on the chair, I rock my hips in time to his rhythm, my tension spiraling out of control.

"Don't stop. Don't stop."

He pulses his fingers deep inside me, then leans down and draws my clit into his mouth. One light nip and I fall over the edge.

The orgasm rips through me, shaking my body, tearing me apart with fierce, unyielding pleasure. So good. So deliciously bad. Almost a sacrilege to my art. But I don't care. The freedom to be so unrestrained is a release in itself.

As I shudder through the last waves of the orgasm, Ray releases me and pulls me into his arms, holding me as I melt, boneless against him.

"Better than lions," I whisper.

With a chuckle, he crushes my lips in a passionate kiss. An erotic shiver winds up my spine when I taste myself on his tongue. Needing more, I slide my hand down, brushing my fingers over his stomach. Ray groans and curls one hand around my ass, driving my hips against the steel of his erection. His eyes are dark with need, and the air between us thick with arousal.

Throbbing, empty inside, I gasp when he twists his fingers through my hair, tugging my head back, making me arch and offer up my breasts for his sucking pleasure. Teasing and torturing first one breast and then the other, his mouth firm but gentle on the little silver ring in my nipple, he holds me tight as I writhe and wiggle against him, my whimpers drowning out the animal cries coming from the TV.

"Ray…" Despite the earth-shattering orgasm of moments ago, I am almost mindless with need, bold with desperation. I slide my hand between us, stroking the ridge of his erection, and then I cup it and he shudders.

Encouraged, I push his shirt up, sliding my hands over his taut pecs to the tattoo outline still waiting to be filled. Like me. Ray rips the shirt over his head, as I tug at his belt and then undo his fly.

"I want you in my mouth," I whisper.

"Not today." He stands and pulls me up with him. "Not after I got a taste of your sweet pussy. I gotta have you now." He digs his hands into my ass and lifts me against him, then crosses the room in three easy strides and slams me against the wall.

"Legs around my hips."

More than willing to comply with his erotic demand, I brace myself against the wall, my arms around his neck, legs curled around his body as he pulls a condom from his pocket, then shoves down his jeans. The crown of his erection presses against my slit and for a moment I am tempted to take him bare. Although I haven't been with anyone for a long time, I'm still on the pill, but do I know Ray—trust him—well enough to take that kind of risk?

Maybe not. Not yet.

So I stay quiet when he pulls back and sheaths himself, and then quiet turns loud when his thick head presses against my entrance and I moan.

"Tell me you want my cock." His fingers dig into my ass as he holds me poised just above the object of my desire.

"I want your cock, Ray."

He eases in just enough to stretch me, his thick head dragging over my G-spot, an exquisite pleasure that makes my eyes water.

"Where do you want it?" His body shakes, his need as great as mine, and yet he has a self-control I envy. If he weren't holding me so tightly, I would impale myself on him without a second thought.

"I want your cock in my pussy. Oh God. Do it now. Fuck me hard." I bite my lip, hoping my inexperience with dirty talking doesn't show. Anything to get him inside me.

"Yesssss." He groans and with one hard thrust, he fills me, so deliciously thick and hard I whimper. Tightening my legs around his hips and my arms around his neck, I hold on for dear life.

"Gonna fuck my girl till she screams." He gives me a bruising kiss, then hammers into me, lifting me in time to his thrusts, until I know nothing but the utter, overwhelming need to come.

"So beautiful." He pants his words. "Wanna watch you come. Scratch me, beautiful girl. Bite me. Show me how much you want it." He slides his thumb over my clit, circling, rubbing, and then he pinches and I'm gone, biting his shoulder as hard as I dare to muffle my screams.

Ray pounds into me as I climax, drawing out my pleasure until he follows me over the edge, his cock pulsing deep inside me.

When I soften against him, Ray carries me to the bedroom and lays me down before going to dispose of the condom. Almost immediately, panic seizes me. Sweat beads on my forehead and my heart pounds. Rolling off the bed onto all fours, I squeeze my eyes shut and try to take long, deep breaths, but my chest is too tight and darkness claws at my vision.

"Shhhhh." A warm hand strokes down my back, and then Ray curls an arm around my waist and pulls me back into his chest, his hand between my breasts.

"Your heart is beating too fast. Gotta slow it down." His voice is low, soothing. Calm. So calm. "Breathe for me."

Shaking violently in his arms, I try to take a breath, but only a whisper of air gets through.

"Wherever you are, you gotta come back, Sia." His voice echoes in the darkness and his arms tighten around me. "Promised Fuzz I'd keep you safe. He'll go fuckin' ballistic if anything happens to you."

Tag. I imagine his face and my heart warms. But it isn't Tag with his arms around me, murmuring in my ear, keeping me safe. It's Ray. Here and now. And my heart warms even more.

"You okay now?"

I draw in a deep breath, and then another. "Yeah. Thanks. I like listening to your voice."

"Had to do something to bring you back." He rests his forehead on my back and draws in a ragged breath. "It was gonna be that or CPR."

We hold each other for the longest time, and then Ray releases me. My cheeks burn and I stiffen, preparing myself for him to walk away from a woman who is so obviously broken. Instead he stands and lifts me into his arms. "Discovery Channel usually has a two-hour special at midnight, and I'm thinking we should stay away from the bed."

"You're staying?"

"'Course I'm staying. I didn't leave you alone after your fight with Tag, and I'm not leaving you alone now."

Stunned and overwhelmed, I say nothing until we get to the bedroom door. "I can walk, Ray. You don't have to carry me."

"I like carrying you. I like everything about you, and I don't just mean your wicked mouth or your lush body or the way I can make you scream with pleasure. I like that you're beautiful, soft, and innocent and artistic. I like that you see the world a totally different way from me. And that you're loyal and loving to your friends and family."

"I'm broken."

He stretches out on the couch and tucks me up against him, then grabs the throw from the back of the couch and tosses it around us.

"So am I. My life has been one fucking tragedy after another. I lost my brother and then I lost my wife, Lisa."

My heart in my throat, I push myself up, but he tightens his hold, hugging me against his chest. "Same as Scott," he says softly. "I wasn't fast enough. We were stationed together in Afghanistan. She was a medic and I was in the infantry division. We'd only been married a couple of months. Base was ambushed. She ran out to help a soldier who'd been badly hit. I saw the rocket launcher on the hillside. And I ran. God did I run. But I wasn't fast enough."

My breath catches in my throat and for a moment I can't move. How does anyone move forward from that kind of tragedy? But he has and he's here, and he needs all the comfort I can give.

"I'm so sorry." I wrap my arms around him, holding on as tight as I can.

"It's part of the reason I don't get seriously involved." Ray strokes his hand down my back. "That and the fact I just can't go through that kind of loss again. I've had enough for any lifetime. And I just can't carry any more guilt. So yeah, I'm broken too."

An ache blossoms in my chest, spreading through my body. So what is he doing with me? With all my hang-ups, I'm hardly worth the effort of a casual relationship. And yet, why worry about it? I don't want a relationship either. I've had enough of opening up and leaving myself vulnerable. I've proved to myself time and again that I can't trust my own judgment with men who take my breath away: Luke; my high school biker, Peter…and Ray.

"Sure. I understand."

And I do. I just wish it didn't hurt so much.

Chapter 13

YOU SHOUTING AT MY GIRL… THAT'S MY FIGHT

TWO MINUTES AFTER I arrive at work Monday morning, exhausted and emotionally drained from spending Sunday with Jess dissecting my previous evening with Ray, Slim walks in the door.

"The boss is back." He tips back his fedora and scratches his head. "Nice new digs we got here. Just had a meeting with Torment, and he said we could stay as long we need as long as Sia sticks around, so everyone play nice with her."

"Why Sia?" Christos gestures his first client to his chair.

Slim shrugs. "If someone offers me free use of a fully equipped studio until my place gets fixed up, I don't ask questions. Maybe he thinks having a pretty girl in the shop will be good for business. Maybe he wants to help out because her brother works for the club. Maybe he has an ulterior motive. I don't care." He turns to me and mocks a frown. "Don't leave."

"Yes, boss." I give him a salute just as Doctor Death walks in the door.

"Morning all." He flashes his brilliant-white smile and Rose almost melts into a puddle on the floor.

"Who is he?" she whispers. "He could give Chris Hemsworth a run for his money."

"Just one of Oakland's preeminent heart surgeons and a fighter and sometimes ring doctor at the gym. But he seems to go for women who aren't available."

"Well, I'm available." She takes a deep breath and pulls down her shirt, exposing her freshly tatted cleavage, now fully healed. "And I've got a heart that needs a little doctor love."

"Sia." Doctor Death joins us at the reception desk. "I found out I'm on call every night this week, but since I need a cover, I thought I'd take the opportunity to spend some time with you and get it done by Redemption's favorite tattoo artist."

Duncan snorts a laugh as he straightens his workstation and Christos, already with his first client, mutters something about golden boys with silver tongues.

"Sure. Rose, do we have any openings today for a walk-in?" I give Rose a nudge, but she doesn't move.

Doctor Death winks at her and then turns up the wattage on his smile. "I'm sure Rose can squeeze me in." The word "squeeze" ripples over his tongue and Rose lets out a sigh. Slim snorts and heads to the back of the shop.

"Yes…of course…I can…squeeze you in," she says, her voice uncharacteristically breathy. "How about now? I can juggle a few things around so Sia has a few hours free."

"Perfect. I am indebted to you. You need a favor, just ask." He leans over the desk and brushes a kiss over her cheek.

"How about lunch?" She lifts an eyebrow and Doctor Death startles. Aha. The master has met his match. Rose comes on all girly, but she's a woman who knows what she wants.

"Lunch?"

"Today. Noon. You did say you owed me."

His eyes glitter and a smile spreads across his face. "Indeed I did. Lunch it is."

Duncan coughs. Christos chokes. I shoot them a warning look as I direct Doctor Death to my chair. Although he is rumored to have slept with a lot of women, Doctor Death is known as a decent guy, a skilled doctor, and a pretty good fighter. Rose could do a lot worse.

"So what do you need covered?" I take a seat as Doctor Death slides into my client chair and then pushes up the sleeve of his T-shirt.

His sunny smile fades when he points to the heart tat on his bicep with the name "Syndee" in the center. "I thought she was the one." His voice is thick with dejection. "First woman I ever really loved. I wanted her inked into my skin forever, so I got two tats with her name on them.

Went by her place to show her and caught her in bed with her second cousin twice removed, Gaylon."

"Oh my."

He lifts an eyebrow. "Not quite my reaction. But I had my justice. Gaylon will never perform that trick in bed ever again."

Eeeep. Doctor Death may be pretty, but he's clearly got a dark side. "I'm so sorry you had to go through that."

His face softens. "Thank you. Means a lot to me. Only had my heart broken twice before. But I don't begrudge Amanda and Makayla their happiness. I've decided the cover for that tat should be a broken heart so I never forget the feeling."

Amanda and Makayla? I'd heard rumors, but I never really believed them. "That shouldn't be a problem. I'll work up a few designs for you. What about the second tat?"

He gives me a cheeky grin. "We'll need some privacy. It's on my ass."

Oh God. Nothing I hate more than ass work, even if the ass is as fine as I'm guessing Doctor Death's ass must be from the way his jeans hugged every taut curve as he made his way to my chair. Doesn't seem to matter how much the needle hurts, you put a guy alone in a room with a woman, close the door, pull down his pants, and you're spending some time in the hall giving him a "moment."

"Duncan actually specializes in ass work—"

"I want you, Sia. This ass is precious. I only want the best hands on it."

Taking a deep breath, I think about Mom and Dad and their mortgage. I think about rent and car insurance and saving for the shop I want to own one day. I think about the difference between big, white, hairy asses and lean, taut, tanned ones. "Okay. I'll take you to the back."

I keep it cool and professional as I direct him to the private ink rooms, while inside I laugh at the irony. I know women who would sell their soul for a peek at Doctor Death's ass and yet all I can think about is Ray and how he cared enough to spend the night holding me, but not enough to want more than a casual fling.

While I wait in the hallway for Doctor Death to undress, my cell rings. I answer when I see it is Tag, and almost immediately he launches into an apology. He doesn't know what he was thinking bringing up the incident with Luke. He's not thinking straight. He just wants me to be safe and happy, and when he saw me with Ray, he was worried I would get hurt. But now, he's not so sure.

"Why?" I lower my voice. "What happened?"

"He was at the gym yesterday when I was prepping for my Sunday Baby Boot Camp class," Tag says, his voice tight. "He said he knew something bad happened to you and he wanted to know what it was."

I suck in a sharp breath, at once annoyed Ray would go behind my back and perversely pleased he cared enough to ask. "You didn't—"

Tag cuts me off with an annoyed grunt. "Of course I didn't. I told him if there was anything you wanted him to know, you'd tell him yourself. But, of course, he's the Predator and he wouldn't give up. He said he didn't want to fuck things up with you by inadvertently doing something that would make you run away."

"He said that?" I walk to the end of the hall where I can't be overheard.

Tag's voice softens. "Yeah. I thought you should know. Still not sure whether I think he's the right guy for you, but none of your other boyfriends ever threatened to bounce me around the ring if I didn't divulge your secret. Tells me he cares about you. A lot."

Reeling, confused, I slump against the wall. "He told me last night he didn't want to get involved."

"That's not the message he sent at Amanda's. He pretty much laid claim to you and warned everyone else away. It's a guy thing." Tag hesitates and then he says, "If you do decide to tell him, bear in mind that you don't tell a man like Ray that someone hurt you and never paid for his crimes and think he's just going to give you a sympathetic pat on the head. That happens with men like Charlie and James. Ray is…well, he's like me. And when someone I care about is hurt and justice isn't done, it's almost impossible to bear."

My breath leaves me in a rush. "I know I've asked a lot of you to keep that secret."

Tag groans. "Sorry, Sia. I didn't say that because I was trying to make you feel guilty. I don't regret the decision we made and I would do it again in a heartbeat if you asked. It's just all coming back because of this case I'm working on. It's driving me fucking crazy. I can't think about anything else. Even going to the gym is an effort because it takes me away from the investigation."

The treatment room door opens and Doctor Death pops his head out. I smile and mouth "one second," and he gives me a wink.

"Do you want to talk about it? We can meet up this week after work."

Expecting him to decline, I am momentarily floored when he says yes he needs to talk about it, but it can't be with me. When I suggest Jess and he says he'll think about it, my heart skips a beat. It must be really bad if he would consider talking to Jess.

After taking a few minutes to calm myself, I check out Doctor Death's tat, a beautifully wrought scroll of Syndee's name on his beautifully taut ass, and make a few suggestions for covers. When we're done, Doctor Death makes a tat appointment with Rose, and I follow him out to grab a coffee from the snack shop, returning to the studio just as all hell breaks loose.

"This is my fucking team." Slim bangs his fist on Rose's desk and glares at a scowling Torment. "I thought we had an understanding. I'm grateful for the use of the space and the equipment but I do have a reputation to protect. Half the clients coming into this shop are my clients. You want to paint a damn car race on the wall, do it when we're gone."

"It's my studio." Torment's growl echoes through the room and Christos and Duncan shudder. "I own it, and I hired Seth to paint. He's here. He's got his equipment. And I want it done now."

Seated on the couch, Seth, a tall, thin redhead with a scraggly beard, swallows hard. "I…can come back another time."

"You will NOT come back another time." Torment folds his arms and poor Seth cringes under the ferocity of his scowl. "I hired you to do it now, and you'll do it now."

"Is it the timing or the design that's the problem?" Impressed by Slim's willingness to stand up to the man whose name alone instills fear into the hearts of most fighters, I touch him on the arm to draw his attention.

Slim grabs a picture from Rose's hands and thrusts it at me. "Look."

Although I try not to grimace at the brightly colored scene of a NASCAR race, my mouth curls.

"It's a...very nice piece," I say to Torment. "But it's not really right for a tattoo studio. You've been in other studios before. Usually the feel is edgier, more offbeat, something to draw people's attention away from the pain of the needle, and take them out of their everyday life. Tattoos aren't mainstream. And the people who get them want to feel that they are making a statement. The shop is part of that statement. A stock car race scene isn't really the right vibe."

"Don't recall inviting you to be part of the conversation." Torment's voice rises to a shout. "This has nothing to do with you, so stay out of it."

"Voice."

Torment's head jerks up, and I look back over my shoulder. Ray is standing in the doorway, arms folded, one ankle crossed in front of the other. Artlessly casual to anyone who doesn't know him. A warning to those who do.

"Oooooh," Rose whispers. "The cavalry has arrived."

"Not your fight, Predator. Move on." Torment dismisses him with a jerk of his head, but Ray doesn't move.

"Sia wants this fight, she's got this fight." His gaze flicks to me and back to Torment. "But you shouting at my girl, that's my fight."

Torment's lip curls. "Man's agitated, he'll speak however he wants. And Sia interfering in my discussion with her boss is agitating."

Emboldened by all the support, Slim steps forward. "That's 'cause you know she's right. And I'll tell you something else. You have Red over there paint a fucking car race in the shop, and we're outta here."

"I'm doing you a favor letting you work here."

"We're both benefiting from this arrangement," Slim says. "And I'm only asking for a coupla weeks, then my shop will be fixed up and we'll be outta your hair for good. But in the meantime, we've got an image to uphold. We're Rabid Ink, not fucking Race Car Alley. A gal who comes in to get her clit pierced or her boobs inked doesn't give a damn about race cars."

Rose snorts behind her screen. She held my hand when Duncan pierced me. Jess, of course, held the other.

"Why don't you let Sia do it?" Ray says quietly. "She paints. I've seen her work, and it's damn good. Edgy stuff, although she might have to tone down the color."

"No." I glare at Ray. "I don't paint anymore. I haven't painted for years. I'm not interested."

"You painted the other night."

My stomach clenches at his betrayal. I opened myself up for him and only him, and he's exposing me to the world. Why doesn't he just tell them what else we did?

Torment studies me, considering, and then looks at Slim. "Sia or the car race. I'll expect an answer in fifteen minutes. And if neither of those work for you, feel free to clear out." He stalks toward the door, pausing only because Ray doesn't move. "Predator, I'll see in the ring Friday night. No one fucking tells me to lower my voice in my own gym."

Ray gives him a curt nod and steps to the side to let him pass. Red grabs his art bag and scurries after him. The room heaves a collective sigh.

"I'm not doing it," I say to Slim. "Duncan's an amazing artist. I'm sure Torment will be happy with whatever he comes up with."

"He said it had to be you." Slim puts a gentle hand on my shoulder. "Come on, Sia. We're making a killing here. The next coupla weeks could cover us for the clients we've lost since the shop was closed."

"I don't care if we have to leave or if we have to work in a shop with a car race on the wall. And it's totally unfair of you to put this on me. I won't do it. I won't even consider it. I don't paint anymore. So leave me alone."

A shocked Slim puts up his hands in a warding gesture. "Hey. Chill. I didn't realize it was such a big deal."

"It is." Nausea curls in my belly, and I head to the staff room, painfully aware of Ray following behind me. He closes the door and I can't bring myself to turn around. Usually this room is an oasis, furnished with soft, caramel sofas, a plush beige area rug, and dark wooden tables. Torment spared no expense and fitted it out with a fridge, sink, hot plate, and a coffee maker so complicated we all go to the café for our caffeine fix.

"What's going on?" Ray's voice echoes in the quiet space.

"What's going on? How can you even ask that question?" I turn to face him, my body shaking with anger. "When I painted the other night…it was supposed to be just between us. I thought you understood that. I wasn't opening a door that I closed years ago. This is who I am now. Ink is what I do." My hands tremble and I swallow past the lump in my throat. "Just because I let you see that side of me doesn't mean that's who I am anymore. You saw what happens to me when I open that door. I felt exposed out there. Vulnerable. I promised myself a long time ago I would never feel that way again."

He studies me for so long, I look away. Finally, he folds his arms and leans against the doorjamb. "Why?"

"Why what?"

"Why does letting people know you can paint make you feel vulnerable? Everyone in the shop knows you're an artist. They see your work every day. Is it such a stretch to let them know you paint too?"

"You don't understand." My voice rises in pitch. "You don't know me or why I stopped painting. I can't go back. I have to keep moving forward. You can't just railroad through my life and decide I should paint again. Just like you can't go behind my back to find out what happened to me. It's not that simple."

"I don't understand because you won't talk to me." Ray lets out a breath and turns to the door. "The problem isn't that I don't know you, but that you don't trust yourself enough to let me in."

—⁓—

The shop is inundated with fighters for the rest of the week. We are so busy that Christos cancels his gig, Rose divides her time between reception and sterilizing equipment in the autoclave, and I am partially distracted from the fact Ray hasn't called, but then, coward that I am, I haven't called him either.

Doctor Death comes in for his arm cover, and I ink my best broken heart ever into his skin while he tells me that relationships are not worth the heartache and it is easier and safer to just sleep around. When I tell him I think he just may be right, he squeezes my hand and tells me we can have a more intimate conversation about it next week when we're alone in the treatment room and I'm doing his ass.

Friday morning, we get a new walk-in off the street, Yuri, who makes even Rampage seem small. The massively muscled, tall, blond Dolph Lundgren look-alike watches Rose and I from the client sofas while we rejig the morning schedule to fit him in, his ice-blue eyes so piercing I shiver. Rose whispers that his gold bracelets, blockhead haircut, and the multiple gold rings on this left hand, coupled with his dark, fine wool suit, scream Russian mafia. She thinks he is more terrifying than attractive and not worth the effort of her making a play. I whisper back that she has made a wise decision. She has enough men to juggle, and Yuri doesn't seem the juggling type.

Although I have a slot free, when he pops his knuckles and cracks his neck, I foist him off on Duncan. I get enough nonverbal aggressive communication from Tag and Ray. I don't need any more.

Turns out Yuri is a talker. While he waits for Duncan to finish with his client, he tells us he's been in the U.S. for five years and is very interested in MMA fighting. He asks lots of questions about the club and some of the fighters. He even knows of the Predator, which is curious, since Ray only fights on the underground circuit and not for the club. But if he's interested in fighting, it makes sense that he'd know about the underground fights.

Slim returns that afternoon, after spending the week trying to speed up the renos at the old shop. I catch him in the staff room and apologize again for not being able to do the mural and forcing the team out of our new digs. He tells me it isn't my fault, and this wasn't his first altercation with Torment. They've been butting heads over the division between managing and owning the shop, but mostly over me.

"Me?" I pause on the threshold of the doorway and look back over my shoulder. "What do I have to do with it?"

"He wants you to run this shop. He's been angling to poach you away from day one."

"You're crazy." I gesture vaguely around the tattoo parlor. "Look at this place. It's every artist's dream shop. He could get anyone. He could pull in some big names, make it one of the top shops in the city."

Slim's forehead wrinkles with consternation. "He wants you and he's the kind of man who gets what he wants. Anyone with half a brain can see you're a gifted artist, and you're building a client base here faster than you ever did at my studio. He sees your potential, same as me. If you want to stay, I won't get in your way. But if you really don't want what he's offering, you'd better be prepared when he walks through that door. He's not going to take no for an answer."

We finish our last clients just before eight p.m., and I offer to tidy and lock up just for the opportunity to have some time alone before the big fight. After I'm finished, I sit on the client couch and stare at the bare wall where the mural is supposed to be. If this was my shop, I wouldn't paint a mural on the wall. Instead, I'd fill the space with paintings from local artists. Give people a chance to be seen.

If this was my shop. Am I really even considering it?

The door opens and my breath catches when Torment walks in and joins me on the couch. He's wearing only his fight shorts with a towel around his neck, no doubt ready to tear Ray limb from limb at the fight tonight. He is broader than Ray and more muscular. Taller too. But for some reason, his toned body does nothing for me—especially when he's intending to pound on Ray.

"Busy day?"

"Yeah." I look over at him and raise an eyebrow. "Slim thinks you sent all those fighters this week to keep us too busy to pack up."

"He's right."

Startled by his candor, I bite my lip. "He also says you're trying to steal me away from him."

"True. You're wasting your time in his shop. You have the drive and personality and talent to make this place great. I don't want to see you throw it away."

My hand clenches by my side. "I'm happy with Slim. And he would never forgive me if I abandoned him."

"Slim is safe," he says. "His shop is comfortable. You have a pretty good idea who's going to walk in the door every day. But he's got no ambition, no drive. Safe is good when you're starting out, but it won't let you grow. You need to spread your wings. Take a risk. Grab this opportunity with both hands even though it scares you."

"So, is this your poaching technique?" I raise an eyebrow and lean back on the comfy leather couch. "Tell your target it's for her own good and her life will be better if she comes to work for you?"

"I do what it takes," he says with a laugh. His smile fades. "But it's not just me. Slim knows it's time for you to go. He sees how you've changed since you've come to Redemption. That's why he's overreacting."

Squirming in my seat, I stare at the wall. He's right. I do feel different since I started working here, but I chalked it up to being in a beautiful shop and knowing most of the clients. And Ray. He has awakened things inside me I thought I'd locked up with my paintings so long ago. Hope. Desire. And a longing to be free.

Torment waits while I lock up and we walk through the gym, toward the ring set up for his match with the Predator. Despite our altercation this afternoon, I would never miss this fight, especially since he's fighting because of me.

"I've known Ray for a few years," he says, stopping when we reach the ring. "Keeps his personal business to himself. He's never once asked me for anything." Torment stares at me and I shiver under the force of his gaze. "He came to see me on Monday. He asked me to take back my ultimatum."

A ball of emotion wells up in my throat, tightening my chest. "Oh."

His face softens. "Actually, he didn't ask. He told me that's how it was going to be. I thought you should know."

My heart swells at the thought he tried to make things right. "Thanks."

Torment smiles an evil Torment smile. "Of course, I said no."

———

"He said no?" Makayla's voice rises to a shriek when I share Torment's parting words with her, Jess, Shayla, and Amanda on the bleachers overlooking the fight ring. Soft and curvy, with auburn hair and bright green eyes, Torment's girlfriend is almost his opposite in every way.

"Oh my God." Her brow creases in a frown. "Sometimes Torment can be such an ass. Just wait until I get him home. I'll bet he said no to wind the Predator up. He likes to psych out his opponents before a fight." She grabs my hand and gives it a squeeze. "Don't worry about anything. You won't have to leave the studio. I'll give him a no he won't forget. One night alone in his bed after he's all revved up after a fight will teach him a lesson. I'll have him eating out of my hand by morning."

Shayla pulls out a bottle of vodka and some Dixie cups and pours us all a shot. As we drink, Torment, Renegade, Blade Saw, and Tag amble over to our bleachers and then stand semi-clustered below us.

"What's going on?" Jess frowns when Blade Saw looks up over his shoulder and winks.

"They think we're going to be ravaged by a horde of inebriated, overexcited fighters so they've set up a defensive zone." Amanda twists a strand of her long, blond hair around her finger. When I first met her, I knew right away she was the woman who had broken Jake's heart. Not from her breathtaking good looks, but from the way he stood, shielding her with his body, protecting her from me.

Jess chokes on her vodka and her smile fades. "Blade Saw isn't like that. He's more of a friendly protective type. He'd be like, 'Hey, guy, you want me to buy you a beer so you have something else to do with your hand than put it on my girl's ass?' And then he'd be all cool about it. Become best friends with the dude. Not much gets him riled up. He's probably down there because he feels he should, not because of some primal protective instinct."

"So are you with him or not?" Makayla tilts her head to the side and gives Jess a questioning look. "I saw the two of you together at Amanda's party."

Jess gives a noncommittal shrug. "We're sort of together, but it's pretty casual. I like to leave myself open to options."

I snort and almost choke on my vodka. Jess looks over and frowns.

"What's with you and Ray?" Amanda leans back on the bleachers, her lips quivering with a repressed smile. "You guys put on quite a show at my place. Never thought I'd see Ray hook up with someone."

Now it's my turn for noncommittal. "We've hung out a couple of times. It's nothing serious. Neither of us wants a relationship."

Amanda and Makayla share a glance, and then Amanda lifts an eyebrow. "Really?"

My stomach clenches. Ray does PI contract work for Amanda and, according to Tag, they are also good friends. Does she know something I don't know?

"Really."

She gestures to the alpha male cluster at the foot of the bleachers. "So why is he switching off with Tag down in the defensive zone?"

Twisting Jess's ring around my finger, I look down and spot Tag heading to the other side of the gym. Ray is talking to Renegade, just below us, his beautiful body, clad only in fight shorts, gleaming under the overhead lights. In the space of a heartbeat, four days' worth of longing sweep over me, stealing my breath away, and in that moment, I want him more than any man I've ever wanted before. Ray looks up as if he knows I'm watching. We stare at each other for what seems an eternity, and then he turns away without so much as a smile.

Crushed, I sigh and meet Amanda's sympathetic gaze. "See. Nothing serious."

We join the crowd in a cheer as Torment and Ray enter the cage. Torment is about an inch taller and two inches broader than Ray, but Ray's muscles are sleek and more defined. He's wearing purple fight shorts with yin-yang symbols down the sides, an odd choice for a fight. Doesn't Taoism advocate unity?

Shayla blows a whistle and Ray throws a few jabs at Torment, then follows up with a hard shot that drops Torment to his knees. The crowd gasps, and so do I, but for a different reason.

"Something's wrong." I grip Jess's arm. "He's not fighting the way he usually fights. He never feints, and his punches weren't controlled. Usually he feels out his opponent. Dances around the ring a bit. And look how tense he is. His face…his stance. If I had to guess, I'd say he's angry, but usually in a fight he keeps his emotions contained."

"Then maybe Makayla's right." Her gaze is fixed on Tag and not the fight. "Maybe Torment said something else to him, wound him up on purpose."

Torment rises quickly to his feet and returns fire, coming after Ray with a dizzying barrage of fists and feet. Ray dodges every blow and snaps off a kick to Torment's midsection that sends Torment staggering back two steps. But Ray follows him with another vicious kick, followed by a massive punch that drops Torment to the mat.

Makayla shoots out of her seat, her hand clamped over her mouth, and then descends the bleachers and runs out of the gym. My heart squeezes and I stand to go after her, but Amanda pulls me down.

"Don't worry about it. She's a paramedic and can handle blood and trauma, knife wounds and broken bones, but she can't handle watching actual violence. Torment likes her to watch him fight, so she shows up, stays for a few minutes, and then has to leave. Usually, he gives her a bucket."

Torment is up again, his face curled into a scowl, but before he regains his balance, Ray thrashes him with a brutal knee. An ache forms in my chest. This isn't him. This isn't the way he fights. There is no artistry in the way he is moving today. Only anger and pain.

Doubled over, Torment wavers and Ray follows up with a hard left and then a right, dropping Torment back to the mat. He follows Torment down, dropping hammer fists until Torment taps out.

The room stills. No one has ever beaten Torment on home ground before. And no one could have imagined the fight would be over in only one round. Finally someone claps. And then everyone is clapping and cheering. But Ray doesn't take Shayla's hand for the victory salute. Instead, he kneels beside Torment, says a few words, and pats him on the back. Then he leaves the cage, stepping to the side for Makayla to rush in with her medical kit.

"He's not himself," I say to Jess.

"Go talk to him. He needs you."

I twist the ring she gave me around my finger. "What if he doesn't want to see me?"

She gives my arm a squeeze. "Then I'll be here to pick up the pieces. Just like you've always done for me."

Chapter 14

SOOTHING THE SAVAGE BEAST

"SORRY. RULES ARE RULES. I can't let you into the men's changing room, and especially not the VIP area." Rampage points to the bench. "You can wait there."

"Is he alone?" My nails dig into my palm as I try to think of a way inside. If I wait until he comes out, it may be too late.

"Yeah. We closed the gym for the fight, and Torment's in the first-aid room with Makayla so there's no one else there."

"Please." I grab Rampage's hand. "He shouldn't be alone. I just want him to know I'm here."

"I can tell—"

"Don't make me beg. You know I wouldn't ask if it wasn't important."

Rampage hesitates, then shakes his head. "Even if I was inclined to break the rules, it's probably not safe for you right now. Never saw him so wound up before. That was a vicious fight."

"I can take care of myself." I sigh and throw down my only chip. "I could do a piece for you for free. Something on your arm. Maybe a symbol that represents your fight name…"

He mocks a frown. "Are you trying to bribe me?"

"Yes. Absolutely. Whatever it takes."

A grin spreads across his face. "A bull. That's what I want. With a ring through its nose."

Relief washes through me and I have to hold back from giving him a hug. "You tell Rose when you want to come in."

He pushes open the changing room door and his face softens. "I'll be right here 'case you need me or 'case someone tries to get in."

"Thanks."

Rampage gives me a wink. "See ya, Sia."

When I walk into the changing room, the scents of sweat and un-washed gym clothes make my nose wrinkle, but I forge ahead and find the VIP room through a red door at the top of a small flight of stairs. Clean and bright, and smelling faintly of sweat and lemon cleaner, it houses two rows of beige lockers, wide benches, floor-to-ceiling mirrors, and shelves of fluffy towels.

Ray is at the back, facing away from me, a towel wrapped around his narrow hips. He must have just stepped out of the shower because his hair is wet, and the air is thick and fragrant with the sharp scent of the shower gel I have smelled on his skin.

Seemingly oblivious to my presence, he mumbles something to himself then pounds on the locker. The loud bang makes me gasp, and I step back into the door with a soft thud.

His head jerks up and he spins to face me. But it isn't Ray who meets my gaze, but the Predator. In the flesh.

"Go, Sia." His voice is rough, hoarse as if it is an effort to force the words out. "Get out of here."

Goose bumps prick my arms and I twist my hands together. "You weren't fighting the way you usually fight. You seemed…angry. Out of control. I just wanted to make sure you were okay."

He closes his eyes and pinches the bridge of his nose, as if in pain. "Please."

"I'm not leaving you alone. Not like this."

His hands curl into fists at his sides and his eyes narrow. "Man hurts someone he cares about, he should be alone."

"Yes, you hurt me," I say, taking a step toward him. "I felt betrayed when you told Torment I was painting. I felt like you exposed me to the world when you shared that piece of me that I had only wanted to share with you."

A groan erupts from his throat. "You don't think I realized that after I saw your face. Christ, if I could take it back…"

"It was my fault." I stop two feet away from him and tug my T-shirt over my head, the only way I can think to calm him down. "I know you were just trying to help. And you were right. You couldn't have known how it would make me feel or why it was important because I never told you."

Under his shocked, heated gaze, I unclip my bra and slide it off, dropping it to the floor. Then I undo my jeans and shimmy them over my hips along with my underwear. Ray doesn't move. Doesn't speak. But his eyes sweep my body with a feral gleam.

"What are you doing?" His breathing is raw, ragged, and thick with need.

"Soothing the savage beast." I close the distance between us and slide one hand around his neck, while I whip off his towel with the other and dig my fingers into his ass. Already thick and hard, his cock presses against my hip as I lean up and nuzzle his neck. "I know we're not in this for the long haul, but I want to tell you what happened to me. I will tell you. Just give me time."

"Sia." He groans my name and threads his fingers through my hair. "Do you know what you're doing? After last time…"

With a soft sigh, I rock up to kiss him, sliding my tongue along the seam of his lips until he opens for me. But one kiss is all it takes. Within a heartbeat, I am no longer the predator.

I am the prey.

Heart pounding in my chest, I stare up into his eyes, caught in the fire that matches the burning in my veins. His fingers stroke my neck, over the pulse point at the base of my throat, then he cups my jaw, tilts my head back, and lowers his mouth. There is no gentleness in his kiss, no fleeting meeting of lips or dancing of tongues. Instead, his mouth is hot and hungry, his tongue thrusting deep, devouring me even as I struggle to breathe.

He pulls back, rasping his breaths, and then curls his hand around the back of my neck, immobilizing me with his touch. "Anything I do hurts you or makes you panic, you tell me to stop. Understood?"

"I'll say stop. I promise."

He grunts his approval, then fishes around in his gym bag on the bench and pulls out a condom.

"Door locked?"

"Yes."

Wrapper torn, cock sheathed, he pulls me into his chest. "Who's at the door?"

"Rampage."

"Fuck. He's got the biggest fucking mouth in Redemption. I'll be surprised if there is anyone in the gym who doesn't know by morning."

Hand trembling I follow the soft trail of hair down his abdomen with my fingers, then wrap my hand around his shaft. Just the feel of him, hot and hard and throbbing in my hand, makes me wet. I tighten my grip and stroke.

Ray growls his approval and I stroke harder, watching his face in case I hurt him. But the harder I stroke and the tighter I hold, the more he seems to enjoy it, so I lean up and bite his shoulder too. His cock swells in my hand and he groans.

"Jesus Christ. You want this to be over before it begins?"

"I want to make you feel good. The way you do for me. Tell me what to do. I want to get you off."

"Harder."

Gritting my teeth, I squeeze his cock so hard my knuckles whiten. Ray's body tenses and his hips jerk forward into my hand.

"Fuck." He clamps a hand on my wrist, then gently pulls me away.

"Not with you, Sia. You're soft and sweet and everything that's good in my life. Don't want you tainted with any of that. That side of me, you don't need to see."

Before I can ask what he means, Ray settles himself on the bench and pulls me up onto his lap, my back to his chest, his erection pressed against the cleft of my ass. "This feels good."

Shivering, I lean back against the solid wall of his chest and catch a glimpse of us in the floor-to-ceiling mirror, my small body nestled against Ray's massive chest, his arm curled around my waist. It's so erotic, I can't tear my gaze away.

Ray hooks my thighs over his, then widens his legs, spreading me, until my sex, pink and glistening, is on display. A whimper escapes my lips and I try to turn away, but Ray captures my jaw and gently turns me back to the mirror.

"Look how beautiful you are. You are the most beautiful fucking thing I've ever seen. I could spend an entire day just looking at you." He cups my breast in his palm and draws his thumb over the nipple. "Perfect."

My cheeks burn, and I squeeze my eyes shut. I make a point of not looking at myself naked in the mirror. I am more exposed now than I have ever been.

"Open your eyes." He pulls out my ponytail holder and smooths my hair over my shoulders. "See what I see. Look at your sweet curves and how perfectly my hand fits over them." He strokes his hand down my side, in and out of my waist and over my hips. "So soft," he whispers.

My eyes flutter open just as his fingers graze my stomach and brush over my mound. "Love these curls and what you've got hiding underneath." He spreads his legs farther, opening me obscenely wide, and I turn into his shoulder and try to press my legs together.

"No." His voice drops to a husky growl, and he turns my head back to the mirror. "I want you open when you're with me. I like to see how wet you are, and know you're wet for me. And I want you to see it too." He strokes his finger along my folds, spreading my wetness up and around my clit; then he parts me wide with his fingers and whispers in my ear. "This is where I'm gonna be. I'm gonna be inside your hot, wet pussy, taking you so high you'll be begging me to come, and when I take you there we'll both watch you come all over my hand."

"I can't." My voice drops to a murmur. "I can't watch."

Ray's hand drifts down to cup my sex, his fingers rubbing, stroking through my soaked folds until I whimper. Then he works his fingers inside, deliciously deep, making me arch as his free hand toys with my breasts.

"You can, and you will." His voice rasps in my ear. "You like to watch. I can feel it here"—he curls his fingers inside me and pulses against my sensitive inner tissue—"and I can see it here." He rolls my peaked nipple, and then cups my breast and squeezes.

Oh God, he's right. But it feels so wrong. So naughty. So deliciously bad. "I've never watched before." I swallow past the lump in my throat. "But…I want to watch you fuck me."

He growls softly, then lifts me, his hands tight on my hips, and pulls me down over his cock, one slow, thick inch at a time.

"Ah ah ah." My body tenses as he stretches me, fills me, and my gaze is riveted to his thick, ribbed shaft sliding between my folds. Heat pools in my belly and I moan at what has to be the most arousing sight I have ever seen—Ray's dark head bending over me, his lips pressed to my temple, his thick, muscular arms dark against my pale skin, holding me safe. Lowering my gaze, I watch his thigh muscles bunch and flex as he lowers me another inch, and my legs bare and smooth, twined around his calves.

"You good?" He looks up and I melt under the heat of his gaze in the mirror. Dark. Carnal. A reflection of my own inner desire.

"More." I shift my hips, try to lever myself up, but he must have chosen this position for a reason. No matter what I do, I have to take what he gives me and no more.

"Ray…please."

He hisses out a breath and pushes in another inch. "Tell me what you want. Use the dirtiest words you know."

"I want your cock in my pussy. Buried deep inside me, right to the hilt. I want you to fuck me while I watch. Hard and rough. I want bruises on my skin tomorrow so I can remember tonight, and every time I move I want to remember you were inside me."

"Anything you want, you can have from me." Ray's arms shake as he eases me down a little more and he slides to the edge of the bench, until my feet are on the floor. "Take it. Take what you need."

So I do. With one downward thrust, I take him all in, as far as he will go, watching his thick, ridged cock sliding between my folds, flushed and wet in the mirror. And then I ease up and slam down again. But it isn't nearly enough. Not enough force. Not enough pressure. And I am too free. Unrestrained. Untethered.

I take him one more time, sliding over his thick shaft, and a groan rips from my throat as the sharp movements jerk my piercing, setting off a cascade of lightning bolts that sizzle straight to my clit.

"I can't do this anymore." I pant my words. "I need—"

"I know what you need." He toys with my piercing and my pussy tightens around him. "The way this makes you feel…I should make you feel. Only me." He tugs on the ring in my nipple and growls when my nipple peaks. "You don't need these, Sia. I can make you feel more than they ever will."

He slides his free hand up to my neck and closes his hand around my throat with a gentle, unyielding pressure, forcing my head back against his chest as he rocks inside me.

Arousal crashes over me in a thunderous wave. I am possessed. Controlled. Dominated by the subtle threat of his hand and the rhythmic thrust of his cock.

"Hands behind you, around my neck. Clasp them together and don't let go. Open yourself to me."

Drunk with lust, I do as he asks. Although I have never been so exposed, I feel no fear. His hand on my throat makes me feel perversely safe. As I watch in the mirror, his dark fingers splayed across my throat, the careful way he watches my reaction, his strong body supporting mine, I am struck by the intense beauty of the moment. Dark and light intertwined. We are the yin and yang on his fight shorts, now abandoned in the corner.

Ray slides his free hand over my hips and strokes his finger gently over my clit, over and over, his touch as light as a butterfly wing until I can think of nothing but the relentless build of pressure in my core.

With his hand still around my throat, he tilts my head back and kisses me, a full open-mouthed kiss as he drags me down onto his cock for another thrust. Before I can catch my breath, he pinches my clit. My body tenses, then convulses. I squeeze my eyes shut as moisture floods my sex and the orgasm thunders over me. With a breath, I scream into Ray's mouth.

He gives me only a minute to come down before he lifts me and helps me turn to face him, his cock sliding easily back into my wet pussy.

"You didn't do so well last time, when you couldn't see me behind you," he says softly by way of explanation when I protest the change of position. "And I like to watch you come."

His hips rock on the bench and his cock thrusts deep. My arousal builds quickly again, relentlessly, until I am panting and moaning, my arms wrapped around his neck as I near my peak.

Hands on my hips, Ray lifts me up and hammers me down, angling me so my piercing thuds against him with every stroke, making my clit throb and ache. This time I know what he wants. This time he doesn't have to tell me what he needs. My Predator likes pain, and after what he told me about his wife, I think I know why. Guilt is a hard master.

My fingers dig into his shoulders, and I scrape my nails down his back as hard as I can. Ray gives a strangled yell and slams me down, pumping deep inside me, the jolt on my piercing all I need to be swept up in another wave of pleasure. He tenses and climaxes with me, his shaft thickening and throbbing against my inner walls.

But this time when I come down, his arms are tight around me, his body is warm against me, and my face is nestled in the crook of his neck, where I can feel his pulse beating steady against my skin.

"Never had sex in a men's changing room before." I breathe in his rich, masculine scent of sex and body wash. "You sure know how to treat a girl right."

Ray chuckles and brushes a kiss over my forehead. "The shower is next. And maybe if you're good, I'll do you over the table."

"Does that mean my Ray is back?"

"It means you'd better not have any plans for the rest of the night."

But what about the night, the day, the week, and the month after that?

Chapter 15

SHOW ME WHAT ELSE THOSE SWEET LIPS CAN DO

"I'VE GOT A REQUEST for a full ass piece on my voice mail." Rose looks over at Christos, Duncan, and I as we drool over the latest gadget Torment has procured for us, a Cheyenne Hawk Thunder. The new gun mimics the feel of a pen with the grip and needles in a disposable cartridge and is perfect for the 3-D designs people have been requesting.

Christos shakes his head. "I'm no good with ass work unless it's a girl's ass. And we had a bad gig last night. I'm feeling delicate."

"Sia?" Rose raises a perfectly plucked eyebrow and I glare. She knows I hate ass work.

"I've got an ass today, thanks. And I'm surprised you forgot. I thought you and Doctor Death had lunch the other day."

Rose turns three shades of red. "Actually, we skipped the lunch part."

"Rose! You dog. A lunchtime quickie. Never thought you had it in you." Duncan chortles, but his smile fades when he catches Christos's scowl. "Come on, Chris. Aren't you happy for Rose? She's had a dry spell of what…two months?"

"Three," she says, now recovered from her uncharacteristic moment of embarrassment. "But who's counting?'

"Me."

The room chills at Christos's icy tone, and without another word, he storms out of the studio.

"Uh…did I miss something?" Duncan scratches his head.

"Unrequited love." I give Rose's arm a squeeze when her brow creases in a frown. "Don't worry about him. Jealous is good. Jealous means he cares. Jealous means he might get his head out of his ass and tell you how he feels."

"Sure." Rose shrugs. "I've only been waiting three years."

Duncan's Russian client, Yuri, drops in while Rose and I are going through the schedule for the day, to see if anyone has time to ink some crosses on his knuckles. Rose says Christos can fit him in and excuses herself to go and find him. Yuri looks down at me sitting in Rose's chair, his unblinking ice-blue eyes making my blood run cold.

"So you work here every day?"

I shake my head. "I take a day off every week, depends when we're not too busy."

His golden bracelets clang when he folds his arms over his massive chest, and I will him to go and sit where clients are supposed to sit—in the client lounge and away from me. Unfortunately, Yuri doesn't hear my silent plea.

"You ink all the fighters?"

"Some of them."

"You ink the Predator?"

Again with the Predator, and he doesn't look like the fanboy type. The skin on the back of my neck prickles, and I look back over my shoulder to where Duncan is inking a client. At least I'm not alone.

"Yeah, I inked him. Not finished the piece yet though."

Yuri nods. "I saw the outline. Very nice. So, he'll be back for more?"

"I guess so."

Mercifully, Rose returns with a calmed down Christos, and they whisk Yuri away to Christos's chair. For a moment, I toy with the idea of adding a note to his virtual file that one or two fighters should be present anytime he comes in. But why? Although he looks threatening, he has only ever been polite and cordial when he's been in the shop, albeit a tad inquisitive.

Half an hour later, Doctor Death arrives for his appointment, and Rose's melancholy fades as she basks in the glow of his smile. Christos glares when Doctor Death whispers something in Rose's ear that makes her blush.

"He's gonna use her and throw her away, and she's gonna get hurt." He mutters obscenities under his breath along with conjecture about what might happen if he ever met Doctor Death in a dark alley.

"You've got it wrong," I whisper. "Rose is him but in female form. And she's the one pulling the strings. He didn't have a chance from the moment he first stepped through the door. My money is on her using him and me getting to do a new broken-heart piece on his other ass cheek next week."

Doctor Death's ass work is largely uneventful, although I have to step outside to "give him a moment" a few more times than with the usual ass. I keep the private room bright, the music loud, and my needle humming. There is no more talk about sleeping around nor is there any more talk about Syndee. At first I think it is because he is smitten with Rose, but while I'm applying the bandage, he mentions Ray.

"So, Rampage says you and Ray—"

"I don't discuss my personal life with clients." I pat the bandage a little too hard and his ass cheek tightens when he winces. Doctor Death looks back over his shoulder. "I'm hardly just a client. You're part of Redemption. We're family here."

"Nosy family."

He chuckles. "Guys like to know where they stand when there's a beautiful woman on the premises."

"You mean Rose?" Shifting uncomfortably in my seat, I apply the last piece of tape and hope he gets the message.

He doesn't. "I mean you, Sia. I've had my eye on you since Fuzz brought you to the first Redemption party. Rose and I had fun together, but we're too much alike."

Backing my stool away from the client chair, I shake my head. "I'm flattered but I'm with Ray."

"Really?" He pushes himself to his side, and I look away just in case I get an unexpected visual treat.

"He ever take you out on date? In public? Have you gone to a restaurant or a movie? Or anywhere that isn't secured with a door?"

Puzzled, I frown. "We went for a walk once."

"Somewhere deserted and in the dark no doubt." He snags the towel from the back of his thighs and adeptly manages to push himself to sitting while keeping decently covered.

The hair on the back of my neck prickles. "What are you saying?"

His face softens and he sighs. "I'm saying there's more to Ray than he lets on."

My hand clenches into a fist, and I back up into the door. Oh God. Have I misplaced my trust yet again? "Like what?"

"Not my place to say. He doesn't know I know. I just…don't want you to get hurt when he walks away."

"Then why did you bring it up?" My voice rises in pitch. "You hardly know me."

"I know you well enough to want to get to know you better," he says. "And I'd be lying if I said my motives were entirely selfless. But even if I weren't interested, I would have said something. We look after each other at Redemption."

Pulse pounding in my ears, I shake my head. "Ray's part of Redemption too."

"He trains here, but he doesn't fight here," Doctor Death says. "He's not part of the fight team or the staff. And he's made it clear he doesn't want to be one of us. But you are, and we'll always have your back."

"Why do I feel like I've suddenly inherited a club full of Tags?" I reach behind me for the door handle and turn away.

"We were always here," Doctor Death calls out. "You just weren't looking."

After Doctor Death leaves, I call Jess at work. She says I shouldn't trust him since he clearly has an ulterior motive and instead of assuming the worst, why not just put it to the side and ask Ray about it the next time I see him? I tell her she is too levelheaded and clearly doesn't understand that artistic types thrive on emotional drama. Jess says she has enough emotional drama in her life for both of us. Tag showed up at her place last night.

We make plans to meet up for a drink after work, so she can share all the details, and for the first time since Doctor Death stepped through the door, my anxiety eases.

I spend the afternoon on two small walk-in pieces and yet another Redemption logo. But I don't mind doing it and, in fact, I admire the loyalty the fighters have to the club. I suggest to Slim we all get Rabid

Ink ass tattoos to show our loyalty to his shop. He suggests we get his name inked in our skin instead. Christos says Slim would look good on his ass. Many filthy comments ensue.

Ray walks in as I'm cleaning my station at the end of the day. He nods to Slim and Rose as they head out the door, then he sits on my chair and says he's come to have his tat finished. I tell him I have plans with Jess. Christos and I are closing up for the night, and if he wants a tat, he needs to make an appointment with Rose. He leans over and whispers in my ear that he's fucking the artist so he doesn't need an appointment, and if I have a problem with that, he'd be happy to pull me over his lap and spank my ass until I'm ready to work. I tell him there seems to be a lot of talk about spanking but no real action. Ray grabs my shirt and yanks me over his lap. Then he whacks my ass so hard I gasp.

Scrambling off his lap, cheeks burning, I turn around. Far from being shocked, Christos is laughing. He tosses me the keys and heads out to his gig. I am left alone with Ray, a lungful of mortification, and a burning ass.

"I'm never going to live that down." I gesture toward the closing door. "He's going to tell everyone."

Ray turns in the chair and pulls me between his legs. "I'll make it up to you. You can ink me while you're naked and sitting in my lap."

"I'm thinking that's going to be more for your benefit than mine. And there's no way I'm stripping down in the studio or doing a tat from your lap."

He lifts my shirt and presses a warm kiss to my stomach. "We'll see."

Half an hour later, after securing the door and sending Jess an apologetic text, I'm still clothed, but straddling Ray's lap on my client chair with the tattoo machine in my hand.

"This is so unprofessional," I say after I put away the disinfectant. "I can't believe the things you talk me into."

He cups my breast in his palm over my T-shirt and licks his lips. "If I remember correctly, I didn't have to talk."

My cheeks burn at his reference to our moment in the staff room when he kissed me so hard my knees went weak and I moaned into his mouth.

"Yeah," he says, his voice soft. "She knows what I'm talking about."

Despite Ray's protests, I have plugged my iPod into the sound system and the first mix starts off with Coldplay's "Viva La Vida."

"Christ." Ray grimaces. "You sure know how to take a mood down. You got any hard rock? Linkin Park? Isn't the client supposed to choose?"

"I'm sitting on your lap," I say with a little grind over the bulge in his jeans for effect. "I'm also working instead of going out with my bestie. You've pretty much gotten everything you want from me. Is it too much to ask for a little musical indulgence?"

His hooded gaze rakes over my body. "Maybe if I were inside you—"

"Seriously?" I hold up the tattoo machine. "The tat is forever. If I slip up, it is a permanent mistake. I don't want to do that to you. Also, you know it can be painful. You might not be able to…you know…keep it up."

He lifts an admonishing eyebrow.

"Okay. I take it back. You are all lion all the time. But I have to draw the line at having sex while doing a tat."

"Fine. I'll give you a break."

"Gee, thanks."

"Pleasure."

"You probably already know this," I say, "but the shading can be much more painful than the outline, so let me know if you need a break."

He raises his eyebrow again, higher this time.

"Right. Forgot you are too manly to feel pain, just like every man who comes in here. However, when the pain overrides your pride, let me know." Taking a deep breath, I try to ignore his cock pressed up against the curve of my sex, his body warm beneath me, and his hand caressing my breast as I begin shading. I manage to relax into the design and listen to the music, but after ten minutes of silence, I sigh.

"We call clients who don't talk cadavers."

"Can't talk." Ray's voice is husky and low. "It's taking all my energy not to rip off your clothes and fuck you till you scream."

"Don't hold back." My voice drips with sarcasm. "Tell me what you really want to do." I wiggle on top of him. He is indeed harder than when I started. I wiggle again. Ray groans.

"Stop. I'm barely hanging on."

"This was your idea." I look up and grin. "And FYI, I'm going to be at least another hour."

He grits his teeth and nods. "Go for it, but don't move."

But it is almost impossible not to move. Inking skin is, by its nature, an intimate experience, but with Ray it goes beyond intimate into the divine. In this position, with one hand braced on his chest, I can feel every beat of his heart, hear every rasp of his breath, soak in his warmth as I inhale the scent of fresh ink and the musk of Ray's skin.

"Sia." My name is a tortured groan on his lips, and when I look up, I see both pain and pleasure etched across his face.

"You need a moment?"

He shakes his head and strokes his hand through my hair, a gentle, caressing gesture that turns my body liquid.

"If it hurts…" My words trail off when he tightens his hand in my hair.

"Like to hurt. Need to hurt. But when you're doing the hurting…" His voice breaks. "Hard to stay in control. Just…finish it."

So I do. I pour my soul into his tat, sweeping the wolf down his shoulder and over his pec. Although I usually prefer color to semi-tribals like this one, I think it is one of the best tats I have ever done. I show Ray in the mirror and he nods his approval. "Fucking awesome."

After I've bandaged the tat, I sit back and give him a questioning glance. He has been so quiet, his body so tense… "You okay?"

He rubs his thumb along my bottom lip and groans. Taking a hint, I draw his thumb into mouth, wrap my lips around it, and suck, tasting Ray on my tongue.

"Christ. I can't…" He eases me off his lap and then slides out of the chair, his body tense, quivering, as if he's fighting for control. A tiny shiver winds its way down my spine when I glance at his face. It's a cold, hard mask of concentration without the usual warmth I see when we're together.

"Ray?"

He seats himself on my artist's chair and grabs my hips, pulling me until I'm standing between his spread legs. Then he pulls me down, urging me lower until I'm kneeling in front of him.

"Suck me, beautiful girl. Show me what else those sweet lips can do."

Oh God. That voice. Commanding. Sexy. Utterly dominant. My body tightens, need curling deep in my core.

Ray exhales when I help him ease his pants over his hips. His erection springs free, bobbing gently in my direction, and I lean forward and take a little lick.

He grips my hair, tilting my head back, and growls. "Don't play."

"Okay," I whisper, torn between excitement and a niggle of concern over my ability to handle him taking so much control.

Ray wraps his hand around mine, curving us both over his thick shaft, and strokes hard. The feel of him hot and throbbing in my palm sends spasms through my groin.

"Harder." He barks his command as he squeezes my hand around his shaft, his tone so gruff and unfamiliar my heart skips a little beat. Is this the dark side of him he didn't want me to see? The Ray who likes pain?

We stroke him together until his cock is rock hard, and then Ray releases my hand and I lean forward and take him into my mouth, my tongue stroking up and down his length, praying my inexperience doesn't show. But whatever I'm doing must be right because he grips my hair and arches into me.

"That's it. Take it all."

His words make my clit tingle, and I take him deep, my cheeks sucking inward as I increase the pressure. Oh God. It's so deliciously, illicitly dirty to be kneeling at Ray's feet in the studio with his cock in my mouth, the wooden floor hard beneath my knees. How many times did I fantasize about doing something like this, never imagining for a second it would ever come true?

Wrapping one hand around the base of his shaft, I work it in counterpoint to my mouth. Ray's breathing turns ragged and his erection thickens, becoming impossibly hard. I inhale his scent of soap and musky male, and try to focus on the slide of my lips over his smooth skin and not the ache at the juncture of my thighs.

"Touch yourself." His rasped command is almost a relief. Without hesitation, I slide my hand between my legs and toy with my piercing.

"Fuck." He wraps his hand around mine and squeezes, my grip on his cock at least twice as tight as before. Shocked at how hard he wants to be touched, I look up at him. Ray stares down at me, his fingers still in my hair. My breath catches at the raw hunger in his eyes—and something else, hiding in the shadows, feeding on his pain.

"Did I tell you to stop?"

Heat rushes between my legs, and I let out a moan as my clit pulses and throbs. God, I could come just from the filthy things he says.

"You like that." He tugs my head back, forcing me to look up at him.

"Yes."

"Good. 'Cause I'm gonna hold you still and fuck your pretty mouth, and you're gonna dig your little claws into my thighs as hard as you can."

"I can't hurt you like that."

"Pain pays for the pleasure." He reaches down and pinches my nipple, finding my piercing through my clothes and pulling it so hard I gasp. "Pleasure me. Take me deep."

And I do. I lean forward and take him in my mouth again, trying to relax my throat when he pushes in so far I gag. He pulls back just enough for me to recover, then holds my head still and plunges in again.

Pressure builds inside me, and I rock my hips frantically against my hand as he drives deep and withdraws, his thighs taut and quivering beneath my other palm.

Sweat beads on my forehead as I fight back the fear of losing control. This is what I fantasized about. Rough, not gentle. Used, not pampered. Dominated instead of dominating. I wanted the Predator—raw, wild, untamed. And now I have him.

"Do it," he rasps, pressing my hand against his leg. "Now. Let me feel your claws, kitten."

I grip his leg, digging my nails into his skin. This is as much pain as I can give, and even this is too much for me.

Ray's entire body goes rigid and the sound that comes from his chest is at once a growl and a groan. His hand tightens on my hair so hard, my eyes water, and his shaft thickens until it is a struggle to take him all.

"Sia." He arches into my mouth, yanking me forward to meet his impatient thrusts. So rough. So dirty. So damn confusing. But I feel—every emotion, every sensation.

His cock swells; then he comes with a groan, driving so deep I gag as he spurts down my throat.

"Jesus. Fuck." With a roar, he rips himself away, leaving me stunned and panting on the floor. And then I see the blood, four little crescents from my nails in his skin.

"Oh God. I hurt you. I'm so sorry. Let me wash it. I didn't mean for it to go so far."

"Neither did I." His voice flattens. "That's a side of me I didn't mean to share."

Fear and confusion give way to anger. Why doesn't he want to share himself when he asks the same of me? "I know you like pain. I know you get off when I use the tattoo machine on you. It's okay with me. Why don't you want to share it?"

"Because when I'm around you, I lose control. I don't know how far I'll go." He grabs his jeans and yanks them over his hips.

"I like who you are, Ray. I want to know about you and what you need."

He pulls on his T-shirt, wincing slightly from the fresh tattoo. "I don't want you to be part of my pain. I failed the people I cared about most, and I gotta live with that for the rest of my days. You've got your own demons to deal with. I won't give you mine."

Stunned speechless, I watch him turn and walk away.

Chapter 16
WHO IS HE? GIMME A NAME

Priority: Confidential
Bay Area Underground Fight Club (BUFC) Fight Night
Abandoned Church. Fell and Fillmore. 8 p.m.
Headlining: Fuzzy vs. Renegade
Code Word: Styx

"WHAT THE HELL IS he thinking?" Heart pounding, I push myself out of my seat and slam the door to my Volvo, now parked outside Tag's apartment building. On the other side of the vehicle, Jess does the same.

"He can't fight anymore. His arm"—my voice catches, breaks— "and his shoulder. They never healed right. The doctor told him he couldn't fight again."

"We'll talk him out of it." Jess catches up with me on the walkway to Tag's apartment and gives my arm a firm squeeze. "Or…you'll talk him out of it and I'll back you up."

"Did he say anything to you about it when he went to your apartment the other night?" I press the buzzer for Tag's apartment. "Did he say anything that would explain why he decided to challenge Renegade?"

Jess shakes her head. "It was just…strange. He came to my place, totally distraught, but he didn't want to talk. I suggested we watch TV, so we sat on the couch for a few hours. Then he said he had to go. I got the feeling he wanted to say something and needed to work up the nerve, so when he called again the next day, I invited him over. But it was just more of the same. If you ask me, he needs some serious help."

I press the buzzer again and again. "I think you're right. He's too deep into this case. He wouldn't talk to me, so I called my parents, but they had no luck either."

But Tag isn't at his apartment or the gym, and he isn't answering his phone. And by the time we get to the abandoned church for the fight, Tag is already in one corner and Jake a.k.a. Renegade is in the other.

For the first time, I don't have the usual pang of longing when Jake rakes his hand through his blond curls. Instead, I imagine dark hair, thick and neatly cut and sky-blue eyes. And then I remember spending the last two nights at Jess's place because I couldn't bear to be in my apartment alone. Despite my best intentions, I got involved—so involved that the thought of never seeing Ray again is a physical, tangible pain that takes my breath away.

"Tag." I race around to his side of the makeshift ring. "What are you doing? You know you can't fight."

A pained expression crosses his face. "I was meant to be a fighter, and I left it all behind seven years ago. I need to get back in the ring, do what I was meant to do. Who knows when I may need these skills again?"

What the hell is going on with him? This is what happens when I spend all my time obsessing over a mercurial fighter who easily walked away, and turn my back on the people who have always been there when I needed them the most.

"You have police skills. You have a gun. And I have no doubt you can defend yourself in a fight. Please don't do this." I reach up and grab his bicep. "You haven't even trained properly. Renegade is near the top of the amateur league."

"So was I." He jerks out of my grasp. "And I will be again."

But I can't let this go. Nausea roils in my belly. "I don't understand what's going on with you. What do you need to prove? You aren't acting like yourself. And Jess"—I look back over my shoulder at Jess standing in the spectator's area with Rampage—"she's worried about you."

He swallows hard. "I have nothing to say to Jess. She's with Blade Saw. I'm happy for them."

"Why don't we all go for a drink and talk?"

"Sia." His voice rises to a loud bark and Jess looks over in alarm. "Go."

"Let him fight." Ray's voice is a low murmur in my ear, his hand warm on my hip. "There's nothing you can do to stop him."

Still reeling from seeing Tag in the ring, I don't question Ray's sudden appearance at the fight. "You don't understand. He's injured."

"Then he'll know the extent of his injuries better than anyone." He grabs my hand and tugs me away. "When a man decides to fight, he's gonna fight. All you can do is be there for him at the end."

Jerking out of his grasp, I give Tag one last pleading look, but when he shakes his head, I sigh and head back over to Jess with Ray on my heels.

"Where did you come from anyway?"

"Got the message about the fight. Knew you'd be here. Figured you wouldn't be too happy."

I edge away when we turn to watch the fight. I don't want his hands on me. I don't want to be tempted by his too-perfect body or the strength of his arms. I don't want to think how he came here tonight for me even after he pushed me away.

The ref blows the whistle, and Tag opens with a low kick followed by a mid-level that throws him off balance. Renegade moves in fast with a hard left to Tag's nose, and Tag topples backward. Renegade is on him before he even hits the mat, swarming him with punches. My stomach churns, and Ray leans over and murmurs in my ear.

"Renegade's pulling his punches. Fuzz will be okay."

"Doesn't look like he's pulling any punches to me." I swallow as bile rises in my throat. "Tag's lip is bleeding and Renegade's not letting up—"

"If it were a real fight, he'd already be unconscious."

"That doesn't make me feel a whole lot better." I scrub my face with my hands and take a deep breath. But although I can block out the sights, I can't block out the sounds of flesh hitting flesh, Tag's grunts and groans, and then a howl.

"Oh God." I rip my hands away. Tag is writhing on the mat, clutching his shoulder, his face contorted in pain.

Ray frowns. "Renegade was trying to put him in submission,

helping him save face, but Tag twisted out of it. Was it a shoulder injury that did him in?"

"Yeah. A bad one. He fell out of a second-story window and broke his shoulder in three places. It wasn't set properly and never really healed."

An underground medic waves to Tag from outside the ropes, but he shakes his head and pushes himself to his feet. His left arm dangles by his side and his face is contorted in pain.

"I'm going to be sick," Jess whispers.

"I'm going to kill him."

Renegade speaks urgently to Tag. Clearly he wants Tag to tap out. But Tag refuses. Instead, he attacks, using his feet and his good arm. Renegade goes on the defensive, backing away.

"Fuck." Ray swears through gritted teeth and mutters to himself. "C'mon, Fuzz, give in. He's trying not to hurt you."

But he doesn't know Tag the way I do. Tag isn't thinking anymore. He's on autopilot and his goal is to take Renegade down. The last time I saw him like this was the night he injured his shoulder. And all because of me.

Finally Renegade has had enough. He sweeps Tag's front leg and Tag goes down. But he can't brace for the fall on his left side. He tries to recover and staggers back, then loses his balance. His head hits the post and he slumps to the ground.

"Tag." I am running, pushing away the crowd, crawling through the ropes. I get to him at the same time as the medic. She gives him a quick check and whips out her phone. One of the organizers blows his whistle, calling for an emergency evac. The crowd scatters. Once the ambulance arrives, the police will follow, and no one wants to be caught at an unsanctioned fight.

Jess joins me beside Tag and then Renegade crouches down beside us. "I'm sorry. I tried to stop him. I thought he'd just go straight down. Stubborn ass just wouldn't give up."

"How could you?" I shove him in the shoulder, and he falls back. "You knew about his injury. You knew he hasn't really fought in years. I thought you were his friend." My anger comes out in a frenzy of fists, and then Ray is behind me, holding my arms, his voice a soothing rumble in my ear.

"Shhhhh. It's not his fault. Fuzz challenged him. Renegade tried to set it up at Redemption, and Torment said no for all the reasons you spelled out."

"Well, at least someone had sense." I glare at Renegade, and he returns my glare with a pained expression.

"It was me or a stranger," Renegade says. "And the reason I agreed is *because* I'm his friend. I knew I could control the fight. I could pull my punches. I could take him down when I saw he was going to get hurt. Any other fighter in this ring would have done him some serious damage. I tried to save him from himself." He looks at Ray. "*We* tried to save him. It was Ray's idea."

"You knew about it beforehand?" I spin to face Ray.

"The promoters tell the fighters a day before the event, so they have time to prepare." He strokes his hand down my hair, and I close my eyes and grit my teeth.

"You knew and you didn't tell me?" I rip myself out of his arms and my hands clench into fists. "How could you not tell me? I could have talked him out of it."

"We had it under control. I didn't want you to worry."

Turning away, I snort. "Yeah. This is having things under control. So much better than me convincing him not to come here in the first place. Thanks for that, guys."

The ambulance arrives, and I ride with Tag while Jess follows behind in my car. Tag is whisked away once we hit the emergency room doors, and Jess and I sit together in the waiting room. My stomach churns at the familiar scent of antiseptic and I am assailed by memories of the night I sat here with Tag. The night I met Jess. I squeeze her hand when I see her bottom lip tremble. She has bad memories of this waiting room too.

A short while later, we are joined by Rampage, Blade Saw, Torment, and Ray.

"He'll be okay," I say to them when they settle themselves on the seats across from us, more to convince myself than anything else. "He's knocked himself out twice before. Once when he was playing touch football, and then again when he fell out of a tree house when we were little. He has a hard head and no brains inside it to speak of."

Jess manages a half smile. "Are you going to call your parents?"

"After they tell us he's okay. I don't want them to worry."

A tear slides down her cheek. "It makes my heart hurt to think he wanted to fight so bad he'd take that risk."

I nod, but my heart doesn't just hurt; it feels shredded and torn. He's here because of me. He left fighting because of me. He deserved justice too, but he gave it up because I asked him to do it.

Ray sits with the other fighters, but he doesn't talk to them. Instead he watches me. Far from making me uncomfortable, his presence is soothing, and the fact he is here makes me confused all over again.

Tag regains consciousness after an hour. The doctor says he'll be okay but because he has a concussion, he'll have to stay in the hospital overnight. I call Mom and Dad and they freak, but not as badly as they would have if I'd called before he woke. I let Jess go in to see him first, and then the fighters who are chomping at the bit. Ray stays in the waiting room with me.

Blade Saw offers to take Jess home, and she gives me a farewell hug. She says Tag was happy to see her and asked her to come for the next Sunday dinner to distract Mom from harassing him about the fight.

After everyone leaves, I step into Tag's room. He's pale and clearly in pain, but his anger is still there.

"That was fucking humiliating. How am I going to teach now?" He shifts on the bed and winces.

"There weren't that many people there. Mostly just the people who know you well." I pause, wondering if this is really the best time to bring up his crazy behavior, and then I do. "Why did you do it?"

He hesitates, and then shrugs. "I wish we could live that night all over again. I wouldn't take the easy road. I'd do everything I could to make that bastard rot in jail."

My breath leaves me in a rush, and I sit on the chair beside Tag's bed. "We didn't take the easy road. At least, it wasn't easy for me. But I don't regret our decision to keep it quiet. Mom and Dad would never have recovered. They would have lost their house and their jobs, and who knows what would have happened to us? You remember all the threats and the bullying. Luke's family has too much power."

He scrubs his hand over his face and sighs. "I just can't help thinking it's dragging us down. We changed our lives, moved on, but it's still there. He's there. He took something from us that night. Maybe you would have wound up being a famous artist with shows all over the world. Maybe I would have become a pro fighter. We never had a chance to become who we were meant to be. Tonight, I thought I'd try and take it back. But it was too damn late."

I've never heard Tag sound so defeated. He's my rock. My fighter. My protector. My everything. Chest tight, I squeeze his hand. "Dad just texted. They're just parking the car. I'm not up for seeing them, so I'm gonna take off. Do you want me to go by your apartment and pick anything up? I can come back later."

"You can't go to my apartment." He cuts me off with a sharp tone. "I told you before."

"But…"

"No."

"Should I come back after Mom and Dad leave?"

He shakes his head. "I just want to be alone."

I swallow past the lump in my throat. "Call me if you need anything. I'll be back tomorrow."

Tag nods and I make it out the door and partway down the hallway before I am overwhelmed by emotion. Fear, anger, remorse, and guilt wage a war over which of them should destroy me first. My chest tightens and I lean against the wall and struggle to breathe. But this time the air doesn't come.

Someone puts a hand on my shoulder. I hear words in the distance, a woman's voice, white disappearing into a sea of black. My knees hit the floor but I feel nothing. I am at once empty and filled with pain.

And then warm arms enfold me, lift me, carry me. A heart firm and steady beats against my chest. The rumble of a voice, the creak of leather, and the rich masculine scent of Ray.

He strokes my hair and talks, holds me against him. I can't make out his words, but his voice pulls me out of the darkness. I draw in a breath of sweet, cool air and look up into a sea of blue.

"There she is," he whispers.

"And here you are." I bury my face against his chest, breathing him in, resting my cheek against the soft cotton of his Twisted Sister T-shirt as he leans back on the bench in the hallway.

"What happened to Tag is my fault." My voice chokes with tears. "He wanted his life back. The life I stole from him." And then, because he came when I needed him, because he says he is broken too, I tell him what I should have told him before. "I was…" Raped. But no, I've never been able to say that word. Even now. "Sexually assaulted."

"Raped." He says it for me, his voice calm, soothing, but I can hear a tightening in his tone.

"Yes. When I was eighteen." I tell him everything: how Tag told me not to go to the party, but I went anyway, how I trusted Luke because he was Tag's teammate, how Tag saved me and fought with Luke and they both fell out the window. And then I tell him about the threats that started when we got to the hospital—phone threats, email threats, a smear campaign on social media that suggested I was setting Luke up to get his family's money. I tell him how we decided not to go to the police or tell our parents, to protect our family and to make it all go away. But, of course, it didn't go away. I couldn't paint anymore. Tag couldn't fight. And our parents knew something was wrong and were hurt we didn't let them help us.

Ray strokes my cheek as I talk. His hand is warm against my palm. He doesn't shout or yell or cry or look at me as someone who needs to be pitied. He is simply there. And that is exactly what I need.

"I get panic attacks when I feel like I'm losing control or something that reminds me of that night." I close my eyes and lean into the warmth of his palm. "I have trouble with trust and getting close to anyone—and I have real trouble with intimacy."

"You trusted me enough to tell me." Ray leans forward and presses a kiss to my forehead. "Means a lot to me."

My cheeks flame. "Well…you're different from the guys I was with. Charlie and James treated me like I was made of glass. They would get…overly emotional. They were so gentle, kind, and considerate, and I tried, I really did, but I always felt like a victim. I never felt normal. And

Peter, another guy I went out with… I didn't tell him what happened because I didn't want to be treated that way again. But something about him set off my triggers, and when I finally told him, he cut things off and said he couldn't handle my baggage. After that, I kinda gave up."

"And then you met me." He gives a satisfied grin and I laugh.

"You seem to think quite highly of yourself."

"I got the hottest tat artist in California sitting in my lap. She's got the biggest heart and the most beautiful face, and hell, when she gets going, you should hear her sass. Guy like me with a girl like you, yeah, that's worth a smile."

For a single irrational moment, I am insanely jealous of his wife. She didn't just have his smile; she had his heart, and if they hadn't suffered a tragedy, she would have had it forever.

"You know why I like you?" I stroke his cheek, rough with a five o'clock shadow. "Aside from the fact that you're hot, sexy, an amazing fighter, always there for me, understanding, and good in bed?"

He lifts an eyebrow. "I'm waitin' to hear more."

"You're everything I ever wanted a man to be."

Ray kisses my forehead and chuckles. "And here I thought it was just about the sex."

Not anymore.

"He live around here?"

My brow creases in a frown when the rumble of Ray's voice pulls me out of my thoughts. "Who?"

"The bastard who raped you."

My heart quickens, and I will him not to be thinking what I'm pretty sure he is thinking. "He did, but then he disappeared. Tag tried to find him. He wanted to keep tabs on him just for my peace of mind, but even with all his resources, he couldn't track him down. We figured he must have left the state."

"Walking the streets like he has a right to be anywhere but jail?" His voice rises to a threatening growl.

"Ray…"

"Who is he? Gimme a name."

Stomach churning, I push myself up to sitting and shake my head.

"It's finished, Ray. I made my choice and I've moved on. Don't think I haven't been through this already with Tag. I just want to live my life like it never happened."

"But it did." He cups my jaw in his broad hand and tilts my head back, forcing me to meet his gaze. "And you're not living life like it never happened because you've locked part of yourself away."

"Except with you," I whisper. "Because you make me feel safe."

A pained expression crosses his face. "You should feel safe every fucking day of your life. You and Tag should have justice. I got the resources to make that happen."

Dread claws its way through my belly and I wrench myself away. "Justice isn't going to change the past."

"Maybe not. But it can give you a better future."

My hand clenches into a fist against his chest. "Please, Ray. I didn't tell you because it was a problem that needed to be fixed. I told you because I wanted you to understand why I am the way I am and why I do some of the things I do. I wanted to share my past with you but not to get you involved."

"I am involved." His voice tightens. "And you should know by now I'm not the kind of man to let something like this go. You'll have justice, Sia. I promise you that."

Chapter 17

YOU CAN'T PROTECT ME FROM EVERYTHING

TAG IS RELEASED FROM the hospital the next morning and decides to hide out at my apartment to avoid Mom chasing him down while he's on sick leave. He watches TV beside me on the couch and grumbles about how he can never show his face at Redemption again. I pull out my sketch pad and start to draw.

"You doing up a stencil for someone's tat?" He rests his feet on my glass coffee table, then lowers them when I raise an admonishing eyebrow.

"No. I just…wanted to draw."

He nods at my dining room table, still set up with my easel and the half-finished painting from Ray's visit. "Like you just wanted to paint?"

My cheeks burn and I shrug. "Yeah. Ray was here the other night and he opened my closet and everything fell out. He asked me to paint something for him." My throat tightens with emotion. "It had been so long…and… Oh God, Tag, it felt so good."

His face softens. "I'm happy for you, Sis. I missed your art. I mean, I see your tats on the guys at the gym, but it isn't the same."

Holding up the sketch pad, I flip through the pictures. "I started drawing too. Every spare minute."

He looks at the pictures and laughs. "I see a common theme. Are they all of Ray fighting in the ring because he's the one who opened the door?"

"I love watching him fight. He's so confident in the ring. So utterly competent and in control. I used to watch him and wish I could feel like that."

Tag's smile broadens. "You ever want to learn to fight, just let me know. I'm your man. Starter class is called Get Fit or Die and even though you're my sis, I'll show you no mercy. Love that class. Love running the newbies into the ground."

"So does that mean you're going back to Redemption after all?"

Tag leans over and ruffles my hair. "If you're gonna learn how to fight, I'm gonna be there."

For a moment I feel like I've got my old Tag back. The lines are gone from his forehead and he hasn't mentioned his case since he left the hospital. I lean into his shoulder and sigh. "I guess we've got a deal."

Tuesday morning I walk into the studio with a happy smile only to discover our time in paradise is almost over.

"You missed one hell of a fight on your day off yesterday," Rose says as she hands me my schedule. "Torment found out Slim had ordered his own supplies, and they weren't the quality Torment wants for the shop. It got so loud that a couple of the fighters came in and pulled Torment away. Slim's had it. He says we're outta here at the end of the week. His shop isn't finished, but he says it's good enough to get things going."

"It's going to be hard to leave."

"Hard?" Rose rolls her eyes. "It'll be impossible. I'm ruined for tat studios for life." She motions me forward with a crooked finger and then whispers in my year. "I'm gonna ask Torment to keep me on. He'll need a receptionist who knows the business when he fills those chairs."

My breath catches in my throat. "You can't. We're a team. Slim will be devastated."

Rose shrugs. "I don't think his heart is in the new shop or he would have pulled out all the stops to get it done. He never liked the business side. He's too much of an artist."

"Then why does he keep going head-to-head with Torment? This is the perfect setup for him. Torment handles the business and he handles the art."

"Pride." She pulls her chair up to her desk and taps on her keyboard. "It brings the best of men down."

Before the clients arrive, Christos, Duncan, and I sit down to check out the modeling programs Torment has had installed on our new superpowered computers for the increasingly popular 3-D surrealistic tattoos. By the time we open the shop, I am so nauseated by the 3-D images of guts, muscles, and flesh that are all the rage, I am perversely grateful when Doctor Death walks in the door.

"Good morning, beautiful ladies." He beams and Rose laughs.

"Good morning, beautiful man. To what do we owe this pleasure?"

"I was looking at my ass in the mirror the other day," he says, his expression growing serious, "and I had an idea for an addition to the cover Sia did for me." He hands me a piece of paper with a drawing of a bird perched on a broken heart. "Hope." He points to the bird. "From the Emily Dickinson poem. I thought the broken heart might be a bit depressing for the ladies, but if we add the bird—"

The door opens and closes behind me, and I shiver as cool air brushes over my skin.

"It's lovely." I hand him back the drawing. "I'll be happy to add it. Do you want me to make a stencil from your drawing or make up one of my own?"

Doctor Death tilts his head to the side and gives me a questioning look. "I was hoping you could do it freehand."

Rose coughs and bangs her coffee cup on her desk.

"Freehand?" Very few artists will do freehand work because, if the client doesn't like the tattoo, there is no going back. It is the ultimate statement of trust between a client and the artist. And something Slim has always claimed for himself.

"Slim doesn't let anyone in the shop work freehand except him. If you don't want a stencil, he'll have to do it for you."

Doctor Death strokes a finger over my cheek. "I trust you, Sia. You do great work. I was almost disappointed I'd asked you to do that cover on my ass because I would have liked to show that piece around."

"Sia!" Rose shouts even though I am only a few feet away. "Someone is here to see you."

Only then do I turn around.

Ray is sprawled on one of the big, brown leather client couches, taking up the space of four clients. This I know because the four clients that were there are now huddled on the other couch, clearly afraid to ask

Ray to take his arms down from the back of the couch or perhaps close his legs so his manliness is not on full display. His posture is powerful, aggressive, controlling. And maybe he seems a tiny bit annoyed.

I make the wise decision to ask Doctor Death to come back another day, and I keep his attention focused on Rose and her appointment book so he doesn't see Ray glowering in the corner. Catching on, Rose positions her screen so Doctor Death's back is to the reception area. But I can't stop Doctor Death from giving me a final peck on the cheek when the appointment is made and saying he looks forward to having my hands on his ass again.

Glancing over my shoulder, I see Ray watching this exchange with avid interest, although his face remains an expressionless mask.

"Your boyfriend is pissed," Rose mutters from behind her screen as she writes out the appointment card. Doctor Death's phone rings, and he stands by the desk as he takes the call.

"How can you tell?"

She shrugs. "Oh, I don't know. Maybe it's the extremely aggressive, intimidating alpha-male gonna-getchu posture, or the way his eyes drilled into Doctor Death while he was flirting with you. Or it could have been the 'When the fuck did he get here?' he growled at me when he walked in before heating the place up so much I thought he was going to combust. But that's just me. I might have it totally wrong."

"You do." I draw frowny faces on her notepad as I mentally prepare myself for an unexpectedly irritated Ray. "He's not my boyfriend. Well, sort of. Anyway, it's work. No big deal."

"If you say so." She lifts a perfectly manicured eyebrow and turns away. "Although I think someone forgot to tell him that."

Doctor Death ends his call, and Rose hands him the card. But just as he turns for the door, Ray pushes himself off the couch and closes the distance between them in three easy strides of his long legs. Positioning himself between Doctor Death and the door, he folds his arms and glares.

My heart thuds in my chest. Rose gasps and grabs my arm. Seemingly unaffected by the raging male in front of him, Doctor Death sighs.

"Excuse me."

Ray doesn't move. "I see you here again or anywhere near my girl, I'm gonna rip off your balls and shove them down your throat."

"Ray!" I take a step forward. "He's a client. You can't speak to my clients that way."

"He wants your hands on his ass." Ray bites out each word.

"Actually, I already had her hands on my ass." Doctor Death smirks. "I came back for more."

Ah. Doctor Death has a death wish.

Before my mind has even registered he has moved, Ray has Doctor Death by the collar and up against the wall. "I know about Makayla," he growls. "And I know about Amanda. You got a problem keeping your hands off another man's property. But I'm telling you now, this ends here."

"Ass work is part of my job." I fold my arms and scowl. "So it ends when I've done the work my client asked me to do."

Ray doesn't take his eyes off Doctor Death, but his words are directed at me. "No more ass work. You don't touch any man below the belt for any reason. And you don't touch them above the belt unless you're out in the open. And this fucker you don't touch at all."

"This is just like in the movies," Rose whispers under her breath. "And he's not joking. Look at his face. I thought Torment was scary but Ray is terrifying."

"Put him down." I raise my voice almost to a shout. "You're being ridiculous."

Ray glances over at me, but it is not Ray I see in his eyes, it's the Predator. He loosens his grip on Doctor Death and lets him slide down the wall; then he lifts him and body slams him on the ground.

"Stop it." But my words go unheeded as Doctor Death struggles on the floor. The four clients on the couch all have their cell phones out and are filming the action. Duncan is shouting into his phone for someone—hopefully not Torment—to come and break up the fight. And Christos has Rose by the arm and is trying to pull her to safety.

Luckily Doctor Death is not just a pretty face. He has moves of his own. With a quick twist, he breaks Ray's hold and jumps to his feet.

"Come on, Predator." He waggles his fingers toward himself. "Hit me. Show Sia who you really are. Show her just how much you're going to hurt her in the end when you walk away."

"Don't you dare." My voice cracks the silence. "You touch him again, Ray, and it will be the last thing you ever do. This is my place of business and you are totally out of line."

The door opens and Rampage and Blade Saw step inside, their faces covered in sweat. Rampage takes in Ray and Doctor Death squared off in the client lounge and looks over at me. "Everything okay here? Need a hand?"

"No, but thank you for coming. We're fine. Doctor Death was just leaving."

Doctor Death straightens and does the alpha-male side-to-side neck crack before taking his gaze off Ray. His mouth opens, and I just know he intends to goad Ray again, so I step between them and usher Doctor Death toward the door. "Thanks for coming in. If you give me the drawing, I'll make a stencil of it, just so we can be sure you get exactly what you want."

Doctor Death hands me the drawing and smiles. "I know what I want. I just don't want to see her get hurt."

Rampage and Blade Saw follow Doctor Death out the door. Rampage thumps Doctor Death between the shoulder blades and asks him what the fuck he was thinking, but before I can hear his answer, the door closes behind them. The clients return to their couch to compare videos of the fight. Duncan grabs the ringing phone, since Rose and Christos are nowhere to be seen. I gesture Ray over to my chair and then spin around to face him.

"What the heck was that? He's a client. You can't go around threatening to rip the balls off my clients."

"Don't like him."

"You don't like him? Oh. Well…that's alright then. Pound away. Maybe you want to break his fingers too." I can't keep the sarcasm out of my voice as I fight for calm. "How about we get something straight? I don't give a damn whether you like my clients or not. I have lots of clients I'm sure you won't like. Some of them scare me. Some of them make lewd comments. Some of them cop a feel. Lots of them ask me out. It's the nature of the business, and I can deal with them. I don't need protecting, and I don't want you to interfere with my work."

Ray stiffens. "Which ones?"

"Which ones what?"

"Which ones scared you, made comments, touched you, and asked you out? I want a list."

"Did you not hear anything I just said?" My brow creases with my fiercest frown. "Do not interfere."

"Heard it. Processed it. Ignoring it. Now I'm gonna deal with it. After what you went through, you should be kept safe. I'm gonna make sure no one hurts you ever again, in any way."

My blood chills. Oh God. This is like Charlie and James all over again. He's going to want to wrap me up and hide me away. He'll be afraid to touch me the way I want to be touched. He's going to think I'll break. "What I went through was over a long time ago. It doesn't mean I need protecting now. It doesn't mean I can't handle men like Doctor Death. I don't want you to treat me any different than you did before."

Ray shrugs. "Can't help it. This is who I am. Man sees someone touching what's his, he's gonna do something about it. Man thinks his woman is threatened, he's not gonna hold back until she's safe."

"He hardly threatened me."

"You don't know him like I do."

With a sigh, I sit on my artist's chair. "Actually, the person I don't know is you. If I did, I would have known how you would react and I wouldn't have told you what happened to me. But you don't talk much about yourself. You don't let me in. I hardly know anything about you. We never...go out and do stuff together." Like Doctor Death said.

Tension coils in the air between us, and my head starts to throb in time to the pounding bass of the Metallica song Duncan is streaming through the speakers.

Ray folds his arms across his chest. "What do you want to know?"

Really, there is only one thing I want to know. The question that has been burning into my brain since Doctor Death first talked about Ray. "Why does Doctor Death think you're going to walk away? Why did he say you aren't the man you appear to be?"

His eyes darken, and then he shrugs. "Don't know."

Defeated, I try an easier question. "What kind of work do you do as a PI?"

"Surveillance mostly. Spent the morning watching a building. Gotta get back out there in an hour. Came by to see if you were okay after what happened at the hospital. I would've come by yesterday, but I was on a job and had to keep radio silence. Sent a text."

"I got it. Thanks. Anything else about what you do?"

"Nope."

With a sigh, I say, "Well, I really feel like I know you better now. Guess I'll see you around."

Ray stares at me for a moment like he wants to say something, but then he just nods. "Later."

When he turns away, I grab my purse from the counter where I dropped it before going to check out the modeling software, and a rolled-up picture falls out.

Ray's picture. Even though I'm annoyed, I want him to have it.

"Ray. Wait."

He turns, and I hold out the picture. "This is for you."

He closes the distance between us and takes it from my hand. "What's this?"

"Take a look." My face heats and I bite my lip. What if he doesn't like it? I was so excited to be finished that I never thought about how he might react.

Ray unrolls the picture and his body stills.

"It's you." My voice wavers. "The first time I saw you fight. You were so beautiful to me. I've had that image in my head since that night. And that's me standing by the pillar."

Long seconds pass and he doesn't look up.

"It's okay if you don't like it." I fill the silence with my anxiety. "It's the first non-tat drawing I've finished since…you know. I'm a little bit rusty."

He looks up, jaw tight, eyes burning bright with repressed emotion. The drawing shakes slightly in his hand. "It's…" His voice cracks, breaks. "Perfect."

My tension eases and I smile. "I'm going to finish the painting of your bike next."

"Knew it was my bike." His corded throat tightens as he carefully rolls up the drawing. "You wanna come?"

"Where?"

"Surveillance. Tonight. You said we never go out."

I glance up just as Slim walks in the door. He frowns at the clients on the couch with Duncan, Rose's empty desk, and me clearly having a personal conversation. "Someone want to tell me what's going on?"

Duncan shoots me a glance, takes in the moment, and then waves Slim over to help answer one of the clients' questions.

"Surveillance isn't a date. I just thought...maybe we could do something that didn't involve sex or me having a panic attack or you beating the crap out of someone."

"I'll bring potato chips."

My betraying mouth waters. "Chips?"

"You said they were your vice. We'll chill in my vehicle. You'll have your vice. I'll have mine."

Despite my best efforts, a smile tugs at my lips. "I didn't think you were paying attention."

Ray's eyes soften, and he cups my jaw and strokes his thumb over my cheek. "I pay attention to everything about you. I want to know what to do to make you happy. I wanna be there for you when you're sad. I want to make this world beautiful for you again. I want you to know when you walk out the door that nothing will harm you."

"You can't protect me from everything, Ray.

He leans down and kisses me lightly, sending an electric current through my body that makes my toes curl. "I can try."

Chapter 18

YOU'RE GONNA BURN UP MY JEEP

LATER THAT EVENING, RAY and I are parked in a dimly lit side street in the Tenderloin, one of the seediest areas of San Francisco. Ray's target is somewhere to the left, which is all I can gather from the direction of his binoculars and the occasional click of his long-range camera lens.

My stomach growls softly, and I glare at the empty chip bag. Two last-minute walk-ins meant I didn't have a chance to grab dinner before Ray showed up, and although delicious, the chips aren't quite enough to sustain me.

From my vantage point in Ray's Jeep, I can see through the brightly lit windows of the apartments surrounding us. I've never sat and stared at an apartment building for any length of time before, and I am amazed at how few people think to close their curtains when they engage in illegal activities like freebasing in their kitchens, selling drugs in their living rooms, and counting huge piles of cash.

But really, it's the nudies who capture my attention. Even though I live alone, I don't make a habit of standing nude in front of my window with the light streaming out behind me, like the couple going at it like there's no tomorrow. I make a mental note to strip off and stare out into the night as soon as I get home to see what I've been missing.

"This must be a PI's dream." I point at the couple. "I mean…who does that? Don't they know everyone can see them?"

Ray looks up from the redbrick building on the left he has been watching since we arrived. "Might just be their kink, or they're just so hot for each other they don't care. People often forget they can be seen even if they are a few stories up."

"Their kink?" I shift in my seat as the man, tall and dark with a hard, ripped body, pushes the woman against the window. Hmmm. Not very flattering. Would my ass look like that squashed from behind? From the movement of his arms, I imagine he is squeezing her breasts and my skin prickles. Although I never thought of myself as a voyeur, something about the couple going at it in full view is making me hot. Or maybe it's Ray, so cool and calm beside me, his jeans a feast of tight seams in all the right places.

The side door to the brick building opens, and he lifts his camera and snaps a picture when a man walks out, but I'm guessing it's not the object of his interest because he immediately deletes the pictures and drops the camera to his lap.

My stomach tightens, and I squirm in my seat. A naughty part of me hopes it's not over too soon. Maybe I have a kink I never knew I had. Or maybe I did. Watching us in the mirror at the gym made me feel almost the same way. Slick, desperately aroused, and unable to sit still. Is this normal? Seems to me Peeping Toms are arrested and disparaged by society, so maybe not.

I turn my attention back to the couple in the window. The woman places her hands on the man's shoulders and slides them around his neck. But he is having none of that. In a heartbeat, he rips her hands away and pins them to the glass above her head with one hand.

I draw in a ragged breath and clench my fists so hard my nails dig into my palm. Oh God. That is what I want, what I dream about, what Ray offered me and I couldn't handle. I shouldn't want to be dominated after what happened to me. I need passive and gentle, not hard and rough. I need to be understood, not controlled. I'm so damn messed up it isn't funny. Not normal in any sense of the word.

"Um…are you done?"

"Nope." Seemingly oblivious to my unchecked arousal, Ray continues to watch the redbrick building and I watch my show. Now the man is sliding his free hand down the woman's body, cupping the curve of her sex. His touch is not gentle as he pushes her hips against the glass, forcing her up on her toes.

Moisture pools between my thighs and my back arches in the seat. My nipples are tight and hard, clearly visible through my T-shirt, if Ray was so inclined to look, and the urge to slide my hand down between my thighs and relieve the throbbing in my clit is almost overwhelming. I grab the seat belt and snap it in place, giving Ray a wan smile when he frowns.

"Good to be safe at all times."

From this distance, I can't see what the man is doing with his hand, but from the way she stiffens against the glass, I imagine his fingers are inside her the way Ray's fingers were inside me, thrusting and spreading, pressing and curling, pumping into her until her body is coiled tight with need. He bends down and takes her nipple in his mouth and she squirms and writhes against the glass. In my mind I do the same. But it is Ray's mouth on my nipples, sucking and biting, Ray's breath in my ear.

Crossing my legs to get some necessary friction where it needs to be, I focus on taking slow, deep breaths and slowly rock my hips as the man pulls away. The woman slumps against the glass and then he grabs her hair and forces her to her knees.

I draw in a sharp breath and everything below my waist turns liquid. *Don't watch. Don't watch.* I shoot a frantic glance over at Ray, now photographing a man in the alley, as I claw my thigh trying to relieve the pressure. "Are you...done? Do you have enough pictures?"

Ray shakes his head. "Shouldn't be long."

"Sure." My voice rises to a squeak. My fevered skin burns, and sweat trickles between my breasts. *Normal. Normal. Normal.* I repeat the word over and over, a mantra to keep me on the right path.

Ray's gaze slides to mine, and I thank the city for not installing bright lights in the alley because my cheeks feel like they're on fire. "You okay?"

"Yup. Good. Just...enjoying the view."

Ray returns to taking pictures of the guy in the alley, who is now talking on his phone. I glance up once again at the couple and...oh my God. He's holding her head still and fucking her mouth, his hips rocking back and forth as he thrusts. Although her hand is wrapped around his shaft, he is the one in control. My chest tightens and my breath comes in short pants as I remember Ray's hand in my hair, his cock in my mouth...

"I think I'll get some air." I reach for the door handle, and Ray clamps a hand around my wrist.

"Not if you're wet."

My heart skitters to a stop. "Pardon?"

"Open for me, beautiful girl."

A violent shudder wracks my body. *This.* These words. His authoritative tone. This is what turns me on like nothing else. And it shouldn't. I should be running as far and fast as possible. "Ray…"

"Now." His tone invites no disobedience and God help me I want to play this game. Swallowing hard, I part my legs, sending my skirt riding up my thighs.

"Good girl." His approval sends a torrent of need pounding through my body until it centers in my clit. How does he know the exact words to say to get me off? It's like he's inside my head, delving into my most secret fantasies, my deepest desires.

Gently, he traces his finger slowly up my inner thigh, his hooded gaze never leaving my face. His hand brushes over my panties, a feather light touch that drives me crazy. Desperate to rock my hips, I reach for the seat belt, but Ray stays my hand.

"I like you restrained."

"I can't… I mean, I don't." I release the seat belt, which only serves to make the situation worse because now my hips can move, and move they do, seeking out the pleasures only Ray's fingers in my panties can give.

As if he can read my mind, Ray traces along the lace edge, then shoves the wet fabric aside and glides his finger along my wet folds.

"Christ, you're wet. And hot. You're gonna burn up my Jeep."

I writhe, hungry for his touch. A stroke, a thrust, a pinch—anything to give me release. Finally, a whimper escapes my lips.

"You like to watch." He glides his finger through my folds again, this time, spreading my moisture up and around my clit.

"Ray…" My voice is a pained whisper. "I need to come."

"I know. But not yet. Maybe you should watch some more." He thrusts one thick finger inside me and I drop my head back on the seat and moan.

With a low chuckle, he changes the angle of his hand, pressing two fingers into my sex. Desperate for release, I press his hand hard against me and shamelessly grind against the heel of his palm.

"Watch," he commands. I obey. And for a moment I feel free.

My eyes flutter open, and I stare at the balcony. The man is holding the woman face-first against a table with her hands pinned to her lower back. Every light in their apartment is on, and their curtains are fully open. How can they not know people can see them? Or maybe it is as Ray says, and they do.

He spanks her with his free hand, his arm rising and falling in a steady rhythm. A low groan tears out of my throat, and I rock my hips violently against the fingers curled inside me, struggling to keep my grip on reality under the raging tide of arousal and the desperate, almost painful need to come.

But wicked Ray is in a teasing mood. He thrusts his fingers deep, spreading them inside me, then withdraws, leaving me aching and bereft, over and over again, bringing me up and taking me down until my body is trembling and I am writhing against his hand, my sweat-soaked clothing sliding over the cool leather seat. "Please…Ray…it hurts."

With a low growl, he leans across the seat and covers my mouth, his tongue brushing over the seam of my lips, forcing them open. And I open. I give him everything, tangling his tongue with mine, threading my hands through the silky strands of his hair.

"So fucking sexy." He curls his hand around the back of my neck and pulls me to him, his breath hot on my cheek. "I want you like that. Naked, wet, restrained for my pleasure, begging me to make you come. I want your ass pink from my hand. I want to claim every part of your sweet body until you know nothing but me and the pleasure only I can give you."

He pounds his fingers inside me and circles his thumb around my clit until my tension builds and peaks.

"Scream for me, beautiful girl." He slants his mouth over my lips as he presses his thumb hard over my clit. And I come, hot and wet over his fingers, a burst of pleasure so intense the world sheets white as Ray swallows my scream.

Exhausted, my body still quivering, I slump back in the seat as he withdraws his fingers. "What made you wetter?" Ray's voice drops to a husky rasp. "Watching them fuck or the way he controls her?"

"I don't know. I watched a couple of porns on TV with Jess, but they just made me laugh. Other than that, I've never watched anyone. Never imagined it would turn me on. Maybe it's a bit of both, but mostly I think it's the control. But it's that side of me that got me into trouble in the first place. Luke—" I suck in a sharp breath at my slip and pray he didn't catch the name. "The guy who assaulted me was rich, handsome, charming, a daredevil, and utterly thrilling. Almost irresistible to an eighteen-year-old introverted artist with an overprotective family. That's the night I learned I couldn't trust myself. I learned I couldn't trust these feelings I had around men who took my breath away because I couldn't handle men I couldn't control."

"You control me pretty well." Ray glances up at the redbrick building. The alley is empty, and I hope he didn't miss out on something important because of me.

"Seriously? You're the Predator. Not even Torment can control you."

"One drawing and you almost had me on my knees." Ray threads his fingers through mine and holds my hand to his lips. "You got a kinky side. Nothing wrong with that, especially when our kinks fit together. You got a need to give up control and I got a need to take it. I can feed your soul and you can feed mine. But you will always be safe with me." He kisses each of my fingers and warmth flows through my body, spreading out to my fingers and toes.

"You don't understand." I swallow hard. "Even if that's my kink, I'm not normal. Normal people have normal sex in a normal way. They don't worry if they're going to have a panic attack afterward or if something might trigger a bad memory and send them spiraling off into a black hole, or that something bad will happen if they give in to their secret desires."

Ray turns on the ignition and puts the Jeep in gear. "I'm gonna show you that you're wrong about normal. And that you can enjoy your kink and be who you want to be without worrying about anything else. You went through a nightmare I wouldn't wish on anyone, and now I understand your panic attacks, and we can work through them. But I know you've got needs and you're afraid to embrace them. That's 'cause that bastard took something from you. And I'm going to give it back." He puts the Jeep in reverse and glances in the rearview mirror. "Christ."

"What's wrong?"

Ray's demeanor changes in a heartbeat. His body stiffens and his face smooths into an expressionless mask. Cool and calm, he reaches down and unholsters the gun strapped to his leg.

My eyes widen in alarm. "What's going on?"

"Stay in the Jeep. Lock the doors. I'm leaving the keys. If I don't come back or something happens to me, you get out of here as fast as you can." Even his voice sounds different. His tone clipped, professional, and so cold I shiver.

My skin prickles as he steps out of the Jeep. "Tell me what's going on."

"I said I'd keep you safe. And I will."

Chapter 19

Don't want to let you go

Famous last words.

Turning in my seat, I watch Ray through the back window of the Jeep as he stalks over to a black sedan parked two cars behind us. The driver must see Ray too, because the vehicle's lights go on and I can hear the faint grind of an engine starting. Ray's steps become longer and then he runs at the car, launching himself at the vehicle before the driver has time to pull away. He yanks open the door and drags the driver out, then pummels him to the ground. From this distance, I can't see the driver's face, but I catch a flash of blond hair and blue jeans and white streaks on a black T-shirt that remind me of the Viva la Vida shirt I got when Coldplay played San Francisco's Warfield Theatre.

Nausea roils in my belly. Who is the man in the car, and why was he following us? Should I get out and stop the fight? But this is no street brawl. Ray is fighting with one purpose in mind, and that seems to be to kill. Every strike is vicious and precisely directed to where it could do the most damage.

Anger doesn't even begin to describe what I see in his face.

However, the man from the car is holding his own. He manages to roll away and push himself to his feet. Ray charges and slams him against the vehicle, his hand around the man's throat. His shout echoes in the quiet street. I catch a few words: "nothing to do with this," "stay the fuck away," and "I'm done with this shit." He raises his fist and the man puts up his hands in a warding-off gesture and begs for his life. My heart squeezes in my chest, and I silently beg Ray not to make that final strike. He doesn't. Instead, he smashes his fist on the hood beside the man, so hard I'm sure he'll leave a dent.

After slamming the man one last time against the vehicle and watching him slide to his knees on the ground, Ray returns to the Jeep and bangs the door so hard the vehicle shakes. For a moment, he doesn't move, save for the violent quivering of his body. Lips pursed in suppressed fury, hands gripping the steering wheel so hard his knuckles whiten, he glares at the rearview mirror until the black sedan pulls away from the curb and speeds past us and into the night.

I've been to enough fights, talked to Tag enough times, that I know better than to speak to or even touch Ray until he's calmed down. But I can't slow the pounding of my heart or deny my instinctive desire to run from an angry Predator. A familiar prickle crawls across my skin, and I grit my teeth and fight it away. The last thing Ray needs right now is me having a panic attack, so I dig my nails into my thigh and take a deep breath and tell myself it will be okay.

Without a word, Ray turns on the ignition and pulls into the road. He doesn't look at me, and I wonder if he's so far into the zone that he has forgotten I'm sitting beside him.

We drive and drive. I break and ask if he's okay, but he doesn't answer. Finally, he pulls over at a historic hotel at the edge of the Claremont Canyon Regional Preserve and reaches over me to grab a flashlight from the glove box.

"Take this."

When he slides out the door, I sling my purse over my shoulder and tuck my phone into my jacket pocket.

Not that I think he'll hurt me, but I like to be prepared.

Ray fishes around in the back of the Jeep and produces another flashlight, bigger than the one he gave me. Then he takes my hand and tugs me toward the back of the hotel.

"If we're going up the Stonewall Fire Trail, I'll need to change my shoes." I point to my black sling-back pumps. "I've got a pair of running shoes in my gym bag in the backseat."

After a quick shoe change, I follow Ray to the back of the hotel. I haven't been up the Stonewall Fire Trail in years, and never at night. I hiked into the hills a few times as a teenager and occasionally with Jess for the incredible, expansive views of the East Bay and San Francisco. But the steep one-mile ascent is a killer.

Ray holds my hand as we make the climb. Creatures scurry in the underbrush, and birds swoosh overhead. I startle at an unfamiliar noise in the darkness and squeeze Ray's fingers. But I am more worried about not sounding like a freight train than being attacked by a wild animal—especially since I've got one holding my hand.

When we reach the top, Ray sits on the grass and pulls me down between his legs, my back against his chest, his warm arms wrapped around my waist. The city spreads out below us, soft lights fading to the inky black bay.

"Do I get to know what's going on?" I look over my shoulder, and Ray leans down and presses his cheek against mine, rough with a five o'clock shadow.

"Don't want to let you go." He pulls me in tighter and buries his face in my shoulder.

"I'm not planning on going anywhere." And then my blood chills. "Are you ending this? Is that why we're here?" Was Doctor Death right when he said Ray would walk away?

Ray doesn't answer. Instead he draws in a deep, shuddering breath and I try to connect with him in the stillness. Closing my eyes, I sink back into his body. My breath is his breath. Our hearts beat as one. We are in full contact. But I can't sense him in the darkness. How can he be so close and yet so far away?

"I shouldn't have taken you with me," he says after an interminably long silence.

"I wanted to go."

"It was too dangerous. I knew that. Every other time, I've stopped myself from taking you out in public. Even this afternoon, I made myself walk away. But when you gave me that picture…" He squeezes me so hard, I can barely breathe. "Fuck. It was so beautiful. After all the beauty I destroyed in my life, you gave a piece of it back to me. And the way you drew yourself…that's what I see. The real you. And you gave me that too."

"Ray." I turn my head and rest my forehead on his cheek, rough with stubble. "You're scaring me. Talk to me."

A tree frog croaks in the distance, and something scurries in the tall grass. We are alone but not alone. Even the silence is not silence because I can still hear the hum of traffic, the wail of sirens, and the occasional faint blare of a car horn. But the breeze is soft and cool, fragrant with the smell of grass and a kiss of the ocean. And Ray still has his arms around me, protecting me in the darkness.

"When I moved to the Bay Area a couple of years ago and started up as a PI, it was the first time I had control over my work." His voice drops to a soothing murmur and I relax into his arms. "I got a job working at the law firm where Amanda used to work. Met Amanda. Liked her. She was a good person caught in a bad situation. Turns out power corrupts at all levels, and when I saw they were doin' her an injustice, I did my best to help. Got to know her very well, and Penny, her secretary, and the boys at Redemption. Before that, my life had always been about duty, never staying in one place long enough to have friends. Lisa was my first and only serious relationship and we hooked up only because we were stationed together."

"In the army?"

He brushes a kiss over my cheek and sighs. "I started thinking about staying here, and Torment hounded me to join the Redemption team, but duty kept calling. I had assignments that kept taking me away. I joined the underground league so I could fight without letting anyone down. And then one day, I saw you at a fight."

"You saw me? I kinda stayed in the back."

"Couldn't see anything else. That was the day I decided I wanted a real life. I wanted a chance to be with a girl who took my breath away, to have friends, to answer only to myself. But the job I do, it's not that easy to walk away, so I tried not to get too close to you. When you gave me that picture, I realized I'd lost that battle a long time ago. Suddenly I wanted to take you out so bad—more than anything I've wanted before. Just for a night, pretend it was real."

"It is real." I brush my hand over the cool grass.

"Tonight says it can't be real." Ray releases me and pushes himself to his feet. "I put you in danger. It can't happen again, especially after what you've already been through. It was a stupid dream and I should have known better." He stalks away through the darkness. I hear rocks clatter, swearing, a strangled cry. I shine the flashlight in the direction of the noise and find him seated on a rise, his arms crossed on his knees, head down.

Although not very reassured by his words, I can't ignore his pain, so I make my way up the little hill and kneel in front of him.

"Let me in." I ease his legs apart and he lifts his head as I shuffle close and wrap my arms around him.

"Shhhhh." It's my turn for shushing now and, curiously, he doesn't resist. Instead he wraps his arms around me and pulls me tight against him, shuddering against my body.

"Look at me," I whisper. "This last month we've been together, I've done things I never thought I'd do before. Things I thought would destroy me. I'm stronger than I thought I was. I've been leaning on people for too long. I don't know what threat that guy was to me, but whatever it is, I can deal with it, Ray. We can deal with it. Together."

"My beautiful girl." His words are a soft murmur against my neck. "Never wanted anything as much as I want you. Never wanted a normal life as much as I want it now. But I can't go through losing someone again. What if, one day, you turn the corner, and he's there and I'm not fast enough? The guilt never goes away. It eats at my soul."

Kneeling, I stroke his hair, soft and silky under my palm. "You need to forgive yourself. What happened with Scott, and with Lisa too, wasn't your fault. They made their choices. Just like I've made mine."

The sound that comes from his throat is part sob, part groan. A prickling sensation shoots up my spine and for some inexplicable reason, I feel like I'm about to lose him. So I don't let him go. I hold him tight while in the back of my mind I wonder if this will be the last time.

"Where were you last night?" Tag paces beside me on the mat in the warm-up area of Redemption as we wait for the rest of his Get Fit or Die class to arrive. "I thought you were joining Renegade, Rampage, and me at the Protein Palace after work."

"Something came up." I pull my ball cap low on my forehead,

hoping to hide the last vestiges of swollen eyes and a sleepless night. "So are you and Renegade tight again?"

"We're good." He frowns and tips up the visor on my cap. "You okay?"

"Yeah. I was with Ray. It wasn't such a good night. Something happened."

Tag stiffens, instantly on alert. "What happened?"

"I'm not sure. There was a guy in a car. Ray thought he was following us. He beat him up and afterward, he said he was a threat. He wouldn't talk about it, but I don't think it had to do with his work as a PI."

Tag glances up as two women join us, both wearing tight Lycra bike shorts and tank tops and looking as if they've taken the class multiple times and have mastered the Get Fit part of Get Fit or Die.

"Ladies." He smiles the smile that got him voted king of the high school prom. "We're meeting over by the exercise mats."

After the women leave, he says, "Why don't you just ask him?"

"He won't tell me. He's always very vague when he talks about his work." I bite my lip. "Would you be able to check him out? I mean, find out what else he does for a living other than being a PI, and other…stuff like that? I'm beginning to wonder if that rumor about him being in the CIA is true."

"Are you fucking kidding me?" Tag leans against a lat machine and folds his arms. "I can't believe he's a fucking spook. That just sounds crazy. His work as a PI is legit. Ask Amanda or Renegade. And what else do you want to know about him?"

"Anything."

"You don't trust him."

I scrub my hand over my face. "I thought I did, but now I'm not sure anymore."

Tag pats my shoulder. "Then you should think about moving on. You've got nothing without trust."

I follow Tag back to the mats, where the rest of the class is waiting. Maybe nothing has changed over the years. Maybe I'm still exercising the same poor judgment I showed when I was eighteen. One thing I know for certain, Tag is motivated only by the desire to protect me.

Or not.

Fifteen minutes into Get Fit or Die, I change my view. Tag doesn't give a damn about protecting me. He wants to hurt me. Badly. Does he seriously think I can run ten laps of the gym, then do fifty starfish jumps followed by twenty burpees without a break? Does he think I'm not going to tell Mom and Dad about his filthy language as he hurls abuse at us for being too slow? And what the hell does this have to do with fighting?

"Move that ass, O'Donnell," he shouts. "You're at the back of the class. You know what we call the people at the back of the class? We call them losers. That's you. So get the lead out, so we can have another loser to laugh at before the class is done."

I look at the clock. Forty-five minutes to go. I'm not going to survive. Wheezing, I stumble over the mats and mentally write my epitaph, *Fuck you, Tag.*

Tag's phone buzzes. As if possessed by a hive mind, the class stops as one. Tag jogs over to Doctor Death and Shayla, a.k.a. Shilla the Killa, who are spotting each other in the free-weight area. A few minutes later, he jogs back and scowls. "Did I tell you to stop running? Laziest class I've ever had. I gotta go take a call. Shill and Doctor Death will take over until I'm back. Show them what you've got. Ten more laps around the gym followed by fifty crunches and twenty push-ups."

He looks over at me and the other women. "And don't give me any bullshit about women's push-ups. Only things on the floor should be your hands and your toes." He looks over at Shayla and barks. "Show them the drill."

Shayla laughs and drops to the mat. She does twenty push-ups, clapping in between, without her knees ever touching the mat. Then she bounces up and grins. "Who's next?"

Not me.

Tag disappears and we run our obligatory laps, but as we position ourselves for the crunches, Doctor Death holds up a hand.

"Most of you are here to learn some MMA fight skills, isn't that right?"

Most of us nod. Doctor Death smiles. "I always think it's a good idea to give people a little taste of what they think they want, so they can be sure that's what they really want. So while you all catch your breaths, Shilla and I will split the class into two and teach you a few fight moves."

In that moment, I love Doctor Death even more than potato chips. But the moment doesn't last.

"Sia, I could use your help." He gestures me forward, and I push up off the floor with a groan. Surprise. Surprise. I'm in Doctor Death's section of the class. Good thing Ray isn't here.

"First move I'm going to demonstrate," he says as he lies on his back on the mat, "is a basic triangle submission." He motions for me to mount him, which involves sitting astride his hips, knees to the mat. When I'm in position, he curls one leg over my neck and yanks my right arm across my body until my body weight drops and his thigh is pressed against my throat. I stiffen as the pressure restricts my airflow, but before I can panic, Doctor Death winks.

"Always wanted to get you in submission, Sia. I am a submission specialist, after all."

Indignation replaces fear, and I huff as he releases me and explains the move to the class. While I recover, he pulls up another victim…er, volunteer and demonstrates a dominant position, which I boil down to "man on top."

Next it's time for us to practice our mounts. I try to get my mind out of the gutter when Doctor Death says he wants to mount some volunteers. I manage to avoid him by pairing up with one of the "Fit" girls for the full mount and half mount, but when it's time for the rear mount, Doctor Death calls my name.

Moments later, I find myself prone on the mat with Doctor Death sitting astride me horsey style. He tells the class the name of the game is control. The rear mount is one of the most dominant and controlling positions because it leaves the person on the bottom in a very vulnerable position. I don't feel vulnerable, just tired after too much physical activity. And since I'm lying cozy on the mat, I consider having a little nap until Doctor Death yanks me up to all fours and kneels behind me with his hands on my hips.

Still not feeling vulnerable, but hoping that whatever Doctor Death is now grinding into my ass starts with the letter *C* and ends with the letters *UP*, I look over my shoulder and glare. "What's this called?"

He gives me another wink. "Having fun."

"Don't have too much fun, or you'll be getting a nasty surprise on *your* ass the next time you come in to the tattoo parlor."

Doctor Death laughs. "Sia. I'm shocked. I never thought you had it in you."

"I'm discovering I have a lot more inside me than I ever knew."

"From this position, I can demonstrate a rear naked choke." Doctor Death leans over my back and slides his arm around my neck, pulling me up to my knees until my throat rests in the crook of his elbow. My body tenses. I've watched enough fights to recognize this powerful and super-difficult-to-escape submission, and I'm pretty damn sure being held immobile with my air cut off is going to set off my triggers.

And yes, when Doctor Death pulls me back so I'm lying flat on top of him, my ass pressed against his "cup" and my windpipe tight in the crook of his elbow, I hear the familiar roar of blood in my ears, much like the roar of the crowd when the Predator had the Meat Grinder in this same hold. Everyone thought it was all over for the Meat Grinder, until he went Tasmanian Devil, wiggling, squirming, shrimping, and bridging until the Predator was forced to release his hold. Of course, the Predator still took him down, but I can be a devil too.

Taking a deep breath, I fight back the panic, and thrash and wiggle against Doctor Death like my life depended on it. I use every move I've seen in the fights, struggling the way I wish I had struggled with Luke. That night I froze, unable to process how someone I trusted implicitly could betray me so profoundly. This time, exhilarated by the fact I've fought back the fear, I fight. Moments later I am free and crouched in a defensive position on the mat.

Doctor Death pushes himself to his side and quirks an eyebrow. "And that would be a way to escape a rear naked choke if one were in the ring, although it was entirely unnecessary during a class demo."

"Saved you from losing a coupla limbs."

I look over my shoulder and my stomach does a back flip. Ray is leaning against the wall, arms folded, one leg crossed over the other, as if he's been there for quite some time. He's wearing his purple fight shorts and a gray T-shirt stretched tight over his deliciously hard body. But when he catches my gaze, I look away. I want to see him, but I don't. Last night was enough heartache to last a lifetime.

"Come." Ray holds out his hand to me, and I shake my head.

"I'm in the middle of a class. I'm learning how to fight." Then I lift an eyebrow. "Might be useful if I found myself in a dangerous situation."

He swallows hard. "You want to fight, I'll teach you."

Hands clenched, I push myself to my feet and close the distance between us so the rest of the class doesn't get an unexpected show. "I thought we were done," I say, keeping my voice low. "You said you were a danger to me. You said you couldn't go through losing someone again. Then you just dropped me off at home and didn't answer my texts."

"Man finds himself in a situation where his heart is trying to rule his head, he needs to take a step back. Get some focus."

My bottom lip quivers. "Well, while you were getting focused, I was thinking we were over. So I'm moving on. I don't want to play this game where you keep secrets and pull away, then show up again and think everything will be okay. I need trust, Ray. More than anything else."

He scrapes a hand through his hair and exhales, his forehead creasing as if he's in pain. "Last night, I drove around and thought of ways I could keep you safe, starting with finishing the job I'm doing and not taking on anymore. As of this morning, that's in the works. And I got you this." He puts his hand in his pocket and pulls out a necklace, dark-colored amber teardrop on a silver chain.

"You got me a present?"

"Didn't make it, but I thought it matched your eyes."

My chest tightens with emotion as I take the necklace. "It's beautiful. I won't take it off."

"That's the idea." He gestures for me to turn and then clasps the necklace around my neck. The teardrop sits lightly on my skin. I look up and catch Tag watching us. He winks and I bite back a smile.

"Does this mean you're going to tell me what's going on?" I say, turning to face him.

He shakes his head. "Better if you don't know."

"It has nothing to do with your PI business, does it?"

A pained expression crosses his face. "Sia…"

"What if I guess?"

"I'll have to lie to you. I don't want to do that."

With a glance back toward the class, I sigh. "Thank you for the necklace. I've gotta get back to Tag. Maybe we can talk later."

Ray cups the back of my neck and pulls me closer. "Fuzz is just gonna make you jump up and down for another half hour. You want to learn to protect yourself, I'll show you how."

"I don't think—"

"Please."

My Predator said "please." "Okay."

He walks me over to a secluded corner of the gym, stopping along the way to tell Tag he's taking over my training today. Tag shoots me a questioning glance and I shrug. It's only half an hour. What could possibly go wrong?

Ray runs through some grappling basics, and I surprise us both with the amount of info I've picked up just watching the fights. Yes, I know about armbars and kimuras, foot bars, triangle chokes, and guillotines. Not that I have the technique down, but I know a gogoplata when I see one.

Amused by my interest in the more complicated holds, Ray grabs a Submission Master from the rack and makes me lie on my back, positioning the grappling dummy on top of me.

Weighing in at eighty pounds, the black nylon–coated dummy is anatomically correct but lacks the humanlike appearance of the less sinister Grapple Man. However, eighty pounds is no small amount of weight, and by the time Ray has finished bending the Submission Master's limbs into position, I can barely breathe.

"I submit. I submit."

Ray laughs and locks the dummy's arms so it bears some of its own weight. "I'm trying to teach you something. Don't distract me."

"And I'm not supposed to be distracted with the Submission Master lying on top of me?"

Crouched down beside me, Ray gives the dummy a considered glance. "Hmmm. Now that you mention it, I don't like the way he's lookin' at you." Ray lifts the dummy and tosses him to the side as if he weighed eight pounds, not eighty, then he lies on top of me, taking the dummy's place, his weight on his elbows, his legs between my thighs.

My body responds in an instant, heating from zero to boiling point in a heartbeat, and I melt beneath the intensity of his gaze.

"We've never done this before." I soak in his warmth, the weight of his body, the safety of his arms.

Ray frowns. "Grappling?"

"No, silly. We've never made…" Love. But I can't say it if I don't feel it. And I can't feel it if I don't trust him. So I try again. "We never had sex lying down. Like in a bed."

His eyes soften, warm. "Thought you couldn't do beds."

"Thought I couldn't defend against a rear naked choke or handle having someone lying on top of me, but I seem to be doing okay tonight." I bite my lip and take the kind of risk I would never have taken before. "Maybe we should try three for three."

"Anything your heart desires, beautiful girl." He leans down and kisses me, soft and sweet. So gentle. I forget for a moment he is the Predator because all I see is the man.

"Christ. Not again. Every time a guy hooks up with someone in the gym…" Rampage coughs indiscreetly a few feet away, and Ray looks up and scowls.

"Not your party."

"It's never my party." Rampage sighs. "But one day, it's gonna be me on that mat pretending to teach a girl moves so I can catch some quick nookie in the middle of practice."

Ray's scowl deepens. "You here for a reason, or you just haven't been punched enough today?"

"Yeah. I'm here with a message from Torment." Rampage snorts. "He says 'get a room.'"

Chapter 20

I DIDN'T HURT YOU

"Wow."

I don't know what I expected Ray's apartment to look like, but it certainly wasn't this eclectic feng shui–inspired loft conversion with its dark, polished hardwood floors, exposed beams, and matching support pillars along the center of an open-plan living space. Ornately carved doors line one wall, and a small bathroom is inset in the exposed brick beneath the white-painted piping. A crown-shaped teardrop chandelier hangs over a long, wooden dining table surrounded by a patchwork of quilted chairs, and a bright purple rug brightens up the living area, dominated by an enormous, overstuffed, velvet-covered couch.

"Friend of mine is a designer. I told her what I wanted, gave her a coupla things I collected when I was abroad, and we worked it out together."

"Well, it's incredible." So incredible I hope she lives far, far away. "If I lived here, I would never leave."

A smile ghosts his lips and he heads for the kitchen. "That means a lot coming from an artist."

"Doesn't take an artist to appreciate beauty." I take a seat on the zebra-fabric covered chair at the kitchen island and Ray pulls out a bottle of vodka.

"Saw you drinking this at the fight."

I hold up my hands in a warding gesture. "Ray...me and vodka... it's not a good relationship. It's like me and potato chips. I can't stop with just one."

"Don't worry. I'll stop you before you pass out. No fun drinking alone." He pours two shots and hands one to me. Our fingers touch and a zing of anticipation shoots straight to my core. We're going to have sex on his bed, and although for most people it is hardly a noteworthy event, it is such a big step for me that I feel like I did my very first time—except I won't have to worry about Tag interrupting and chasing my man away with Dad's gun.

"So this is where you bring women to seduce them." I sip my drink and wander through the dining area, trailing my fingers over the smooth wooden table. "Ply them with alcohol and then what?"

He studies me, his gaze focused, intent. "Never brought a woman here. Take off your shirt."

"Why?"

A slow, sensual smile spreads across his face. "I wanna pour vodka all over you and lick it off."

I stare at him for a moment as my brain tries to sort that one into a "known sexual practices" box. Failing miserably, it shoots out a "strip" command and I whip my T-shirt over my head. "I thought we were going to do, you know, something else that involved a certain item of furniture."

"Can't do something else with your clothes on."

Cool air brushes over my skin, tightening my nipples, and I head over to the shelves inset in the brick wall, ostensibly to check them out, but really to put some space between us and calm my thudding heart. "Well…good to know you aren't wasting time with social pleasantries. See a girl you like, invite her home, then tell her to take off her clothes so you can get down to business. Very romantic."

"Not big on romance when I finally got you where I want you. Take off your bra." He takes a few steps toward me, and I retreat to the far end of the room. A warning niggle at the back of my mind suggests he's doing what predators do, forcing me to retreat until I am trapped with no hope of escape.

Heart thudding against my ribs, I slip off my bra. My nipples peak under his heated gaze, and I scramble for a neutral topic of conversation when he takes another step toward me.

"Lots of interesting furniture here. Where's it from?"

"China and Thailand, mostly." He puts down his glass and strips off his shirt, baring his chest for my viewing pleasure. "Took a leave of absence after Lisa died and did some traveling. Lived with some monks in Thailand and learned about balance and harmony, finding peace when the world is fucked up and you're messed up inside. Take off your skirt."

"Do you have a better seduction technique when you're not in your apartment?" I feign an exasperated sigh as I remove the offending article of clothing. "Something more subtle than 'take off your shirt' or 'take off your skirt'?"

"Not for you, 'cause all I can think about is getting you naked. Take off your panties."

Ray is standing on the threshold of the living room, blocking my only exit unless I want to crash through the glass doors I am now pressed up against and hurl myself off the patio. For a brief moment, I wonder if he wants to have sex against the glass, where everyone can see. Too bad I took off the skirt. Smushed ass is so not a good look.

"I see someone has no restraint." My lips twitch, and I try to douse my inner fire with the combination of vodka and the cool glass door behind me. But it doesn't work. Need burns through my veins. Tension electrifies the air between us.

"Oh, I got restraint." He leans against one of the wooden support pillars, his gaze locked on me as I shimmy out of my panties. "I'm just choosing not to exercise it right now."

"What happened to the whole peace and harmony thing?"

"I never said I was good at it."

His deadpan statement makes me laugh and my tension eases. "Can I have more vodka?" I brave the distance between us, stopping when I am near enough to feel his heat.

Ray looks down at his empty glass and makes a move as if to head back to the kitchen, but before he can go, I place my hands on his shoulders and rock up to lick his lips. "Like this."

My touch sets him off—the Predator unleashed. Heedless of the shot glass falling to the ground, he cups my face between his hands and kisses me so hard, so long, so deep that I fear he has forgotten I need to breathe.

"Bed?"

Releasing me, he smooths his hands down my back to cup my ass. "Gotta get you ready first."

My lower half tightens. "Naked isn't enough?"

His breath is warm and moist in my ear as he follows my curves up my body, his thumbs brushing the underside of my breasts. "Not even close."

"The necklace?" I touch the amber pendant, now hanging between my breasts. "Should I take it off too?"

"Never." He positions me at the edge of his beautiful, polished wood table facing into the room and eases me back until I am lying on the cool surface. The chandelier swings lazily overhead, the crystals tinkling with the slight tremors of the building. I cringe at the thought of marring the perfect surface of the table with my naked body, but when Ray presses up against me, the ridge of his erection beneath his jeans rough on my folds, I imagine other terrible things that could be done on the surface of the table, and my mouth waters.

"Knees bent. Legs apart. Feet at the edge of the table." He stands in front of me, watching, as I follow his commands.

"Like this?"

He nods his satisfaction and eases himself between my legs. "Rules. First, that thing where your heart tries to beat out of your fucking chest and you can't breathe—"

"Panic attack."

Ray's eyes narrow. "Not happening again."

My lips quiver with repressed amusement. "I'll let my sympathetic nervous system know."

"Your heart starts pumping from anything other than the fact that you're hot for me and wanting to come, you tell me right away."

"Okay."

He leans over me, placing one hand on either side of my shoulders, the bulge in his jeans a deliciously stimulating rub against my sex. "I find out you didn't tell me right away, then I'll throw you over my knee and spank the fucking daylight out of you."

"Are you trying to turn me on?"

He slicks his finger through my folds, then holds it up for me to see it glisten. "Looks like I already did."

"Beast."

Ray grins. "Predator."

He leaves me on the table and returns with a long, soft rope which he strings across the table and ties to the table legs behind me.

"Hands over your head. Spread 'em wide. Hold the rope."

"Um…Ray…rope?"

His face softens. "Go with me on this. You're not restrained, just holding on. You feel panicked, you let go. Any other reason—"

"And you'll spank the daylight out of me?"

A slow, sensual smile spreads across his lips, and he leans down and presses his lips to my ear. "She gets it. I can hardly wait."

He leaves me again, displayed on his table like a Christmas feast. When he returns, he has a bottle of Polar Ice vodka in one hand and a bowl of ice cubes in the other. It takes only a moment for my lust-sodden brain to clue in and a shiver runs down my spine. "You're not…"

"Brace yourself. This is gonna be cold." He plucks an ice cube from the bowl and places it in the hollow at the base of my throat. Almost immediately, little water drops trickle down the sides of my neck, a cool, erotic tickle that makes me shudder. Ray leans down to lick away the droplets, then sucks so hard on the sensitive skin between my neck and shoulder that I gasp.

"Marked you." He gives a satisfied growl and licks the wound. Predator indeed.

Leaving the ice trickling over my throat, he takes a second ice cube and runs it down my body, circling each of my breasts and then my nipples until they peak from the erotic slide of ice on my skin.

"Like you all wet and sexy." Ray settles the ice cube in my belly button. Ice water trickles down my sides, sending me arching off the table.

"Down, beautiful girl. Need you to stay still. That is just the warm-up." He places a warm hand over my hips and presses me back against the table.

"What do you mean, a warm-up?"

He takes a third ice cube from the bowl and rests it just above my pubic bone.

"Ray...I don't think..."

"Shhhh. Let it happen." When the first droplet slides its way over my mound, he follows it down, over my clit, and along my folds. Then he parts me wide and pushes the ice cube deep inside my pussy.

"Ahhhhh." I arch off the table, terrified about getting freezer burn in my most intimate area, but the ice feels naughty and slippery inside me, sliding over my swollen tissue, and almost immediately water trickles along my inner thigh. "My hotness is too much for the ice cube." I give him a smug smile.

Ray laughs and plucks another ice cube from the bowl. "Well then, we'd better try two." He pushes another ice cube inside me and quickly follows it with a third. I gasp at dual sensations of being hot and cold, the obscene thickness inside me, the sensation that is at once pleasure and pain. Writhing on the table, I beg him to take them out. Ray lifts an admonishing eyebrow.

"They stay in until they melt. You let one go, and I replace it with three." He teases my piercing with his finger and I whimper.

"Breathe through it."

Tangling my hands in the rope above me, I take deep breaths as my sex throbs, whether from heat or cold, I no longer know. But when he kneels between my parted legs, spreading my thighs impossibly wide to lick his way up and around my clit, warmth spreads through my body and the burn of the ice cubes begins to fade.

"Better?"

When I nod, he stands and fills a shot glass with Polar Ice and then tips it over my breast.

"Ahhhhhhh!" A stream of freezing cold vodka splashes over my nipple, hardening it instantly. Ray bends down and draws my nipple into his mouth, warming it with his tongue. The combination of cold and heat sends my arousal skyrocketing, and I moan.

"It's gonna get a lot worse than that." Ray tips the glass over my other nipple and I brace myself between the rope and the table. "I've only just begun."

He teases me for what seems like hours. No part of my body is safe from the trickle of freezing cold vodka and the rasp of his warm tongue. He laps the cold liquid from the pulse point at the base of my throat, licks his way down my sternum, laves every part of my breasts, and then fills the glass up again when he reaches my stomach.

"You're gonna be so drunk, you won't be able to perform."

He raises an eyebrow as he drizzles cold vodka over my stomach, the cool liquid sending shivers through my body as it trickles down my sides. "I ever let you down?"

"Well…no."

"'Course not." He thrusts his finger into my sex and water from the melted ice cubes dribbles over my skin. "So wet. And I'm about to make you wetter."

"I don't think that's possible." I look up at his handsome face, his eyes hooded, gleaming with the promise of a challenge.

"Oh, it is." He drips the vodka over my clit, one freezing drop after another and my panting turns to moaning as my nerves try to decide whether the burning sensation spreading through my lower half is pleasure or pain.

"Don't move."

He strips off his clothes, then removes the gun and holster strapped to his leg and places them on the kitchen counter.

"Did I ever tell you I think it's hot that you carry a gun?"

Ray frowns. "Guns aren't hot. They are dangerous weapons. Not to be taken lightly."

"Hot," I whisper.

He laughs and drizzles vodka over my folds. "Well then, let's cool you off."

While I wiggle and squirm on the table, Ray disappears behind me, returning moments later, sheathed and fully erect, a tantalizing treat just out of reach.

"One last lick." He bends down and licks his way along my slit, lapping up the vodka until he gets to my piercing. "This is the hottest fucking thing I've ever seen." He waggles the little barbell with his tongue, and I groan and tug on the rope.

"But I like this better." He draws my clit into his mouth, sending me into sensory overload. Cold. Hot. Wet. Warm. Sucking. Nipping. I hold on to the rope for dear life as tension coils deep in my belly.

With one last lick, Ray backs away and places his hands on my knees, spreading me wide. "Open for me, sweetheart. Show me how wet you are, how much you want me."

Straining, I part my legs as far as they will go, clenching my belly at the feeling of being so totally exposed.

"Fucking beautiful." He rubs his cock against my cleft. "Love seeing you restrained and open for me."

"I'm not restrained. I'm just holding on." But when I look up, my hands are impossibly tangled in the rope. My breath catches in my throat. He left all that slack for a reason. But before I can panic, Ray thrusts, pushing deep inside me.

"You've restrained yourself, beautiful girl. You're in control."

But I don't have time to dwell. Ray glides his hands down my body, tweaking my nipples, then sweeping his palms in and out of my curves and over my abdomen. With a low groan, he cups my ass with his two hands and yanks me against him. "I'm gonna take you every way. Everything you ever imagined or secretly desired, I'm gonna give you. And then I'll do things you never imagined. I'm gonna be everywhere inside you, so deep you won't know where I end and you begin."

"Soon?" I rock my hips against him and he growls.

"Now."

And then he thrusts so fast and hard, my back arches and my head hits the table. If I weren't so wet, so needy, so utterly consumed by the desperate need to come, I might have been frightened by his intensity, the rough movements that border on pain. But fear beats a hasty retreat before the rush of desire pumping through my veins and the sheer and utter thrill of being taken by the Predator.

"Tell me what you want." He drags me down until my backside is partly off the table and then he brushes my clit with his fingers.

"I want you to take me," I say, panting. "Fuck and don't hold back."

The sound that erupts from his throat is part groan, part growl and all approval. Then he drives deep as he curls one arm around my right thigh, and lifts my leg, spreading me so wide that his every thrust slams against my piercing, sending pulse after pulse of pleasure through my clit.

"Ray…" I want to ask him if he needs me to let go and hurt him, but desire steals my breath away and I want to know—does he really need it?

Faster. Harder. He drives me to my peak with dizzying speed until the pulses in my clit become one long burn and I am gone. Shattered. Screaming Ray's name as I climax around his throbbing cock.

Vaguely I am aware Ray has withdrawn and instead of the delicious hardness of his cock filling me, he has curled two fingers inside my sex and is stroking them against my G-spot.

"Again, beautiful girl."

"No. I can't." I writhe, trying to escape the incessant press of his fingers as a different pressure builds inside me, low in my womb, deep, uncontrollable.

"Shhhh. Don't fight it." With his free hand, he spreads my moisture up and around my clit. The dual sensations, coming so fast after my climax and before I have fully come down, make my body tingle. The pressure builds until I'm shaking, grateful for the solid table beneath me.

"I love to watch you come," he whispers. His muscles ripple as he moves, abs tightening as he leans close. But it is the intensity on his face as he glides his fingers inside me, the softness in his eyes as he smooths his hand over my skin, and the powerful thrust of his hips as he leans close and rubs his cock over my throbbing nub that send me over the edge. Again.

Moisture gushes from my sex, trickling down my cleft, and my lower body convulses in a slow rolling, powerful orgasm, different from anything I've experienced before. I am swept away in a rush of pure sensation so exquisite I don't want to move.

"Tempted to keep working your G-spot," Ray says, his voice a soft growl. "But I don't think I can last with you so wet."

"Now your turn."

"Now bed." He untangles the ropes, then lifts me easily off the table and carries me to his bedroom, yet another feast of sensual delight in a large alcove, hidden behind thick, gray plush curtains. As he climbs up beside me, I take in the dark-blue Thai print wallpaper, the twinkly overhead recessed lights, and the enormous soft bed covered in a cool, navy silk duvet.

"Gonna love you now, beautiful girl," he whispers as he kneels between my legs. "Gonna love you until you don't ever want to let go."

And before I feel even a flicker of anxiety, he thrusts into me, his cock a painful pleasure as it glides through my sensitive inner walls. "You are mine, Sia." He withdraws and drives in again, deeper this time, ripping a groan from my throat. "I want to look after you. Love you. Protect you. Everything I have, everything I am, I want to give you. I wanna be there when you wake. I wanna be holding you when you fall asleep, and I want to be inside you every minute of every day whether I'm in your head or in your heart or in your very sweet pussy."

His words sink into me, cover me, warm me. Dazed with pleasure, on the brink of release, I reach up and wrap my arms around his neck pulling him down for a kiss. This time there is no teasing, no violence, no heat. His kiss is soft and sweet, his fingers stroking my face in an almost reverent gesture.

"Sia." My name is a murmur on his lips, a whispered prayer.

When he moves again, he gentles his stroke, holding me on the brink, giving me enough to keep me on edge but not enough to tip me over. Bracing himself with one hand, he sweeps the other down my body, then up again to caress my breast.

"I can make you feel good without this." He flicks the piercing in my nipple. "Or this." He reaches down to my hood and tugs on the little barbell. "You don't need them. I can give you back what he took from you. Reclaim yourself through me."

I answer with a kiss, sweeping my tongue through his mouth, tasting him as he drops his weight and we sink deeper into the bed.

"You okay?" He covers my body with kisses and caresses, firing my nerves with sensation and my heart not with fear but with warmth.

"Love me," I whisper, as he tortures me with yet another slow slide of his deliciously thick, hard cock. "And do it fast."

One last gentle kiss, one promising quirk of the lips, and then he grips my hips and pounds into me, so hard, so deep, so fast that my orgasm crashes through me in a tidal wave of pleasure, washing away the last of my fears as it ripples out to my fingers and toes. Ray stiffens, hammers deep, and climaxes, his fingers digging grooves into my skin as his cock pulses inside me.

"My beautiful girl," he whispers as he collapses on top of me, his hard body over my soft curves, his sun-darkened skin a contrast to my paler complexion. But we fit together—our bodies mold together in an eclectic contrast worthy of this room.

"You did it," he says softly.

"So did you. I didn't hurt you."

My eyelids grow heavy and sleep falls over me, a thick, black, warm curtain scented of Ray and me and sex, and surrounded by the deep rumble of his voice.

The only thing spoiling this perfect moment is his whisper just before I drift off.

"But you did hurt me."

Chapter 21
CUT ME

THE NEXT MORNING, DOCTOR Death comes in for his ass addition. I tell him I don't want to have to worry about Ray ripping off his balls, so Duncan has agreed to take over. Doctor Death is not pleased. He says he prefers my soft hands. Duncan offers to rub some lotion on his skin. I crack up, but no one seems to get the joke. Maybe they don't like psychological thrillers like me.

Yuri stops by for another tattoo. He is wearing a black humming-bird tie over a white shirt and baggy black pants. Rose regretfully informs him that we're booked solid for today. She suggests he make an appointment, which is what most people do. For the first time, Yuri loses his cool. He thumbs his nose, showing off the heavy, gold bling on his fingers, then removes his dark sports shades and glares. Spending a lot of time around fighters has made me proficient at interpreting nonverbal aggressive communication. I quickly join Rose at her desk and tell Yuri I have an hour free, and if he doesn't need a complicated piece, I will be happy to help.

Mollified, Yuri settles himself in my chair. He wants a small pink rose tatted on his bicep above the most evil-looking skull tat I have ever seen. While I prepare and ink his arm, he peppers me with personal questions about where I live, places I hang out, friends, boyfriends, and days I have off, all of which I struggle to avoid answering. He is unfailingly polite, never pushes when I am evasive with my answers, and doesn't flirt in any obvious way. My mind says there is no reason to mistrust him, and yet instinct has other ideas, making my skin prickle and my pulse pound until the tattoo is finally done.

Slim arrives just as Yuri is leaving. He grumbles about the renos at the old shop. He wants everything to look the same as it was before and has been sourcing used chairs and equipment to replace the furniture that was damaged. He wants character, not shiny new. As he talks, I look around the shop. Although we haven't been here long, it feels like home to me. Not just because it's the kind of shop I had always imagined working in, but because of the fighters who have become my friends and how safe I feel when I walk in the door.

"At least Torment scared away that damned idiot who was going to defile the shop with his car race mural." Slim gestures to the blank wall and snorts a laugh. "Hopefully we'll be outta here before Torment finds someone to replace him."

"What would you put on that wall?" Christos comes up behind me and rests a hand on my shoulder.

"Paintings," I say softly, so Slim doesn't overhear. "I'd show local artists. Change them out every week." Maybe even start with my own work. A thrill of excitement slides down my spine at the thought of painting canvases big enough to fill the space.

"I heard Torment offered you the shop."

"Yeah. I turned him down. I don't think I have what it takes to run the place."

"But you've taken a business management course," he says. "You do great work. The fighters who come here all ask for you."

Turning, I frown. "Christos…"

"I'm not trying to get rid of you," he says. "The place wouldn't be the same without you. But how can you pass up this opportunity?"

"I don't always make the best choices. What if I fail?"

"Then you come back to Rabid Ink." He puts his arm around my shoulders and gives me a squeeze. "You'll always have a place with us, Sia. Hell, I'll drag in an extra chair myself if Slim fills yours."

"To be honest, I've been thinking about it—"

"I hope so," he says. "You're a great artist, and you'll be a great manager. Everyone in the shop sees it. You just need to believe in yourself."

Believe in myself the way Jess believes in me, and Tag and Ray. I've watched Slim for years. Maybe I should take that step. Maybe I should stay.

Hands shaking, I text Jess to tell her I'm going to do it. I'm going to talk to Torment when he comes in tonight and take him up on his offer to run the shop. And then I'll talk to Slim. Of course, she's ecstatic. She says she always knew I could do it, but it's been a long wait.

After work, I show up for Tag's Grapple and Groan class, but Tag isn't there. Rampage is subbing for him and tells me Tag never showed up. The skin on the back of my neck prickles. Tag is nothing but punctual and reliable, and if he didn't even bother to call to say he wasn't coming, something is seriously wrong. I call his home, his cell, my parents, the station, and his detective partner, Lou. No one has seen Tag. Rampage suggests I call Ray. He is a PI after all. So I call Ray. He says Tag is with him. They can't talk right now, but everything is okay.

By the time I return to the class, everyone is partnered up except me. Rampage explains that no one wants Ray to tear off their limbs, so I have to use a grapple dummy. He gives me the lifelike Grapple Man who looks like Doctor Death but with his eyes closed and lacking a little something between the legs. I like Grapple Man. He is totally without pretense. Right from the start, he makes it clear he likes to bury his face between my breasts, and he does this until Rampage comes over and straightens his arms. After that, Grapple Man kisses me instead.

While I'm stretching after the class, Tag and Ray arrive. Tag goes straight to Torment's office and closes the door. Ray stops me before I leave the mats to chase after him. In full view of everyone in the gym, he wraps his arms around me and holds me tight as if something terrible has happened and he doesn't want to let me go.

Full contact. This is how Ray speaks when his emotions overwhelm him. I melt into his stillness. His body is hot and hard, his breath warm on my neck. He smells of leather and sweat. He smells of sex and sin. And another scent, sharp and tangy... Blood? Memories of being sweaty and panting on his table hit me in a rush. All the pent-up emotion I've been harboring all day tightens my chest, and after giving him his moment, I try to push away.

"What the hell is going on?"

Ray tightens his grip. "Something came up. I needed Tag's help."

"Great. Another cryptic explanation. You sure know how to win a girl's trust." I push harder, but it's clear there's no way he's letting me go. So I put my lessons to good use. I use my new grapple techniques to break his hold. When he loosens his grip, I twist and whirl away.

For a moment I think it was that easy. My illusions are quickly dispelled when I find myself on my back on the mat with Ray on top of me, pinning me with the weight of his body, his forearms on either side of my head.

"What just happened?" Dazed, I stare into his eyes, now a deep azure blue.

"Leg sweep. Carried you down. Now I got you in submission."

"This girl isn't submitting to anything, especially not with someone who steals my brother away and doesn't tell me what's going on."

A pained expression crosses his face. "I promised Tag I wouldn't say anything. We just want to protect you."

My chest heaves as I try to contain my emotions. "I'm tired of being cosseted and protected. I'm tired of everyone thinking I'm going to break. I know now it's partly my fault. I liked that Dad and Tag looked out for me, but it meant I wasn't looking out for myself. So when I did step out of line with the biker and with Luke, I wasn't prepared for what could happen. And after that, it was easier to go back to the way things were. I let Tag protect me, and when you made me feel safe, I let you protect me too. But I don't want to be like that anymore. The price is too high. If it concerns me, I want to be respected enough, thought strong enough, to be involved."

"Gotta talk to Tag first."

Not what I want to hear. I press my arms against his chest, motioning him away with my chin. Ray pushes himself to sitting, straddling my hips.

"No. I want to hear it from you," I say. "Tag would never ever forget to call in if he couldn't make it to work, and given our relationship, that means he'll never tell me."

"I gave my word." He frowns and touches my neck. "Where's your necklace?"

"I took it off to work out. I didn't want it bouncing around and getting lost."

His brow creases. "Promise me you won't take it off again."

"Ray...that's nice in theory, but sometimes it just isn't practical."

"Promise."

With a huff, I thud my fists against his rock-hard stomach. "Okay. I promise. Now get off me."

Ray grabs my wrists and pins them to the mat over my head, his body angled over me. My breath catches in my throat, and I steel myself for the memories, the black rush, the heart-pounding fear, but it doesn't come. Instead, a red haze settles over my vision, and I press my lips together and buck my hips, throwing him slightly forward.

Bad plan. Now his groin is only inches away from my face. He's still wearing his jeans, which means that bulge isn't a cup.

"Ray..."

His face softens. "I hurt you."

"Yes, you hurt me. Keeping secrets hurts me. It makes me feel like you don't respect me. And it makes me feel like I can't trust you. So maybe you could return to your proper seat now. Tray table up."

He shifts down, settling his weight over my hips, but he doesn't release my hands. "I hurt you. Means you care."

I swallow hard and meet his gaze. "You hurting me means I was being stupid. Things were going where I didn't want them to go. Now I've had a wake-up call. You have secrets you can't share. You need to protect your secrets. I need to be with someone I can trust, and I need to stand on my own two feet. It's just not going to work between us."

His gaze darkens, searing me to the core. "You want to be done? Or are you scared and trying to push me away?"

The air shifts between us, electrifying, tightening my nipples and heating my blood. I am hyperaware of his thighs tucked against my hips, carrying most of his weight as he sits astride me in a dominant MMA position. My wrists, hot under his palms, press against the cool mat, restrained in a way I could never have imagined allowing them to be restrained. My chest rises and falls twice for every one of Ray's breaths, and my core tightens. The innuendo isn't lost on me. God, yes. I want to be done in the carnal sense of the word. But only by Ray. And I don't really want to let him go.

"I don't want to lose you."

Ray's hands tighten on my wrists, and he leans down and brushes a kiss over my lips. "I don't want to lose you either, but I live in a dangerous world. I've got stuff in my life that would make your head spin. I need to protect you from that, and I'll do what it takes to keep you safe, even if it means you hate me for it, because for the first time in my life, I want something more than doing my duty. I want a life and I want you in it. I've got one bad guy to catch and then I'm free. And after I'm done and after what went down this evening, you'll never have to worry about being safe again."

Finally, he releases my hands but I don't move. Heat sweeps through my belly. I feel both vulnerable and curiously safe lying beneath him. My gaze shifts from his intense gaze to his sensual lips, and my breasts swell, remembering the touch of his hands, the gentle press of his lips. He wants me. Not just today, but tomorrow and the tomorrow after that.

"You make it sound like I don't have a choice about being with you."

"You don't." He leans down and kisses me with a savage fierceness that takes my breath away.

"I suppose that's a good thing since I have a history of making bad choices, and if I chose to believe you, it would probably be a bad idea."

Ray stands, then holds out a hand to help me to my feet. "You think coming with me now would be a bad decision?" He pulls me up and into his body in one smooth fighter move.

Behind us, exercise machines whirr and weights clang. Rampage barks orders like a drill sergeant and someone laughs. But Ray's gaze is focused entirely on me, and now his hard, masculine body is pressed up against me, and all I can think about is how much better it would feel if we weren't wearing clothes.

"Yes."

"I'll prove you wrong." He cups my jaw in his broad palm, stroking his thumb over the apple of my cheek. "I can show you things, Sia. Things that will take your breath away. Things that will make you so hot and wet you won't remember your name. Any dream, any kink, any fantasy, anything you want to try, I'll make it happen and I'll keep you safe."

"It's not about sex. It's about my heart."

"I'll look after that too."

Butterflies flutter in my stomach at the heated interest in his eyes, and I draw in a ragged breath. "Any fantasy?"

Footsteps thud on the mat nearby. I catch sight of Tag walking toward us out of the corner of my eye, but he's not close enough for me to see his face. And I am distracted by the beautiful fighter in front of me who is sliding his hand under my hair to curl around my neck.

He pulls me close. "Anything. What do you want?"

"I want to know what happened tonight."

"I found Luke."

—⁓—

The thunderstorm rolls in just as we leave Redemption.

I haven't been able to speak since I sat with Tag and Ray in the café and heard how Ray had managed to track Luke down using only the details I'd given him and the name that had slipped off my tongue. Of course he went to Tag to verify his information. And somewhere along the way, they had decided justice should be done and they would do it together, with Tag disguised and on lookout because of the risk to his job and Ray throwing all the punches. Justice was done, and they were pretty sure he was still alive.

Pretty sure.

Ray wraps his leather jacket around me, but after fifteen minutes on his bike, we're both soaked through, and with no sign of the rain letting up, he pulls off the main road and into an alley behind a fancy hotel. After parking his bike beside a Dumpster, he leads me to the protected alcove of the emergency exit. A mouse scurries away from a pile of old clothing in the corner, and the scent of stale piss and alcohol makes my nose wrinkle.

Ray places our helmets in a dry corner and then pulls a bandanna from his jacket pocket to wipe my face. Pat. Pat. Pat. His touch is so gentle that I know he is feeling guilty for making me wet. But dammit, he should be feeling guilty for a hell of a lot more.

"I can't believe you did that." My words, when they finally come, slip and slide over each other as they rush off my tongue. "I can't believe you went behind my back and did what I explicitly asked you not to do. This wasn't your fight; it was mine. The decision to let it lie was mine. And Tag…I didn't want him involved anymore either. He sacrificed enough for me. I destroyed one of his careers, and now it looks like I'll destroy another."

Ray steps back, stunned. "I thought you'd be happy."

"Happy?" My voice rises in pitch. "Happy for him to know I'm still around, and that there's still a possibility I might report it to the police? Did anyone ever tell you an animal is more dangerous when it's wounded? Now he'll come looking for me. What if he recognizes Tag? You don't know his family—the power they have, the things they said they would do."

"I know all about them. I don't go into things half-assed, Sia. I've covered our tracks, and you don't have to be scared. If they ever threaten you or your family, I have the resources to make sure those threats never come to fruition."

"I thought you were giving it up, whatever it is that you think puts you above the law and gives you access to information and powers other people don't have."

He flinches as if I hit him, and I wonder if he's really thought through what he intends to give up for me.

"But that's not even the biggest issue," I say, my voice shaking with emotion. "The issue is trust. I trusted you to respect my decisions. I trusted you to respect my wishes. I trusted you to let me live my life the way I wanted to live it. This is exactly what happened with the mural in the tattoo studio. I didn't tell you so you could do something about it. I just wanted you to know."

"But you're not living your life the way you want to live it." Ray scrubs a hand through his hair. "You're hiding behind the tats and the leather and the piercings. But I see you, Sia. I see the softness and vulnerability you try to hide. I see your pain and I want to take it away. I see an artist who has stifled her own creativity, and I want to set her free."

"By beating a man half to death?"

His eyes narrow. "I told you I would keep you safe, and there are no limits to what I would do to make that happen."

"What you did is a limit for me. Breaking my trust is a limit for me."

"Don't." His voice breaks and he takes a step toward me.

But I'm on a roll, and my pain and frustration need an outlet. "For the longest time, I just wanted to be normal. I wanted to forget about the past. I wanted to be with a man and have sex the way I always fantasized about and not worry about panic attacks and PTSD. And then I met you, and I realized there is no such thing as normal, that maybe the problem was I had never let anyone get close. And I could have what I wanted as long as I felt safe and protected. I realized what I had really wanted was to be able to trust again—not just someone else, but myself. I trusted you. I gave myself to you. And now I realize it was all a mistake."

He reaches for me and pulls me into his arms. "Please, Sia…"

"I know what you did came from a good place." I try to pull away, but he tightens his grip. "I understand what you were trying to do, but it wasn't what I wanted. I can't deal with this anymore. I can't handle the secrets. I don't want to get hurt more than I already am. You're not the right—"

Ray cuts me off with a kiss, hard, desperate, wanting. "Don't push me away."

"God, Ray," I whisper. "I don't want to. I have to. But I wish I were wrong. I ache for you."

And then, because I want him so much, and it feels so right to be in his arms, and this might be the last time we're together, I kiss him back, trying to let him know what is in my heart that my head won't let me say, while the rain thunders down outside the alcove, washing the alley clean. *Please, rain, wash my pain away.*

Sliding my arms around Ray's waist, I tug him out into the alley and push him against the wall. "I wanted you from the moment I saw you. I never stopped wanting you." I brush my lips over his, sliding my tongue over the seam until he opens them for me. "I want you now more than I ever wanted you before. And I'll never stop wanting you, even when I can't see you again."

"Here?"

"Yes, here." I place his hands on my hips. "Or is it still too dangerous? I thought you had that sorted out."

He looks up and down the alley and shakes his head. "I do."

Frustrated by his unmoving hands, I slide them up farther and place them on my breasts. "No one is going to be out in this rain, much less see us in a dark alley. Please, Ray. I need you. One last time. I want to remember what it feels like to be yours."

He groans and pulls me closer. "I'll take you home first, get you dried off—"

"No. Fuck me here, with the rain beating down on us and the thunder crashing. Fuck me where people might see because you want me as badly as I want you. Make my heart pound. Make me feel alive. Take me, Ray. I'm yours."

He gives no further protest. Instead, he pushes me back against the brick wall and slants his mouth over mine. His kiss is hard, deep, and hungry. Savage. Water streams down our faces, trickling into our clothes, cool and refreshing in the hot, muggy air.

With brusque, efficient movements, he shoves up my bra and T-shirt, then helps me shove my jeans over my hips, tugging them quickly over my feet, so he can toss them into the dry space in the alcove.

"Touch me." He grabs my hand and presses it against his hardened length, where it's straining against his fly. I stroke until he growls, and then I yank on his fly. The zipper parts, and I slip my hand inside and wrap my fingers around him. He is rock hard and hot in my palm, but his skin is silky smooth.

He groans and pulls a pocket knife from his jeans. Then he flicks open the blade and slides it into my free hand. "Cut me."

"I thought...you didn't need that anymore."

"Never like this before, but I need it now, beautiful girl."

Ray's sodden shirt sags under the weight of the rain, and I yank it up and over his chest, and then off, tossing it into the alcove.

"Here." He touches over his heart, the center of the wolf I inked into his skin. Water streams over his tattoo, the beads of water trickling from the wolf's head like tears.

"I can't."

Hands trembling, I reach around his neck to pull him close, skin to skin, cool and warm with only water drops between us, holding the knife away from his body. My nipples harden against his chest and Ray wraps his arms around me and digs his fingers into my ass.

In the distance, cars splash through puddles and someone honks a horn. Faint lights illuminate the alley then disappear. But I am focused only on the rasp of his breath, the warmth of his body against me, and the rigid length of his erection pressed tight against my belly.

"You're so fucking hot." Ray lifts me, bracing my back against the rough, wet bricks as he cups my ass. I wrap my legs around his hips and grind my sex against his shaft.

"Hell." His word is swallowed by the patter of raindrops on the cement and a distant clap of thunder. But I'm not afraid. Naked, wet inside and out, I am truly alive. Heart-pounding, pulse-racing, clit-throbbing life.

"Now, Ray. I need you now."

He groans. "Don't have a condom."

"Me either but I'm on the pill. Are you safe?"

Ray nods. "But if you want to stop—"

"No. Please don't stop."

He must sense this isn't the time for games. With a low groan, he drives his shaft inside me, impaling me, making me his.

Trembling, I cling to him, the knife still in my hand, hopefully forgotten as he thrusts, savoring the feeling of being as close as we can get, the friction of his unsheathed cock sliding against my inner walls.

Raindrops spatter on my mouth and I lick them away, tasting Ray and me and tears on my lips.

When he bends down to take my left nipple in his mouth, my head falls back and I close my eyes. Wanton, uninhibited, and totally unrestrained, I give myself over to the storm and to the man who has made me feel again. "Take me."

Ray releases my breast and grips my hips so hard I know I will have bruises tomorrow. His thrusts are fast, hard, and deep, merciless in their rhythm, making my necklace bounce against my chest. I am drawn to my peak by his passion and the violence simmering beneath his glistening skin.

Lightning flashes. Thunder roars. Rocking my hips, I meet Ray's thrusts until I am mindless, awash in sensation. Free.

He slides a hand between us and presses the pad of his thumb over my clit, releasing me. My body uncoils with such violent intensity that I forget to breathe. Shaking, convulsing, I climax hard. And then he curls his hand over mine, tightening my fingers around the knife, and slides our joined hands to his chest.

"No."

He pounds into me, and then he leans forward and swallows my scream as he cuts himself with our joined hands, piercing the wolf's heart. Moments later, he stiffens and groans, his shaft pulsing as he spills hot and deep within me. And then we hold each other in the rain until our hearts no longer beat as one.

Chapter 22

THIS IS NOT A GAME YOU WANT TO PLAY

Priority: Confidential
Bay Area Underground Fight Club (BUFC) Fight Night
Empty lot. Shipley. 8 p.m.
Headlining: Krakow vs. Raptor
Also on the card: Predator, Rampage, Dark Knight, Anarchist
Code Word: Revolution

"WHO ARE YOU?" JESS sniffs and turns away when I join her in the empty lot on Shipley Street to watch Rampage fight. A makeshift ring has been set up in the grass about ten feet away, marked off by ropes and poles. The lot is far off the beaten path and lookouts have been stationed on either end of the small lane leading up to our illicit fight ground.

"Your BFF." I slide my arm around her waist and she pulls away.

"BFFs don't ignore their BFFs. They respond to texts, answer phones, and don't forget Thursday drinks at Clive's Bar."

My heart skips a beat. "I'm so sorry. I was with Ray."

"Of course you were." Her cold tone makes me cringe. "I guess he's more important than me or helping me decide if I should break up with Blade Saw, since he's decided he wants to get serious."

"How serious?"

"Wouldn't you like to know?" She huffs and steps away. "I waited an hour for you and had to fend off groping hands and bad lines and the worst martini ever poured. Where were you? Why didn't you answer your phone?"

"Ray...and Tag..." I tell her what happened. How they found Luke. Even the part about sex in the rain, and how Ray drove me home and we said good-bye. And how, when I walked into my apartment, I couldn't bear to see the half-finished painting on my table or my sketchbook on the table or even the paintings on the wall. Now my walls are stripped bare. My art supplies are in the closet. And I'm resolved to focus on my tattoo work, find new clients, and stay with the team when Slim gets us back into his shop.

For the first time since I've known her, Jess is speechless. She stares at me aghast for a few moments and then finally finds her tongue.

"I thought you were happy painting again, and that you were going to take Torment up on his offer to run the Redemption shop."

"I can't, Jess. I let Ray get close, I trusted him, and look what happened. I don't make good decisions. I have no clue about managing a shop. I have one business course under my belt and a few years of watching Slim. If I'm really serious about going out on my own, I should take a few more courses and spend some time with him, learning the management side, perfecting my techniques, and getting better at bringing in clients. Plus, what if it's not a success? My parents need my help. This way I know I'm always guaranteed a steady stream of income."

And I don't have to worry about bumping into Ray every day, or seeing him with someone else, or wondering if he's going to walk in the door. But I don't say it, because I'm sure she already knows.

"So you're just giving up?" Her voice rises so high people turn to stare. "One knock and you fall down? That's not the Sia I know. Luke gave you the hit of your life and you bounced back. You remade yourself. You gave *me* the courage to go on."

"I don't want to remake myself again. I can't do it. This Sia is the one I'm comfortable with, so this is who I'm going to be."

"Seriously?" She scrapes a hand through her hair. "I have never seen you happier than when you were with Ray and painting again. And that day you texted me to tell me you were going to take over the shop and put your art on the wall, I almost exploded with happiness. It was like you were breaking free and you'd found a way to be Sia now and Sia then."

"He broke my trust."

"Because he cares," Jess says. "Because he wanted to protect you. He loves you."

My breath catches in my throat. "He doesn't love me. I'm not a lovable type. Too many hang-ups."

Jess shakes her head. "People don't do what he just did because of friendship."

Tears prickle my eyes. "I would do it for you."

"And I would do it for you." Jess's eyes water and she looks away. "But that's because we love each other. Which is entirely my point."

We shuffle to the side as more people join the crowd. Blade Saw waves from the other side of the ring, where he is done prepping Rampage for his fight. Rampage looks over at us and grins before he climbs through the ropes to face his opponent, the Dark Knight, who looks anything but dark with his pale skin and light blond hair. He also looks like a child beside Rampage, who has about five inches and one hundred pounds on him.

The ref signals for the fight to begin and Rampage picks up the Dark Knight and tosses him across the ring. The crowd roars. Jess and I cheer. The Dark Knight staggers to his feet while Rampage smirks. Then the Dark Knight launches a full-on assault, running at Rampage like a battering ram. I brace myself for the inevitable. The inevitable happens with the sickening thud of the Dark Knight against Rampage's chest. Rampage looks down and swats him away. The Dark Knight falls to his knees. We cheer again.

"This is painful to watch." Jess scrunches her nose. "I like there to be some sport involved. What was the Dark Knight thinking, challenging Rampage? He's a middleweight at best. Who's next on the card?"

"I've got the lineup on the invitation email." I paw through my purse, looking for my phone. Damn. Everything is still wet from my little jaunt in the rain. My hand closes over a small plastic disc, and I pull out my pills. Double damn. Not only did I forget to take one last night, but they've also turned into little wet smudges of beige. I find my phone and send myself a reminder to pick up a refill tomorrow. If I go first thing, I'll only have missed two.

After showing her the evening lineup, I tuck my phone away just as Blade Saw saunters over to join us.

Jess frowns. "Aren't you supposed to be watching Rampage's back?"

Blade Saw throws an arm around her shoulder and pecks her lightly on the cheek. "Waste of time. Rampage is just toying with him. When the crowd gets bored, he'll put him out of his misery." He looks over at me and winks. "Heard a rumor you'd hooked up with the Predator. He's fighting next."

"Uh…yeah…it's just casual." I roll my eyes at Jess. Redemption is notoriously bad for gossip, worse even than high school. The last thing I need is for Blade Saw to run around telling everyone I confirmed the rumor, when in fact, we're no longer together.

"That why he told everyone at Redemption to stay away from you this morning?"

My breath catches in my throat. "He didn't."

"Guys at Redemption need to know when someone has staked a claim." Blade Saw peers around the dude in front of him to check out the situation in the ring. Rampage has the Dark Knight on the ground in a painful submission. The Dark Knight struggles and strains for all of three seconds and then taps out. Rampage wins. He fist pumps the crowd as if he actually had to exert himself or use any skill, and receives the concomitant praise.

Jess frowns. "She's not a piece of land."

"She's taken." Blade Saw pulls her into his side. "Just like you."

Jess's eyes widen, and she shoots me a glance. I know what she's thinking. Maybe Tag didn't make his move because of the unspoken rule at Redemption about trespassing on a teammate's territory. But, oh, poor Blade Saw. He is totally enamored with Jess. I don't want to see him get hurt.

Before I can intervene, Ray steps into the ring. His opponent is the Anarchist, an amateur from a rival club in Menlo Park. Physically they appear compatible, although the Anarchist is maybe an inch or two shorter and much broader in the chest. He wears a black mask with eye-holes that makes Jess laugh and Blade Saw groan. Masked competitors get no respect. MMA is about the fight, not theatrics.

Ray takes the center of the ring. His muscles ripple, his six-pack gleaming under the lights as he shakes the Anarchist's hand. He is wearing blue fight shorts with nothing on the sides. I've never seen him wearing anything plain and my heart tightens just a tiny bit.

The second the ref signals the start of the fight, Ray plants his right hand on the Anarchist's jaw and tugs down the mask, covering the Anarchist's eyes. The crowd roars in appreciation. The Anarchist flails, throwing a kick and trying to knee Ray in the stomach, except by the time his knee gets there, Ray's stomach is nowhere to be found. Blind, the Anarchist attempts a takedown, but is easily thwarted by Ray's solid hammer fist.

So much aggression. So much power. I want that power used on me, holding me, restraining me, fucking me. My cheers distract Ray, and his gaze flicks in my direction. The Anarchist manages to straighten his mask and throws another knee to Ray's body and then another. As he hammers his knees home, Ray wails on him with elbows until the Anarchist sinks to his knees and taps out—a win for the Predator and the shortest fight of the evening.

We stay for the rest of the fights, but I am distracted searching for Ray. What if I've made a mistake? What if I shouldn't have pushed him away?

After the last fight, Rampage meets us on the street, and we decide to head over to the Dirty Diva's bar where Christos is playing tonight. I take one last look around the empty parking lot and sigh.

Jess gives my hand a squeeze. "The first few weeks are the hardest."

"I know."

Dirty Divas is hopping when we arrive, and even more hopping when it is swarmed by testosterone-fueled fighters fresh out of the ring. Rampage flexes his biceps and growls at a crowd of college freshmen, then scores us a booth at the back with an awesome view of the stage.

"I thought you said Christos's band wasn't any good." Jess flips her quarter at the collection of shot glasses in the center of the table. She's killer at Quarters and seems determined to get me drunk tonight.

"They weren't. But they got a new keyboardist and vocalist a few months ago, and it's been a major improvement." An understatement if there ever was one. Their first set of hard rock covers blows me away. Maybe I shouldn't have been so reassuring to Slim when I told him Christos would never leave.

The quarter bounces off the edge of one shot glass and then slips inside. "Score." Jess pumps her fist in the air and then points to me. "Drink up."

With a sigh, I take the glass and down the shot, then pull my quarter out of the game. Two is my limit. Any more and I'll be drunk texting Ray and all the boyfriends I've ever had.

The band takes a break and a DJ takes over. He throws on some Lady Gaga and Jess grabs my hand. She can work Lady G like there's no tomorrow. Slightly dizzy with the vodka rush, I grab Rampage's shoulder to steady myself.

"You okay there?" His brow wrinkles in concern.

"I'm good. Just stood up too fast."

Rampage frowns. "Tag and the Predator will have my head if anything happens to you." He glares at Blade Saw and Hammer Fist across the table, both of who are trying to flip a coin into one of the glasses. "I think we'll end the game and I'll order you some water."

My stomach clenches and I glare. "Why does everyone think they have to look out for me? I'm a big girl. I go drinking all the time. I know when I've had enough. And I've changed. I'm living on the edge now."

"You're not big." Rampage snorts. "You're little. Go live on the edge on the dance floor." He points toward the heaving crowd and Jess dancing alone in the center.

"I'm not liking you very much right now."

Rampage laughs. "I didn't think it was possible, but you're even cuter when you're angry. Go, before I do something the Predator will make me regret."

"He doesn't own me." I throw out the words over my shoulder as I stomp away.

Rampage's smile fades. "Yes, he does."

Jess and I dance up a storm until Blade Saw decides he wants in on the action, leaving me without a dance partner. But never mind. The dance floor is packed. I wiggle and shimmy with a few of the non-Redemption fighters from the event, showing off my moves as best I can in the three-inch silver stilettos and skirt I always keep in my trunk in case of an emergency dance trip, which with Jess, happens every week.

The band returns to the stage and launches into a cover of Atrocity's "Let's Dance." Good song. My fighter buddies think so too. One of them is so happy he gives me a hug. He disappears. Oh, he hasn't disappeared. He has turned into Ray.

My new fighter friends run away. One of them is holding his hand over his eye. He doesn't look so happy anymore.

And neither am I. Ray closes in on me. His hair is wet like he just showered, and he smells deliciously of citrus-scented body wash. My entire body aches for him, and I am tempted to open my arms until he scowls.

"What the fuck are you wearing?"

"Clothes."

Ray shakes his head. "No one should see you dressed like that but me."

"Not anymore."

People dance around us. Someone bumps into me, and Ray grabs him by the shoulder and pulls back his arm.

"Watch where you're dancing."

Heart thumping, I step between them, pressing myself against Ray's body as I push down his arm. "Calm down. We're the ones who shouldn't have been standing on the dance floor."

Ray growls deep in his chest but he doesn't move. "We need to talk."

"There's nothing left to say."

The music segues into a cover of Orisha Sound's sultry "Own Ya." Ray's eyes burn into me, and he tangles one hand through my hair and yanks my head back, leaning close to whisper in my ear. "I am fucking wound up tight after that fight. It took me this long just to come down enough to walk in the door to find you so we could talk. This is not a game you want to play with me right now."

"I'm not playing games. I meant what I said last night."

"Jesus Christ, Sia." His free hand tightens around me, his fingers digging so hard into my skin that I'm sure I'll have bruises tomorrow. "Then what are you doing in my arms?"

Emotion wells up in my chest. I can't bear to pull myself away. His body feels so right against mine. Warm. Safe. Solid. Unyielding. This is where I want to be.

"I don't know," I say. "I can't walk away."

He looks down at me, his expression dark and hungry. "Do you have any idea what you do to me?"

I slide my hands over his chest. "If it's anything like what you do to me, then you can't walk away either, so maybe we should dance."

His hand slides down my spine to my ass, and he holds me against him as we sway in slow circles around the dance floor. I press my cheek against his chest and wrap my arms around him and pretend last night didn't happen—pretend he didn't break my trust and all is right with the world.

"Ray." I whisper his name.

He tips my head back, firm fingers under my chin, then he leans down and slants his mouth over mine. His kiss is possessive, demanding, leaving no one in the bar in any doubt that I belong to him.

And he belongs to me.

The band segues into Beyonce's "Drunk in Love." I finally try to pull away, but Ray holds me tight. His heart beats steadily, his hips sway gently to the music, and his arms are firm around me. Who was I kidding when I told Jess it was over? I'll never get over Ray. He is the missing part of me. Hard to my soft. Dark to my light. Rough to my smooth. Heart of my heart.

"So quiet." He nuzzles my neck. "What are you thinking?"

"I think we should go talk." I rock up and brush my lips over his. Ray groans softly and cups my nape with his hand, and moments later we are caught in a passionate kiss that I feel through my heart and deep into my soul.

The band switches gear to an Anthrax cover. I mentally take back my comments about their improvement. Musically, they are better, but they don't have a clue about putting together a set. The dance floor clears, and Ray excuses himself to take a call. By the time I get back to the table, Doctor Death has joined the party along with Shayla and a few other Redemption fighters I don't know. I suffer through five minutes of good-natured abuse about taming the Predator, and then Doctor Death pulls me to the side.

"Did you think about what I told you about Ray?"

I give a casual shrug. "I know his secret." Not entirely true. I have made a reasonably intelligent guess that he's some kind of special agent, maybe black ops or FBI or even, if the rumor is true, CIA. And I've watched enough TV to know that if I'm right, he can't reveal his secret to me without putting me in danger. Which, although kinda frightening, is also kinda cool. My Ray. A spy.

"So you know it can never work." He pulls me into his arms as if in sympathy, except when you're consoling someone, you don't cop a feel of their ass.

"Hey! This ass is taken." I slap his hand and pull away.

"Hands off."

But they aren't my words. They are Ray's words, and he is bearing down on us in a rage like I've never seen before. Face taut, muscles quivering, danger oozes from his pores and people scatter, clearing his path.

"Christ." Rampage looks up at Doctor Death. "Do you never learn?" He slides out of the booth and motions for Blade Saw to join him. "I'm guessing there's gonna be trouble."

"What the fuck?" Ray growls, keeping his voice low. "I thought I told you to stay away from her." He tosses a chair out of the way and shoves Doctor Death in the chest. Black-shirted bouncers head in our direction, and I tug on Ray's arm.

"Ray…it's okay. I had it under control."

Doctor Death staggers back, but moments later he pulls himself up, going head-to-head with Ray. They are instantly swarmed by bouncers, and within minutes they are both outside on the patio.

"I'm leaving." Doctor Death holds up his hands palms forward in a gesture of surrender. "Not causing any trouble. If I was out of line, I apologize. Just calm down."

"Calm down?" Ray hits him with a left hook. Doctor Death dodges the blow only to meet Ray's right. His head snaps to the side and blood trickles from his nose.

"Predator. Stand down," Rampage shouts. "He apologized."

But Ray doesn't stop. He is kicking and punching without mercy. If Doctor Death wasn't a fighter too, he would, no doubt, be unconscious on the ground, but he manages to hold his own, albeit in a totally defensive mode. Still, he is clearly suffering, and when Ray raises his hand for a hammer fist, I can't take anymore.

"STOP." My voice rises to a shriek, and I take a step toward them. Rampage grabs my hand and pulls me back.

"You, go over there. You'll just get hurt."

"If I go over there, Doctor Death will be Doctor Dead." I step forward and grab Ray's arm. "Please. Stop. He's down. He apologized. He's not a threat."

"Get back." Ray sweeps his arm back to free himself from my grip, and the force of his swing sends me flying into some empty patio tables. I hit the ground hard.

"Sia!" Ray looks down at me aghast, his opponent forgotten.

But when he takes a step toward me, I hold up a hand. "I don't know you. Just leave me alone."

Hammer Fist and Blade Saw run to help Doctor Death, and Jess and Rampage help me up. Staggering to my feet, I grab Jess's hand. "Let's go."

She glances back over her shoulder to where Ray is still standing. I can feel his eyes burning into me, willing me to turn around.

"Are you sure?"

"I've never been more certain."

Chapter 23
UNDRESS ME

JESS DROPS ME OFF at home. A storm hits just as I wave good-bye. Thunder booms overhead and lightning sheets the sky. How perfect.

My apartment door is unlocked and light streams from underneath. The stolen "Do Not Disturb" sign on the door handle is Tag's way of letting me know he's decided to crash at my place, a necessity after I almost had a heart attack the first time I walked into the dark apartment and found him on my couch.

"Got a pic from Rampage." He holds up his phone with a picture of me and Ray on the dance floor. "Didn't think you'd be home tonight."

With a sigh, I dump my stuff and join Tag on the couch. "Doctor Death squeezed my ass. Ray went ballistic. He totally overreacted. I thought he was going to kill him. So I left. I couldn't deal."

"I guess not. You okay?"

A ball of emotion rises in my chest, and my throat tightens. "I don't know what to do. It feels so right when we're together. He can be so gentle and passionate, and he has this dry sense of humor that cracks me up. He just…gets me. Sometimes he knows what I want before I do. But every time I think I know him, I find out something that makes me second-guess myself. I just wanted to be able trust someone, but he has so many secrets. And the violence… Even though I love the fights, sometimes I think he isn't in control. He knocked me down tonight. I know he didn't mean to do it, but it happened."

Tag's face softens in sympathy. "He's crazy about you, Sia. He pulled all sorts of strings and called in all sorts of favors to find Luke. That guy has connections like you wouldn't believe. And he did it for you. It should have been me in that alley making sure justice was done.

But Ray wouldn't let me near him. He said he didn't want me to mess up my police career. And that was for you as much as it was for me, because he thought you'd blame yourself if I did."

"He was right."

"My police work is all about catching guys like Luke and putting them in jail," Tag says. "It's about me finding justice and getting over the guilt of not being there to protect you. But Ray was there for you and only you."

"Tag…" My voice wavers. "It's not your fault. You warned me about Luke. You did everything you could do. You can't feel guilty for my choices, and you can't feel guilty that there are people like Luke walking the streets. You're a good person. The best. Why do you think Jess has stuck it out for so long?"

"Lack of a better option?" He turns away and his shoulders heave.

"She has an option. Right now. And she's still waiting for you to get your head out of your ass."

"Seems to be a family trait," he says, leaning back against the cushions. "I've got this sister who's in love with this guy, but she says she can't be with him because she doesn't trust him. So she keeps pushing him away. She doesn't realize you can't trust someone if you don't let them close enough to see what kind of person they really are."

"So, what happens to this sister of yours?"

Tag shrugs. "Don't know. She's got her head stuck up her ass pretty damn far and it's a long way down."

"Very sweet. But very crude."

"That's me." Tag grins. "That's what keeps the ladies coming back."

With a snort, I grab the remote and flip through the channels. Tag likes sports, sports, and more sports. He doesn't know other channels exist. Just for fun, I stop at the Discovery Channel. They are doing a special on apes. We watch as the dominant ape tosses a lesser ape across the jungle floor and steals his woman. Ape shenanigans ensue.

"Would you go crazy if someone pinched your woman's ass?" My cheeks heat as the apes get it on. Even though I'm a grown-up, I still get embarrassed watching sex of any sort with Tag or my parents.

"I might. Depends on the situation. And after a fight, when the adrenaline is still pumping through your body and all your instincts are heightened, some things you just can't let slide, especially anything to do with your girl."

"I'm his girl."

Tag holds up the phone. "Yes, you are."

"Are you okay with that?"

He twists his lips to the side and sighs. "Aside from the fact that he has a secret job he won't share and he scared you tonight, sure. After what he did for you with Luke, I'd say he's a good guy. The best."

My lips quiver with a smile. "So that's a no."

He laces his fingers together and rests them behind his head, settling in for hours of hogging my TV. His feet go back up on the coffee table. I glare. They come down.

"So what happened to your pictures?" He nods at the blank wall. "And all the art supplies you had strewn all over you dining table last time I was here. I thought you were painting again."

My stomach clenches. "I thought it would be better to focus on things that made money, so I could help out Mom and Dad. I figured I shouldn't have opened that door and things were good the way they were."

"Like I said. Head. Ass."

"You might want to tone down the language. One day you might slip at Sunday dinner and you'll have Mom washing out your mouth with a bar of soap."

Tag sighs. "I'm wondering if they really need us to help them out. Now I see you standing on your own two feet, learning to fight at the gym, doing so well at the tattoo parlor, and taming the Predator, I've started thinking I might be a bit overprotective of the people I love. Every time I offered Dad the money, he wouldn't take it. He said they don't need a big house anymore, and they would rather downsize and spend some time traveling. I didn't believe him. I thought he was just being proud—just like I didn't believe you could look after yourself. Did you know they've never cashed one of my checks, and those envelopes you've given Mom are stashed in the letter holder?"

No, I didn't know. Just as I didn't know Ray had so totally won Tag over. With my emotions all over the place, I can't sit with Tag and watch football, so I pace up and down my covered balcony with a bag of potato chips. Have I really been pushing Ray away? Can I trust him despite his secrets? He is everything I have stayed away from. Everything I have feared. And yet he is everything I've always wanted.

I love him.

"Sia."

Hands trembling, I look down. Ray is on the back lawn one story below me, rain drops sliding down his face like tears.

"Sia." His voice breaks on my name, and he just stands there looking up at me, his leather jacket glistening in the rain, as if he wants to say something but the words won't come.

My lungs tighten so hard, I can barely breathe. How many times have I pushed him away only to have him come back? He never gives up on me, despite all my hang-ups. Even when he thought he would have to leave to keep me safe, he found a way back. And if that isn't a statement about how much he cares, if that isn't the essence of trust, I don't know what is.

"Talk to me." His chest heaves.

"Go," Tag says from behind me. "If a man like Ray stands in your backyard in the rain calling your name, he's got something damn important to say. Plus, I've suddenly thought of somewhere I need to be. If you need me to come back…just call."

Best. Brother. Ever. I give him a kiss on the cheek, grab a towel, race down the stairs, and push open the back door.

Ray stalks toward me, pausing under the overhang.

"You want to come in?" I hold out the towel, but he makes no move to take it. Instead, he stares at me, panting as if he just ran a great distance, water droplets clinging to his skin.

"You walked away."

"You scared me," I say. "Watching you fight for sport is one thing, but violence against someone who puts up his hands for mercy, beating a man when he's down…those aren't things I can handle."

"You don't walk away." Ray's voice rises above the patter of the rain. "You don't leave me. Something's wrong, you talk to me." He rips the towel from my hand and tosses it on the ground. "You don't leave."

My body trembles, but I stand my ground. "And you don't lose control."

"I can't help it around you. When you walked away from me last night and tonight…" His voice breaks. "When I saw the pain in your face…I realized I could lose you, just as easily as I lost everything else beautiful in my life. Just because of who I am. It almost killed me. I've never wanted anything in my life as much as I want you. You are the light in my darkness, Sia. I'm lost without you."

A million thoughts race through my mind, but the only one that lingers is the way I feel when I'm with him: safe and protected, cherished and cared for. He makes me laugh. He makes me feel normal in a way I never thought I'd feel again. And Tag thinks I should give him a chance.

"You want to come inside?"

Tag is gone when we reach my apartment. Ray walks in and pulls up short when he sees the bare walls. "Where's your artwork?"

"I put it all away."

His jaw tightens. "Because of me."

"No, because I thought opening the door to the past wasn't the right thing for me."

Ray strokes my cheek. "How can you move forward if you don't deal with the past?"

"I don't need to move forward. I'm happy where I am."

"Where are you, beautiful girl?" he whispers. "Not here with me."

Not anymore. And yet somehow my arms have found their way around him and I'm holding him tight. Ray draws in a shuddering breath and strokes my hair. He's silent. But I can feel the emotion rippling through his body. I squeeze him hard, breathing in his familiar scent, committing everything to memory: the feel of his body hard and unyielding against mine, the steady thud of his heart in his chest, the rasp of this breath, and the certainty I trust him as I trust myself.

And then I let him go.

Ray exhales a gasp, as if I've punched him. But before he can speak, I hold out my hand. "Come."

He follows me to the bedroom and I turn to face him. Myriad emotions play across his face but settle on confusion when I clasp his hands and put them on my hips.

"Undress me."

Ray's gaze burns into me, but when I raise my arms, he lifts my tank top over my head, his broad, warm palms sweeping up my body in a caress that takes my breath away. Swallowing hard, I drop my arms. "Keep going."

He reaches around me and flicks the catch on my bra with strong, steady hands, sliding it down over my arms and tossing it on the bed with my tank top. When I nod, he unfastens my skirt and then kneels, reverent, as he slides it down over my hips.

For the first time since Luke, I feel no fear.

I touch him then, my hand on his head, steadying myself as I step out of my skirt. Ray lifts my right foot after the skirt is gone and brushes a kiss, whisper soft, over each of my toes.

Biting my lip to hold back my smile, I push his head back enough for him to meet my gaze. "Panties."

Still kneeling, he slides his index fingers beneath the elastic waistband and eases them gently over my hips. But with each tug, he kisses me. First my stomach. Then my mound. A feathered kiss over my clit. And then the tiniest lick along my folds. By the time he has my panties off, I'm wet, and from the gleam in his eyes, he knows it.

He kneels and looks up at me, curious, expectant, wanting. But beneath his calm demeanor, I can sense the predator in him pacing, need rippling beneath his skin. I know this predator. And I know I can hold him back just a little bit longer.

"Everything." I touch the piercing in my nipple, giving it a final good-bye tweak, and Ray sucks in a sharp breath. But he doesn't speak. He understands this game that isn't a game. He gave me a gift, and in return I am giving him everything.

He stands and cradles my breast in his palm, caressing my tender flesh with the pad of his thumb. I close my eyes and breathe in the scent of his cologne and leather, the essence of him. Ever so gently, he peppers kisses across the crescent of my breast, and then he draws my nipple into his mouth. Warm and wet, his lips tease, every suck making my sex throb. When my nipple is a taut, hard peak, he carefully unfastens the little silver ring and slides it out.

"Oh." Whether my gasp is from pain or pleasure or a lightness I've never felt before, I don't know, but the sudden rush of heat between my thighs makes me stagger. Ray is there to catch me. His hands grip my hips and he holds me firm. Then he walks me a step back and seats me at the edge of the bed. The intensity of his gaze melts me inside. In this moment, he is utterly and completely mine.

And I am his.

Lying back on the cool silk comforter, I raise my arms and cross my wrists over my head. "Hands."

Ray is quick to comply. He ties my wrists with a scarf from my dresser. Then he returns to the foot of the bed and drops to his knees between my thighs.

There is no rush of blood in my ears, no prickles on my skin. I feel nothing but the slow, steady beat of my heart and a warmth that suffuses my soul. "One more," I whisper, bending my head to watch him. Ray looks up and smiles.

He licks his lips before he starts, and then he trails kisses down my stomach and over my mound. His lips are soft, like butterfly wings, but his body is tense, muscles bunching beneath his shirt, and if I imagine hard enough, I can see the Predator's tail flick. I have pushed my predator far. Soon I will set him free.

Skirting over my piercing, he glides his tongue along my slit, then flicks inside. My body tightens and my breath comes in pants. But he doesn't stop. Over and over again, he teases me, his tongue circling my clit and then sliding through my folds until my wetness trickles from me, and I am moaning his name. Only then does he attend to my throbbing clit, licking and sucking until I am writhing on the soft covers. His fingers find the piercing and he gently works it free, then he nips my clit ever so lightly and I climax, screaming his name as he draws away the little barbell.

I am free.

Ray strips off his clothes as I sink into the bed, and then he lies down beside me and brushes his lips over mine. His kiss comes from the heart, deep and steady, grounding me from the maelstrom of emotion swirling through my body.

"I'm yours," I whisper. "Keep me safe."

"I love you, Sia. You will always be safe with me. I promise."

When I go into work the next morning, I expect to see everyone packing our equipment for the move back to Slim's old shop. Instead, it's business as usual. Christos is perched on Rose's desk, telling her about the gig last night. Duncan is walking a client through our sample book. Slim is nowhere in sight.

"What's going on?"

Rose smiles. "The workers found asbestos in the ceiling of Slim's old shop. They reported it, and the regulators came in and told him he has to pay big bucks to have it properly removed. He can't even knock down the building until the asbestos is gone. He says he can't afford it, and he doesn't want to start all over again. He's talking to Torment right now."

"We get to stay?" My heart leaps in my chest, and I have to hold myself back from dancing around the room. Only now do I realize just how much I didn't want to go.

"Depends on what work out together, if it's possible for them to have a civil conversation," she says. "But they seem to be best buddies now, so I'm guessing it might just work out."

An hour later, Rose receives a call. Torment wants to see me. She laughs about his inability to walk the fifty feet between his office and our shop, but her smile fades when he calls back ten seconds later and barks "now" into the phone so loudly I can hear him from my chair.

My mouth goes dry when I knock on Torment's door. If he's already offered to keep Slim and the team in his shop, why does he want to see me?

"Come."

I enter the room and Torment gestures to the chair in front of his desk. "Sit."

Swallowing hard, I lean against the wall and fold my arms. Then I fix him with a stare. When you challenge a predator, you have to look them in the eyes. I've learned a lot since coming to Redemption.

Torment raises an admonishing eyebrow, but I don't budge. His lips quiver and he leans back in his chair. "I won't beat around the bush," he says, steepling his fingers. "You've got what it takes to run the shop. You're highly skilled, clients like you, Slim says you are incredibly organized and efficient, and you have a good manner with people. He says you've wanted to run your own shop since you joined him and now, after getting your license and experience under your belt, the only thing you're lacking is confidence. Although I'm thinking he might be wrong about the confidence part."

"Slim said that?"

Torment gives an irritated snort. "Yes, he said that. He said many other flattering things about you, which I won't relate because I don't want his praise to go to your head. In my view, the best way to deal with your confidence problem is to throw you into the fray. The shop is yours to manage if you want it."

"What about Slim?"

"He says he's decided to go freelance and I've bought out the business. I've hired him as a consultant, and he has a chair whenever he needs one. He asked me to keep the team as a favor, although the shop is now mine to do with as I will. I asked him who he thought would be the best manager and he named you. If you want to keep Rose, Christos, and Duncan on staff, I'm fine with that. If you want to hire new people, you can do that too."

My own shop. And not just a shop, but Torment's incredible, state-of-the-art, beautiful shop where I could see my fighter friends every day. But what if I screw it up? What if I run it into the ground, and I don't have the money to help my parents? The old worries still niggle, but what really holds me back is Torment. I know now what it takes to control an alpha male like him. If we do enter into a business relationship, he needs to know he doesn't scare me, and I won't jump every time he snaps his fingers—or barks at Rose.

"It's an incredibly generous offer," I say. "But I need some time to think about it."

Torment scowls and I almost take back my words.

"Tough. But I like it. You got a month, then I hunt you down."

I take a step toward the door, and then I turn back and give him a half smile. "How does Makayla put up with you?"

Torment doesn't miss a beat, nor is he in any way offended. His face softens, and he leans back in his chair. "Love. It works out all the kinks."

Chapter 24

SOMETHING SCARED THE PREDATOR

Priority: Confidential
Bay Area Underground Fight Club (BUFC) Fight Night
Railway Station, 51st & Main 8 p.m.
Headlining: The Predator vs. Dirty Dancer
Code Word: Swayze

AFTER STOPPING AT THE pharmacy to pick up my pills on my way home from work, I walk into my apartment just as my phone vibrates with a text message from BUFC. Trust Ray to forget to tell me he's fighting tonight. I text Tag, and we arrange to meet up for a quick bite at our favorite steak house before the fight. Then I text Jess. She's already made plans to attend the fight with Blade Saw. I tell her that Tag will be there. She says she knows, but she's decided it's time to move on.

Anticipation ratchets through me as I rifle through my wardrobe. What to wear? What to wear? I want to look special tonight. For the first time, I'm going to stand front and center and watch the Predator fight instead of hiding at the back.

After texting pictures of at least six outfits to Jess, I eschew my usual black for a pleated red chiffon dress with a fitted bodice, spaghetti straps, and a sweetheart neckline that my mother bought for me one Christmas in an attempt to get me to wear something other than black.

Jess approves the dress and especially approves of the ankle-high black stiletto boots and the chunky black goth necklace—the Sia she knows with a splash of color. Exactly how I feel.

Ten minutes later, I'm in my underground parking garage, my

heels echoing in the quiet space. Friends, fight, Ray. It's gonna be a good night.

My skin prickles as I reach my Volvo. Heart racing, I spin around, just as a hand clamps on my arm.

"Sia?"

Relief floods through my system when I recognize Duncan's client from the shop. "Yuri? I didn't know you lived here."

"I don't." He jabs a needle in my arm and the world goes black.

I don't know what wakes me.

Maybe it is the rumble of a truck outside, or a sound in the room. Perhaps the rasp of a breath. My eyes open and adjust slowly to the semidarkness. Gradually, I make out a bland lacquer dresser; flat screen TV on the wall; small, ornate table; and Yuri, sitting in a chair reading a newspaper beside my bed.

I'm on a bed.

"Finally awake," Yuri says, as he swings his legs off the small, wooden coffee table, his Russian accent now so thick I can barely understand him.

My heart thuds against my ribs. This is happening all over again. I didn't listen to my instincts and now I'm going to die. Terror builds inside me, a living, hungry beast.

"What is this? Why am I here?" My words come out in a croak.

He shrugs. "Your man needs to learn a lesson. He got too close. Thought he was invincible. But there is more pain in heartbreak than death, and we're all about pain in this business."

"He's not in the business anymore." I scan the room for a way out and some kind of weapon, since he hasn't tied my hands. "He's out."

Yuri laughs. "There is no out. There is only death. And that will come for him. But first, the pain." He pulls a knife from a holster on his belt, and a sickening wave of terror wells up from my belly. I take a deep breath and then another. I steel myself. This time, I won't panic. This time, I will save myself. Yuri is still talking, and if he's talking, he's not hurting me. So I need him to talk some more while I figure out a way to get free.

"What is the business you're in?"

He snorts again. "Tragic you have to die without even knowing the reason, but duty means more to him than love. That is the way it is with CIA scum."

My pulse roars in my ears. It was true after all. I wish Tag were here so I could tell him. I wish I could say good-bye. I wish I could tell Ray I love him, even though he's a CIA spy.

Yuri doesn't seem too concerned about my ability to move, so I pull up my knees and push myself to sitting, my back protected against the headboard. My purse is on the dresser, too far to reach, and Yuri is between the window and the door, my only possible exits. I glance over at the nightstand for a weapon, anything that would buy me enough time to get out the door, but my only option is a small digital clock, flashing ten p.m.

Ten p.m. The fight will be over. Will Ray have missed me? Will Tag think I ditched him again? What about Jess? Will anyone be looking for me?

"What are you going to do?" My voice wavers, despite my attempt to keep it steady. Already my body is shaking with the adrenaline rush, and my attempts to slow my breathing are in vain. But I've been here before. And I won't make the same mistake I made with Luke. I will not panic; I will not freeze.

"What would hurt him most, do you think?" Yuri cocks his head and gives me a lascivious grin.

"I think you've already decided," I say through gritted teeth. "Otherwise I would already be dead."

"So entertaining." Yuri reaches for his belt. "I enjoyed you in the tattoo parlor as well. Charming, pretty, and talented. Such a shame you have to die. But that was his choice. I'll let him know you gave me a little something to remember you by." He pats his arm where I tatted the rose, and I bite my lip to fight back a scream.

Yuri laughs as he undoes his belt. "Don't fight it. Scream away. No one will hear you. This entire wing is empty. And I like the sound of a woman's screams. I also like a little fight, which is why you're not restrained."

Not restrained. Hands free. Legs free. Mouth free. I hear the voice of the Discovery Channel narrator in my head: *Biting, charging, kicking, and scratching are effective forms of defense that can chase potential predators away or force them to release their prey.* I remember Tag's self-defense moves, Doctor Death's grapple techniques, and Ray lying on top of me, keeping me safe. And I remember the feel of my teeth piercing his skin.

I don't want to be prey. I want to be the predator.

Yuri whips off his belt, and I form a quick plan. When he leans over and grabs my hands, holding them over my head against the scratchy bedspread, I lick my lips.

I am the predator.

He drops his head closer, and I rear up and bite his lip.

Yuri screams and pulls back. The acrid, metallic taste of blood on my tongue makes me gag. But still I hold on, driving my teeth into his flesh. Only when he slaps me across the face, do I let go. Holding his lip with one hand, he crawls on top of me. He smells of smoke and stale sweat, and my stomach lurches. When he reaches for my hands, I Tasmanian Devil him, wriggling, writhing, and shrimping on the bed. Yuri pushes himself up, dodging my blows, but before he can reassess the situation, I bring up my legs and smash them into his chest.

Yuri falls off the end of the bed. His eyes harden, and he pulls a gun from the holster at his side.

I scream.

Pain rips through my shoulder.

The door crashes open.

Ray bursts into the room. Yuri turns and raises his weapon, but he's too slow. Ray fires twice and blood blooms across Yuri's chest. He collapses on the bed, then rolls to the floor.

Agents in black with FBI vests flood into the tiny space. Ray kneels beside the bed. "It's okay. We got you now."

But it's not okay. Breath doesn't come to my lungs. My heart doesn't stop pounding. Sweat doesn't stop trickling down my forehead, blurring my vision. "My shoulder…"

Ray's face is pale, stark. His eyes burn with a fire I haven't seen before. He turns and yells. "Medic. Now." And then he squeezes my hand. "It's just a little flesh wound. Talk to me."

But I can't talk, can't breathe. The fire in my shoulder burns hotter than the fire in his eyes, consuming me, pulling me into the darkness.

"Fuck." Ray turns and shouts for a medic again. He strokes my head, and the pain subsides as I slide into a dark, safe place.

"I didn't panic," I whisper. "I fought back. Like a predator. Like you."

"You did good, beautiful girl." Ray kisses my forehead. "You held him off. I came as fast as I could."

"But…" I swallow past the lump in my throat as I struggle toward the light.

"Where's the damn medic?" Panic infuses Ray's voice. "Medic!"

His panic defeats me and the world fades away. "You weren't fast enough," I whisper.

Something scared the Predator.

I think it was me.

Chapter 25

EVERYTHING BEAUTIFUL...

THIS TIME WHEN I wake, the room is light.

White. Bright. Medical equipment on the walls. Machines beeping. Heavy, cloying scent of disinfectant.

An IV tugs my arm when I try to move, and when I turn my head, I see Ray.

We stare at each other. His face is deeply lined. Worn. Haggard. He needs comfort, but I can't give it to him. What do I say to the man who promised to keep me safe, and instead made my worst nightmare come true?

A tear trickles down my cheek. My mouth is dry, so dry. But I manage to get out one word. "Tag."

He nods as if he was expecting me to say just that, and he pushes himself out of his chair. His leather jacket creaks as he makes his way to the door, and then he pauses, looks over his shoulder, and meets my gaze. His eyes are dull, so pale they are almost gray. Haunted. Broken.

And then he's gone.

A nurse comes to see me next. She gives me water, checks my vitals, and raises the bed so I can sit. Her name is Mary, and she tells me I'm in a private, federally funded hospital outside Oakland. I had an operation to remove a bullet from my shoulder yesterday, and everything went well. Tag and Jess are outside. My parents are meeting with the doctor in charge. Two agents are waiting to talk to me.

"You haven't been alone for a minute," she says gently. "Your family and friends were here during the day, and at night Mr. Black sat beside you and held your hand."

When I give her a puzzled look, she frowns. "The agent who just left."

Ah. Ray. I didn't even know his last name. And I didn't really know he was an agent.

After Mary leaves, my room becomes a revolving door of visitors. First the doctor who tells me I'll be fine and will be able to go home the day after tomorrow. Next, Mom comes in for a bout of weeping followed by a lecture on how being a tattoo artist exposes me to the criminal elements of society and I need to rethink my career. Overcome with emotion, Dad just pats me on the head and fills the silence with football stats.

Jess and Tag come in holding hands after Mom and Dad leave. Like Dad, Tag is too emotional to talk, so Jess talks for him. She knew something was wrong when I didn't show up at the fight, and when she called Tag and found out I hadn't shown up for dinner, she told Ray and they went to my apartment. Tag was already there. He'd found my car keys under my car and had called his police buddies. But before they even arrived, Ray had the FBI on the scene. That's when she knew it was really bad.

Tag makes a noise, a cross between a sob and a growl, and Jess gives his hand a squeeze and tells him, "Look, she's here. She's okay. Ray saved her."

"She wouldn't have been in that position if not for him. This is all his fault." Tag stalks out of the room. Jess races after him, telling me over her shoulder that she's spent the last few days trying to keep them apart, because every time Tag sees Ray, he goes crazy.

Strangely detached, I watch them go. Maybe it's the drugs or shock, but I feel nothing. No happiness. No sadness. No relief or anger. I just sit as people come in and out, say little, feel less, and pray the circus will end.

"You okay, Sia?" A man enters the room and pulls up a chair beside me. He is tall and thin, with sandy-brown hair parted to one side. His dark suit and white shirt are impeccably pressed. Everything about him screams agent, and I tense in the bed.

He holds out his hand. "I haven't properly introduced myself. I'm Special Agent Jack Harris. FBI. I just wanted to ask you a few questions about what happened and commend you on your bravery."

Giving his hand a limp shake, I shrug. "I'm hardly brave. When I saw him in the parking lot, I didn't run away because I knew him from the tattoo parlor. And in the hotel room, I knew all sorts of self-defense and fight moves, and all I could come up with was to keep him talking, kick him, and bite his lip. If you hadn't come, he would have killed me. I trust all the wrong people. I make myself vulnerable over and over again, and I get hurt. I'm pathetic."

The self-loathing and bitterness in my voice shock even me. Maybe this is why I haven't been able to talk all day. These are the words that I needed to say and I couldn't let my family or friends hear them.

Jack appears to be unfazed by my outburst. His bland expression doesn't change. "Sometimes talking is the bravest thing you can do," he says in a calm, even tone. "It buys you time, it keeps the assailant calm, and it makes him see you as a person, not a victim."

"He saw me as a message for Ray." I spit out each word. "And I bought myself maybe a few minutes."

"That was enough time for us to get to you." Jack smiles. "Those were minutes where you stayed calm and didn't panic. Not easy to do. And don't beat yourself up for not running away. He had been watching you for a while. His visits to the tattoo parlor were for the sole purpose of ensuring you didn't run when he finally took you. We found surveillance pictures on his computer."

"How did you find me?"

He shifts uneasily in his chair. "There's a tracker in the necklace Ray gave you."

My hand flies up to the amber pendant hanging around my neck. God, this just gets worse and worse. "Ray knew about it?"

"He put it there. After he caught one of Yuri's men following you, he came to us for assistance and arranged for the tracker. We raided Yuri's hotel room the next day. There was an explosion, and we thought he died in the blast, but he must have escaped out a back exit."

The urge to rip the necklace off my neck and hurl it across the room is so great, I have to fist my hands in my lap.

Seemingly oblivious to my despair, Jack asks detailed questions about what happened, starting with Yuri's visits to the shop and ending with what I now know was a motel room near the San Francisco International Airport. Finally, he closes his notebook and we say good-bye.

"Jack?"

He turns at the doorway, eyebrow raised.

"Yuri said Ray is with the CIA. Is that true?"

A tight smile crosses his lips. "I wouldn't know."

———

He comes in the night, as I knew he would.

Visiting hours don't mean anything to a man like Ray, and no one is going to turn him away.

The monitors beep softly in the dim light. Something gurgles behind me. Ray's jacket creaks as he leans forward and touches my hand.

"I was waiting for you," I say.

"Wasn't sure if I could come back." His voice is rough, hoarse, and so gravelly I know he hasn't slept for a while.

Steeling myself to keep my emotions at bay, I look over, studying the lines and planes of his haggard face. "Did you have something you wanted to say?"

He scrubs a hand over his face and shudders. "Everything beautiful…"

"Ray…"

"I've destroyed everything beautiful in my life. But you"—his voice tightens—"you are beyond beautiful to me. The last thing I ever wanted to do was hurt you. I failed you in the worst possible way. I broke my promise."

"Yes, you did." I hand him the necklace I removed after Jack's visit, my anger now smoldering instead of a raging inferno. "You promised to keep me safe, but—"

"I put you in danger." Self-loathing fills his voice as he takes the necklace. "Danger I will never put you in again." He tightens his fist and holds the necklace to his heart. "I'm sorry, Sia. I wanted you so much that I lost you. I wish I could turn back the clock so I could make all the right choices, spare your suffering, and keep you safe in my arms." He draws in a ragged breath, then perches on the edge of the bed and pulls me into his arms, holding me so tight I can barely breathe.

"I made that wish about turning back the clock for years. It never came true."

"Maybe when I'm gone."

My heart stutters. "You're leaving the city?"

"It's the only way I know to keep you safe." He brushes a kiss over my forehead. "This way I'll know you'll never be in danger. Because you won't be with me."

A black hole opens in my chest. For all the anger and disappointment I feel, I can't imagine life without him. I open my mouth, but the words I want to say don't come.

"I'll join a different gym until I leave," he says. "I'll stay away from the places you like to go. I…won't see you again." He begins to pull away, and I tighten my arms. *Not yet*, my heart screams. I'm not ready.

"Don't go." My voice wavers. "You don't go. You don't leave. You don't walk away."

Ray buries his face in my neck. "I have to."

We hold each other in the darkness. I breathe in his scent, soap and leather and the essence of him. I commit him to memory, the feel of his hard body pressed up against me, the warmth of his embrace, the slow, steady beat of his heart, the words he whispers into the night.

I wasn't fast enough.

I must have fallen asleep in his arms, because when I wake, Ray is gone.

Chapter 26
You are a survivor

"Sia? You ready to go?"

Jess walks into my apartment, and her steps slow when she sees me sitting on the couch. "I thought you were packing up the stuff you were going to sell at your mom's garage sale."

"I can't do it." I haven't moved from the couch all morning. Instead, I've spent three hours staring at the painting of Ray's motorcycle and wondering if I made the right decision four weeks ago when I let him walk away.

Not a day goes by that I don't imagine that I see him on a street corner or hear his voice in a café. Every time the bell rings in the tattoo parlor, my heart jumps, hoping it's him. I can't watch the Discovery Channel without bursting into tears, and I haven't touched a potato chip in weeks.

"What about that?" She sits beside me on the couch and gestures to the painting. "It's beautiful. You caught a side of him I've never seen before. But if it's going to make you catatonic for an entire morning, maybe it should go."

Frowning, I glance over at Jess. "How did you know that red streak was Ray? Even he didn't know."

Jess shrugs. "You love color."

"Well, it's not finished." I ball my hands into fists in my lap. Jess has a way of poking where I don't want to be poked. "If I'd caught his real nature, maybe I would have run away when I still had the chance of not getting my heart broken."

She gives my arm a squeeze. "You and me both. Tag is totally withdrawn. I haven't seen or heard from him in weeks. I thought we'd made some progress in the hospital, but I guess he just needed a friend."

Immediately I feel guilty for not giving her the attention I know she needs. Although she called it quits with Blade Saw after she and Tag became close when I was in the hospital, I think she's come to the end of her rope.

"I'm sorry." I draw in a deep breath. "I haven't been a good friend these last few weeks. It's just…the pain won't go away. I thought it was part of the PTSD, but my new therapist says it's grief. She says I lost someone I love and it doesn't matter whether he died or walked away, I still have to grieve. I just wish she would tell me how long. This last week, I've been bursting into tears at the stupidest things and I've totally lost my appetite. When I do eat, I feel like throwing up. It seems to be getting worse, not better."

"Then why don't you just forget about selling this stuff?" Jess says, waving her hand at the pile of easels and paintbrushes outside my hall closet. "There's no burning urgency to get rid of it. Your mom is planning to have a sale every week until they've downsized enough for their new condo. We'll just put it all back, and when you're ready, you can sort through it again. I think you're making an emotional decision that you're going to regret."

With a sigh, I push myself off the couch and pick up the painting. "I loved him."

"I know you did."

"I never loved anyone like that before."

Jess sighs. "That's why I stopped the whole loving thing. It fucking hurts."

⌁

Duncan and Christos are both tidying up when I arrive at Redemption later that afternoon. Slim is in Rose's chair, pounding away on the computer. He gives me a wave and I stop at the desk.

"You doing Rose's job now?"

"My last day. I'm doing all the things I wished I could do. And I've just realized I was overpaying Rose. This job doesn't require a whole lot of skill."

"You were paying her for her people skills, not her typing skills.

She gets people in the door. She makes them happy to be here. And she makes them happy to pay. You can't put a price on that."

Slim laughs. "Very true. That's why I'm going to focus on what I do best. All art. All the time. And no young bucks like Torment trying to push me around."

The bell rings and I look up just as our long-lost artist, Jay, walks into the shop. It's been over two months since I've seen him, and he looks thinner, his long, sandy brown hair messier, and his thin face even more peaked than usual. He's wearing a beaded hemp shirt, torn jeans, and a pair of flip-flops. So not Redemption style.

He gives us a sheepish smile and shrugs. "Hey."

Slim and I share a glance. Then Slim folds his arms and leans back in Rose's chair. "Hey? You leave us to the mercy of a vicious street gang and over two months later you walk in and all you can say is 'hey'?"

"Yeah." Jay scratches his head. "I heard they shot up the shop. Sucks. But I had to get them off my back, so I told them I lived in the apartment above it."

Slim grits his teeth. "Sucks indeed. What are you doing here?"

Jay stuffs his hands in his pockets. "Saw the sign on the door of your old place that you'd moved here. Since I never really quit…just took a bit of a break, I thought I'd…um…just get to work."

Duncan gives a snort and Christos mumbles, "You've got to be fucking kidding me."

Jay's mouth gapes, and he looks at Slim. "If that's…okay."

"Don't ask me. Ask the boss." Slim points to me.

I look at him aghast. "I'm not the boss."

"Are you seriously going to turn down Torment's offer?" Slim says. "You've got what it takes to run this place. Everyone likes you. They respect you. You're a talented artist. And you have a way with people that puts them at ease. Wasn't that your dream?"

"I had a lot of dreams."

He lifts an eyebrow. "So melodramatic. Redemption is full of dreams just waiting for you to grab them, and they don't all look like a rough fighter who would move heaven and earth to have you." He gestures to Jay and then winks at me. "Come on, Boss. At the very least, make my dream come true."

My lips twitch, and then I scowl at Jay. "You're fucking fired."

———

Priority: Confidential
Bay Area Underground Fight Club (BUFC) Fight Night
Underground parking lot. 543 Marine Drive. 8 p.m.
Headlining: Fuzzy vs. Devastation
Also on the card: Petis Pois, Jackhammer Jones
Code Word: Cataclysm

"Are you going to the fight?" Jess's nose wrinkles when the waitress serves my double cheeseburger tofu deluxe. We've found a new place for lunch only four blocks from Redemption. The Kosher Vegan Steak House boasts that even a meat lover won't be able to tell the difference between their tofu burgers and the real McCoy, so I'm putting their claim to the test. So far, so bad.

"No."

"Not even to see Tag?" Her voice rises in pitch, and I sense a guilt trip of epic proportions coming on. "He's your brother. And look what happened the last time he fought. He needs our support."

Nausea roils in my belly as I contemplate the food in front of me. This was a bad idea. I won't be able to keep it down. And only this morning did I figure out why.

"I thought you were done with him. Again. Why don't you go out with Rampage? He's funny, nice, loves to gossip, but has good alpha, protective instincts. He's also cute, has a good sense of humor, and can leap tall buildings in a single bound."

Jess sighs. "I can't go out with Rampage. He's a friend. Plus, my dentist's third cousin's sister's husband's brother just broke up with his girlfriend. My dentist thought we'd be perfect for each other. I told her to go ahead and set up a blind date."

"You look thrilled."

She toys with her spoon. "How is Tag, by the way?"

"Tag never talks to me." I push the burger toward Jess and lean back in my seat. "He's totally consumed by this case he's been working on. I thought it was bad before I was in the hospital, but now it's ten times worse. He calls every few days, asks if I'm okay. I say yes. He says 'good' and hangs up. He doesn't even come for Sunday dinner."

"Are you going to eat that?" She points to the burger and I shake my head.

"I haven't been able to eat anything except bread and crackers."

Jess's eyes narrow. "Not even potato chips?"

Emotion wells up in my chest. "Oh, Jess." I reach into my purse and pull out the plastic bag with the pregnancy test I took this morning and shove it across the table. "I missed two pills and then I was in the hospital for the next few days and totally forgot."

She stares at the little pink cross and then slaps her hand over her mouth. "Oh my God. What are you going to do?"

"I want this baby like I've never wanted anything before," I say, my voice hoarse. "Twice in my life I thought I was going to die, and this was something that would never happen. This baby is a gift I never thought I'd have."

Her eyes tear, and she reaches across the table and squeezes my hand. "I'll be with you all the way. You're like a sister to me and I'm going to be the best auntie ever. And you know your parents and Tag will be thrilled. But are you going to tell Ray?"

"I don't know." I crumple my napkin in my lap. "He doesn't want to be with me, Jess. He thinks he destroys everything he loves and he thinks he failed me and that I'm safer without him because of what he does and who he is. And he's right. I couldn't go through that again. How do I know someone else from his past isn't going to pop up and try to kill me? He couldn't keep me safe. And he never told me the truth about who he is. I didn't even know his last name."

Jess purses her lips and huffs out a breath. "You're my best friend and I love you like a sister, but you're being crazy. You love him. He loves you. You're having a baby together. Yes, he's got a dangerous job. But so do a lot of guys. And of course you don't want to go through that shit again. But guess what. You did go through it. Not once but twice. And you survived. You're a survivor, not a victim. I watched you go through it before, and I'm watching you go through it now, and there's a huge difference. And do you know why?"

Shocked by her impassioned speech, I just shake my head.

"The difference is that this time you had justice. You had closure. It was all there, out in the open for everyone to see. It wasn't buried in the shadows, eating away at your soul."

"You sure you're just a vet's assistant," I say, "and not a psychologist in disguise?"

Jess just laughs. "I'm a best friend and I'm still in love with your brother and I hope one day I'll be Auntie Jess for real."

———

"Look at this place." Jess grabs my arm as we push our way through the crowd in the underground parking lot of a derelict apartment building on Marine Drive. "I've never seen a BUFC so busy. Who is Devastation? He's a real crowd-puller. Look! Even Torment is here."

"That's not a good sign."

When I spot Amanda and Shayla in the crowd, I grab Jess's hand and drag her toward them. "What's going on?"

"Devastation broke his wrist," Shayla says. "The organizers asked Fuzz if there was anyone else he wanted to fight, and he named the Predator."

I look at her aghast. "He can't fight the Predator. He'll be slaughtered."

"The Predator accepted the fight." Amanda stands on her tiptoes and waves Jake over. "He's been moping around my office for the last few weeks, so when he said he had a fight tonight, I was happy he would have something to pull him out of his funk. But when I found out he was going to fight Fuzzy, I tried to convince him to drop out, but he wouldn't do it."

"Can't Torment stop it?" Jess, still in total awe and fear of Torment, breathes out a sigh as he cuts a path through the crowd with the ferocity of his stare.

Shayla shakes her head. "Underground has its own rules. Only thing Torment can do is threaten to ban the fighters from training at Redemption if they decide to participate."

"I think that's his plan," Jake says, coming up behind Amanda. "He's worried about Fuzz. We all are. He's just not been himself lately." He looks at me. "Do you know what's wrong?"

"He won't talk to me." I drop my voice so only Jake can hear. "Redemption is the only thing in his life outside of work that keeps him going. If Torment bans him, I don't know what he'll do."

"If he steps into that ring with the Predator, there won't be much he can do." Jake's voice tightens and then drops low. "Ray's wound up like I've never seen him before. I don't think he'll be able to pull back."

A whistle blows and the crowd gathers around the makeshift ring in the center of the parking lot. The air is thick with the scent of gasoline and cigarette smoke. Floodlights have been set up around the perimeter, but there is nothing on the ground to cushion a landing if the fighter falls hard. Already the organizers have had to drive three fighters to the hospital. I hope they won't be driving any more.

Tag steps into the ring wearing a pair of red fight shorts. I am momentarily stunned by how lean he is. Although not fat, Tag has always been solid. But he's not solid anymore. Although his muscles are well-defined, his skin doesn't seem to sit right on him, and he looks gaunt and pale. He's not my Tag anymore.

A murmur in the crowd heralds the Predator's arrival and I hold my breath waiting for my first glimpse of him as he climbs into the ring. Over the last few weeks, I have imagined every inch of him, touched every part of his body, held him in my arms. But when he steps into the ring, he takes my breath away. He's even more beautiful than I remembered. Emotion wells up in my throat. I miss him so much I ache inside.

The ref stands between them and holds up a red flag, but before it drops, Ray holds up his hands and gestures Tag to the side of the ring. I push through the crowd until I'm close enough to hear but behind Ray's back, unable to be seen.

"I'm not gonna fight you, Fuzz," Ray says, keeping his voice low. "I'm here so you wouldn't fight anyone else."

Tag startles and then growls. "You aren't getting out of this fight. No one leaves the ring unless they tap out or can't tap out." His voice rises to a shout. "You almost got Sia killed. I trusted you to protect her.

I gave her to you, and you let us both down. You hurt her, betrayed her, and lied to her. You broke her, and I'm gonna make you pay. For once in her life, she deserves real justice."

A sob rips from my throat. "Tag. Please. Don't do this."

Ray spins and sees me. His jaw tightens and his eyes turn to ice, sending daggers through my heart.

If Tag heard me, he doesn't acknowledge my plea. He and Ray join the referee in the center of the ring, and the moment the flag drops, Tag charges and hits Ray with a right uppercut. Ray's head snaps to the side, but he does nothing to defend himself. Tag hits him again in the face and then in the chest, his punches hard and fast—relentless.

"Tag." I am at the ropes now, so close I can hear the smack of flesh on flesh, hear Ray groan. But my scream is swallowed by the cheering crowd.

"Fight, dammit," Tag bellows, and knees Ray in the stomach. "Why won't you fight?"

"Because it will kill Sia if I do," Ray mutters.

Tag backs off, panting, and snorts a laugh. "You couldn't possibly hurt her any more than you already did."

Ray wipes the back of his hand across his mouth, and it comes away covered in blood. "I was trying to protect her."

A fight official clamps a hand on my shoulder and tries to pull me away, but I won't let go of the ropes. Even if they won't stop, I can't leave them like this.

With a howl, Tag launches himself again at Ray, this time sweeping his leg. Ray goes down. On purpose. I know this because I've seen him defend this move a hundred times. If he doesn't want to go down, he won't.

The moment his back hits the concrete, Tag is on him, pummeling him with elbows and punches. The crowd goes quiet. There is no sport in beating a man who is down, especially when he's made it clear he won't defend himself.

"Enough, Tag. He's down." I slide a leg through the ropes, but one of the fight officials pulls me back.

"Rules say no one goes in and no one goes out until someone yields."

"You don't understand." I pull at the official's blue shirt. "He won't yield. That's not who he is."

"Nothing I can do."

"Fuck you." I shove him aside and step into the ring.

"Tag. Stop. Please. You're going to kill him." But Tag doesn't stop. He sees me, but he doesn't. Eyes glazed with bloodlust, he swings his arm back and pushes me away.

I stagger and hit a massive chest. "It's okay," Torment says. "I got this."

The crowd boos. The fight officials holler. But Torment stalks across the ring, grabs Tag from behind, and rips him away. The fight zone descends into chaos. People shout and curse. Rampage joins Torment, and they drag Tag away. I run over to Ray. He has pulled himself to sitting and is leaning against one of the pillars. His face is cut and one eye is swollen shut.

"Oh God. Ray? Are you okay?" I kneel beside him, running my hands over his body, checking for breaks.

"I'm fine. Just go."

"You're not fine. Look at you. I'll take you to the hospital."

"Go, Sia. Please."

He winces when I touch his forearm, and I suck in a breath. "At least let me get the medic."

Drawing in a deep breath, he shouts, "Sia. Go."

His words echo through the parking lot, stilling the crowd. Shaking, I push myself to my feet and take one step back and then another.

"Okay," I whisper. "I'm gone."

Chapter 27
DON'T GO

SUNDAY MORNING AFTER THE fight, I go to Tag's apartment, determined to find out what the hell has been going on with him. I push the buzzer. No answer. I call and text his cell. No answer. I go around the back and find his car parked in its spot. Then I return to the front and hang around until one of the tenants who knows me lets me in.

Minutes later, I'm banging on Tag's door. I shout and holler that I'll keep it up and disturb his neighbors until he lets me in. Tag has been brought up too well to allow me to disturb the neighbors. It only takes a few minutes before he opens the door.

Before he can protest, I push my way inside. Then I freeze. Usually highly organized and meticulously clean, Tag's apartment looks like a hurricane just blew through. His clothes are everywhere. Papers, books, and old CDs are strewn across every surface. But it isn't the mess that makes me gasp and step back, but the photos pinned to every wall.

Women. Young. Sixteen, maybe eighteen. Their faces and bodies battered and bruised.

"I didn't want you to see this," he says, his voice flat. "I didn't want you to know about it, especially now."

"Who are they? What happened to them?"

Tag sits heavily on his couch. He's wearing a pair of pajama pants and a T-shirt, a pen stuck behind his ear. His right hand is bandaged over his knuckles—knuckles that hit my Ray.

"The same thing that happened to you." He twists his hands in his lap, then meets my gaze. "By the same man."

My stomach clenches and my mouth goes dry. "Luke? He raped all those women?"

"I'm pretty sure it was him. Some were before you and some after."
I sink down onto his paper-strewn couch. "How did you get involved?"

Tag rubs his hands down his thighs, just like our father does when he's stressed. "The night you met Ray, I was assigned a new case. The victim was an eighteen-year-old student he'd met at a bar—he'd drugged her drink, but she was so drunk she threw it up when she went to the bathroom and he didn't know. She remembered most of the details but not his name, and filed a police report. At first I didn't know it was him. But then she started getting the threats…"

He rubs his thighs harder now and stares at the floor. "God, Sia. It was so hard to watch. I knew exactly what she was going through. So many times I wanted to talk to you about it, but I didn't want to put you through it all again. It took a long time to trace the threats, but when we did and I realized it was him, it was worse than I imagined. Our local DA said there wasn't enough evidence to run the case without a witness, and the girl changed her mind and refused to testify. Not only that, but at the time of the incident, he was out on bail after being arrested last year on a similar case in a different jurisdiction."

"Oh God."

"I've been working to help build a case against him. I reopened old cases where he was named as a suspect. I visited the victims and begged them to tell their stories. No one would. Some were too afraid. Some had moved on. Some had been threatened. Even when I told them just one victim testifying could make the difference, they wouldn't do it. And I didn't blame them. I understood. But I became totally obsessed. Even though Ray went after him and did what I'd always wanted to do, I wanted real justice. I wanted him behind bars. I told Ray to make sure he left him alive, so I could put him away."

Tag sighs and shoves a pile of paper aside to sit beside me. "I finally found someone who would testify and his trial is scheduled to start next week. But a few days ago, she backed out. We've built a good case on circumstantial evidence, but the DA is reluctant to proceed without a witness. When I found out he might walk, I just lost it."

My heart aches for Tag. He is everything that is honorable and good about the system, and I've asked him to carry this burden far too long. It has weighed us down, held us back, prevented us from being who we are meant to be. We have waited a long time for the justice he craves, the justice that will set us free. I reach out and squeeze his hand.

"One victim or one survivor?"

Tag's face crumples. "You were always a survivor, but you don't have to do this. I didn't tell you because I didn't want you to be involved. I don't want you to have to relive it again or be ripped apart by the defense team. If they let him go, I'll find another way."

"If it's not too late, I want to do it. It's time for us to be free."

He scrubs his hand over his face. "I can't...I can't let them put you up there. They'll destroy you."

"They can try." A smile tugs at my lips. "But after what I've been through, they won't succeed."

"You're the bravest person I know." He chokes on his words. Tag is so not a sentimental guy. "I've never met anyone with so much courage. You could have let him ruin your life, but you didn't. You found a new way forward. And now, after you've just been through it all again, you're willing to try and bring him down."

"That's 'cause I have you standing behind me." Something niggles at the back of my mind and I frown. "That's my only worry. You may be considered a witness to the crime. Wouldn't you get in trouble for not reporting it? And didn't you have to report the conflict when you found out it was him? What'll happen to you if I come forward?"

He stands and walks over to the wall of pictures. "I would willingly give up my career if it meant even one woman would be spared what you went through. I would be proud to go to jail for it. Maybe once the DA knows why we made the decision we did, I'll get off with just a warning. But even if I don't, I won't let you stand up there alone. If the DA agrees, I'm going to testify too. The truth will be out there, and the lawyers can sort out whether our testimony stands or not."

I join him at the wall and wrap my arms around him. "We're going to do this, Tag. After all these years, we're going to be free. Together."

"You're going to do it," he says. "I'm just along for the ride."

Monday morning I walk into Torment's office.

Without knocking.

Torment looks up and scowls. I meet his scowl with one of my own.

"I'm taking the job managing the Redemption studio." I fold my arms and lean against the wall. "I'll start on Friday, after I take care of a few legal matters. I'm keeping the team. I expect you to leave me alone with respect to business decisions unless I ask for your help. That includes hiring, firing, selecting and ordering equipment, marketing, and decor."

He lifts an eyebrow. "Decor?"

"That's right. I'll be hanging paintings to showcase local artists on the walls. No car race murals allowed."

Torment's eyes twinkle with amusement, and he leans back in his chair and laces his hands behind his head. "Anything else?"

"I'll need a few months off about seven months from now. I'll make sure there is someone fully trained to run things in my absence. Nonnegotiable."

His gaze drops to my stomach and he raises an eyebrow. But ha-ha, Torment. There is nothing to see yet.

"I choose the name," he says. My heart skips a beat because for a moment I think he's figured out my little secret, but then I realize he's talking about the studio.

"Not if it sucks."

Torment chuckles. "Redemption Ink?"

"No."

"Torment's Tats?"

"Definitely not."

"Forbearance?"

I sigh. "Is that a joke?"

"Yes. You're almost as difficult to handle as Makayla. But maybe I don't need to be reminded about it every day. How about Phoenix, since you're starting new?"

"Hmmmm."

"Phoenix it is." He slams his hand on his desk, and I jump. "I'll get my people on that right away. Look for your new sign tomorrow. But I have a condition." He strokes his chin and studies me for a long moment. I take deep breaths and pray my bravado doesn't give out. This was just supposed to be a quick in and out. My nerves are already stretched to breaking.

"What is it?"

"The first set of paintings to go up will be yours."

My heart sinks. "That might take a while."

"As long as it takes. But I'm hoping the blank wall will be a motivator."

"Thank you. For everything."

"You're welcome." He smiles an entirely benign, un-Torment-like smile. "Took you long enough. I was beginning to think I might actually have to hire one of the people I interviewed."

"I had a life to sort out first."

"You have a man to sort out next," he says. "He's taking out his frustrations on my fighters. I had to arrange for an ambulance to be on permanent standby."

For the first time since I walked into his office, I manage a smile. "That's on the agenda."

The next day, I go to Ray's apartment. My heart drums in my chest as I stand outside his door. What if he doesn't want to see me? What if I don't get a chance to make the speech I've had running through my head for the last few days? What if he doesn't want the baby?

Taking a deep breath, I push the what-ifs away. No matter what happens, I'll survive. And once I testify against Luke, I'll really be able to move on. I'll live the life I've always wanted to live. I just hope I don't have to live it alone.

I knock.

Silence.

Then, footsteps.

My heart pounds when the door swings open.

Oh God. He's so banged up—black eye, swollen cheek, tiny bandages on his temple and chin. Instinctively, I reach out to touch him and he steps back. Away.

Swallowing my fears, I stiffen my spine and push past him into the apartment. "I need to speak to you. I'll take five minutes of your time and then I'll leave."

He nods and closes the door, turning to lean against it, his thick arms folded. "Okay."

"Okay." My hands clench and unclench by my sides. He's wearing the sexiest damn pajama pants I've ever seen, navy blue with the Redemption logo on the side, tight in all the right places, and nothing else.

The nothing else is distracting. I feast my gaze on the hard planes of his chest, the solid ripple of muscle in his abs. So delicious I want to lick him all over.

"Sia?" His soft voice draws me away from that fantasy.

My cheeks flame. "Sorry."

"You want a drink?" He peels himself away from the door and brushes past me as he heads toward the kitchen. My body heats, trembles at his touch, and I follow him across the floor.

"I'm not drinking anymore."

Ray pauses beside the fridge. Frowns. "Water?"

"Sure. Water is good."

"You want to eat something?" He fills a water glass from the tap and hands it to me, the slight touch of his finger sending a zing of electricity through me.

"I'm…uh…not really eating anymore either."

He stills, then plucks the water glass from my hand and places it on the counter. "What's going on?"

My heart bangs in my chest, and I curl my fingers around the cool concrete counter. "I…I'm…pregnant," I blurt out. "That night in the rain. I missed my pill the next day, and then I was in the hospital, and by the time I told them, it was too late to catch up."

His eyes darken almost to black and a sliver of panic winds its way through my heart. "I didn't mean for it to happen, but I want this baby.

After what happened to me, I never thought I'd be able to have children, and to me it's an incredible gift."

He stares, silent, unmoving. His face gives nothing away. Although I had prepared myself for rejection, I can't help my heart from sinking through the floor, nor can I help the ball of sorrow from lodging itself in my chest.

"I'm not asking you to be involved unless you want to be," I say quickly, desperate now to get out. "I've taken the job at Redemption, so I'll have enough to get by, and my parents decided to downsize, so they don't need financial help." I'm babbling, but I can't stop. "I just…thought it was the right thing to do to let you know. I love you. More than anything I want to have this baby with you. I'm not afraid anymore. Not of you. Not of your job. Not of me. Jess made me realize I'm a survivor. And tomorrow, I'm going to testify against Luke at his trial and I'll really be able to put the past behind me."

He still hasn't moved from the kitchen. A sob wells up in my throat and I turn for the door. "Good-bye, Ray."

"Don't go."

"What did you say?"

"You don't go. You don't leave. You don't walk away." His voice, deep and raw, slides over me like a warm blanket. Hope flutters in my chest, and I turn around and find myself in his arms.

"Did you really think I would let you leave?" He kisses my forehead, then cups my jaw in his hand, brushing his thumb over my cheek.

"You did before."

"Biggest fucking mistake of my life." He teases my mouth open, grazing his tongue along the seam of my lips. My fingers curl into his shoulders, and I lean up for more. He tastes lemony and sweet. He tastes of Ray.

I arch closer to him, my body coming alive at the feel of those hard muscles against me. I want him so badly, I can barely breathe, and yet I need to clear the air.

"What I said at the hospital…about you breaking your promise and not being fast enough. That was wrong of me, and I'm sorry. It wasn't your fault and yet you took all the blame."

"I've always blamed myself." He buries his face in my neck. "For Scott. For Lisa. For you. For not being there when the people I cared about most needed me. I wanted to be worthy for once in my life. Worthy of your love."

"You have my love," I whisper in his ear. "I love you. And although there is nothing to forgive, I forgive you. But you need to forgive yourself and move on, just like I'm going to do. Not just for me, but for Scott and Lisa. For our baby." I slide my hand down his chest to rest over his heart, where we cut him together that night in the rain. "That's what the pain is about, isn't it? Guilt. If we have any hope for a future together, you have to let it go."

He frowns. "It's not that easy."

"Come with me." I clasp Ray's hand and lead him to the alcove. Then I slip off my dress and underwear and hold out my arms. "Make love to me. Kiss me. Hold me. Hug me. Take me. But do it without the pain."

Ray groans. "It's been so long, and I want you so bad. I might be rough."

"I can handle rough."

"And I'm gonna be hard."

"I love it hard."

"And fast."

This time I laugh. "Not if I have anything to say about it."

Ray takes me in his arms. "I'm gonna give it to you sweet, beautiful girl. Soft and sweet."

Nuzzling his neck, I murmur, "What about the pain?"

"I never really knew pain until I woke up each morning and knew I wouldn't see you. I never knew love until I held you in my arms."

"I knew you loved me when you wouldn't fight Tag," I say. "That meant everything to me."

Ray slants his mouth over mine and kisses me so deeply I feel it in my toes.

"I loved you a lot longer than that. Just took me a while to realize it." He slides his hand into his pocket and pulls out the necklace. "Wear this for me. I spent an entire night driving around the city trying to think of a way for us to be together and to keep you safe when I couldn't be with you all the time. I stopped for a coffee and I saw this in the window of a little jewelry shop beside the café. The stone reminded me so much of the color of your eyes, I went in and bought it, and then I thought of attaching the tracker so I could always be with you, always keep you safe. It came from the heart."

I spin around and lift my hair so Ray can fasten it around my neck. Then I turn and close my eyes as the tiny weight settles between my breasts. "Welcome home," I whisper.

This time his kiss is gentle, soft nibbles and licks, caressing my mouth. A wave of heat rushes through me. And something else—a fierce rush of emotion and a certainty I am where I belong.

Chapter 28

I'M PRETENDING THEY CAN'T SEE

"MOM. DAD. WE HAVE something to tell you."

Sunday night before Luke's trial, Tag and I have an emotional talk with our parents. We tell them what happened with Luke, and why we decided to keep it quiet. I tell them how putting the past behind me was the only way I could cope, and how the tats and piercings gave me the armor I needed to make it through each day. Mom dissolves into tears and tells me she's sorry for giving me such a hard time, and if only I'd told her, she could have helped. Dad shakes his head and says he wishes he could have been there for us, and he would never have let anyone threaten his kids and get away with it. And where is this guy now, anyway?

So we give them the good news. Tag has been working hard to collect evidence against him, and we're going to testify at the trial. They promise to be there. Dad says he wants to look Luke in the eye, so that if Dad ever meets him in a dark alley…

I tell him, actually, I have a new boyfriend who beat him to it.

When we've talked everything through and dried our tears, I call Ray. He is the first boyfriend I have ever invited for Sunday dinner. With his usual confidence, he walks into the house and shakes Dad's hand. Dad asks him about his fights. Five minutes later, they are on the couch in front of the TV with Tag. Best friends forever.

Ray sits beside me at dinner and throws a casual arm over the back of my chair. Mom's lips quiver as she tries to repress a smile. I have never seen her so sad and so happy as I have this evening. I could make her even happier if I told her about the baby, but since it hasn't been three months yet, we've decided to wait.

"So, Ray. What do you do besides fight?" Dad leans back in his chair and I tense. My parents aren't big on evasiveness, especially Dad, because he's a straight-up kind of guy.

"PI work." Ray strokes my shoulder. "I also served in the military and did a few other things. Moved around a lot. Not anymore. I found a girl who made me want to settle down."

Dad nods and grunts his approval while Mom gives up on trying to hide her feelings and beams.

"You treat her right," Dad says. "She's my little girl, and Tag and I will always have her back."

Ray gives me a gentle squeeze. "That makes three of us, but I don't think she needs us anymore."

—⁓—

That night, before the trial, I leave Ray asleep in his bed, pull on one of his T-shirts, and stand by his balcony window, looking out into the night. Barely visible through the smog, stars prick the dark gray sky, and ten stories below, the streets are empty and quiet. Danger lurks down in the darkness, but here, high in Ray's tower, I am safe.

My hand drifts to my stomach. We are safe.

"People can see you in the window." Ray curls an arm around me, pulling me into his chest. The room is dark around us save for a faint light streaming from his alcove.

"I know, but I'm pretending they can't see me. That's what I'm going to do tomorrow. I'm going to sit in the witness box, tell my story, and pretend no one else is around."

Ray eases up the T-shirt and slips a hand underneath, cupping my breast in his warm palm. "I'll be there. And your parents. And Jess too."

I look back over my shoulder. "Okay. I'll pretend no one else is there except the people I love."

He tugs the T-shirt higher in the back and works his way underneath until he cradles both my breasts in his hands. "Luke will be there."

"You're ruining the moment."

Ray laughs and rolls my nipples between his thumbs and forefingers. "Look him in the eyes when you say your piece. Show him your courage. Let him know he didn't break you."

"Only one man has come close to breaking me." I grind against his hardened length barely concealed by his pajama pants, and Ray groans.

"And only one woman has ever brought me to my knees." He slides both hands down my hips, and then grabs the edge of my T-shirt and whips it over my head.

"Ray!" Naked, in front of his balcony window, I am in full view of the apartments across from us and perhaps from the street below. And, *oh God*, what a thrill.

"Pretend they can't see you, beautiful girl." Ray reaches around and pinches my nipples. "We'll practice for tomorrow."

"I'll be wearing clothes."

Ray chuckles. "Not in my mind. When I think of you, I always think of you naked."

"Nice. I'm glad this relationship is only about sex."

He laughs again. "Nothing wrong with sex. And since I have yet to take you out on a real date, taste your cooking, listen to your music, watch your movies, or read your books, I'll take what I can get."

"Well, then I just may be persuaded to put out tonight."

Ray slips one hand between my legs and strokes his finger along my wet folds. "I don't think it will take much persuading. My girl likes to be watched."

"Shhhh." I look back over my shoulder and press a finger to his lips. "I'm pretending they can't see."

He kicks my legs apart and presses his lips to my ear, his breath hot and moist against my skin. "But they can see. They see my hand stroking your pussy. They see your breasts swollen and your nipples peaked with arousal. They see your skin flushed, and your lips pink and plump and waiting to be kissed."

"What else do they see?"

"They see the present I'm going to give you." He pulls away, leaving me bereft, but returns moments later with a small silver box.

"I got these for you, to replace what you gave up." He opens the box and pulls out a pair of nipple clamps with tiny glass beads dangling from the fine filigree silverwork.

I let out a whimper of fear and Ray laughs. "Lookit those wide eyes going all green on me. Yeah, they'll hurt, but they'll feel good too." He gently turns me to face the window and then pulls me into the safety of his chest. "Let them see you, Sia. Show them how much you like your present."

Gritting my teeth, I look out over the city. Few lights shine through the windows at this late hour, and surely no one can see us. And even if they could, would anyone know me, naked, aroused, and in the arms of the man I love?

Ray rolls my right nipple between his thumb and forefinger, then reaches around me with both hands and carefully slides the clamp around the tip before tightening the rubber ring.

"Aaaaah." I shriek and step back into his chest, but he drops his arm to my waist and holds me tight. "The more you move, the more it will pinch. Now be a good girl and stay still." He repeats the process with my other nipple, rolling it first, then affixing the clamp carefully just below where the piercing was. I give a small murmur of appreciation that he has remembered it is still tender, and then I gasp as a zing of pleasure pain shoots straight to my clit.

"Look at yourself," Ray whispers in my ear as he points to the window. "So beautiful, I want everyone to see you. So precious, I will never let you go."

Trying to ignore the throb in my nipples, I change my focus and catch a glimpse of myself in the window, my soft, curvy body against the hard planes of Ray's chest, my skin pale against his darkness— and the twinkle of silverwork dangling from my nipples, brighter than the stars.

"I'm gonna fuck you against this window." His voice drops to a husky growl. "And you're gonna think about everyone watching. And it's gonna make you hot. And it's gonna make you wet. And when you come, you're gonna scream so loud, everyone will hear you."

"Soon?" I wiggle my ass against him. "I need to come so badly, I ache."

"I know." He strokes his thumb over my cheek. "And I know it hurts. But you'll have to wait. You aren't ready yet."

A whine escapes my lips. "I'm so wet, it's dripping down my thighs."

"And it's a beautiful sight." He twines his hand through my hair and pulls my head back, then leans down and takes possession of my mouth. Hard, demanding, his kiss melts my body and my knees tremble. He tightens his fist, and his tongue plunges deep as he tugs gently on the right clamp with his free hand. With every tug, a bolt of lightning shoots straight to my core and my vision blurs.

Ray releases my hair and slides one hand over my throat, resting a finger in the hollow of the base as he continues to play with the clamps with his other hand. My breath catches as he increases the pressure ever so slightly.

"Easy, beautiful girl. It's a lot to take. I'll go slow."

His erotic words spark a slow burn between my legs that spreads through my body like wildfire. I rock my hips, but all he does is turn his attention downward, cupping his hand over my sex and stroking along my folds, avoiding the one place I so desperately want to be stroked.

"You are mine, Sia. Mine to play with. Mine to love."

"Yours." Arousal rushes through me. The feeling of his hand on my neck, possessive and controlling, and yet safe and protecting, sweeps away the last vestiges of my anxiety about our show in the window and my body softens against him.

"That's right," he says. "Give it all to me."

"Make me come."

Ray laughs. "As you command, but I'm gonna take the clamps off first, and I won't lie, it will hurt more than when they went on."

He takes one off.

He does not lie.

I gasp as blood rushes to my breast. Ray leans down and draws my burning nipple into his mouth, soothing it with gentle licks of his tongue until I'm panting with need. Reaching down, I cup the steel of his erection in my palm, stroking him through his pajama pants, hopefully into a painful, desperate need to come. Like me.

The removal of the second clamp is even worse, his tongue even more arousing, and within moments, I am writhing in his arms, my only thought how I can get him inside me.

"Ray. Please."

A slow, sensual smile spreads across his lips. "There we are. We're gonna take back the night."

He strips off his pajama pants and kneels naked in front of me, his erection huge and heavy between his legs. With infinite patience, he traces lazy circles along the sensitive skin of my inner thighs in a slow, tortuous tease, then parts my folds, holding me wide open. "I like to see your pussy all pink and wet and dripping for me."

"I like to see your cock thrusting into my pussy," I say, my usual reticence giving way to desperation. "I like to see it hard and hot and throbbing, sliding in and out, making me yours in every way you can take me."

With a low growl, he shoots to his feet, cups my ass, and lifts me against him until I am braced between the window and his body, his shaft pressed tight against my clit. "You want me to fuck you against the window? You want everyone to watch me claim you, make you come?"

My body tightens, and I grind my clit against his shaft. "Yes, Ray. Like this. Love me like this with the whole world watching."

Meeting my gaze for a heartbeat, he lifts me and thrusts his way deep into my sex. His thickness thrills me, fills me, and my overly sensitized tissue swells against his hardness.

"Harder. More."

With a chuckle, he pulls me closer, opening me to him as he pulls out and thrusts in again. And then he is everywhere—warm lips on my nipples, firm fingers on my clit, and his cock so beautifully thick and hard pounding into me in a ceaseless rhythm.

Sensation builds on sensation, until I am thrashing against him, clinging to his shoulders, as I teeter at the edge of release. When he finally pinches my clit, I overload. My sex contracts and convulses, my body tightens, and I come so violently, I shriek his name.

Ray hammers into me, drawing out my orgasm, and then he climaxes, his shaft becoming impossibly hard before he swells and throbs inside me. With a shuddering breath, he leans forward and rests his head against mine, his breathing hot and hard, his heart pounding against my chest.

"Think of that tomorrow, when you're pretending no one is there."

"Think of how you loved me without any pain."

Ray smiles. "It seems my plan was a double success."

My lips curl into a smile. "This was your plan? Make me think of sex instead of worrying about what I'm going to say?"

He nuzzles my neck and pulls me closer. "Man sees his woman standing by the window, her hair tousled, her beautiful long legs bare, wearing his shirt, he gets a little emotional. He finds out that she's worrying about something when she should be resting, 'cause she's carrying his child, he's gotta do something about it."

"So kinky sex was your solution?"

"Loving you was the solution." He kisses the sensitive dip between my neck and my shoulder. "Sex was a bonus."

"Promise you'll be there tomorrow." I brush a kiss over his lips.

"I'll be there tomorrow," Ray says. "And every tomorrow after that."

<center>~~~</center>

Party time.

The Redemption boys love to party. And tonight is no exception. After Tag and I testified earlier this week, his other witness came forward and testified too. Luke is in jail. His family is under investigation for threats. The trial made the evening news, and more women are coming forward. Justice is done and served on a silver platter. And Redemption wants to celebrate.

After christening Phoenix Ink, now managed by me, Torment shouts that protein shakes are on the house. Fighters stampede toward the little café, and the owner's eyes widen in fear. Lucky for him, Shayla and Doctor Death have offered to help out, and they run the blenders like there's no tomorrow.

Glancing quickly around the gym, where fighters are dancing, chatting, and, of course, fighting, I lean against a lat machine, slide my hand into my handbag, and pull out a handful of contraband potato chips. One whiff of greasy goodness and my mouth waters.

"Bad." Ray snatches the chips out of my hand. "Chips are full of unhealthy fats and chemicals. My boy needs good, healthy food." He waves to Rampage and shouts, "Get Sia a whey protein shake. Extra wheatgrass."

My lips tighten into a thin line. "First, your boy may be a girl. And second, I'm not a dog, Ray. Or a small child. If I want to eat potato chips, I—"

"Won't." He clasps my hand and kisses my palm. "'Cause you don't want your man to worry. A man who isn't worrying is a happy man. Happy men buy sexy presents. Sexy presents lead to sexy times."

"I see." I lick my lips, imagining the taste of potato chips on my tongue. "Somehow it always winds up being about sex."

Ray leans in and kisses me. "Wrong. It always winds up being about you."

Rampage joins us and hands me a protein shake. I don't ask how he managed to get the shake before the fifty people lined up at the café. Maybe it's because Rampage is the ears, eyes, and heart of Redemption. He is also the café owner's cousin.

"So we're gonna have a kid running around the gym," he says.

Ray hisses out a breath, and I look up and frown. "How did you know that? We only just told my parents and Tag today."

Rampage shrugs. "I know everything that goes on at Redemption, and we need a few kids around here. Liven the place up. Fuzz can teach some junior MMA classes and make the kiddies cry."

"Hey." Homicide Hank joins us, with Blade Saw and Doctor Death on his heels. "I got kids. Two of 'em."

"Everyone knows they aren't yours," Doctor Death says, winking at me. He is fully recovered from his fight with Ray and, surprisingly, holds no grudge. In fact, he caught us one night on our way out of the gym and apologized for his behavior. Ray said he understood. His girl did, indeed, have a damn fine ass. But if Doctor Death ever touched her ass again, he'd break all his fingers.

"Fuck you, Death." Homicide makes a rude gesture, and Doctor Death laughs.

"I do, in fact, get fucked over quite regularly, but that's my love life. In the ring, it's you who is going down."

Homicide Hank takes a swing at Doctor Death. Someone yells "fight." The fighters leave the café and run over to the mats, where the two miscreants are now going at it full tilt.

"So, this is a Redemption party," Duncan says, coming up beside me. "Not quite what I expected. When you said most of them didn't drink when they were training, I imagined the party would be more sedate."

Ray snorts a laugh. "They're just getting warmed up. Just wait until those protein boosters kick in."

"He's big into the health thing," I say to Duncan. "He gets up at five every morning, goes for a run, then works out, makes a protein shake, cooks up a healthy breakfast, and he's ready for work before my alarm has even gone off. It's so annoying. I wish he'd warned me before we started going out. I'm so not a morning person."

"You will be." Ray winks. "I'm gonna whip my girl into shape so we can run together in the morning."

Before Ray can start his lecture about the healthy benefits of starting the day with exercise, I excuse myself to look for Jess. Although she doesn't train at Redemption, she never misses a party.

I find her sitting alone in the bleachers, watching Tag and Shayla talking over by the free weights.

"She has a crush on him," Jess says as I sit down beside her.

"Yeah. For a long time. But Tag isn't interested. She's not his type."

Jess shrugs. "Neither am I, apparently."

"You're wrong." I squeeze her arm. "Now that Luke is behind bars and my parents are in their new condo, and he's about to become an uncle, he's changed. He's happy."

"I've never known him happy," Jess says.

"If you liked him sad, anxious, and stressed, you'll definitely like him happy."

As if on cue, Tag looks up and smiles. He gives Shayla a pat on the back and then jogs over to us, climbing the bleachers two at a time.

"Hey, Sis." He ruffles my hair. "I'm surprised Ray let you out of his sight."

"I'm not out of his sight." I roll my eyes and gesture toward the lat machine where Ray is talking to Blade Saw with his gaze fixed on me. "You think he'd take his eyes off me in a gym full of protein-boosted fighters?"

"Good point. If you were my girl, I'd be watching you too." His gaze drops to Jess, and I catch the slightest reddening of his cheeks, so faint only a sister can see.

"You…still with Blade Saw?"

Jess freezes, and I poke her in the side.

"Uh…no. Didn't work out."

Tag smiles the devastating smile I haven't seen for years, the one he used to charm his way into all sorts of trouble. "You want a protein shake? Everyone's watching the fight."

Jess gapes. I nudge. She stumbles on recovery. "Uh…yes. I like protein. In shakes. And out of shakes. Generally, protein is good. But not meat. I don't eat meat."

I cringe on her behalf, but Tag doesn't seem to notice her sudden awkwardness. Instead, his face softens and he holds out his hand.

"I know."

After being abandoned by Tag and Jess, I head back to the studio to lock up. Christos and Rose are making out on Rose's desk, clearly visible through the glass door.

"Hey. Get a room," I shout.

"That's my line," Torment says from behind me.

"Except you used Rampage to deliver it." I knock on the door, and Christos and Rose break their clinch.

"Gotta keep Rampage out of trouble. He knows too much about what goes on here." Torment lifts an eyebrow as Christos and Rose push open the door and murmur their apologies on their way out.

"Never got a chance to say congratulations." Torment follows me into the studio and stands by the door as I turn off the computers and make a quick check to make sure all the equipment is off. Our new Phoenix Ink, Redemption logo—flames with a phoenix rising from the ashes and the studio and gym names in script below—is everywhere. Torment spared no expense.

"And I never said thank you for taking a chance on me."

"I don't take business risks unless I'm fairly certain of the outcome. I know you'll make this place a success." Torment stands to the side as Ray pushes open the door. Ray's got his leather jacket on, so I guess he wants to go.

"How?"

"Because once you find the path to Redemption, you never go back." He nods at Ray and then disappears out the door.

"He's a bit of an enigma." I turn off the back lights and push in Rose's chair. "Sometimes he just comes across as a mindless, ruthless fighting machine, and other times he seems to see into your soul."

Ray scowls. "You're mine. Only person who should be seeing into your soul is me."

I slide my arms around his waist and pull him close. "Yes, I am yours. All yours. Only yours. Forever yours."

"Good." He kisses my forehead and then pulls an open bag of potato chips from the pocket of his leather jacket. "Got you something."

"That's very sweet." I take the bag from his hand. "I know how hard this must have been for you. After all, they are filled with salt and bad fats."

Ray shakes his head. "You got no idea. Eat them."

Laughter bubbles in my chest. He seems so earnest, I hate to turn him down.

"I still have a bag of chips in my purse."

"No. These. Eat them."

I glance down at the bag in my hand. "Why? I thought you didn't want me eating unhealthy food."

Ray heaves a sigh. "Please. For me."

"Okay." I pull out a chip and eat it slowly, my cheeks heating under Ray's intense scrutiny. "That was delicious. Thank you."

He waves at the bag. "More."

"Are they poison?" I lower the bag and frown. "Are you trying to get rid of me? Is that why you're pressuring me to eat them?"

"Siahhhh." He draws out my name, his voice a plea I can't ignore. I put my hand in the bag and grasp something that is definitely not a chip.

"What's this?" I hold up a ring bearing an oval-shaped diamond surrounded in a lattice of tiny diamonds that twinkle—nothing ostentatious but quietly different. Like me.

Ray beams, puffing out his chest like he's just won the underground championship belt. Although now that he's formally joined the Redemption team, it might one day be the state title.

"Ray Black." I grab a tissue from Rose's desk and clean off the ring. "Are you proposing to me?"

"Man loves a woman, wants to spend the rest of his life with her, raise a family together, he asks her to marry him."

"It's beautiful."

A smile spreads across his face. "Does that mean yes? 'Cause my mom said I'd better make an honest woman of you or she'd whup my ass."

I wrap my arms around his neck. "I didn't know CIA agents were afraid of their moms."

"Don't know anything about CIA agents," he says. "But I am afraid of my mom."

"Well then, I'd better say yes." I lean up and kiss his cheek. "If anyone's ass is getting a whupping, it had better be mine, and I know just where I want it to happen."

"Naughty girl," he says.

"The naughtiest."

Ray's lips brush over mine. "My beautiful girl."

"Yours."

His smile lights my heart and truly sets me free.

—◦◦◦—

Priority: Confidential
Bay Area Underground Fight Club (BUFC) Wedding Night
Redemption. 8 p.m.
Headlining: Ray "The Predator" Black and Sia "Phoenix" O'Donnell
Code Word: Forever

ACKNOWLEDGMENTS

Many thanks to all the MMA fighters who generously shared their stories, and especially Animal, Chainsaw, Rhino, and Blizzard—you rock! To my wonderful editor, Cat Clyne, who loved Ray right from the start, and my agent, Laura Bradford, who so patiently indulges my need for long, detailed explanations. To CaRWA and the Secret Group of Awesome for all their support. And to my family, who have all learned how to cook out of necessity.

ABOUT THE AUTHOR

New York Times and *USA Today* bestselling author Sarah Castille writes contemporary erotic romance and romantic suspense featuring blazingly hot alpha heroes and the women who tame them. A recovering lawyer, she once practiced at one of the world's largest law firms in London, England, during which time she traveled extensively, wrote moderately, and developed a taste for tea, satire, and hard-bodied soccer players. After her first book, *Legal Heat*, won numerous awards in romance-writing contests, Sarah traded in her briefcase and stilettos for a handful of magic beans and an untrustworthy laptop. Her books have been named as *Publishers Weekly*'s "Top Ten Picks" and "Best Summer Books" and have appeared on the *New York Times* and *USA Today* bestseller lists. Sarah lives with her husband, munchkins, and a family of owls in the shadow of Canada's Rocky Mountains, where she is currently working on her next novel.

Against the Ropes

Redemption
by Sarah Castille

New York Times and *USA Today* bestselling author

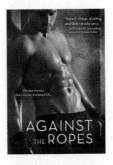

He scared me.
He thrilled me.

And after one touch, all I could think about was getting more...

Makayla never thought she'd set foot in an elite mixed martial arts club. But if anyone needs a medic on hand, it's these guys. Then again, at her first sight of the club's owner, she's the one feeling breathless.

The man they call Torment is all sleek muscle and restrained power. Whether it's in the ring or in the bedroom, he knows exactly when a soft touch is required and when to launch a full-on assault. He always knows just how far he can push. And he's about to tempt Makayla in ways she never imagined...

Praise for *Against the Ropes*:

"Smart, sharp, sizzling, and deliciously sexy."
—Alison Kent, bestselling author of *Unbreakable*

"*Fifty Shades of Grey* meets *Fight Club*." —*RT Book Reviews*

For more Sarah Castille, visit:

www.sourcebooks.com

In Your Corner

Redemption

by **Sarah Castille**

New York Times and *USA Today* bestselling author

He rules in the ring

Two years ago, Jake and Amanda were hot and heavy. But when Jake wanted more, Amanda walked away. Jake immersed himself in mixed martial arts, living life on the edge. But that didn't dull the pain of Amanda's rejection—until a chance encounter throws them together again.

A high-powered lawyer, Amanda was a no-strings-attached kind of girl. But two years after her breakup with Jake, she still hasn't found anyone who gets her heart pumping the way he did. And then he shows up in her boardroom, hot as sin and needing help…

But can he rule her heart?

Jake is darker, sexier, and impossible to resist. As their chemistry builds, Amanda's not sure if she can stay in control, or if she's finally willing to let him claim her body and soul.

For more Sarah Castille, visit:

www.sourcebooks.com